I0654542

The Girl Who Danced with Snakes

Daniel Basil Lyle

LylePublishing

Sulphur, Oklahoma

The Girl Who Danced with Snakes

Copyright © 2015 by Daniel Basil Lyle

ISBN 978-0-9794101-7-8

Published by LylePublishing
505 W. 12th Street, Sulphur, OK 73086
(www.LylePublishing.com)

Printed by CreateSpace, an Amazon.com company. Available from Amazon.com and other retail outlets. Also available as an ebook on Kindle and other devices.

LCED09282018

DISCLAIMER and FORWARD

Although this book draws heavily from some of the author's own experiences, all characters are fictitious. Any resemblance to real persons, living or dead, is purely coincidental. Although the historical Socrates is depicted in this book, his words and behavior are fictionalized. This book is a sequel to *"The Girl Who Tempted God,"* beginning where that book left off.

Chapter 1

GARDEN OF EDEN

If only mankind might have survived
Its fatal encounter with the Tree of Knowledge
When given the power of gods, they stupidly fumbled
Instead of awe and gratitude they gave back Arrogance
And stumbling and falling where they might have flown
They watched their Paradise drift slowly into the past
Losing forever that which they'd held in their hands
Turned now to dust, draining through fingers
Wafting away on the wind, forever lost
Remaining just as a vague memory
An unobtainable, aching longing
For when they were young
And everything seemed
Within their grasp
They thought...

Homo sapiens Eulogy, 1:23-27

Sally sat on a rough wooden chair.

She was afraid to move.

She was looking out over a magnificent valley.

She saw a thick wood splashed with color: green, yellow, gold, and red—the colors of early fall. A pristine river ran down the middle of the valley, complete with white-water cascades. Extensive green meadows, spotted with patches of blue and white flowers, hosted grazing animals. Sheer mountains rose up, towering on both sides.

1

And overhead—against a brilliant blue sky—drifted peaceful, white clouds.

The sun was larger than she remembered, and redder?

"It's so beautiful," she whispered, her big green eyes wide in amazement.

She felt she dare not move lest she wake up from what could only be a wondrous dream.

But there was a hard reality clutched in her hand. She still held the *black super-gun* that'd saved her and Dave by opening up a Portal to the future. In one immense discharge it unleashed energy stored up across two millennia. Its solid weight both comforted and frightened her.

After the nightmarish events of her recent past, the present reality seemed too good to be true.

Yet she missed her own world—as bad as it had seemed. In particular, she missed Dave's mother, Jean King—and her dear friend Eashoa. But she clung to the knowledge that they'd both died heroically, holding back hordes of demons, allowing Breep to throw her and Dave into the closing Portal.

Tears welled in her eyes as she realized that her own mother and all her previous friends were long gone, turned to dust in the "purification" of Earth's surface by God—a billion years in the past!

Dave reached over from his chair beside her and gently stroked her long red-brown hair. The pull of his strong hands on her fluffy locks felt real. It was true that he was a middle-aged man versus her present teenaged body, and her ingrained biological imperatives urged her to reject his advances for someone closer to her own age. But he was still attractive, in a mature and fatherly way.

"It's all true," he patiently reassured her. "Everything I told you really happened. The Portal threw us *one billion years* into the future. Somehow, though, I arrived before you did. I've already been here now for several years."

"Your hair is longer," she softly observed, now focusing on his wild "mountain man" shaggy beard.

"Yep," he happily admitted. "There's no classrooms full of students here for me to be neatly-'professorial'. But worse than that, Sally, I thought I was going to be here all by myself—the last human on

Earth. Then you finally came through. Wow..." he paused, choking back happy sobs until he could continue. "Well, maybe I'll cut my hair if that's what you want. *You're* my whole world now."

She laughed good-naturedly.

"So, we're 'Adam and Eve'—is that it?"

"Well," he grinned at her, raising his eyebrows, "we *could* be, that is—if *you* wanted?"

She sighed.

"You *are* a little old for me," she grinned, looking at him flirtingly.

"Hey, and *you're* a whole lot older than you look," he laughed back at her. "But what choice do you have? I'm literally the last man on earth. We're certainly close enough in physiological age to make *great* sweet love together...that is," he repeated again, "if *you* wanted?"

She felt the warm sunlight caressing her body. She saw Dave lean back in his chair, looking at her expectantly.

Well, at least he wasn't pouncing on her like a horny mountain goat.

"I'd have to...think...about that," she sighed, her head spinning from everything that had recently happened. "Remember, Dave, for me just a couple days ago I was back in the 1st Century A.D.—watching *Jesus* being scourged by the Roman occupiers of the Holy Land. After that I...died. And then I woke up finding that Jesus had preserved me in suspended animation for over two thousand years! Remember, Dave, for me this was just a couple days ago."

Dave nodded in appreciation at the gigantic changes she'd experienced.

"Well, that was quite a jolt to me as well," Dave admitted, "a very pleasant one, though, when I saw your 'mummified' body returning to life in that Jerusalem tomb."

She snickered, imagining his reaction. She'd been so groggy it'd taken her a while to get her bearings, so she didn't remember his expression.

"And then we had to battle what looked like Satan," she continued, slowly enumerating the recent incredible events, "in an apocalyptic Nuclear Winter on Earth," she sighed, shaking her head in amazement, "only to then be thrown through the Portal by Breep, my pet dinosaur, to wind up...here! It's a lot to take in all at once, Dave."

"Of course it is," he said, standing up and stretching. "But we've finally got time, Sally," he said. "We don't have to rush into anything. Before, we were thrown from one crisis to the next, just barely managing to survive. Here, we're long past the Wrath of God. We're back to just being two people living out our lives in peace. How about that? I guess miracles *do* happen after all."

"In peace," she sighed. "I don't even know the meaning of that word anymore for..."

Her voice trailed off. She was tired. Her head hurt. She couldn't think straight. She needed to sleep for about a week.

"Well, I assure you that you don't need that *gun* anymore," Dave smiled at her, looking at the heavy black pistol in her hands. "There's nothing in this world big enough to threaten us. And the nonhuman intelligent species from the other past Dimensions of Earth—those that also made it through the Portal—are very gentle. They've long ago evolved past senseless, stupid conflict. It's rather refreshing."

"Yes, I know of them," Sally agreed. "They're good neighbors. In fact, they guided us to surrender everything to God. I'm convinced that's what made the difference in the end—so that He took pity on us and sent us here."

But she still couldn't put down the gun. Maybe it was just her frazzled instincts from the last few days of intense conflict, but the gun assured her she still had a grip on reality.

"I think I'm in shock," she admitted in a small voice. "It's going to take me a while to come to terms with this new world."

"I admit it's been quite an adjustment for me as well," Dave agreed, "even though I've already been here for several years. I still wake up in cold sweats from nightmares of those giant Reaper Robots about to grab me!"

He visibly shuddered.

"But you say that there are cities out there of our friends from the other, nonhuman Dimensions?"

"Yes, quite fascinating!" Dave said, getting up and walking to his single-room hut. "The brief Portal you created appeared in all their Dimensions simultaneously. It allowed most of Snake's small population of reptilian people to cross over—they were hoping and prepared for it. Also a lot of George and Alice's Dinosapiens from the city that another Sally saved from being destroyed by the alien Harvester got across. Then there's a scattering of other nonhuman intelligent Earth races from other Dimensions as well."

"But how do they regard us?" she asked, now worried. "After all, it was us *Homo sapiens* that caused all the trouble in the first place—inventing and then misusing Dark Energy Generators. It was *us* that caused God's full attention to focus on us, not the gentle reptilian and dinosaur races. *We* caused Armageddon! If I were from the other linked Earth Dimensions, I think I'd probably take us by the scruffs of our necks and..."

"—*don't* think like that!" he sternly admonished her, cutting her off. He entered his hut and quickly emerged with two wooden tumblers. He handed one to her.

"What's this?" she asked, surprised.

"It's a type of 'tea'," he grinned. "I brewed it up myself from bush leaves I discovered out in the woods. It's kind of bitter, but definitely has a caffeine-like molecule in it."

"Ah, yes...*coffee*. We didn't have that in my Dimension. But I did acquire a taste for it when I was the High Priestess on Mars."

She took a sip and grimaced. But then she took another sip.

"Not too bad," she gratefully smiled up at him. "Thanks, Dave."

"After Earth's surface was destroyed a billion years ago in the Day of Judgment—from God causing a solar super-storm to sweep over the Earth—there's been enough time for complex plant and animal life to re-evolve," he explained. "So everything's different, yet surprisingly similar."

As if to give an example, Dave reached down to his feet and lifted up a strange animal.

"What's that?" Sally said, gasping at the six-legged animal that looked like a cross between a cat and an insect.

It had a long snout like an anteater, complex multi-facetted black eyes like a spider, and stiff spine "hairs" like those of a porcupine.

"This is '*Grindle*'—my pet...*something*," he laughed, stroking it from its head down to its pleasurably twitching tail. "It started coming around for handouts. And then it just stayed. As long as you stroke it in the proper direction, it's quite harmless."

"And if you don't?"

"Well, those quills are mildly poisonous, so you'll get a badly-swollen hand. I got several puffed-up digits before I learned how to treat it properly."

She grimaced as he handed the "purring" creature to her.

However, it was indeed very friendly, snuggling down contentedly into her lap.

"He likes you!"

"Well, sure," she said, gingerly stroking his thick quills in the proper head-to-tail direction. "Nice little...cat-spider-thing."

She carefully handed Grindle back to Dave, who put him down on the ground.

"So—I know it's been a long day," he said as they both watched the strange animal scamper off into the bushes.

Yes, the swollen, reddish sun was sinking low over the mountains, starting to cast long shadows.

"But what about Breep out in the...?"

"I suspect he'll be just fine," Dave said. "He'll come around when he's finished exploring the valley. I've crops out in a field. He'll want to munch on them. He's an omnivore, right?"

"I used to feed him caviar."

"Well, there's fish to be caught in the river. Plus, the Dinosapiens brought seeds with them through the portal. So I've got real past-Earth potatoes, beans, corn, and carrots. There's enough food just from my crops to feed all three of us. Also there are various fruits and nuts out in the forest. There are less now that it's fall, but sufficient for snacks. As you know, I've plenty of nuts that I've 'squirreled' away by the bushel. I'll bet Breep will like them. He was hatched in a tree like a bird, right? So we're in good shape snack-wise, hah!"

She was fascinated by this new farm life, knowing there was much to learn. But that would have to wait for another day.

"I'm exhausted, Dave," she widely yawned, stretching her arms up over her head.

When Dave brought her to his homestead after she'd materialized in the meadow, she'd bathed herself in the stream, washing her filthy corpse-clothes. Then she put on new, rough-hewn clothes he'd made himself during his years here. They were scratchy but warm. Plus she'd gotten a good meal of the delicious, but strange-tasting nuts and fruits. Then—after it was hung in the sun to dry—she'd put back on her more comfortable red jumpsuit.

It was tattered but soft from being "tenderized" on a corpse beneath the collapsed Church of the Holy Sepulchre in Jerusalem. It was probably on some tourist girl that took shelter there when the Aliens descended down upon the Earth.

She shuddered, momentarily overcome.

Terrible memories threatened to suck Sally back into the past horrors.

Now, though, she was aware of just how dead tired she was—here in a "paradise" a billion years in the future.

"Like I said, Sally," Dave kindly smiled at her, "we've all the time in the world to make good decisions. Whatever you want, I'll support you. If you want to go and immerse yourself in the science or societies of our nonhuman friends, that's fine with me. They're even building a Starship to attempt interstellar travel! If you decide to enlist on such, I'll be right there with you—though after all we've been through I kind of like my little hut and valley."

"You're a good friend, Dave," she said, pushing her body up from the wooden chair—then almost falling over as the world seemed to spin around her.

He grabbed her arm, steadying her.

"*Or* should you want to 'retire' here to make babies with me—that would be fine too, heh?" he grinned in a half-joking, half-serious way.

Sally knew that he was truly handsome, a youthful-looking middle-aged man. But still, something inside her young body still longed for a fellow near her own age.

She realized her reluctance to accept the "Adam and Eve" thing was emotional, not logical. But to settle down here with the older Dave seemed...premature. Then again, they'd already experienced incredible adventures together. And now there was a whole new world to explore!

It was all too confusing, too much to absorb. And the still-fresh nightmares she'd just escaped were still just inches away in her mind, threatening to swamp her fragile mental equilibrium.

She gently disengaged Dave's strong hand.

"Well, I'm just a 'little' girl," she jokingly replied, steadying herself now by grabbing onto the back of her chair while bracing herself mentally, "who's chronologically somewhere around a hundred and fifteen years old..."

"—and not looking a day over one hundred!" Dave grinned back.

"—and still looking like a *teenager*," she good-naturedly huffed back at him, "thanks to a massive dose of Optimmune anti-aging retroviral systems still rampaging around in my blood system," she added. "But perhaps it is time to fulfill my biological imperative. Maybe I've put it off long enough. I'll have to think about it, Dave. Ok?"

"—and the 'biological imperative' part I'm happy to help you out with," Dave grinned widely. She again felt his strong hand taking her arm to support her as she wobbled toward the entrance to the hut. "That is," he hurriedly added yet again, "if that's what *you* want, Sally."

She appreciated his continually reminding himself not to jump on her, pin her to the ground, and rape her. She squeezed his arm affectionately.

"Right now I just want to collapse and sleep for several days," she wearily said as he led her to the one, straw bed inside. "But where are you going to...?"

"I've a shed outside that I made where Snake sleeps when he occasionally visits me," he gallantly explained. He helped her onto the one bed, drawing up the thick blankets to her chin. "If it gets chilly I'll come in and light a fire in my rock 'stove'. I'll be out there in the shed—it's very comfy...unless you want me to...?"

"Good*night*, Dave," she firmly replied, placing the gun comfortingly under her pillow—while drifting off toward a delicious, stress-free sleep.

Tomorrow there'd be plenty of time for her and Dave to sort out their present situation and future objectives.

But she had a nagging doubt that itched at the back of her mind.

It seemed, somehow, *too* perfect. After all, in the ancient Creation-accounts weren't there always evil 'Devils' lurking about?

But they'd left Satan behind on the other side of God's time-barrier a billion years in the past...hadn't they?

She had a sudden, terrible feeling that she was lucky to have that black gun under her pillow.

It certainly wasn't to protect her against Dave, but to protect *both* of them in ways she could not yet imagine.

Regardless, it was one of the few things that tied them to the past and to the future. It acknowledged their violent animal heritage while helping them forge a path forward.

But she could contemplate that at her leisure.

Finally, she had time to let down her guard and just peacefully fall asleep...

—hopefully without nightmares!

Chapter 2

<u>ORIGINAL SIN</u>

Did you think they'd forgot
The hurt and pain you caused them
When you lashed out in anger or fear
Or, worse yet, out of jealousy or greed
And imposed your Will upon them
Regardless of their Wants or Desires
Making their Pain a path for your Pleasure
Oh, the depths of such abysmal Evil
Especially when others weren't even considered
Their presence, dreams, and lives ignored
As if they did not even exist or matter
Or, worse yet, were mere objects of your Pride
There only to fulfill your own selfish Orders
How can you now be angry or surprised?
That they regard you as what you are
A dangerous, scary presence
No longer tolerated or pampered
But cast out, banished, and rejected
Condemned to stew painfully
In your own vile juices...
Homo sapiens Eulogy, 2:19-25

Dave woke up with a feeling of foreboding.

Normally, Gringle—his cat-spider pet—would be happily "snoring" (clicking and snorting, both at once) on Dave's chest or off to the side of the bed.

Today, the shed was abnormally quiet. Outside, Dave heard no chirping of four-winged "birds" in the trees. There was no rustling of the fallen leaves as six-limbed small "squirrels" ran through them. Even the ever-present gentle breeze that swept across the camp from the elevated mouth of the valley was absent.

"*Sally?*" Dave gasped—the feeling of dread growing—as he jumped up from the rough bed in the shed and ran out into the morning sunlight.

The door to the hut hung open.

The previous evening he had carefully shut it and latched it, leaving Sally sleeping securely inside—to be doubly certain that no animals came ambling in during the night to disturb her.

He ran into the opened doorway to see lying there on the rough bed...

—nothing!

The blankets were there, but pushed to the side.

She was gone!

But...?

Gringle came ambling in, hopping up on the bed to nervously sniff around. Its multiple-black-eyed snout was trembling. Even he seemed worried.

"She's probably just walked to the stream," Dave said to the creature, giving it a couple of gentle strokes along its back to comfort it. "I'll go get her. Then we can have a nice breakfast, all three of us. How's that sound?"

Gringle "chittered" agreeably, the noise coming from its long mouth opening and closing rapidly, causing the flat teeth to "clank" against each other.

First Dave jogged out to the garden plots to see if Sally was looking at his crops or flowers. She was nowhere to be seen. In fact there were no footprints in the soft, tilled dirt. She hadn't been there!

Dave then rushed through the woods to the sparkling mountain stream.

But Sally was also not there. In the soft, fertile ground around the stream, again, there were no fresh footsteps. She'd not been there that morning.

Where could she be?

"Sally!" Dave yelled loudly into the woods. "Sally, where are you?"

Nothing...

There was no answer. There was only silence. And the trees bearing yellow-red leaves, poised to fall, gave no response either. Narrowing his eyes in puzzlement, Dave looked up at the canopy. It was frozen in place. Nothing wavered. It was very peculiar.

Dave grew acutely aware that the air was not moving. There wasn't a trace of a breeze.

And then, through a gap in the canopy above, Dave saw the sky...

"What the hell?" he gasped.

The normally pristine air glimpsed through the trees above him was...blurry! The deep blue of the sky was strangely shimmering.

Then he realized what it was.

"Oh, God," he gasped, running back through the woods and stumbling into his hut.

He frantically rummaged around beneath the tossed-aside pillow and bunched-up blankets. Then he dug down into the straw "mattress." Finally, he dug beneath the elevated bottom of the "bed."

There was no doubt at all. Sally's energy-gun was missing along with her.

That was ominous, chilling.

Dave grabbed up the only thing he might use as a weapon, his crudely made guitar. In a pinch, he could slam it down on someone's head.

He raced up the path he'd worn into the hillside, toward the elevated mouth of the valley.

This was the path out of the valley and from thence across a wide plain. On the other side of the plain were low hills. Beyond the hills was a Dinosapien city where his old friends George and Alice lived. To get to the city was a leisurely walk of three days, stopping and camping at night. Without pausing to sleep, he could make it there in maybe a day and a half.

But right now he meant to climb to the top of the gorge to get an unobstructed view of the entire valley. If Sally was still somewhere in the valley, he'd be able to spot her bright red jumpsuit. If she was in trouble he could run to her rescue.

And right at the mouth leading out of the valley, he SLAMMED into an *invisible, unyielding barrier.*

"No, no, no!" he yelled, jumping up from where he'd fallen. Gingerly he reached up and felt along the invisible barrier.

It was just as he'd feared.

It reached upward beyond his height, curving slightly inward.

He knew what it was.

It was a Dark Energy-powered force field. And by its curvature it stretched upward to contain the entire valley within its half-orb. Indeed, that was what Dave had recognized in the sky above him. It was the same appearance that Dave knew from when he and his Resistance organization managed to encase the entire Earth in a Planetary Shield to keep out the alien armada of Harvester spaceships.

Except, in this case, it was *trapping* Dave inside his valley.

That's why the air inside was not moving, the ever-present breeze absent which normally swept in through the mouth of the valley.

"Sally!" he yelled again, vainly thumping his fists against the impenetrable barrier.

They'd taken her...

Those bastard snakes took her away from me!—he groaned to himself in agonized acceptance.

He slumped down onto his butt, sitting in the dirt with his back against the barrier. He cried bitterly.

Why?

Why did they do this to him?

He picked up the guitar he'd dropped. For a moment he almost jumped up and slammed it into the barrier to try and beat it open. But he knew that'd just destroy his homemade instrument. So he began to strum it, defiantly *shouting* an ancient song from a billion years in the past: "OH MY DARLING, OH MY DARLING, OH MY DARLING CLEMENTINE—YOU ARE LOST AND GONE FOREVER. DREADFUL SORRY, CLEMENTINE."

He continued shouting the old ballad, hoping somewhere someone was listening. He sang all the verses. And then he sang it through one more time.

It was both a protest and a release. He wasn't the first human to endure the unexpected loss of a girlfriend. But it looked like he'd be the last.

Hoping he was wrong, Dave climbed to the top of the mountain peak on the inside of the force bubble such that he could look back over the entire valley.

As far as he could see there was not a glint of Sally's red jumpsuit.

But that didn't stop Dave from descending to methodically search every cranny and nook of the valley, in a vain hope that she was still out there somewhere.

After several days he ran into Breep.

Quite literally, he *ran* into him—jogging along a narrow trail in the thick woods and *tripping* over the supine body of the man-sized creature.

"Breep?" Dave said, scrambling to his feet. He crouched down beside the fallen dinosaur. Standing up the animal would have been six feet tall. Now laid-out on his side on the trail—from the tip of his nose to the tip of his tail—he was a good nine feet long.

His breathing was labored. He weakly raised his bird-like head, staring blankly at Dave. The big black eyes were unfocused. Patches of his scaly hide were hanging out. He was clearly having trouble shedding.

Breep was in distress.

Dave managed to grip the animal around its big chest and haul it up to its three-toed feet upon which it wobbled uncertainly. The small dinosaur was very unwieldy, much like a featherless ostrich with a long reptilian tail. Also, Breep felt cold and clammy to Dave's touch.

"Hey, boy, it's me—Dave!" he declared, as with difficulty he helped the dinosaur wobble along the path. Its long front arms clawed futilely at the air, trying to gain purchase.

And dripping from sharp teeth in its beak was yellow pulp and seeds.

"Ah...I see," Dave nodded grimly. "You ate the yellow fruit. Now if you'd come and asked me politely, Breep, I'd have told you that they'd hurt your tummy. Those are bad fruits. Not everything re-evolved in ways that fit with us time-traveling ancient species from a billion years in the past. I myself was sick for a week after eating those. They tasted great in my mouth, but then they almost killed me. Nasty stuff!"

"B-breeeeeeeppppp?" the dinosaur weakly replied, laying its long neck across Dave's shoulders.

"That's good, Breep," Dave reassured him. "You just lean on me. I'll get you back to my hut where we can put you next to a nice warm stove. Otherwise you'll probably get further chilled, sicker, and then die. Us time-travelers from the past have got to stick together. You, me, and Sally...uhm, well, not her..."

"Brrrrrrrreeeeep?" the animal queried, perking up at hearing Sally's name.

"She's ok, Breep...I hope..." he quietly answered. "She's not here though—at least not in our valley anymore. I don't think she'd voluntarily leave us without saying goodbye. So I'm sure that the other 'people' here took her away against her will. Well, don't worry, boy. We'll find her and get her back."

But his brave words belied his fears. What could he do if the superior nonhuman races had her? Clearly, they'd trapped him here in his 'cage' with the force field that shimmered-down implacably from above.

Yes, it was a wonderful jail, but a cage nonetheless. Apparently the upper layers of the force field were engineered to be permeable to air because he was still breathing ok after several days, plus birds could still fly in and out of the valley. But he had no advanced technology. There was no way he could climb or fly several thousand feet up in the sky to escape the valley through the thinning layers above.

Back at his hut, he helped Breep flop down right beside the rock stove, in which Dave had a small fire going. The dinosaur would warm up quickly. Dave put a big wooden bowl of water beside him in case he got thirsty, plus a rough pillow of straw under his head.

Breep closed his big black eyes and snuggled closer to the warmth, clearly happy to be rescued.

"Rest well, kiddo," Dave said, patting the now-snoring dinosaur on his big green head.

Even the red thatch on the back of Breep's head—his "Mohawk" was drooping and dull-looking. Dave hoped that his old friend would recover. He wouldn't replace Sally, of course, but he'd remind Dave of her every single day.

As Dave walked sadly out of the hut, he saw another old friend, "Snake" walking up...

—who Dave ran up to and *punched* him straight in his thin face, *knocking* him to the ground!

"Hey man, what the...?" Snake gasped, holding his bruised cheek with a frail-looking hand.

Snake didn't look like much lying there on the ground. He appeared to be a scrawny, teenage kid. He had long black hair, a scraggly goatee, and arms covered with numerous tattoos of every color and shape.

And tattooed on the left side of his face was a black cobra, etched from his forehead to his throat.

That's where his name came from.

But Dave knew full well that Snake was not what he seemed.

In reality, he was a shape-shifting *actual* nonhuman Snake from another Dimension—an intelligent race that originated on Mars before escaping to earth via the red Obelisk eons in the past. The Obelisk was a sophisticated transportation device, capable of moving across time, space, and Dimensions.

Snake was an ancient, reptilian, Martian.

"Why did you take Sally?" Dave *screamed* in rage at him, grabbing him by the scruff of his shirt and hauling him back to his feet.

"Hey, D-Dave, man—it wasn't me, it wasn't me!" Snake protested, fearfully raising his thin hands to ward off any further blows from Dave.

Disgusted, Dave tossed him into the shed where he fell down onto the straw.

"Then why did 'they' take Sally?" Dave yelled again at him. The anger and frustration of the last few days seethed up, making him see red!

Snake shakily got to his feet, came out of the opened shed, and sat on the same wood chair Sally used just a few days before.

"Hey, man," Snake said, indicating for Dave to come sit beside him, "I'm here to tell you what I know. In fact, I just heard about it myself this morning. I came right over to..."

"Oh...well then..." Dave sighed, his anger rapidly draining away. Snake was the artist that had originally inked Sally's Turtle Tattoo—which saved both her and Dave a number of times. He was an alien nonhuman, but a friend nonetheless. Dave couldn't stay mad at him.

Dave slumped down in the other chair, still shaking from his repressed fury.

"So then tell me what you know. Sorry about hitting you."

"It hurts," Snake gulped, feeling gingerly at his cheek. "But I guess I'd do the same if someone snatched Sally from me—'specially since we thought she didn't make it across the time-barrier in the first place. It *sucks*, man."

Snake shakily drew a pack of cigarettes from his shirt pocket and stuck one in his mouth. It dangled limply from his thin lips as he struck a match and lit it up. He inhaled deeply.

"Why do you do that?" Dave irritably asked, cringing backward from the white smoke blowing from Snake's nostrils. "Don't you know it's filled with carcinogens and tumor promoters?"

"I got used to it the years I wuz in your Dimension," Snake sighed. "So I took a few packs with me when I made it across the Portal. I only smoke one now and then, when somethin' big is happening, you know, that..."

"—or you get real nervous: like when you encounter an angry mammal whose mate's been *stolen* away from him?"

"Y-yes," Snake nervously replied. "Jist like that...uh, Sally and you mated?"

"None of your damn business!" Dave yelled at him, half-rising from the chair with his fists clenched. Then, more softly as he settled back down, "No, we didn't. We talked about it—but Sally was still shook up from the trip and didn't make any commitment."

"Man, that's good to hear," Snake sighed. "If you two mated you'd be in even bigger trouble."

"Trouble?" Dave snapped at him. "What's up, Snake? Where the *hell* is Sally?"

Snake took a long drag on the cigarette before answering, holding the red flaring end out in front of his face. Then he popped the business end of the cigarette back in his mouth, letting it dangle from his thin lips.

"It wuz the 'Council of Elders' that done it, man," he reluctantly admitted.

"Go on," Dave grated.

"It's...like...well, you know...the highest ruling body on New Earth now—a group of the top leaders from the civilizations that made it across the Portal. They saw Sally arrive here in your valley, and..."

"—they *saw* her?"

"Sure," Snake said in his soft, nasal voice. "There's camera-phone-things stuck all around here, tracking your every movement, man...even what you say."

"I don't have to shout to get their attention?"

"Not even sing dorky old folk songs, man."

"And are they watching and listening to us right now?"

"Sure...I mean their operatives—everything we do or say, man. I can't believe you're surprised. You're like a celebrity. And they kept hopin' that Sally might show up also to..."

"So they've been spying on my every movement," Dave ominously said to Snake in a very low, controlled voice. "Even now—*everything* that we say or do—they're listening and watching?"

Snake took another deep drag on his cigarette, blowing another cloud of white smoke—this time right at Dave's face.

"I *told* you that, man," he now huffed irritably back at Dave, looking like he was getting angry himself. "Ain't you been listenin' to me?" But then, more conciliatory, seeing Dave's frustrated expression and apparently not wanting to get hit in the face again: "But it's mostly for your own good, man. You ain't got nobody out here to help you if you fall and break a leg or get sick or something. We wuz comin' when you ate that yellow fruit before, until you looked to be recovering."

"You were?" Dave said, confused. Maybe they weren't so cold-hearted after all?

"Sure! You are...ah means you *were*...the only human left alive, man. They wuz jist lookin' out fer you."

"Like a prized animal in a cage at a zoo?"

"Uh, well..."

"Ok, ok," Dave waved a hand dismissively. "So they knew that Sally finally arrived through the Portal. But then they kidnapped her and slapped this force field around the valley. *Why?*"

"Jesus Christ, man!" Snake grated, shaking his thin face in fierce denial. "They didn't snatch her...jist took her for a checkup and such. She's like a hero to them. She saved all of us! If it wuzn't fer her tempting the Creator, we'd all be billion-year-old ashes, man. They gonna give her a big parade soon, stuff like that. There's 'nothin to worry about. You jist gotta be patient. Simmer down..."

He weakly grinned at Dave but Dave grabbed Snake again by his shirt, knocking-away the still lit cigarette.

"Hey!" Snake protested. "I ain't got that many of..."

"Don't give me any crap!" Dave now yelled in his face, his anger returning. "They didn't have to kidnap her to give her a medical checkup! We'd have readily agreed. Maybe your reptile friends are watching right now—but I'll bet they can't get here in time to stop me from *snapping* your scrawny neck. Now tell me the truth or you're going to be sorry!"

"Alright, alright!" Snake said, trying to push away Dave's strong hands. "You want the truth? Here it is: you can't *breed!* You're a middle-aged guy and she's a young gal. You're both still fertile. And if the Council let her stay longer than jist her first day here, you'd sex her up, man! You know you would. And since we ain't got no contraceptives for you humans in New Earth...well, that's exactly how you make *babies*, right?"

"I know how to make babies," Dave growled at him. "But that still doesn't explain...?"

"Doesn't it? The Council knew you had this very thing in mind to do and would try to hide it from us!"

"You heard when Sally and I first talked...about my book?"

"They sure did, man. It's a cool title: '*The Luminary Chronicles.*' Nice."

"Thanks..."

"You wanna have hobbies like writing poetry stuff and singing songs, that's totally fine, man. But the 'take-home' message of leaving a record for further generations of humans sure says your intentions with Sally. Plus you talked about hiding your intentions from your nonhuman friends 'cause you knew they wouldn't like your plans."

"Uhm...I guess I did. I didn't know I was being spied on."

"It's for your own good, man," Snake repeated. "But you see how they felt they had to immediately sneak Sally away from you or you'd knock her up before they could get here for some formal sit-down chat session."

"But still..."

Dave sighed deeply then released Snake, settling back in his chair, looking up at the bizarrely shimmering sky. Yes, he knew full well how the nonhuman races on New Earth regarded both him and Sally. But that still didn't make it right! In fact, he *had* hoped to hide the "coupling" from them. That was obviously now a futile hope. Well, maybe he could still reason with them?

"We're not a threat to..."

"You hit me! You choked me! You threatened me with bodily harm, man, to 'snap my scrawny neck'!" Snake protested. "And that's you—one of the smartest humans of them all—to me, a long-time friend of yours. The Council can't let there be *any* chance, no matter how slight, of you crazy humans proliferating upon New Earth ever again! Get used to it, man. Your species is like...an abomination! They're tolerating your presence, but *not* for starting up the human race again. There's no way that they'll let that happen, man—*no way* at all!"

Dave had suspected as much, but in the absence of Sally there hadn't been any point to being concerned. Now that Sally was here, though, his worst fears were being realized.

"But that's racial genocide," Dave softly replied, looking bitterly up at the shimmering force field in the sky. "I thought you 'wise' ancient races were more enlightened?"

There was a long silence broken only by the "snoring" sputters of Breep in the hut. The shouts from Dave and Snake hadn't disturbed his fevered sleep.

"Dave, man," Snake finally replied, seemingly sorrowfully, "you and Sally saved us—we're all grateful. But talkin' about 'genocide' it wuz *Homo sapiens* that caused millions and billions of both us and you to die in the first place! We gave you this nice valley to live out yore days in. It's all yours, man. We've kept away from it, haven't we?"

"Ok, but that still doesn't give you the right to..." Dave started to argue.

"—and now Sally's bein' very well taken care of also, gettin' her dreams finally to come true!" Snake continued hastily. "But we're *never* going to let her and you get together ever again—it's jist too dangerous, man!"

"But if we promised to..."

"You know we can't kill things," Snake grimaced. "We don't have the genetic wiring for it anymore. So we can't stop conceptions or do abortions. Once you and Sally 'got it on' then we'd be stuck with the results. The only way for us to guarantee that the human race doesn't get re-established is to separate the last male and female, you and Sally. You gotta understand our position, man. You kin live out your lives, both you and Sally. But there ain't no way we'll let you 'mate'—which means you can never be allowed to be together *ever* again!" he firmly repeated.

Dave deliberately stood up, went over and picked up Snake's still-smoking cigarette, brushed the dirt off it, and handed it back to the scraggly young man.

As Dave sat back down, he tried to suppress the fury raging in his skull. He wanted to appear calm. He knew he was arguing not just with his old friend Snake, but unseen officials observing the two of them.

"I see your position," Dave carefully replied. "I don't agree with it, but I understand your fear. But even if what you say is true—that the human race is fatally flawed—we can improve! Now that we're together on this planet, you can help guide us to be better. Isn't that a 'righteous' task? You don't have to kill off the human race. You can use your enlightened wisdom to help us to properly mature, right?"

"I don't know, man," Snake said, slowly shaking his head in the negative as he stuck the twisted cigarette back in his mouth. "I wuz in yore Dimension for years and never saw you humans gettin' better. In fact, you seemed to get *worse* all the time that I was there."

Dave knew that his and Sally's fate hung in the balance. He carefully considered his next words.

"But we, as a species, *did* do some great and noble things," Dave protested.

"Yep, that's true," Snake said, sucking deeply on the bent cigarette. "But at the slightest threat or problem you *reverted*, man—killing and hurting and destroying both yourselves and yore friends. You even savaged the world around you. You wuz killin' off the entire planet, man!"

"But that's our animal heritage speaking, that you wiser races could..."

"Yep, that's again true," Snake nodded, "and which you could never get beyond, man. *We* did it! We and the other nonhuman races, man, we *did* it. We rose above our animal origins. You humans, however, aren't truly 'intelligent' or mature—jist smart animals, man. That's all you are...or ever will be."

Snake's words were intense, his skinny hand holding the cigarette shaking.

"But you've had a lot longer to mature, right?" Dave pressed his argument. "Aren't you and the other races tens of millions or maybe even billions of years old? Mankind just came down out of the trees only a couple millions years ago! We deserve time to develop, don't you think? And with wise guidance we could..."

"Man, that's jist the point," Snake sorrowfully broke in, brushing back his long greasy black hair with one hand. "You *think*, man! You're not jist driven by instinct. You make decisions on yore own. And your people did *awful* things, man—things they *decided* consciously to do. You ain't got no excuses. It don't matter if you get to 'mature' or not, you're *fatally flawed*."

"But...but," Dave tried to protest.

He fell silent. What could he say? His people at all levels of society *had* consciously decided to do terrible things to themselves, to friends, and to relatives—not just so-called "enemies". And they'd pushed their short-sighted selfishness and brutality onto Nature as well, poisoning and destroying their own environment.

And it was "justified" in the name of...what?

Security...the most primal of instincts: to live yet another day. If paying a few bucks extra for a carbon tax to combat global warming, or tolerating an "other" group threatening to drain resources, or not launching a "preemptive" strike to stave off a potential conflict...*no way!*

Humans were ruled by the most basic of biological instincts: fear.

Dave was very confused.

Was Snake right? Was the human species fatally flawed? Was mankind incapable of improving? Was there indeed an unbridgeable chasm between its genetics and its higher aspirations?

But—whatever the true nature of mankind's collective motivations—maybe Dave could at least beg for personal mercy.

"So is it possible for them to cut me a little slack?" Dave said, tears welling up in his eyes. "I just can't live in a cage, Snake. You say I'm being constantly monitored, so your people could easily stop me if I tried to leave this valley, right?"

"I suppose," Snake shrugged. "But we're neither fighters nor aggressors. We left all that stupid behavior behind ages ago. That's why they sent me here, me who at least was knocked around on your Earth for a while. Man, I really hated it there—all the violence, savagery, and pain—but I ain't shocked by it anymore. My colleagues here, though, are jist *disgusted* by it, man. To them you really are jist smart animals. Thet's why they slapped the Bubble on you, man. They ain't got the heart to kill you—that's impossible for them—but they can at least keep you isolated and away from the female of your species until you both die off of natural causes."

"Look, Snake," Dave said, getting on his knees before the white-smoke-puffing thin man. "I'm *begging* you! I can't live in a cage. You've got to get them to lift the force field. I promise not to try to escape the valley—and you'll see immediately if I try. You can always slap the 'cage-top' back on. Give me this small favor, please."

"Well..." Snake grinned at Dave. "Actually, I wuz authorized to make things easier for you—they know how your species can't accept no limitations—but only if you agree to a condition, man."

"What is it?"

Snake reached into a small bag at his waist and drew out needles plus small jars of what appeared to be different-colored inks.

"They say if you'll agree to get tattooed like Sally did—so we can always follow you wherever you are—then they'll lift the dome off the valley."

Dave was aghast. That damn *Turtle Tattoo* had terrorized Sally! Sure, it had helped at times—but to be "branded" that way by an alien race, like a horse or a cow?

No, he *wouldn't* do it!

But then Snake *winked* at him. It was so quick, Dave almost missed it. But there was no mistaking what had happened. Dave had no doubt that an alien reptilian species would not notice or even be aware of the meaning of the slight facial twitch. But Dave was perfectly "clued-in" that Snake was *not* saying out-loud everything he knew.

"I'd have a *magic* tattoo?"

"It's got special pigments, man, 'come from my Dimension. It'll be jist like with Sally. The pigments resonate into subspace. We kin use them to track you across large distances, even to...uh...*motivate* you, so to speak."

"So it's an electric collar. If I get out of line you can jerk me back. If I persist you can put me on the ground, writhing in pain. Is that what you're saying?"

"That's about it, man."

Dave sighed deeply, knowing he had no choice. But it wasn't the whole story. Despite himself, he trusted the "hippy" Snake. After all, they had a history...

"Uhm...will it hurt?" Dave hesitantly play-acted that he was hesitantly considering the proposal when he'd already accepted it.

"Sure!" Snake grinned, showing crooked teeth. "It'll hurt like *hell*, man. It's *needles* jammed gazillions of times into your skin—over and over. But it'll be sweet when it's over. You know I guarantee my work, man. You don't like it—I'll give you yore money back. How about that?"

Dave snorted, shaking his head sadly. Then he got off his knees to sit back dejectedly into his rough wooden chair.

"Alright then," he held out his arm, "but do I get to choose the site and selection?"

"Nope!" Snake said, "scooching" his chair over closer and laying out the tools on his lap. "It's on your left wrist, jist like with Sally. But instead of a turtle, it's gonna be a..."

"—don't tell me," Dave stopped him. "It's a *snake*, right?"

"You read my mind, man," Snake laughed. "It's gonna 'brand' you as being under the protection and ownership of us New Earth Martian Snakes, jist like with Sally—a reptile! Now she had a cute little turtle 'cuz she wuz living in an intolerant, suspicious society. *You* get a dangerous, fierce snake. But you kin choose what *kind* of snake. How 'bout that?"

Dave thought for a moment.

"A *green anaconda*," he smiled. "That's my favorite snake."

"You got it, man," Snake laughed as he dipped his needles into the ink jars.

Dave grit his teeth together, closed his eyes, and sat back tensely in the chair.

They thought he was trapped. They thought he was being neatly "branded" by Snake. They thought he was safely contained and controlled. But they were wrong. He was going to find Sally. And together, they *were* going to make babies!

Perhaps *Homo sapiens* would make the same mistakes all over again. But Dave was making good progress writing the *Luminary Chronicles* on the solar-powered laptop computer that he'd brought with him from the past. One way or another, the future human race would have his written guidance. Also they'd have oversight—whether they wanted it or not—from the other intelligent nonhuman races.

But Dave would *not* be denied. Despite its flaws, the human race *would* continue!

Somehow or other he'd find a way.

Chapter 3

<u>ARK TO THE STARS</u>

Away from the earth

Not counting the cost

Into the vastness of Space

Lies a Cosmic Genius

Beneath the vacuum

A wry humor grinning

At the arrogance of Man

And impatience of Woman

When they are kept apart

Fighting to return

To find their way back

To where it all began

But can never be again

New beginnings lost...

Homo sapiens Eulogy, 3:7-9

Sally woke up feeling like she'd been drugged.

Woozily she looked around and realized she was no longer in Dave's hut. Over to the side of her (not straw) bed she saw a porthole. And through that small window she glimpsed stars—*streaming* past!

"I'm...in outer space?" she gasped to herself, dragging herself up off a comfortable white mattress.

She saw her image reflected back in a mirror set into a wall over a sink beside a toilet (looking pristine and never used).

She no longer had on the red jump suit that Dave had procured for her from a skeleton under the ruins of the Church of the Holy Sepulcher in Jerusalem. Instead she wore a simple one-piece white

27

uniform over comfortable underwear. In place of her beat-up black boots she had new red shoes, with rubber soles much like tennis shoes.

Her fluffy long red-brown hair was neatly combed-out. Her skin felt fresh and clean.

She woozily got up and used the toilet. Then she washed her face. Swinging out the mirror she saw a few toiletries, include a comb. She began combing out her tangled long hair.

"I feel remarkably rested," she muttered to her reflection in the mirror. "I must have been sleeping for a long time. How long was I under? It could have been days."

Indeed, her stomach was rumbling. Though she felt energized and strong, she was ravenously hungry.

Perhaps she should go and see if she could find some food?

"SALLY SMITH, PLEASE COME TO THE CONTROL ROOM," a loud voice abruptly reverberated from the ceiling. It was a pleasant though foreign-sounding voice. Although Sally was fluent in several languages, she could not place the accent.

Good! Maybe they'll have some food for me—she thought to herself with relief.

At her feet, a series of large dots suddenly lit up as flashing green lights. Indeed, she saw that her Turtle Tattoo was responding in kind. It clearly wanted for her to follow the lights on the floor.

"Alright, then," she shrugged, her head rapidly clearing from whatever drug they'd given her. "I was going exploring anyway. So let's follow the *green* path to the *green* land of a *green* Oz!"

Jeez...I'm really hysterical—she groaned to herself.

She opened the door of her small cabin and peered suspiciously out.

She saw a high corridor. It was wide enough that a tank could have easily rolled through it. The gravity felt earth-normal, but jumping up she noticed the pull lessened as she approached the high ceiling. Clearly, the gravity was artificial.

"Ok, follow the bouncing green lights," she said to herself, resolved to figure out what was going on.

She followed the lights down the long corridor. Then she walked through an empty chamber. And from there she exited into a large room with a clear canopy that allowed everyone to see unobstructed into what was above and around them.

Her eyes fixated on an incredible spectacle above her—streaks of *every color imaginable* that were slowly streaming past, overlapping, and intertwining!

Lowering her eyes she saw that the room was filled with control panels before which stood an array of large dinosaur-looking bipedal creatures *chirping* and *squawking* at each other in a strange language!

"Sally, it's so good to see you again," a chubby, bald-headed man said as he hurried to meet her, his hand out in greeting.

She automatically took his hand, puzzled.

"Do we know each other?" She said. "And I thought that Dave and I were the only two humans left on the planet. By the way, where is Dave? We were back in that gorgeous valley, and now... Where are we, anyway?"

"All in good time, my dear," he smiled at her. "So sorry, I mixed you up with another Sally that I knew before. She was a real sweetie-pie. My name is Dr. George S. Johnson. In our prior existence, long in the past, I was a Professor of Economics who taught at a small junior college in Edmond, Oklahoma with our much-appreciated Dr. David King. I'm actually also what you term a 'Dinosapien'—*form-shifted* back into a human to make you more comfortable."

Sally nodded politely. That was nice of him. He didn't want to scare her by being a walking, talking, dinosaur. How considerate...what the hell?

Was he related to Snake, who could also transform himself into a human? But Snake was a Martian-derived actual giant snake! This man claimed to be one of the walking, talking dinosaurs that were working out there in the chamber.

Things were moving much too fast for her to keep up.

"And as to your last question," George continued, "please, come over to the astro-display and I'll show you exactly where we are."

He smiled, leading her over to a large computer screen. On it was pictured a spiral galaxy.

"This is our own Galaxy, the Milky Way," he kindly instructed her, sounding very much like a lecturing professor. "It's about 100,000 lightyears across, containing over 200 billion stars. Our earth is located on one of the spiral arms, 27,000 light-years from the Galactic Center—where a mammoth black hole resides."

"And this has to do with us...how?" Sally asked. She was overwhelmed by what was happening but desperately trying to figure out the key "take-home" messages.

"Oh, yes, I get carried away..." George laughed. "We are right now traveling at almost the speed of light, nearing a possible Earth-like planet that orbits a red dwarf star 493 light-years away from Earth. This is what I wanted to show you on the display here. So then when I focus down the view to Earth's immediate area in the Galaxy, you see..."

He punched in instructions and the field narrowed considerably, showing a sphere of stars on which a grid indicated a thousand light-year radius around a central Earth.

"Wait!" Sally said, gripping his pudgy arm under his white uniform tightly. "Did you just tell me that we're nearly *five hundred light-years* away from earth?"

"Yes, I did," he proudly conceded. "This is our New Earth's first interstellar starship's maiden voyage. Doubtless we'll travel to many other interesting solar systems, but we thought our first attempt should be to explore a nearby star system already documented as having an Earth-like world. It was classified back in 2014 as 'Kepler-186f'. It's a rocky world in the so-called 'habitable zone' of its solar system, where water should stay liquid. So there's a chance that..."

"So *where* is Dave?" she sharply interrupted his long explanation.

"Oh, I'm afraid he is long dead, Sally," he sadly but matter-of-factly stated, gently loosening her tight grip on his arm. "You see, he wasn't selected for this mission. You and your mathematical genius were deemed essential for..."

"What do you mean he's *long dead?*" she shouted at him, causing the Dinosapien crew to pause in their work and stare fearfully over at her with their large reptilian eyes.

She ignored them, staring intensely at the portly-looking fake "human."

"Well, I wanted to tell you this as gently as possible, but..."

"*Tell* me!" she shouted again.

The Dinosapiens near to her were nervously edging backward.

"Alright, then, Sally," he said, leading her over to over-large seats where they could sit off to the side out of the way of the other crew-members. "This vessel is powered by bursts from a Dark Energy Generator, yet travels not in subspace but in actual space—where we're now speeding along at near lightspeed. In addition we have a small nuclear reactor that supplies regular power throughout the ship."

"Why not travel through subspace?" she said, desperately trying to understand the magnitude of what had been foisted upon her without her prior agreement.

"Well it's way too unpredictable," he patiently explained. "For short jumps, such as within the solar system, it might work ok. But for anything longer, quantum fluctuations make it increasingly unpredictable, at least in our prototype experimental starship. We could cross over into other dimensions, initiate new timelines, or be thrown back or forward in time. So for this initial interstellar journey we chose to travel through normal space," he politely smiled at her as if addressing a smart but uninformed student.

"But unless you put me into some sort of suspended animation, we couldn't be much further than beyond the moon...?"

"Also, we are—as you'd expect—very careful in how we utilize Dark Energy, doing so sparingly," George continued, frowning at her interruption of his lecture. "Our propulsion-bursts that accelerated our spaceship have little effect on the Universe around us. But if we were traveling through subspace, the ruptures in space-time could quickly and uncontrollably grow very large. Then they'd produce bright flashes throughout the fabric of the cosmos. As you certainly remember, we don't want to come yet again into the Creator's full attention. We'd probably pass inspection without you foul creatures presently contaminating Earth, but why take chances?"

Foul creatures—but she was standing right here! How dare he insult her so casually?

Sally had been listening intently, but now the implication of his revelations hit her like a brick thrown "smack" between her eyes.

"So...you're saying we're traveling in normal space at near the *speed of light*, such that Einstein's *time dilation* is in effect?" she gasped, horrified by the implications of what she was hearing.

"Yes, those selected for this mission—such as my wife Alice and me—knew that the duration of the trip *for us* would only be a total of a few months, including observation and exploration time," he nodded. "That's because traveling at very near the speed of light, time for us slows considerably in transit—but the Earth we left behind would age normally."

While the Earth left behind aged normally—the words ricocheted brutally in her heart!

"So..." she said in an intense whisper. "Nearly *five hundred years* have passed on earth while we've aged only..."

"—well, only a few days, so far," he smiled benignly. "Our Martian snake friends shared advanced technology with us for attaining near lightspeed, so we've..."

"Everyone we left behind, including Dave is..."

"Oh, a few of our long-lived colleagues might still be alive."

"But Dave, with a normal human lifespan...?" she persisted.

"He's long dead and gone, Sally," he sadly admitted, reaching out to take her hand sympathetically in his own pudgy one. "I'm so sorry, Sally, but it's a fact. We'll return to earth in their time-span more than a thousand years after we departed. Our Martian-originated friends who sent us out here have very long lifespans, so we'll likely meet some of them again, such as your friend 'Snake'."

"But...*why?*" she glared at him, not needing to know anything more of the Martian ancient race that'd guided her previous and apparently present path. "Why did you separate us? Why did you take me with you without my consent?" she interrogated him.

She took his shoulders again in her strong grasp and roughly shook him.

"*Please*, Sally," George groaned. "You're hurting me."

She angrily shoved him away.

He staggered and almost fell.

A large Dinosapien ambled over. It stood fully nine feet tall on two large, strong legs. Its arms were free, sporting three nimble fingers each. It wore no uniform but had a large silver chain strung around its long neck, on which glittered five gold stars—clearly ranking it higher than the other dinosaurs in the room. Its head was larger than a human's, with luminous orange eyes.

"YOU HAVE TOLD HER THE SITUATION?" a telepathic voice loudly reverberated in Sally's brain.

"YES, CAPTAIN," George replied, also telepathically. "BUT THE RATIONALE IS DIFFICULT FOR ME TO ARTICULATE. PERHAPS YOU COULD HELP?"

"I AM HAPPY TO DO SO," the Captain said, squatting next to Sally so that his large head was on level with hers.

Sally met his gaze directly with her own angry, unblinking green eyes.

"WE ARE SO GLAD YOU MADE IT THROUGH THE PORTAL TO NEW EARTH, SALLY," the Captain spoke loudly in her head. "YOU ARE GREATLY REVERED AS THE SAVIOR OF OUR ANCIENT SPECIES. YOU CONVINCED THE CREATOR TO GIVE US ALL A SECOND CHANCE. WE ARE FOREVER IN YOUR DEBT."

"Then why did you take Dave away from me?" she fiercely questioned him out loud.

"BUT DAVE IS ANOTHER MATTER," the dinosaur continued, unperturbed by her interruption. "HIS DESIRE TO MATE WITH YOU WAS UNALTERABLE. AS MUCH AS WE ADMIRE THE POSITIVE QUALITIES OF YOUR SPECIES, THE MANY NEGATIVES ALMOST DESTROYED OUR LINKED EARTHS. WE CANNOT RISK THAT HAPPENING AGAIN. SO WE ENLISTED YOU IN OUR CREW, KNOWING THAT DOING SO WOULD SOLVE THE PROBLEM IN A NONLETHAL AND YET IRREVOCABLE MANNER."

"I didn't want to be in your crew separated from Dave!" she spat back at him.

"NONETHELESS," the voice continued reverberating in her head. "YOU ARE NOW OUR VALUED CREWMEMBER, THE LAST LIVING HUMAN. THERE IS NO MORE DAVE. YOU MUST ACCEPT THE FACT THAT HE IS GONE. I AM SO SORRY WE HAD TO DO THIS TO YOU, BUT WE HAD NO CHOICE. I HOPE, IN TIME, YOU WILL COME TO UNDERSTAND THIS. MEANWHILE, WE HIGHLY VALUE YOUR MANY SKILLS AS AN HONORED MEMBER OF OUR CREW—EVEN THOUGH TO MOST OF US YOU ARE STILL A HIDEOUS BRUTE OF A SPECIES THAT BROUGHT DESTRUCTION TO OUR PAST WORLD."

There was a moment of silence.

Sally stared at the intelligent dinosaur for a full minute before responding.

Then she *slapped* it as hard as she could across its reptilian-looking face.

It *sprang backward*, a three-clawed hand stuck to the side of its face in horror, its thick red tongue slipping in and out of its large, many-toothed mouth in shock!

Sally's hand hurt. That dinosaur sure had a tough hide.

This time the entire crew gasped in horror. Sally realized that this sort of behavior was beyond their understanding. Physical assault was likely unknown and abhorrent in their matured, ancient culture.

Well, let them be shocked.

"I'm not helping you in any way," she sobbed, standing up to follow the still-glowing green lights in the floor back to her little room.

"Sally!" George called after her.

But she ignored him, tears streaming down her cheeks, as she strode purposefully away.

She was *five hundred light-years* away from Earth, traveling in a Starship that was about to explore another solar system containing an Earth-like planet.

But she didn't care.

Without Dave her life now seemed empty. Yes, he'd often been a pain. Yes, she'd found him compulsive and excessive. But...he'd been her friend through the most extraordinary adventures imaginable! To lose him forever was a crushing blow.

But there was something even worse. These reptilian bastards treated her not like the Royalty they claimed her to be—but as an inferior *pet* to be ordered around at their pleasure.

Well she wasn't a house-broken cat to be spayed or neutered at the whim of her master.

Damn it, she was a *human being*—maybe the *last* real one existing—but equally as intelligent as them.

She deserved *respect!*

If she'd known they wouldn't allow further human breeding...maybe she could have negotiated a compromise with them. Actually, she was happy being single. She hadn't planned on getting married and having children anyway. And if the result was the end of the human race, so what? She wasn't that impressed with the human race either. Maybe she would have gone along with the prohibition voluntarily.

But to be treated like a stupid animal was beyond reconciliation.

They were just a bunch of dumb dinosaurs.

And they could all go straight to hell!

Chapter 4

HIDDEN TREASURES

Don't forget to dig in the dirt

Looking only for the obvious is boring

When the fun is in the unexpected discovery

A flash to the brain, fodder for one's pallet

A more delicious feast than buttered crabs

Searching the deep, dangerous seas

That sunken chest filled with gold

Jewels and coins from the distant past

Lost forever, but now rediscovered

What an amazing "high" to find them

Not just crumbling remains from wrecks

But the scintillating exhilaration

Of past dead songs resurrected

Their melodies sung one last time...

Homo sapiens Eulogy, 4:19-24

Dave had a hollow feeling in his gut.

It was like Sally wasn't just separated from him, but forever lost.

He hoped that wasn't true, but put nothing past his new "masters".

And he was suffering the humiliation of being "branded."

Trying to ignore the stabbing pain as Snake continued to work on his wrist, he sang beneath his breath "Clementine" over and over.

He particularly liked the verse: "LIGHT SHE WAS AND LIKE A FAIRY, AND HER SHOES WERE NUMBER NINE; HERRING BOXES, WITHOUT TOPSES, SANDALS WERE FOR CLEMENTINE."

He had no idea what most of that meant. But the verse had a nice ring, distracting him from the "operation"—as needles repeatedly punctured his wrist and arm.

But then, finally, Snake was finished.

He'd gone around Dave's entire lower wrist three times. Dave looked down to see inked about his lower arm a *Green Anaconda Tattoo*, seemingly coiled around his wrist. Wow! Studying it closely, Dave saw the familiar black ovals on deep olive green of the coils of the powerful jungle snake. And where the underbelly showed on the snake, it was pale yellow, exactly as with a real anaconda. The head was large and fierce-looking, complete with dark eyes and a flicked-out forked tongue.

"How's it look, man?" Snake said, carefully stowing his gear back into his side-pouch.

"It's...amazing!" Dave said, holding it up to the sunlight. Just like Snake had told him, having the stabbing stop plus the reality of having it on his wrist was exhilarating. It was his first-ever tattoo, and it was indeed beautiful. It looked alive—as if it were going to crawl right off of his arm.

"Well, be careful with it, man," Snake said, now looking critically at his work shimmering brightly in the noon sunlight. "I didn't do all that work jist to have you messin' it up."

"It's so *bright*," Dave marveled, amazed at the brilliant colors. "Did you put something special in the ink—like Dark Matter or something—or is that just how they all look when they're fresh?"

"Dark Matter?" Snake softly replied. "Whut made you say that, man?"

"It just sprang to my mind, Snake," Dave replied, sensing he'd hit on an important topic. "Remember I'm a physicist. When Judgment Day came we'd just recently discovered that the known universe consisted of only about 5% ordinary matter. About two-thirds of the universe is Dark Energy. And the rest—about a fourth of the universe—is an invisible substance labelled 'Dark Matter'. We didn't know what it is. We just knew that it was some sort of not-yet-characterized, mysterious subatomic particle. And since you said it works through subspace, plus Sally's *Turtle Tattoo* was warning us about Time and Dark Energy-related events, maybe..."

"I'm 'fraid that's a 'trade secret'—whut's in my pigments, man," Snake cut him off, curtly closing off the discussion. "It's fer us keepin' tabs on you, that's all you need to know. So if you get in trouble, jist rub it like a genie-lamp. And maybe I'll come rescue you, huh?"

Dave looked at him suspiciously.

"Are you serious?" Dave carefully asked the goateed young man. "Can you really communicate with me through this thing, not just keep tabs on where I am?"

"Not fer you to know, dude," Snake said, refusing to answer directly. "Let's jist say this is the cousin of Sally's Turtle Tattoo—and you know what *it* could do."

Dave glared at him.

"I only saw it glowing and heating up when Sally needed to be slowed, sped up, or moved in one direction or the other," Dave answered, gently touching his own fresh tattoo with a finger of his other hand.

"Hey, man, don't be messin' with it," Snake said, grabbing Dave's hand and moving it away from the tattooed wrist. "It's gonna need time to set. Plus it's like a wound now, easy to get infected. So don't be rubbin' on it or getting' dirt in it. You hear me?"

"Ok, ok," Dave agreed. "I won't bother it. But now that I'm branded, can you please get your 'High Council' to open up my cage?"

"It's already happening, man," the goateed young man said, glancing up at the sky.

Indeed, the ominous shimmer in the sky above Dave was rapidly vanishing.

And he now felt a gentle, cool breeze blowing across his shoulders.

He took in a deep breath, grateful for the fresh air. The air was again flowing through the lip of the valley down across everything inside. Dave hadn't realized how stale the air was getting. Now the fresh air was clearing his head.

"Well, ah've got lots to do," Snake said, standing up. "Gotta go, don't you know."

Dave stood up as well, keeping his newly tattooed left arm carefully away from his own body. He gingerly held it out a few inches from where it normally hung.

"I suppose you've got a lot of training to do for being a crewmember on that first interstellar mission," Dave appreciatively said. "I'll...well, I'll miss you when you leave, Snake. And I'm grateful to you for coming today—sorry again for hitting you. I was very upset when Sally vanished. You understand, right?"

Snake paused as if considering whether to say more.

"There's...no more starships for me, man," he shrugged. "But thet's ok—I'm still gettin' used to New Earth. There's lots to explore right here on the planet, and..."

"What happened?" Dave interrupted him, walking beside him as they headed back up to the lip of the valley. "I thought you were looking forward to traveling out of the solar system? You were going to be a Snake 'ambassador' to the stars, right? Didn't you tell me your other Martian comrades weren't interested, so you'd be the only Snake in the Dinosapien crew?"

Snake ducked his head sadly.

"Please don't attack me again," he replied, cringing.

"What the hell?" Dave gasped. He jerked to a stop and grabbed Snake by his thin arm, spinning him around to be face-to-face.

"Look, I didn't want it to happen and..."

"You said that to me before! Now tell me everything or I'm going to beat you to a *pulp*, weakened arm or not."

Snake hung his head, not meeting Dave's eyes.

"They gave my seat to Sally, Dave," he whispered, so low that Dave could barely hear him.

"What are you saying?" Dave asked, not understanding.

"They put her onto the starship while she wuz still drugged—she didn't know anything about it. She didn't want to leave you, man, but now she's gone, off of New Earth."

"But...but...when will they return?"

"They're traveling at near-lightspeed to a distant star," Snake said, looking about furtively. His head ducked well down. He was whispering, his lips barely moving, apparently to avoid being "lip-read" on some spy-camera.

"You mean...?" Dave gasped, his knowledge of Einstein's famous equations jumping vividly to the front of his mind.

"Yes, man," Snake whispered back. "Our time, they won't be back for around a thousand years. We've lost her fer good, dude. I'm so, so sorry."

Dave saw tears dripping from Snake's eyes.

"You...can't...mean?" Dave gulped.

"Yah, man," Snake quietly sobbed. "I loved her too—jist as much as you, maybe more."

"But the original Sally..."

"Yep, I was jist her inker, not her boyfriend like with your Earth's Sally—but they wuz all *her*, man! I wasn't jist playin' a part when I pretended to be her boyfriend. And now...all of them Sally humans are gone. They're gone for good. We ain't never going to see them again."

"Can't your people get her back? You just told me you control her Turtle Tattoo!"

"It's physics, man...you should know!"

"But her Turtle Tattoo operates beyond known physics," Dave desperately persisted. "Just like with this thing you put on my arm, can't you...?"

"It's limited man. It's not magic. There are things even we can't do. Plus, there are...restrictions."

"Restrictions? I thought your people are super-smart ancient Marian aliens!"

"I wish..." Snake sighed dejectedly. "Man, we've forgotten a lot since those times. Plus our race lost a lot of technology when we were forced to abandon Mars. There are things we know to do and a lot we can't anymore."

"Well, do *something*, dammit!"

"Look, I wish we could reach out to Sally and bring her back. But there's jist nothin' we can do."

Snake now crumpled to the rocky path, sobbing uncontrollably.

Dave dropped to his knees and put an arm around the shaking shoulders of the thin, young man.

He also felt like crying. But he'd already shed too many tears.

Now, he was just filled with *rage*—at the arrogance of New Earth's reptilian and dinosaur rulers! They weren't content with just separating him and Sally on New Earth. They had to take her off the planet such that he'd be long dead whenever she returned.

But he wasn't just a helpless, ignorant human.

Just like Snake reminded him, Dave *was* a skilled Ph.D. physicist, damn it! He was the inventor of the Dark Energy Generator. And he'd had several lifetimes of experience now in the bizarre, *twisted* workings of space-time.

He knew from hard experience that *nothing* was "unreachable."

"Snake, tell me one thing," Dave whispered in his ear.

"W-what?" Snake snuffled, lifting up his thin face.

"*Where* are we?" Dave softly but intensely asked.

"W-what d-do you m-mean?" Snake snuffled.

Dave gripped him tightly around his thin shoulders, so that any spy sensors just saw him comforting the young man—but in reality to focus his attention.

"I know it's been a billion years of tectonic continental drift, of new mountain ranges rising up, of weather remodeling Earth's surface, and formation of new lakes and rivers," Dave calmly stated. "But if you were to correlate this valley with the surface of Earth when we entered the Portal a billion years ago—*where* is this future valley located?"

"Why..." Snake frowned, rubbing at his red eyes with prominent knuckles, "it's where the Portal opened up for you, I guess."

"Can you be more certain?" Dave again intensely whispered as he—to all watching cameras—seemed to be still comforting the crumpled-down Snake.

"Well...yes...now that I do the calculations in my head, that's it exactly," Snake whispered back. "This is where you wuz—in what you people called the *Wilderness of Judea*."

"Thank you," Dave said, helping Snake back up to his feet.

"So...you...?" Snake peered knowingly at Dave with his narrowed, beady black eyes.

"I really do appreciate your continued help!" Dave spoke loudly as he brushed dirt off the knees of Snake's faded jeans. "I guess I'm now your 'Boy with the Anaconda Tattoo', huh? I'm replacing the 'Girl with the Turtle Tattoo', right?"

"Uhm...sure, dude."

"And now that I'm under your oversight and care, will you come back and visit?" Dave continued in a normal voice.

"Well, sure," Snake now stated emphatically. "You kin count of me, man. I'm not gonna leave you all by yourself. Sally wuz both our friends, wasn't she?"

"I know she liked you a lot," Dave agreed, reaching out to shake Snake's hand. "It's hard to lose Sally, but life goes on, right?"

"That's right man. You jist gotta make the best of things."

"Then that's what I'm going to do. I'm going to stay right here and keep at my different projects. I'm not going to make any problem for you or your people or the Council."

"That's real good, Dave. I'm glad you're comin' to terms with all this."

"It's the way it is. I've got no choice. So I'm making the best of a bad situation," he repeated again for emphasis.

"Well, ok then. Good luck to you," Snake said, wiping his eyes as he walked away toward the lip of the valley across which Dave was forbidden to go. "And I liked your singing," Snake called back over his shoulder. "It's good you have them hobbies, helps pass the time."

"I'll keep busy!" Dave cheerfully called back at him, watching Snake trudge over the lip of the valley and away.

Dave knew that Snake understood.

Dave turned back to his hut to check on Breep. He and the little dinosaur had a lot of work to do together—if he was ever to see Sally again.

It was five months later. Sadly, Dave was no closer to taking overt action than when he'd first discovered that Sally was gone.

It was now the dead of winter.

Fortunately, he'd stocked away a very nice crop of potatoes and beans. That plus a shrinking stock of other vegetables plus a stash of nuts should last him through the winter. But his fields were now dormant, smothered under a thick layer of snow.

He was stuck for days on end inside the hut with Breep. There was nothing to do but strum his guitar and type on his laptop, continuing to write the first draft of his "*Luminary Chronicles*." The chapters became lyrical, free-form poems. After finishing a chapter he even slapped in chords and sang them accompanied by his guitar. That helped him to spot lapses in logic as well as his form. He obsessed on tightening up the words and rhythms, making them both thought and emotional-provocative. On one hand it was a total waste of his time. It now seemed doubtful that any future generations of humans would exist on New Earth to read it. But Dave felt compulsed to record the adventures and lessons he'd learned with his dear friend Sally. And at the least it was a way to fill in the time, keep him amused, and ponder the meaning—if any—of what he'd experienced. Fortunately, he'd found a way to extend the solar-charged batteries of his laptop, so that wasn't a limitation. Light from his wood-burning stove was now enough to keep the small computer charged during the dark winter days.

So he typed and typed, on and on. It came out in a rush. It was therapeutic. Plus it was pleasantly artistic. If anyone ever read it, the cryptic words would hopefully challenge people to do their own deep thinking on critical questions. Dave knew that a regular "story" would be quickly forgotten. But a mysterious account might just trigger personal growth in the reader—a "maturation" that might even affect the entire human species!

At least, that's what he hoped.

After all, "cryptic" description was the technique used by many of the writers of time-honored Holy Scriptures. If the Gospels were to be believed in the Bible, this was also a technique that the great Master Teacher himself, Jesus, had used—in order to intrigue and stimulate his disciples and audiences.

And there in the depths of the harsh winter, Dave finally finished the document, saving it onto a disc and carefully tucking it away in a sealed package in his hut.

He wrote a short note on the top of the package: "THE ADVENTURES OF DAVE KING AND SALLY SMITH—TO WHOM IT MAY CONCERN."

"There..." Dave sighed. "If I get trapped by a blizzard out there and die, maybe the lizard races will find it and give it to Sally when she returns in a thousand years."

It was a sad hope.

More likely, no human would ever read what he'd written. He'd poured out his soul to accomplish...what? Nothing—nothing at all. On the one hand it seemed a total waste of time and effort. But on the other hand it had kept him occupied in the cold, boring hut.

Now all he left to keep himself occupied was strumming and singing as many billion-year-old folk songs as he could remember, as lustily as possible. But Breep just looked annoyed whenever Dave started wailing. Perhaps his voice wasn't as supreme as he'd always imagined?

And yet another storm was brewing outside—with very dark clouds accumulating just beyond the surrounding mountains.

It looked particularly bad.

Winter made everything much more difficult. A thick blanket of snow covered everything. The weather had certainly changed in a billion years from what it was in the Wilderness of Judea. What once was a dry hot desert was now a well-watered paradise—except when covered with snow.

But Dave didn't care. The only thing he really cared about was his *search*...

He'd surveyed every inch of the valley. He'd taken the solar-powered laptop with him, running a program he'd written to detect even very weak evidence of three-dimensional "cosmic shear". Normally, astronomers dealt with whole clusters of galaxies to do such calculations. Instead, he was trying to detect the enhanced amplitude of the matter-power "spectrum" of the mountain peaks surrounding the valley. It was almost an impossible task—but the only way he knew to detect a very weak Dark Energy signature...

—of the *Obelisk!*

Sally had previously told him that the Obelisk on Mars was initially powered by heat from the core of that planet. But when that core cooled billions of years ago, the Obelisk's main power source was much-diminished or lost. Consequently, to activate the Obelisk Sally and her scientists on Mars installed a DE-generator within it. But without some electrical power to turn the DE-generator on, even it would remain dormant. But Dave hoped the Obelisk might find power somewhere—enough to produce a faint DE-signal large enough for

Dave to detect. With it, he might be able to triangulate the Obelisk's position in the valley.

After all, the Demon that tossed away the Obelisk in the final fight in the Wilderness of Judea didn't destroy it. It likely fell back down into the sandy hills, to be covered up by the sand yet again. As it was practically indestructible, it just might have survived another billion years buried beneath the ground.

That's why it was so important for Dave to "surrender" to the branding and thereby have the Dome sealing the valley turned off. The massive DE-signature of the Dome would have swamped out any tiny signal that Dave might detect in the valley.

Actually, Dave had no idea that the Obelisk had—or even could—survive another billion years into the future. The last he'd seen of the hundred-foot-tall Red Tower was it tumbling away up into the nuclear-winter clouds—tossed away by the Demon! So it might be totally lost, destroyed a billion years ago when it crashed back down to earth. Or, if it were still intact, could it even function after a thousand million years sitting dormant? But it was Dave's only hope.

He did know, however, that it was one *tough* ancient artifact.

The red Obelisk was an advanced product of the Martian ancient race of intelligent Snakes. They'd used it eons in the past to escape a dying Mars. It survived in a cavern on Mars for *billions of years* to be discovered by Sally. She and her team of scientists had modified it—adding in the DE-generator among other things—to take her 2,000 years into the past, so that she could interact with the historical Jesus in the 1st Century A.D. And then it survived for yet another 2,000 years into the future, buried underground, to be activated by that demon alien from the center of the Galaxy who masqueraded as Satan. If the Obelisk endured all that and still worked—who knew if it might function even now, a billion more years further into the future?

But *where* was it—assuming it still existed?

Likely it was buried beneath deep layers of accumulated rock, like an ancient fossil—waiting to be located and *dug up*. Sure, it was a very "iffy" quest, but it was the only thing that gave him even a tiny bit of hope.

It was getting dark outside the hut. That was when he and Breep normally crept out to do their intensive investigations of particular sites, weather permitting. Dave hoped the Dinosapien sensors would not see them sneaking around in the dark—thus figuring out what Dave was up to.

If the rulers of New Earth removed either him or the Obelisk from the valley, there was no hope of ever seeing Sally again.

"Well, ready to get to work?" Dave asked Breep.

"*Grrrrrrrrrrrrr,*" Breep growled from his ostrich-like beak, refusing even to approach the hut's rough wooden door. He backed off into a corner of the hut.

"What's the matter, boy?" Dave said, walking over to the cowering small dinosaur and patting him on his thick neck.

Then he heard it.

BANG! BANG! *BOOM!*

It was a lightning storm, a *big* one! For the several years Dave had lived in the valley, he'd experience occasional storms, but most were small and brief. This one, it appeared, was different.

Brilliant flashes came through small cracks in the rough-hewn walls of the hut. Dave knew that lightning was *searing* the valley!

The walls shuddered as *whipping, freezing wind* slammed into the hut.

"We're sure not sneaking out tonight, that's for sure," Dave sighed, putting the laptop and his gear under the bed where they'd be safest if the walls blew in. "In fact, this hut might not even be standing here tomorrow," he grimly admitted to Breep, who was cringing in a corner.

He took out his guitar and started singing. He knew it would detract Breep from their present perilous situation. Certainly it would distract him.

He began loudly singing a billion year-old folk song by Bob Dylan: "HOW MANY ROADS MUST A MAN WALK DOWN, HOW MANY SEAS MUST A WHITE DOVE SAIL, HOW MANY TIMES MUST THE CANNON-BALLS FLY? THE ANSWER MY FRIEND, IS BLOWING IN THE WIND...THE ANSWER IS BLOWING IN THE WIND."

Breep stuck his head down on the floor and covered his ears with his two three-fingered paws.

"Ah! So I got you distracted, my friend, by my disharmonious, squealing voice? Hah! Isn't *Bob Dylan* a great song-writer? Don't you just love him, Breep? And I've got a bunch *more* of Bob Dylan's songs rolling around in my head to sing tonight. Yep! We're going to sing this awful night away."

And so Dave kept on singing as the shaking and thundering outside grew louder.

As if in sympathy, Breep raised his head and began *howling!*

Dave had never heard that particular sound come out of Breep: as much participation as pain. So Dave strummed his chords even louder, singing even more lustily.

"IT AIN'T NO USE TO SIT AND WONDER WHY, BABE—IF YOU DON'T KNOW BY NOW. BUT DON'T THINK TWICE, IT'S ALRIGHT!"

Together—in wicked unison with Breep's anguished howling—they tried to drown-out the surrounding hurricane.

But finally, exhausted, they couldn't continue.

And it was getting very, very cold.

The fire in his small stove was struggling to provide heat, but the winter blasts outside were sucking the hut's heat out faster than it could be replenished.

So fully clothed in his winter clothes, Dave crawled up onto the crude straw bed and pulled the covers up over his body.

Breep hopped up and snuggled in beside him.

"Hey, boy, you know you're not allowed up here."

BOOM! BOOM! BOOM!

The *flashes of lightning* accompanying the thunder were intense—lighting up the interior of the hut as if nuclear bombs had gone off outside!

Indeed, the whole hut shook around them. Either an *earthquake* had hit, or the force of the lightning blasts was shaking the very mountains around the hut!

"Breeeeeeeepppppppp?" the dinosaur pleaded, ducking his head under Dave's straw pillow.

"Ok, boy," Dave sighed, letting the leathery beast fully dive under the covers with him. "I sure don't want you to freeze. You're my best friend in this valley since Snake never returned like he promised. And none of the other critters are near as smart as you. Grindle's out hibernating somewhere. So just tonight, let's keep you warm under the covers with me. I know your metabolism isn't 'cold-blooded' like people first thought you dinosaurs were. But you're also not a hot-blooded mammal either."

It was a long night. Dave heard parts of the thick roof above being ripped away by the hurricane-like blasts. The thunder and lightning were fierce, hitting close to the hut.

"Jesus, we're going to die," Dave groaned to Breep.

The shivering dinosaur just moaned in agreement.

The next day, amazingly still alive, Dave couldn't even get the door of the hut open. The hut was entirely encased in snow. Dave had to break through the roof to get outside. He was grateful for the sections in the thick roof thinned by the storm. Otherwise they would have been trapped for days. Then it took most of the rest of the day to dig out the main parts of his camp.

Finally, the dark clouds above were breaking up.

It was getting toward evening when a few shafts of sunlight filtered down through the clouds. Dave immediately got his laptop out, putting it where it could soak up energy. The battery was very low from struggling on firelight from the stove.

"I'll give it an hour to charge," Dave said to Breep, who was now outside in the sunlit snow dashing and jumping around like a little kid.

"Sunlight and snow gives kids a license to play," Dave laughed at the small dinosaur's antics.

Actually, Breep deserved it since he'd used his powerful hind legs to dig out the shed and wood supplies. Now Dave had a strong fire going in the rock "stove" in the hut. It would keep them nice and toasty through the next night.

An hour later as the sun was just sinking to touch the tips of the surrounding mountains, Dave took a careful reading with his laptop of his already-defined reference points around the valley.

"What the...?" he gasped, afraid he'd made a mistake.

He hastily got another set of readings as the sun sank behind the peaks, comparing it to the first.

It was very slight—just the shift of a few millimeters— but there was no denying it. A Dark Energy source had altered the relationships of his reference points! And Dave had enough information to pinpoint the source.

"Damn, it's really true there's always a positive along with the negatives!" Dave excitedly said to Breep, who hopped over and "bopped" Dave with his ostrich-like head.

"Uh...I mean...what a nice storm that was!" he loudly stated, in case a nearby spy-sensor picked up his prior exclamation. Luckily Breep was more suspicious and careful than he, warning him with that bop of his head. "How interesting—the electrical flux was considerable! Perhaps in the future I can find some way to capture and use the energy, maybe power-up my hut?"

But he was really thinking to himself—*all that lightning went into the ground and was enough to power up the DE-generator in the Obelisk. I've got a fix on it. Finally, I know where it is. Wahoo!*

He looked out over the lengthening shadows of the glistening-white, snow-bound valley. Halfway up the slope of the mountain on the other side of the valley was the DE-signature. He didn't know how he'd excavate there without alerting the Dinosapiens to his intentions. But now he was reassured that his project was at least possible.

He and Breep were going to do some *serious* digging.

Chapter 5

<u>**VIRTUOUS BRUTE**</u>

Oh, how you hate them
Those carnivorous "Top Predators"
Prowling outside your room
When you as a little kid shivered
Frightened to death of what might lurk
Out there in the nighttime shadows
Wolves, bears, snakes, and monsters
Ready to pounce on you as you slept
And then to rip you into tiny pieces
And greedily devour your parts
Savoring your bloody remains
Causing you incredible injury and pain
Before happily licking their chops
And slinking away back into the night
And so you relish the return of the light
Signaling you were still with Mommy and Daddy
And civilization was wrapped around you
Comforting, warm, strong, and safe
Protecting you from yourself
You the most vicious Predator of all
That you should have appreciated more...
Homo sapiens Eulogy, 5:8-13

Sally knew that something was very wrong.

She'd been a prisoner in her room for several weeks now within the Starship.

When she tried to go outside her room into the corridor, the door wouldn't open. So she only had the bed, mirror, and toilet to keep her company. It was worse than being in a prison. At least in a prison there'd be sounds, other people, and a routine. Here, the light was the same "day" or "night." There were no noises. There was no variation. It was always the same. It was maddening.

There wasn't even any feeding routine. A dispenser above the sink gave out two-inch cubes of a spongy, protein-tasting substance whenever she put her hand to its sensor-plate. The cubes didn't taste bad, although they were obviously not designed for a human pallet. They were thick and fibrous. Water she had to cup a hand for at the sink.

It was incredibly boring—except for what she saw out the "porthole." There, she saw an endlessly fascinating view of stars streaming past. It was similar to being in an airplane at a high attitude, looking down on Earth's surface—a slowly but ever-changing panorama. Stars were not fixed. Instead they were streams of multicolored light, which mingled and twirled off into the "distance". It was a laser show of the gods!

But she could only stare out the small porthole for so long before she tired.

She wished she had someone to talk with. She hoped that George would come by. But apparently she'd shocked everyone so much with her "bestial" behavior that she was cut-off from the crew.

She almost gave up on her resolve. But she was stubborn. She was still furious about being shanghaied without her knowledge or consent. Perhaps in time she'd relent. But for now she refused to give her Dinosapien captors the satisfaction of cooperation.

So she fought off boredom by forcing herself to go back systemically over everything that had happened since the original Dave noticed her cute little Turtle Tattoo as she worked in the grocery store in Sulphur, Oklahoma.

It was a long list of amazing events.

At the time, they'd all seemed like horrible ordeals. But now, looking back—with apparently endless time to contemplate them— she recognized an incredible series of adventures.

First of all, Dave had "kidnapped" her into a completely new Dimension from her own, where history was markedly different. She'd discovered there a living duplicate of her dead mother. And with the help of a neural matrix from a time-traveler from the future, she'd fixed Dave's invention such that it could crack open subspace and release concentrated Dark Energy in a controlled fashion—plus have other unpredictable side-effects.

And then she and Dave were thrown into the distant past to be chased by giant dinosaurs. After that they'd traveled to the moon in the future to witness God's wiping clean the surface of the Earth on Judgment Day. Trying to change history, they'd gone back to their own time on Earth—but where Sally was required to do the most terrible thing of all, kill Dave! But the ancient race of intelligent Martian snakes gave her another choice—to go back into the past to when she first met Dave and try, with her hard-won future knowledge, to *change history!*

But in the new timeline, *she* ended up kidnapping Dave. Then, separated from him, she was thrown through time to a human city located on Mars, a thousand years in the future, to again witness the relentlessly approaching Wrath of God. Following that, she was thrown into the distant past where she picked up her newly hatched baby dinosaur pet "Breep." Then she was back in the present to earn a couple billion dollars to initiate her *Church of Perpetual Health.* Then she found herself back on Mars a mere five hundred years in the future, again witnessing the time-advanced Judgment Day. Then she was thrown back to the 12th Century A.D. to be a nun living for fourteen years in the German Convent of *Mother Hildegard von Bingen.*

Yes, being a 12th Century nun in a society and religion where women were second-class citizens both secularly and spiritually was a profound and frustrating educational experience. But it also trained her with the inspirational qualities necessary to eventually head up a whole new religion.

Then Breep saved her from being burned alive at a stake for heresy. What a faithful little dinosaur he was! Everyone should have a pet like Breep. Escaping back to the present, Sally then consolidated her new science-based Church and built up a huge fortune—enough to return to Mars and establish a colony for the human race to escape God's Wrath. And by then she was an old woman, thinking she'd succeeded.

But God was way ahead of her...knocking the Martian moon Phobos out of its orbit to smash into Mars and destroy her colony! Where—in a last frantic effort to yet again change history—she used an ancient Martian artifact, the *red Obelisk*, to travel back to the 1st Century to try and stop Jesus from becoming an icon of history, thus indirectly preventing the overuse of Dark Energy! But to survive this particular trip back through time via the unknown mechanism of the Obelisk, she'd had to transmute her body with a dangerously huge dose *Optimmune Retroviral Immune-Enhancer* originating in her future other-dimensional timeline. So she arrived back in the 1st Century as a five year old girl, with no supplies and a dead Obelisk.

She failed in her mission to stop Jesus, instead willingly giving up her own life in that attempt. But, amazingly, Jesus preserved her body to be reanimated 2,000 years in his future. There she battled an incarnation of Satan beside Dave and an elderly warrior Jesus—where she finally totally surrendered to God. This apparently "tempted" God into granting them a reprieve. Thus she and Dave were thrown past the time-barrier that bottled up a condemned mankind, arriving in the far distant future on a revived New Earth!

And so now she was a billion years in the future on a spaceship traveling at near lightspeed to a distant star—forever separated from her friend, the now long-dead Dave.

And along the way, coincidently, the different timelines had spawned at least three other versions of her—all who met untimely but heroic ends.

And through all of these wondrous adventures, the faithful *Turtle Tattoo* on her wrist mysteriously guided her at each step.

"Well, kiddo, why aren't you helping me now?" she wryly laughed, looking down at the now-faded Turtle Tattoo on her wrist.

It just sat there, looking like any other of the number of tattoos adorning her body.

But...did she detect a faint glow from it?

Ah...it was just a sparkle of light coming in from the porthole.

But how was that possible? The starlight was diffuse, not intense.

It was an *ominous* omen.

Then through the inertial-dampers of the spacecraft, she felt a faint tug on her body.

"Oh, are we finally there?" she said to the Turtle Tattoo as she went back over to the porthole and looked out.

The tattoo did not answer her.

But yes, they were definitely slowing. The streaks of light were resolving into individual stars against the black of space—solid and bright. And growing in size ahead of them, just visible to her by peering forward along the curve of the porthole—was a *planet.*

"That must be Kepler-186f," she whispered in awe.

As the planet grew larger Sally saw blue, gold, and white patches on the distant sphere. Clearly, it was an Earth-like planet. And behind it was a reddish, small sun.

She felt a shiver go down her spine.

Sally knew she should be thrilled. They were approaching a whole different world outside the solar system! This was a magnificent achievement. They had traveled to another star!

And yet here she was locked into her room because of her stupid, brutish behavior—both physically and mentally. Was she really just a smart animal who needed to be kept in a cage?

But as the planet grew larger and larger—now clearly showing wide oceans, dispersed continents, and white-caped poles—she saw something else...

A lot of *little black specks* were rising to meet them as they slipped into orbit around the planet!

It looked like a distant swarm of locust, or buzzards, or bats, or hornets, or...

"Oh, hell!" Sally exclaimed to her one friend, the Turtle Tattoo sitting patiently on her wrist. "I sure hope the Dinosapiens are raising their energy shields. That swarm looks like a *fleet of spaceships!* Who knows what their intentions might be?"

Sally was startled to feel a *flash of heat* at her wrist. Looking down, she saw that her Turtle Tattoo was now visibly *glowing*—and pulsating.

"Uh oh!" she gasped, realizing that something very bad was about to happen.

She hopped away from the porthole over to the locked door and starting BANGING loudly on it.

"Hey!" she yelled. "Let me *out!* There are spaceships coming up at us! There's a civilization down there! And I don't think that they're friendly!"

But only silence answered her back.

Sally again jumped back over to the porthole and saw the swarm now encircling her spaceship! And a single scary craft was approaching: totally black, very angular, and covered with *sharp spikes!* The black alien spaceship was only visible against the blackness of space when it obscured the brilliant panorama of pinpoint stars, or when red sunlight glinted off its surface.

"I don't like that 'Spike-Ship' at all," Sally grated as the heat from her Turtle Tattoo continued to increase.

She *gasped* as she saw a cloud of the wicked-looking spikes suddenly *leap off* the approaching craft and *streak* straight towards her!

"Oh hell!" she shouted as she involuntarily ducked...

—as *LARGE EXPLOSIONS* rocked the room Sally was in, the "missiles" *smashing* through the Starship!

Sally was thrown to the floor then floated upward. The artificial gravity gone!

She smelled smoke as she kicked against a wall and floated over to the door, grabbing its handle. She saw it was now warped inward on its frame. There was a large gap along one side. She got her fingers into the gap, stuck her feet against the wall to the side of the warped door, and pulled as hard as she could.

With a loud *"krinch"* sound the door twisted out of its frame, creating a space big enough for Sally to push herself through.

In the corridor Sally felt partial gravity restored, her feet drifting down to the floor. She saw several Dinosapiens floundering in bellowing black smoke, clearly panicked. Their thick, powerful tails flailed-about wildly—smashing into the walls and into each other!

They were making strangled "clicking" and "sputtering" noises.

She ducked beneath the grasping arms of one of the intelligent dinosaurs and felt her way along through the smoke. At her feet she saw again those same flashing green lights flashing...yay! Now she knew where to go.

She followed them again to the central control chamber: where she saw control stations disrupted and scattered-about. The "clicking" and "chittering" noises were louder. And above their heads, the clear plastic dome was ominously *cracked*.

"Sally!" a panicked human voice sounded off to the side.

Sally saw a middle-aged, black-haired woman in the same white uniform as herself hurrying over.

"Who are you?" Sally said, coughing from the smoke.

"I'm Alice, George's wife," the woman said, coughing as well, catching hold of Sally's arm. "I'm morphed just like him to interact with you better. George was hurt in the explosions. The Captain's down as well. We don't know what to do. You saved us before from the Harvester, Sally. Help us now!"

"I did *what* now?"

"Oh, you know what to do!" Alice hurriedly continued, leading Sally through the confusion over to a crumpled-down Dinosapien. "And yes, it was the *other* Sally who saved our city before, but she was still you. Please, help us! We just don't know what to do. We don't understand fighting and battles. We were waiting in a friendly stance when that alien craft fired its spikes at us!"

Sally grimaced.

"So *now* you want me—a 'hideous brute'!" Sally huffed at her. "Before I was just an animal to you, but now you need my animal cunning and brutality, huh? Is that right?"

"YES, THAT IS TRUE," a booming voice sounded in her head, making her wince. "PLEASE FORGIVE US OUR INSULTS...AND HELP US! WE BEG YOU, SALLY."

Sally recognized the captain.

Shrapnel stuck from his heaving chest, around which red blood was swiftly flowing.

"HERE, HUMAN," his voice sounded in her mind, growing weaker. With a trembling three-clawed hand he removed the silver chain with the five dangling gold stars from around his neck. "PUT THIS AROUND YOUR NECK...PLEASE," he concluded, lapsing into unconsciousness, his big oblong head lolling off to the side.

The big Dinosapien crumpled and lay still. The captain was dead.

Alice grabbed the necklace from the Dinosapien's claws and slid it over Sally's brown, bushy hair to settle comfortably around her neck.

"You are now officially in command," Alice urgently pleaded. "So tell us what to do, Sally. We don't understand violence. We approached this world as friends, with open hands!"

"You didn't have any shields up?" Sally gasped. "Is that what happened? You just let those alien ships attack you, defenseless?"

"We didn't know! And we didn't want to seem antagonistic. So we didn't even think to put up shields," she moaned.

Sally shook her head in amazement, quickly assessing the horrific situation.

That black spike-laden ship was still hanging out there, apparently waiting to see Sally's Starship's response to the attack.

The Dinosapien crew was getting the internal fires under control, patching the worst of the damage as best they could. Consoles were being put upright again. But the cracks in the transparent dome above were steadily lengthening!

"Listen up!" Sally shouted into the chaotic room, trusting that they'd hear her telepathic thoughts if not understand her English verbiage. "The Captain has put me in command! Raise the shields! Raise all the shields you have! Get a force-field surrounding the ship! Do it right *now!*"

Sally saw more of the spikes start streaking off of the alien ship—streaking toward them—that *bounced* off of a blue globe now surrounding the ship, *not* striking the already-cracked dome.

"Good!" Sally yelled again. "Whatever else that has to be compromised, keep that shield up. It'll give us time to figure out our next move."

Sally turned to the trembling woman beside her.

"Alice, can you tell me about this ship's weapons?"

"Weapons?" the woman said, shaking her head in puzzlement.

"Sure—like particle guns, or laser beams, or missiles," Sally urgently queried. "Surely after your experience with the alien Harvester spaceships you knew to put ship-to-ship weapons into your Starship, right?"

"Well," Alice shrugged helplessly, "we thought that those terrible Harvesters were just for scavenging planets marked by God for destruction, not the norm of alien intelligences. So we didn't think to..."

"You've got no offensive weapons at all?" Sally gasped in disbelief.

"None..."

"Jesus Christ!" Sally swore angrily at Sally. "For an advanced race you Dinosapiens are really *stupid!*"

"We've l-lost...our c-capacity for senseless...v-violence," George said, staggering up to Alice. He was grimacing in pain. One of his arms hung limply at his side, clearly broken. "Perhaps these attackers w-will just g-go away?" he hopefully stammered, looking upward through the cracked dome.

Nope.

The attacking spaceship was slowly drawing nearer—as were dozens more of the hundreds or thousands of ships that surrounded the lonely Dinosapien Starship!

Sally strode purposefully over to a console where a gaggle of the big dinosaurs were frantically working. Clearly it was the only remaining fully-functional unit.

Behind her staggered George supported by Alice.

"What's the status of the ship?" Sally coldly said to the crewmembers there.

A cacophony of voices echoed all at once inside Sally's head, making no sense while causing her a huge headache.

"George, Alice, what are they saying?" Sally said, holding her hands to the sides of her head.

"We're badly damaged," George gasped.

"We're just barely keeping the shield up," Alice added.

"How long to make repairs so we can start maneuvering this bucket of bolts—before maybe trying to outrun and escape these aliens?" Sally snapped back at them.

"Oh...maybe..." George said, frowning.

"—days or weeks," Alice concluded for him.

"*Days* or *weeks?*" Sally loudly yelled in exasperation, the Dinosapiens around her cringing-back.

She looked up at the encircling mass of spiky spaceships, which were now linking to each other via their spikes!

—and "thudding" onto the protective force field globe were now things that looked like *toilet plungers*, attached to the spiky ships by long cables. And where the plungers attached to the energy shield right above Sally's ship, the force field turned from blue to *red*, grew *thinner*, and began "sparking".

It wouldn't be long and the Starship would be totally exposed.

"Perhaps we could negotiate with them?" Alice hopefully asked Sally, her black eyes wide with fear.

"Yes, we should definitely attempt communication," George added, nodding his bald head repeatedly. "Perhaps despite our welcoming stance they thought *we* were the aggressors. They might be just trying to defend themselves. Any rational beings smart enough to build such crafts must be reasonable. We could try to...?"

"Look up at the planet!" Sally yelled again, focusing their haphazard attentions. The dinosaur heads of the other crewmembers pointed upward also.

From the nearest continent, *fresh columns* of the black dots were rising up.

"Those things may not even be alive," Sally said, observing the swarms intently. "They may be merely an automatic planetary defense, perhaps evolved against attacks from other planets in this system. Whatever, they're trying to box us in, wall us off. We may be like a contagion to them, to seal off then suck dry."

Indeed, the "suckers" on the ship's wavering energy shield were increasing in numbers. The red, thinned areas were spreading. The protective force field wouldn't last much longer.

"Sally, what can we do? You saved us before!" George pleaded with her. "Can't you do it again?"

"How did I—I mean my other self—save you from the Harvester before?"

"You surrendered yourself to them and they left," Alice summarized.

"Well, they're clearly not after me—they're after *you*," Sally retorted.

"Then *we* s-should s-surrender! We could lower our s-shield. That will s-show them w-we're..." George replied.

Sally looked at him with cold contempt, cutting off his sputtering cowardness.

She walked over to an overturned large chair, righted it, and sat solidly in it.

"S-Sally?" George said, stumbling over to her.

"She's thinking, dear," Alice said, holding George back.

"Oh, right."

The "leaches" above kept draining away what little remained of the ship's power. The black ships continued arriving to wall Sally's vessel into a solid cocoon. And Sally furiously calculated in her head. The odds were completely against them, but just maybe...

"Is the DE-generator damaged?" Sally quietly asked Alice.

Alice was silent a moment as she relayed the request.

"The crew says it escaped damage from the spikes that smashed through the ship," Alice said. "It's still powering the force field, but the energy is being sucked away by those things out there!"

"Where is it located?"

"It's in the main engine compartment."

"Take me there."

Alice sat the crippled George down in a chair and waved for other Dinosapiens to help him. Then she placed Sally on the back of one of the Dinosapiens, herself on another, and together they galloped away into the smoke-filled bowels of the ship.

In a large compartment where glowing, pulsating tubes wrapped and convoluted around each other—where energy fields shimmered in various shades of purple—Sally saw something comfortingly familiar.

It was a DE-generator, a large one.

She hopped off the back of the Dinosapien she'd been riding and tore off a panel from the generator's side.

Looking inside, she saw the internal control matrix. It was similar to ones she'd constructed with Dave pre-Judgment-Day—and then perfected on Mars with her team of scientists for inserting into the Obelisk.

"Does anyone have a long screwdriver?" she hopefully asked.

Nothing!

"Ah, hell," she said, reaching in and starting to rewire different connections by hand. It was tight and dangerous to have her hands inside where vast amounts of energy were being generated—but if she could just manage to keep her hands off the key power conduits, then...

"Sally, what are you doing?" Alice said, crouching beside her.

"I'm trying to reconfigure your generator's energy conduits to have the DE-generator create a *large* rip in subspace—*much bigger* than the tiny controlled one which allows spurts of Dark Energy to erupt to drive our spaceship to near lightspeed."

"But won't that kill us?"

"Maybe...but perhaps not," Sally said, reaching far inside now to shift a stubborn module. "We did this with the Martian Obelisk— which allowed the entire structure to do something that was never intended, to fall into subspace. That's how I traveled in a controlled fashion back in time 2,000 years to the 1st Century A.D."

"So you think our *entire ship* could...?"

"Maybe!"

"But...our scientists say that's incredibly dangerous...?"

"Yep!"

"But...how long did it take for you to do that with your 'Obelisk'?" Alice breathlessly asked.

"Oh...it took...a large team of my scientists and me several years of full-time work."

"Years?" Alice gulped.

"Yes, years," Sally answered, painfully reaching even deeper into the large unit. "So...jerry-rigging this one...we've got a good chance to have *anything* happen. Hah! But anything's better than being dead, right?"

"P-perhaps we should a-ask the r-rest of the crew's scientists to...?"

"I'm the Captain now!" Sally yelled-out defiantly as she just managed to drag out two thick dangling wires—and then hold them dramatically above her head. "And when I put these conduits together the whole ship will fall into subspace—maybe...or we'll be instantly incinerated! One of the two! Anyone taking bets? Huh?"

"Sally, I really think we should..." Alice tried to protest.

—as Sally slammed the two ends together...

—and a *very bright white light* blazed through the entire engine room!

—as Sally felt her body being *electrocuted!*

—and she *screamed* in agony...

—as everything faded away and vanished.

Chapter 6

LOST SOULS

None of you want to be lost
But think of the fun of the journey
Not having any idea where you are going
Life just an endless Adventure and expedition
No destination in mind or agenda for tomorrow
Going wherever the tide might take you
Drifting on the wind, everything new
Sure, it's not for the faint of heart
But if you did take that ride
Bobbing so way-up high
What a hot-air balloon
The ultimate trip
Drifting alone
Part of the sky...

Homo sapiens Eulogy, 6:34-38

Dave and Breep continued their "survey" of the valley.

At least, Dave hoped that's what his unseen jailors saw when they tracked his movements.

In reality, Dave and Breep were trudging through deep snow up the mountainside where the DE-signature originated the day before.

The storm was gone. The sky was a deep blue. But it was bitterly cold, with a strong wind whistling down though the valley.

Dave was bundled up as warm as possible, carrying a pickaxe, shovel, his backpack containing supplies plus his laptop, and unlit torches for working into the night. Fortunately he'd been given the farming utensils by the Dinosapiens to use in clearing and tilling his fields. If they had to dig, they'd need those tools.

But obscuring most of those things was his large, home-made guitar, slung over his back.

Hopefully the sensors scattered around the valley would just see him taking a fun stroll, not embarking on a deadly serious archeological expedition!

"You ok, boy?" Dave asked Breep who bounded along beside him, kicking up flurries of white snow.

"*Sqwack!*" the dinosaur answered, clearly excited.

Breep had blankets firmly lashed around his neck and body to keep him warm out in the freezing weather.

"Then right up there is where we saw the...the *iron ore outcropping*...that we'll maybe want to dig up to make, uhm, homemade stove and kitchen utensils and such!" Dave loudly but lamely finished.

Hopefully that would explain their stop at the outcropping to the unseen jailors.

And there it was.

Halfway up the steepening slope, sticking out of the snow was a cliff. And below the cliff was a *freshly fractured opening* leading into the depths of the mountain.

"Jesus!" Dave gasped to Breep as they trudged up to the dark opening. "This ravine is brand new. In fact, I think it happened last night when our hut got tossed around. It must have opened during the earthquake," he explained to the dinosaur that was sniffing suspiciously at the dark cleft.

Dave was very excited. This would make his work much easier. It would have taken weeks or even months to hack his way into the side of the mountain. And if this crack was *due* to the Obelisk, it might really be because of a surge of *activity* triggered by the lightning of the night before.

"*Breeeeeeepppp!*" the dinosaur barked, sticking his head expectantly into the dark opening in the cliff.

"Yes, Breep," Dave loudly replied. "There could be a good vein of *iron ore* revealed inside that crevice!"

Yes, this was what he'd hoped for all along—that the ancient DE-generator inside the Obelisk might still be functional though previously dormant. The unusual lightning storm injected massive waves of electrical current into the ground. Did the lightning surge manage to trigger the Obelisk or its attached DE-generator?

"We're going exploring!" Dave exclaimed to the unseen spy microphones. He lit one of the primitive torches he'd brought with him.

He carefully entered the dark split in the mountain, with Breep right behind him.

It was a deep crack in the rock, angled down. Water was dripping from above, making the torch sputter. And the rough "tunnel" ended about a hundred yards into the mountain. But the rock at that point looked crumbled and soft. Perhaps they could keep digging deeper?

"At least our 'dear' jailors' hidden sensors can't possibly hear or see us under all this rock," Dave said to Breep as he positioned the torch carefully into a small crack on the side of the narrowed, rough tunnel.

He set his guitar and supplies off to the side, unlimbered his pick-axe, and started "thudding" it into the wall at the end of the tunnel, jerking out large and small hunks of rock.

Breep happily jumped forward to fling the debris back into the tunnel behind them with his powerful clawed legs.

So Dave made quick progress forward, digging at least a dozen feet into the rocky hillside before his aching muscles forced him to stop.

Breathing heavily, he lit the second and last torch from the dying embers of the first one. Then he sat down and opened his backpack.

He took out dried potatoes, tossing a couple over to Breep, who happily gobbled them down. Then Dave uncorked a small jug of water and took a few welcome swigs from it.

Finally he took out his laptop and opened the lid...

—immediately seeing a weak RF signal clearly registering now through the much-lessened rock barrier!

"Oh, my God," he said to Breep. "It's the Obelisk! It's communicating with us. It's *alive!*"

Breep "thumped" over and plopped down next to Dave, breathing heavily from his own exertions, putting his head into Dave's lap.

"Let's see now...what if I...?" Dave said, patting Breep on his leathery head while reaching around to try to activate his Internet-like connection mechanisms that'd been dormant since arriving in the distant future from a billion years in the past...

—and an *oscillating line along a three axis grid* suddenly showed up on his laptop screen!

"It's the basic CPU activity-indicator for the DE-generator," Dave gasped, delighted. "That means the Obelisk can't be far away. We've got to keep digging!"

He gently pushed Breep off, put the laptop safely off to the side, grabbed up his pickaxe, and flailed away at the rock.

Then on a powerful swing he *broke through* and *fell forward*, landing on his side...

—in astonishment, seeing by the light of the torch behind him...a large cavern!

"Jesus H. Christ!" Dave gasped as Breep scampered in behind him.

Right there in front of him was the Obelisk.

The *long, rectangular red structure* looked mostly intact. About a third of its lower half was still buried in solid rock. Dave estimated that it was one hundred feet long and twelve feet in diameter, roughly square along its length. The exposed top two-thirds of the Obelisk lay at an angle such that the end of it was lifted up above the flooring of the cavern. The cavern itself was a melted, perfect half-sphere. Likely at some point in the past billion years an energy-release from the Obelisk melted the rock, creating the cavern.

Dave slowly stood up, ignoring the bruises where he'd fallen onto his side, walked back to get the torch, and went on into the cavern.

He held the torch in one hand as he walked across the uneven floor of the cavern, cautiously approaching the Obelisk. He stretched out a hand and put it on the red glassy surface, expecting it to be ice-cold.

Instead, it was *warm.*

"Oh my God!" Dave exclaimed to the prancing-around Breep. "This thing's more than just activated by the lightning, it's *functioning!*"

Indeed, he could feel a steady *vibration* coming from the Obelisk, as if it were poised to do something!

"But where did it get the power?" Dave mused. "A brief electrical jolt couldn't charge its 'batteries' for continual activation, could it?"

"Breep! Breep! Breep!" the dinosaur repeatedly snorted at him.

Yep, the animal felt the vibrations as well.

Oh...right...Sally said it accumulated energy from the fabric of time. And it had lain there motionless for *a billion years!* The bloody thing must be filled to the brim with time-energy! If it wasn't for the lightning triggering the DE-generator inside and Dave finding it, the whole thing might have soon jumped away on its own anyway!

After all, it was semi-intelligent. It had a mind of its own. And now that alien mind was turning itself on.

"Can we get inside?" Dave said, now setting the torch off to the side. He ran his hands across its smooth surface searching for a crack, an opening, a panel.

Breep began "*squawking*" on top of it, having scrambled up to hop along its slanted surface. He was scratching at something with his clawed forepaws.

Dave ran back to the end embedded down in the rock and walked up the slant to where Breep was scratching.

Sure enough, there was a panel that Breep had managed to pop partially up from what before must have been a perfect seal. The massive earthquake must have loosened it. Dave stuck the tip of his pickaxe into the small crack and—using the blade as a lever—forced up the panel...

—which snapped off and fell over to the side of the Obelisk.

Beneath that was yet another, more-solid looking doorway. It looked wide enough to allow either Dave or Breep to go through if they could only figure out how to get it to open.

Dave felt a pain and looked down at his wrist.

His Anaconda Tattoo was *glowing*.

"Of course," Dave nodded, pressing his wrist firmly onto the doorway, which promptly *swung outward* as if on spring-loaded hinges.

"My tattoo," Dave explained to Breep, who was sniffing suspiciously into the suddenly revealed dark space, "was made by our friend Snake, a shape-shifted alien of ancient Martian origin—the very same race that built this Obelisk. No wonder he insisted on 'branding' me. He knew I might find the Obelisk and I'd need a 'key' to get it to open up for us!"

Dave ran back down the slope of the Obelisk, got the torch, and climbed back up.

Holding it above the revealed space, Dave could now see what looked like an equivalent of a storage closet—completely filled with various boxes.

He reached in and grabbed one, pulling it out of a slot. Opening it, Dave was shocked to see what looked like a stack of neatly wrapped *sandwiches*.

Opening one with shaking hands he saw it looked edible.

Afraid of what it might taste like he took a tentative nibble.

"Good Lord Almighty!" Dave gasped in amazement. "It's *tuna*, a tuna sandwich. And there are little bits of celery in it. It tastes like it was made yesterday!"

Having subsisted mostly on dried potatoes and beans for several months now, Dave found the sandwich incredibly delicious.

He scarfed it down. Then he handed the remaining sandwiches to Breep who likewise greedily gobbled them.

"But how is that possible, Breep?" he said in wonderment. "These must have been made by the High Priestess' people for when she arrived back in the 1st Century—more than a billion years ago!

Time-stasis...that must be it—this whole compartment must have preserved everything in it perfectly!

Indeed, there was a faint blue glow from within. Dark Energy was at work here, plugged into the function of the storage area.

Dave began eagerly pulling out more boxes—finding food, water, and other supplies. Then he paused at one small square, pocket-sized box.

Opening it, he saw a hundred large white pills.

"Is this Optimmune?" he gasped. "If I were to take some...the right dosage...might I survive the thousand years to be still alive when Sally returns from her interstellar voyage?"

He gratefully slipped the pillbox into a pocket of his coat.

Now his attention was focused on what he discovered right behind the thick layer of supplies—a solid apparatus.

The torch was burning out.

Dave knew he should call it a night and return to his hut, coming back fresh the next day.

But he was too excited to quit.

Dave ran and got his laptop, using the light from the computer screen to continue his study of the complex apparatus that lay right behind the outer layer of supply boxes.

Yes, it was the *Dark Energy generator.*

"Exactly!" Dave nodded in satisfaction, speaking to the ever-present, faithful Breep. "Sally said that she and her team of scientists installed it in the Obelisk to control its function. This was what allowed her to get the Obelisk to take her to a specified destination. If I can just figure out how it interfaces, then maybe I can also use the Obelisk to take me wherever *I* want to go in space and time. I might even be able to reach Sally!"

And now on his laptop there was more than just a basic energy-usage graph showing. It was his complete array of control apps for DE-generators!

"Oh boy, oh boy," he practically panted in excitement. "This generator is far more complex than anything I ever built, but it recognizes my basic set of control parameters. Wow!"

He excitedly began typing into the apps on his laptop that interfaced with the DE-generator, trying out different combinations to gain control of the device. It was exceedingly complex and confusing. But after a while he felt he was making progress...yes! He was communicating! In fact, the Obelisk *itself* was now downloading *new programs* into the laptop...

Dave was struck by a fantastic revelation.

"Breep, I'm gonna be just like Dr. Who with his 'Tardis' time machine—a master of *'Time and Relative Dimension in Space'*. Hah! This is incredible, Breep...uh, Breep? Where'd you go, boy?"

Breep was gone.

Dave hastily set down his laptop on the slanted surface, grabbed up the still-smoldering, weakly glowing torch, hopped off the Obelisk, and ran back out of the cavern.

Where was Breep? Dave dashed on through the tunnel only to run straight into him!

The small dinosaur was growling at the entrance of the ravine, holding off a frowning *Snake*.

The scrawny goateed man stood there with his hands on his narrow hips, glaring at Breep.

"Uh...hi Snake," Dave grinned weakly at him. "I was just exploring this..."

"Man, they know what you're doing," Snake stated, visibly shivering.

The thin young man was covered with loose snow. His boots were encrusted with ice. And in his hands he held Sally's *black super-gun*—pointed straight at Dave!

"I'm so sorry, man," Snake said, moving forward into the mouth of the crevice as Breep reluctantly backed up while still snarling. "But this was all a set-up. They knew what I was doing, helping you. We wanted you to use your human-cunning and knowledge of physics to find the Obelisk so we could neutralize it. It's the last 'wild card' to get rid of—so New Earth can remain intact and roll happily on into the future."

"But...I thought...you were my friend?"

"It's all for the best, Dr. King," Snake said, speaking formally. He continued to advance while Dave and Breep retreated before him. "I'm sorry I tricked you. But I came as soon as your Anaconda Tattoo alerted me. A full security and science team are close behind me. So you'd best listen to me."

Dave, backing further into the darkness behind him, was fumbling along the wall.

"Do you like *Bob Dylan?*" Dave interrupted him, grinning.

"What?"

Taking the hint, Breep *leapt* at Snake—distracting him while Dave snatched up his crude guitar and SMASHED it down on Snake's head.

"Do you hear ringing in your ears?" Dave laughed at him.

Embedded down to his arms into the smashed husk of the guitar, Snake tried to raise the gun...

—as Dave kicked it viciously, watching it sail away through the cave's opening and bounce away down the slope.

"Please…" Snake gasped before the flat of a snatched-up shovel brutally crashed into the side of his head, dropping him unconscious to the rocks.

Dave scrambled back to the opening of the cave, closely followed by Breep.

Together they furtively peered out the opening.

Dave was startled to realize they'd been inside the cavern all night long.

By the light of the just-rising sun, Dave saw a *large circular aircraft* floating up over the lip of the valley and down toward his hut.

"Oh, Christ!" Dave gasped to Breep, grabbing him by his leathery neck. "Snake or no Snake, they surely saw on their monitors that I was missing—and will see our tracks in the snow, leading them right here! We worked right through the night. We should have gone back before dawn. And once they get here there's no way they won't detect the energy signal from the Obelisk, now that we've dug an opening into the mountain right to it. If we're going to do anything we've got to do it now!"

In a near panic, Dave saw the craft drift down to a soft landing. Several giant Snakes slithering out onto the white snow that covered the fields around his hut. Behind the snakes came a whole squad of the Dinosapiens, pulling behind them a large cage!

Dave had a sinking feeling what that cage was meant to contain…and it wasn't just Breep.

The valley was now too big to safely contain Dave. They were going to put him into a literal prison cell.

Grabbing Breep by the ropes holding the blankets firmly wrapped around his neck and body, Dave dragged him still growling back into the tunnel, pausing only to grab up his pickax.

"What to do…what to do…what to do?" Dave frantically gasped.

The Dinosapiens would be up and on them in minutes.

Dave was now back standing on the sloped side of the Obelisk, poised over the doorway leading down into the side of the Obelisk.

"If we manage to somehow trigger the Obelisk," he said to Breep at his side, "it's likely to just vanish—or incinerate us in a massive energy-burst! Sally was attuned to the Obelisk when she rode it back to the 1st Century. But we're not!"

Then Dave realized what he had to do.

He stood up straight on the slanted back of the Obelisk, lifted the pickax high, and *smashed* it down into the doorway, aiming to the sides of the underlying DE-generator.

If the apparatus was similar to what he and Sally had originally designed, he'd be shearing through the attachment joints. If not, he was destroying it!

Feeling it loosen, he reached in and physically *wrenched* it out of the compartment.

Now there was a small space inside the closet area just large enough for a human to sit alongside a few supplies.

Dave looked at Breep.

Breep looked back at him.

Dave knew that Breep would be ok without him. The intelligent Snakes and Dinosapiens would surely take good care of him. But, that cage he'd seen them unloading from the flying saucer was ominous.

"Shall we?" Dave said, grinning.

Breep snorted.

Clutching his laptop tightly, Dave grabbed Breep by his neck, and flopped into the space.

It was tight.

Breep whined, squirming to get his thick legs inside, his tail flopping around...

They just barely fit.

Dave reached up, found a pull-handle, and solidly closed the "hatch" above them.

By the light of the laptop's screen plastered against his face, Dave barely managed to get his hand up to tap on the keyboard.

He saw a readout-display from one of the newly downloaded programs that looked promising—a *five*-dimensional display. On it was an intersection that was marked with a *pulsating red spot.*

"I sure hope that you are communicating with me, Obelisk—and that spot isn't a forbidden black hole or something equally awful," Dave gasped, feeling gingerly at the mousepad on his laptop.

"If this works," he said to Breep who was crammed up against him, "I think we just might pay a visit to Sally and Jesus in the Holy Land! How about that? Wouldn't that be fun?"

It was poor joke meant to reassure Breep of when they'd last together been with Sally.

It didn't work.

Breep whined, apparently unconvinced.

Taking in a deep breath and holding it, Dave poised the cursor above the blinking red dot in the complex matrix on his screen and double-tapped the mousepad.

Nothing happened.

"Oh, rats, it doesn't work."

And then the world *inverted* upon itself. Dave felt like his guts were thrown outside his body! And in a mind-numbing haze he *fell down* a dark well locked inside a tight suitcase...

—complete with a horrible "shrieking" sound!

—that went on for a long time...

—and then *kept* going on and on and on...

—which Dave realized was his own *screaming!*

Hah! Poor Breep had to hear Dave's not-so-beautiful voice right next to his head.

But it wasn't a laughing matter.

Drained, the laptop light faded away. Dave's shrieking voice also faded, likewise out of fuel.

And now in absolute darkness Dave realized it was getting hard to breathe. He and Breep were both panting deeply, gasping for air.

Dave horrifically realized that the closet was never intended to carry living beings. Their only air was what had been in the closet to start with—which was fast depleting.

Plus, the DE-generator that had apparently fine-tuned the Obelisk's own physical plunge into Time was now missing, ripped out to make space for their bodies.

Dave had the terrible thought that they might fall through time forever.

But, regardless, he and Breep were not going to survive much longer. Breep had already stopped struggling, just barely breathing. He was unconscious.

"Unless..." Dave desperately whispered to himself.

Forcing his arm down along his side, Dave just managed to get his fingers into the side pocket of his coat. He dragged out the pillbox he'd put there, sliding it up towards his mouth.

In the darkness, Dave poured half the content of the pillbox into Breep's opened beak that was stuck right there against Dave's cheek. He closed the toothy beak, holding it tightly shut until he felt Breep compulsively swallow.

Then Dave poured the remainder of the pills into his own mouth and quickly gulped them down.

"Just *one* of these damn things almost killed my mother," Dave whispered to himself as a strange warm sensation spread throughout his body. "And I just swallowed about fifty of them. So I'm probably dead—and what half a bottle of pills will do to poor Breep's dinosaur physiology, who knows?"

But he had to try.

He had no other options.

When the warm sensation became a *burning fire* inside of him, though, Dave regretted his action.

He again *screamed* from the searing pain ripping him apart internally!

But that used up even more precious air.

So he just closed his eyes tightly and drifted off into an utter Hell of accelerating agony.

His last thought was he hoped the alien Snakes would discover the "Luminary Chronicles" in his hut and read it. Maybe they'd finally understand humans. After all, it was now his "last Will and Testament."

He wryly laughed to himself, thinking that they were going to miss him.

His only regret was not to have kissed Sally one last time.

Chapter 7

IN THE BLACK VOID

Nothingness is not nothingness

Indeed, beneath the fabric of empty space

Resides a reality called "subspace"

Where no ordinary matter exists

Just a vacuum to human senses

Actually a strange supporting-matrix

Time, Dark Energy, and something else…

Beyond the comprehension of little humans

A Mystery at once lethal and empowering

Tap into it, if you are brave enough,

Connect with the Mind of God.

Homo sapiens Eulogy, 7:63-66

Tommy was face-down on glistening-white snow.

To all appearances he was dead.

His heart was not beating. He wasn't breathing. If there'd been an electroencephalogram machine handy it'd shown his brain activity at zero.

He looked exactly like a lifeless storefront manikin of a little boy—dropped face-first onto a snow-covered meadow.

He wore a cute little red jumpsuit. On his feet were stubby blue shoes. Beneath the straps of his jumpsuit was a short-sleeved blue shirt. His cherub-like head was topped with a mop of blond curls.

Hurriedly walking up to the motionless form—raising his booted feet high with each step to stomp through the two-foot-high virgin snow—*Snake* was deliriously happy to see the new arrival…

—but not if the newly-arrived boy was dead!

"Hey, hey, little dude," Snake fearfully said, reaching down with a thin arm to grasp the shoulder of the five-year-old boy and give him a gentle shake. "It's time to wake up!" Then, more sharply: "Get those artificial neurons *firing!* Come on outta yore shut-down! You ain't in subspace no more! You're back on Earth again! *Come back* to us!"

The motionless body suddenly twitched.

He was alive.

Tommy blinked his eyes open, looking about in confusion.

Then he grinned.

"Oh...I made it!" he laughed, creakily getting to his feet and flexing his small arms and legs. "That was a *long* ride."

He looked around in confusion.

Standing over him was a slender man with a big bandage on his head.

"Oh, hi there," he said. "I'm Tommy. Do you know where my Mommy is? She's with Dave and Breep. Have you seen them?"

"Hi Tommy. I'm 'Snake'. I'm an old friend of your mother's."

"Oh, that's nice, Mr. Snake. Where is she?"

"Oh, little dude," Snake said sorrowfully, helping Tommy to shakily stand. "Your Mom's gone into *deep space* and Dave...well, we don't know where he is. We think Breep went with Dave, though—in the *red Obelisk.* You remember the Obelisk, right?"

Sure, Tommy knew all about the red Obelisk. That was worrying. The red Obelisk could take Mr. Dave and Breep anywhere.

"Are they ok?" Tommy asked with concern, now carefully straightening each of his rapidly thawing frozen fingers. He wanted to use them to brush clinging snow from his clothes.

"We don't know," Snake sadly replied. Tommy appreciated his help in taking tentative steps forward through the blanket of snow. "I wuz hoping that maybe you could tell *us*, since you're so good at navigatin' through subspace and all."

Tommy looked around in wonderment at the shimmering snow field, the deep blue sky above him, and the towering mountains to each side of the valley.

He breathed deeply of the clean, fresh air.

He was quickly regaining full functionality.

"Oh I *am* good at that aren't I?" the little boy laughed. "I got those dinosaurs to come and help Mommy fight off that mean Demon. I had to go back millions of years to snag them into my time-stream. It was very tricky. If I fell out then I couldn't get back in! I had to grab them into it with me. It was really hard. But I did it!"

"Yep," Snake congratulated him. Tommy gratefully felt the man's supporting arm around his shoulders, guiding him up onto a ridge of rocks where the walking was easier. "You did real good, little dude. Me and my people really appreciated your help. And your Mommy wuz real proud of you also. It looks like you managed to jump through right after your Mom did, just as the Portal slammed shut. That's great! She'll be so happy to see you once she gets back from outer space."

Tommy beamed with pleasure at the praise. He wanted *always* to do a good job.

"Wow, I sure did just make it. I was afraid I was *never* going to get here."

"We were afraid you'd never get here also. But here you are!"

"Yep!"

"And now we need your help to find out where Dave and Breep have gone," Snake solemnly continued. "We think that they used the red Obelisk which your Mommy discovered on Mars to go on another trip into time. But we don't know where they went. You know a lot about that Obelisk, don't you? You were right there when your Mommy altered and enhanced it, weren't you? You paid attention to what she and her scientists were doing, right? And they harmonized you with it, didn't they? I'll bet that you kin figure out where it went, right?"

Tommy was thinking very hard, furrowing his small brow. This friendly 'Snake' looked like a man but wasn't a human. Tommy's scan functions detected peculiar brainwaves emanating from the man's skull. In fact, they were similar to the thinking patterns of the Obelisk!

"*You*...you're one of the Martians who built the big Time-and-Space-Machine in the first place!" Tommy exclaimed in amazement. "Wow! But I'm just a little boy. You know a lot better than me about the Obelisk, don't you? Why do you need me to help you?"

Snake stopped, dropped to his knees on the snow-covered rocks, and put both hands on Tommy's shoulders. Tommy now was looking straight into the man's eyes.

"Look, Tommy," Snake said, speaking seriously and clearly. Tommy noted the man momentarily dropped the pretense of being a stoned-out "hippy." "Yes, I'm a descendant of the Martians that originally escaped to Earth when Mars died long ago. I'm your friend. And I've been helping your Mommy and Dave all along."

"You know my Mommy?"

"I sure do," Snake grinned back lopsidedly. "She's fine, just taking a little trip to the stars. But now we're really worried about Dave and his little pet dinosaur. We don't know where they went. He stole the Obelisk! And that Obelisk has the power to do a lot of things— including *bad* things."

"Bad things?"

"That's right! If he went back in time, he could *change everything*—even if he doesn't mean to, just by accident. He could start a whole *new* timeline. He could even kill our whole world here, making it like it never existed! And we *like* this world. We don't want things to change."

"Why not?" Tommy innocently asked, looking around inquiringly. "Here it's just like where I left—all snowy and cold! Brrrrr! Wouldn't you like to change it so it's warmer? But...I guess the snow here *is* a lot *cleaner* looking," he grudgingly admitted.

He wrapped his little arms around his chest, shivering.

Snake took off his coat and put it around Tommy's shoulders.

"Thanks," Tommy replied with sincere gratitude.

"New Earth isn't all like this, Tommy," Snake kindly smiled. "This is actually a really nice place. You're going to like it. We want to make you happy. We really appreciate you!"

"Thanks," Tommy repeated. He was starting to trust the sincere, harmless-looking Martian.

"But to answer your question," Snake continued, "there is only one single Earth Dimension now, *this* one. And we're no longer threatened by those fatally flawed humans. Your Mommy and Dave are the last of them. We had them safely supervised and contained. We loved them and protected them—but also kept them from hurting themselves or us. So even if God came and took another look at us, we'd probably be ok. You know how humans are, right Tommy? They're lots of fun, but can also be real *nasty*."

Tommy frowned, looking down at his feet. The "friendly" man was insulting his Mommy! Maybe he didn't trust this "Snake" as much as he thought?

"But...*I'm* a human," he gulped fearfully.

"Sure!" Dave grinned in a forced fashion. "But you're also a robot hosting an evolved computer intelligence that your Mom created. So you're not one of those *bad* humans. You're a *good* human."

"I am?"

"Yes, Tommy—a *real* good human, the *best* kind of all!"

"Really?" Tommy doubtfully replied.

"Oh, fer shore!" Snake said, reverting back to his "hippy" disguise. He stood up straight and held out his hand. Tommy allowed Snake to take his small hand and lead him onward. "You never get older, or reproduce without limitations, or fight with other humans over nothing really important, or attack and destroy Mother Nature—you're a real cool dude, little dude!"

"Wow!"

"So you'll help us find Dave and Breep?" Snake urged him as they approached a snow-covered wooden hut. "We sure don't want them getting into any further trouble, now do we?"

Behind the hut loomed a towering, circular hovercraft, floating several feet up off the snow.

Around it were clustered concerned-looking Dinosapiens. Tommy was quite familiar with them. George and Alice were shape-shifted Dinosapiens, who Tommy liked a lot. But also, a non-shifted twenty foot-long snake was smoothly sliding out of a hatch and down a ramp. It had the same brainwaves as Mr. Snake. It was a Martian who was not masquerading as a human.

"Oh, I *do* want to help them not get into trouble," Tommy sighed, deciding to trust Snake—for the time being. "But there's no more Portal. How can I find them?"

"Don't you worry, buddy," Snake grinned widely, revealing crooked teeth. "We're going to open up *another* Portal. And once we do that you can help us to track him down. Won't that be fun?"

"Oh, boy!" Tommy said, clapping his little hands together gleeful-ly. He liked going into the time-stream! "But..." he doubtfully contin-ued, "why don't you just go find Dave yourself?"

"Oh, we would," Snake quickly replied, "but we'd never survive the journey. Our bodies compared to your tough android construc-tion are very weak. Going forward in time, even a billion years, wasn't so bad—since that's the way time naturally flows. But going backward is far more wrenching! It's like going against the flow, try-ing to swim against the tide. And even if our bodies survived, our minds would be destroyed. So that's why we need you to do this for us."

"—because I'm *stronger and stupider* than you!" Tommy ex-claimed happily, yet again clapping his hands together.

"Well...yes," Snake seemingly kindly nodded.

"I'll *do* it!" Tommy laughed, hopping up and down in the snow.

"So you'll find and rescue Dave and Breep?"

"Sure!"

"And you'll give him a *present* from us?" Snake asked as more of the thick-bodied, multi-colored intelligent giant snakes came flowing out of the hovering craft. They crawled up and surrounded the timely arrived visitor from a billion years in the past.

"A present?" Tommy innocently repeated, fascinated by all the fluorescent colors of the giant snakes surrounding him.

"It'll help them a lot—to do good stuff."

"What kind of a present?"

"It's your Mommy's gun...she forgot to take it with her. And now it can help Dave and Breep!"

"Sure, why not?" Tommy said, reaching out tentatively to pat the large snake heads now surrounding him.

This new world was really interesting.

Tommy knew he was going to have a lot of fun.

Snake knew if Tommy realized the magnitude of what he was agree-ing to do, the trip would be off.

The intelligent snakes of the ancient Martian race were all unified in their sad conclusion. If Dave somehow survived his trip back through time, particularly past the God-barrier, the repercussions could be calamitous! There was only one way to insure he was no longer a threat.

Dave was just too dangerous. His resourcefulness in quickly locating and activating the Obelisk proved to the Rulers of New Earth his uncontainable resourcefulness. They'd searched for it for years and couldn't find even a hint it'd survived across the eons. The conclusion of the Council of Elders was firm: they must cause the unthinkable!

Dave must die.

They couldn't do it themselves. To take another intelligent creature's life was beyond their evolved sentiments. So they'd have to do it through an intermediary. And the unexpected but convenient arrival from the past of Tommy was perfect to accomplish their sad objective.

The spunky little robot would do their bidding—thinking that he was traveling back in time to help out his friends.

Instead, he'd kill them.

Snake didn't want to deceive the little robot or have his friend Dave killed—assuming the pesky human was even still alive. Snake counted Dave as a real friend. But Snake had a duty both to his world and to his own kind. Dave, after all, was *not* an equally intelligent sentient being. He was an inferior savage with hardly more status than a beloved but unruly pet.

Once the last human male was gone, the Universe would be better off—freed from the scourge of *Homo sapiens*. If Sally ever returned, she'd be tolerated. Without a male she'd be just a harmless curiosity.

But Snake still missed her and hoped she was well, wherever she was. Without Dave she was no longer a threat. She was now just an Icon to a terrible, well-forgotten past.

Sally saw that they'd gambled and lost.

It was a terrible feeling.

The DE-generator beneath them was fused into one useless lump of inert melted metal. It clearly was not going to be useful ever again.

The two Dinosapiens that she and Alice rode to the engine room both hung limp from a wall where they'd been skewered by jagged exploded shards.

Sally floated in zero gravity in the air of the engine room, slowly tumbling between now-dark energy conduits.

Floating beside her was an unconscious Alice.

"Something's burning," Sally croaked out, puckering up her nose in disgust.

She looked at her hands—which were both burned raw. Smoke was wafting up from them into the air.

"Oh, that's going to hurt," she groggily sighed, realizing that she was in shock, her mind running on sheer adrenalin. She hoped her retroviral Optimmune systems still had enough "umph" over time to heal her hands.

Ignoring the pain, Sally grabbed Alice by her arm and kicked against a conduit, spinning in the zero gravity toward the tunnel leading out of the chamber.

Alice started to regain consciousness.

"What, what happened?" Alice gasped, her eyes blinking open as her black hair drifted out from her head in all directions.

She looked like a bewildered Medusa.

"I don't know if we escaped those spike-ships or not," Sally said. "The DE-generator is toast. Your artificial gravity is off again. But now we've got to get back to the control room. Our guides were killed in the explosion."

"Oh, no," Alice said. The grief in her voice was evident to Sally. Then Alice gathered herself and seemed to focus on the matter at hand, pointing to the correct tunnel leading off the exit.

Sally kicked and drifted, kicked and drifted, over and over—until they finally made it back into the control room.

And as she floated into the large chamber she looked upward.

Fortunately, the cracks in the dome hadn't broken through. If the dome had broken they'd be dead—as there was obviously no longer any shimmering energy-shield around the ship anymore to contain outrushing air.

But there were also no spooky alien spike-ships out there. Come to think of it, there was no planet...and no dwarf red star?

In fact, the few stars out there were extremely faint and distant.

What was happening?

"Get the emergency power turned on!" Sally shouted out into the chamber as the surviving Dinosapien crewmembers regained consciousness. They were also floundered in the zero gravity.

The air...it was stuffy.

Sally realized they'd escaped the attacking spaceships—only to be left drifting helplessly in deep space!

It was very quiet, the normal "throbbing" and "thumping" and "pulsing" of the ship stilled.

A hand reached up and grabbed Sally's leg, pulling her down to a console.

It was George.

"Hi," he croaked at her, reaching up again with his good arm to grab his wife's leg and pull her down also. "I take it that you managed to get the entire ship into subspace."

"Guess so," Sally nodded. "But there was no way to direct our path. Where did we end up?"

"We'll know once we get the astro-charts up," George said, vainly punching at his unresponsive console controls. "They analyze the patterns of stars and galaxies around us and pinpoint our position. That's as long as we're in the known Universe, obviously."

"Is there power to...?" Sally began to ask him.

"You were right, Sally," Alice answered for George. "We do have emergency batteries. They should kick in any minute now. But they won't last long without being recharged by the DE-generator. Hopefully, though, they'll last long enough for us to figure out where we are. Also, we usually have some power from shuttlecrafts, but they're all off-line. The same is true for our small research-level nuclear power plant. Whatever you did discharging the DE-generator blew out just about everything in..."

"*Holy droppings!*" George gasped, blinking unbelievingly at the display that suddenly came to life in front of him.

Sally wished the artificial gravity would start up. She felt queasy, like she was about to throw up.

"Dear!" Alice sternly reprimanded him. "Sally, living in your filthy world for years definitely corrupted my husband. He gained a taste for your profanities that..."

"I've heard it all before," Sally dismissed the "profanity", leaning in close to try and understand the display. It showed an encyclopedia of galaxy shapes: some spiral-shaped like the Milky Way, others round, globular, granular, or diffuse.

"What am I looking at, George?" Sally asked, trying to grasp the situation.

"It's...it's...our immediate vicinity..."

"It's a bunch of different galaxies—I can see that!" Sally snorted with exasperation. "But what does it tell us about where we jumped to?"

Floating up to them was the body of a dead Dinosapien, its big orange eyes glazed over and milky.

Sally gave it an impatient push, making it twirl away.

Its long cold tail brushed her cheek, making her shudder.

"Come on, George," Sally insisted, grabbing him by the shoulder of his broken arm, which made him wince in pain. "Oh, I'm sorry," she apologized. "But our situation is desperate! What does your display say about our location? You don't have to figure it out to the last decimal place. Just give me the 'take-home message'. Are we still near the solar system where those spiky enemy ships attacked us?"

"No..." George slowly sighed.

"Ok, that's good—then where...?"

"We're in Intergalactic space, Sally—somewhere about *thirty billion light years* from the Milky Way," George said in a very small voice, slumping in his chair.

Another Dinosapien drifted by, this time feebly thrashing-about.

Sally didn't even try to push it away, just let it drift on past.

"Say what?" she said.

"The program simulation can't even say for sure where the Milky Way is located...if it's even visible from here at all...we've traveled so far away from the known star maps."

"So we're lost in space?" Sally gulped. She pulled herself down next to George on the same oversized chair—since there was plenty of room for two humans, one real and one simulated.

Alice also pulled herself out of the air to hug onto both George and Sally from right behind them.

"We're...lost in the *Universe*," George said, his voice trembling, "with no way to even know where to go—assuming we had the power to do so."

"The DE-generator is dead," Alice whispered. "Maybe we'll eventually get internal power from the nuclear plant or the shuttlecraft, but they can't power the ship's drive to..."

"—so you're reminding me, my Dear, that all we've got is our ion-drive for propulsion," George frowned, mopping sweat off his bald head with the back of his good hand. "It's a lot slower to accelerate with than using DE-pulses. But the ion-thrusters could get us up to near lightspeed if we ran them continuously for a long enough time period."

"And then...how long to get back home?" Sally said.

"Well—since we'd not actually be at the speed of light but as close as possible—and we're not even sure what direction to go in order in to get back to the Milky Way, and we'd need to do a lot of recalibrations along the way, then..."

"How long?" Sally impatiently asked again.

"Well...if the *Big Rip* theory is valid on how the universe will die—when everything pulls apart from everything else and all distances become infinite—then..."

"Sounds painful," Sally said. She was afraid she already knew the answer to her question.

"—right about that time we should make it back to our own galaxy," George nodded firmly.

"And just when is that, Dear?" Alice politely asked her husband.

"Oh, right, about...*80 billion years* from now, give or take a few billion."

Sally, George, and Alice looked at each other with pained expressions.

Then they all burst out laughing!

The sounds of their hysterical cackling caused the surviving Dinosapiens to look over with confusion and concern.

After a while, though, they stopped laughing and just hugged each other.

"It's going to be a long way home," Alice said in resignation.

"Well, I'm still the Captain," Sally grimly stated, lifting up her head and flinging her fluffy hair around in a circle. "So let's get back down to the engine room. The ship's large DE-generator looked hopelessly cooked. But now it's the only way we'll ever get home. I don't suppose you have a backup unit?"

George shrugged dejectedly.

"No, we don't," he said. "But—we do have spare parts. Do you think that...?"

"Ah!" Sally grinned. "Show me!"

"What about the ship?" Alice said, gesturing about at the cracked dome, floating corpses, and shattered consoles.

"Take care of it," Sally ordered her.

Sally yanked one of the four stars off her "authority necklace" and twisted its supporting wire into Alice's blouse.

"There!" Sally exclaimed as she poised with her feet against the console and pushed off back the way she'd come. "You're now my '#1', Alice. Get to it. Make it so! Do whatever's needed. Onward and up-ward! Get those 'doggies' moving, *yee-hah!*"

Sally knew it was futile to live in the past.

She had lived in the past long enough to have that lesson burned into her brain.

No matter how dire the situation—there were always things to try.

She was determined not to die in the vastness of intergalactic space.

After all, who would bury her body?

Chapter 8

WAR

War, what is it good for?
Nothing, nothing, nothing at all...
The famous song by Edwin Starr
Offensive or defensive it spills blood
The thrill of victory or chill of defeat
Leaving everyone ultimately poorer
Though Men love to run to it with glee
The survivors only creep back broken
The women weeping, angry, and sad
Knowing that they leave a legacy
Forever tarnished and shameful
The "glory" an ugly red stain
Of stupidity, greed, and pain
Never to be washed away!
Homo sapiens Eulogy, 8:1-4

Dave could not talk.
His mouth would not work.
He tried to speak and only "burbling" noises came out.
He must be hurt bad...
"B-Breep?" he finally managed to croak out.
It was dark, it was still, and it was scary—and Breep was gone!
Dave kicked-out frantically, twisting and pushing against the tight quarters—until he realized the hatch above wasn't shut.

It had apparently sprung open! Did Breep get thrown out at the same time?

Diffuse light was shining down. Dave glimpsed above him the moon in a nighttime sky. He'd somehow survived the journey...but to where?

Everything seemed strange.

The compartment seemed much larger. And *big folds of fabric* were wrapped all around him.

Dave managed to stand up and stick his head out of the now strangely enlarged, opened hatch of the Obelisk.

It was then that he realized that both he and the Obelisk were *bobbing* up and down!

"Oh, Jesus...we're in the ocean," Dave gasped. "And we're *sinking!*"

The Obelisk lay on its side, its internal buoyancy keeping it afloat for the moment. But it was slowly going down into the sea.

Indeed, salty waves were splashing up over the red stone side of the Obelisk and wetting Dave's cheeks.

"My beard," he gasped, fumbling at his chin with strangely soft hands, "it's gone!"

This was the worst and most terrible surprise of all. It felt like a piece of his body had been chopped off without his knowledge or consent. What was this new nightmare?

He was brought back to reality by *salty water* now splashing into the compartment.

Dave ducked back down, fumbling around for his laptop—but not finding it. It must be buried under this sudden mountain of fabric that was befuddling and confusing his movements. He squirmed out from under the pile, in the process feeling his hands latch onto a *leathery sphere.*

He grasped it firmly and held it up into the dim light.

It was...an egg?

"Oh, Christ," Dave gulped, looking at it in disbelief. "It's Breep! He g-got turned into an e-egg by the Optimmune I g-gave him! And...me?"

Dave held tightly onto the egg as he pushed his naked body up out of the compartment onto the rocking surface of the sinking Obelisk.

A wave tossed the panel to the compartment shut behind him with a loud "clang"!

"Oh, no!" Dave desperately croaked, trying to get the hatch opened but then *slipping* off the tilting Obelisk into the sea!

He floundered, gasping, sucking in salty seawater, strangling, gasping, and barely able to stay afloat. But he still kept a tight death-hold on Breep's egg...

—as, by the light of the moon, he watched the Obelisk slip gently beneath the waves, its flat red surface vanished into the depths.

"Help!" Dave yelled out, barely able to keep his head above the waves. "Help me! I'm drowning!"

"*Kratiste agori, erchomai!*" Dave heard strange, rough words barked at him over the waves.

"I'm here! I'm here!" Dave called back, desperately trying to stay afloat while not losing his grip on the leathery egg.

"*Echo echeis tora!*" Dave heard excited words calling back to him as a strong hand grabbed his free arm and dragged him up out of the water into the deck of a bobbing boat.

Dave gasped, vomiting salt water onto the deck of a small boat. All around him was the strong smell of fish.

Hovering worriedly above him was a grizzly bearded, gnarled, thin old man. Dave blearily saw, in the moonlight, that the man had only one arm.

"Thank y-you," Dave gasped, huddled naked and shivering on the floor boards. "W-where am I?"

But the man didn't answer, just reached down to take the leathery egg from Dave's shaking hands.

"*Ti einai afto?*" the man said in wonderment, turning the four-inch-long leathery egg over in his calloused hands.

"That's my f-friend," Dave woozily answered, now managing to get up to his knees on the rocking boat's deck, reaching out to retrieve the egg. "He's...a d-dinosaur from the p-past...that to survive the trip from the future b-back to now—w-whenever 'now' is—I had to g-give him s-some pills...a-and he t-turned back into an egg. And I...I..."

Dave looked at his own naked arms, his legs, and his groin.

No pubic hair! His skin was smooth. His arms were small. The man looming above him looked like a giant.

Dave realized that he too had been transformed.

He was now the size and appearance of a *seven year-old boy!*

The only thing that remained from before his leap through time was the Anaconda Tattoo, still brightly wrapped around his small wrist.

"*Irthes apo ta asteria?*" the grizzled man said in amazement, pointing up at the night sky.

"Y-yes," Dave wearily nodded, tightly cradling his round, egg-transformed pet, "I...I c-came...from the s-stars."

In wonderment, the man reached out his hand to lift up Dave's wrist, peering at the bright Anaconda emblazoned there.

"*Boreite skotothikan kai anastithike, opos to fidi theos, tou Ofeos, apo ena magiko votano?*"

"Sure, why not?" Dave mumbled, pulling his arm back.

He slumped to the water-soaked boards and felt his eyes closing—sinking into an exhausted deep slumber.

Wherever he was, he was safe.

But he'd lost everything except for the egg.

Without the Obelisk or any means to generate concentrated Dark Energy, how would he ever find Sally?

She was lost to him...forever.

Sally was struggling with trying to get the various spare parts to the DE-generator to combine into a workable, but much less powerful generator, to replace the burnt-out starship's main drive.

Since she wasn't familiar with the exact design, it was partially a guessing game.

And it increasingly looked futile...but she still persisted. It was their only hope!

It would have been much easier if the engineers in the crew had survived. But, unfortunately, they'd been killed when the spikes first skewered the ship. Now a *geology* specialist was assisting her. The only thing he had going for him was being a scientist familiar with technical terms.

She was grateful for his assistance but contemptuous of his "expertise."

A "rock-smasher," really? That's the best they could find to assist her?

But, if nothing else, he seemed eager to help.

Because she couldn't pronounce his actual reptilian-language name, she dubbed him "Dennis."

Now she was standing chest-deep in her growing collection of haphazardly linked spare parts.

But several key pieces simply weren't present—particularly a central processing unit, CPH, to balance and control the output of the various components. She was now trying to either jerry-rig the missing parts or bypass them, but with little success.

It simply wasn't working.

"Can you hand me the palladium core, please Dennis?" she politely asked the big geologist-dinosaur standing behind her, reaching a hand out behind her back.

"AND THAT IS...?" a voice in her head replied, puzzled.

"The cylinder with the knobs on each end," she replied.

"OH YES, I SEE IT, CAPTAIN," Dennis answered telepathically.

That booming voice in her head was really giving her a headache.

"Dennis, can't you speak with your mouth in my language? You've got a tongue don't you? You talk in your own language, right?"

A scaly, three-fingered hand reached into her vision, holding the cylinder.

"Yes...I can...make your sounds...but it is difficult for me," he haltingly rasped.

"That's much better, Dennis," she replied, struggling to get the palladium core into position. "Thanks."

Fortunately, Alice had managed to get the emergency backup battery power online. For the moment, artificial gravity was restored. A group of industrious Dinosapiens was busily working sealing the cracks in the observation dome.

Even though they'd lost supplies in the decompression blasts, there was still sufficient food and water to last several months, so things were looking up. But according to the astro-charts, the closest "orphan" star with possibly habitable planets was more than *ten thousand light years away* off in the intergalactic void.

Even traveling near the speed of light, time-dilation would not be sufficient for them to survive the journey with their meager supplies.

They couldn't even make it to the nearest star, let alone find their way back to their own distant galaxy!

Regardless, Sally knew she had to get some sort of DE-generator in place. The intensely focused ion-expulsion drive used for maneuvering near a planet just wasn't going to cut it. They had to have massive short bursts from the DE-generator just to approach lightspeed quickly enough to matter. It would take the ion-propulsion system months to build up that sort of speed—by which time they'd be starved to death anyway.

Sally realized that whatever she could build—even if it worked—wouldn't be enough to try another subspace jump. The field would never be big enough to envelope the entire large ship. Perhaps, though, one of their shuttlecrafts might be small enough to slide into subspace...maybe go for help?

But the remaining shuttlecrafts were all still inoperable, damaged in the initial subspace leap into the intergalactic void.

Could they be repaired? Maybe, but that had to wait until they could stabilize the main spaceship.

Sally's musings were abruptly cut short.

"Sally Smith! Captain! Please report to the bridge immediately! It's an emergency! Come quickly!" Sally heard Alice's desperate voice over the ship-wide intercom.

"Oh, what now?" Sally groaned, painfully extricating herself from the complex mechanism she was building.

"Ride on my back, Captain," the Dinosapien geologist said, turning so she could hop up onto him.

She did so, hugging him around his thick neck.

As they bounced rapidly along the narrower corridors, other Dinosapiens flattened themselves against the walls to allow free passage.

In a couple minutes they were back on the bridge.

"What's so important that...?" Sally said, stopping her query as she glanced upward through the now-sealed, transparent dome.

Hanging there ominously against the backdrop of faint stars and distant galaxies...was a black *spike-ship!*

"Oh...hell," she gasped.

"It must have somehow followed us here," George said in a small voice, sitting trembling at his console.

"It just appeared a minute ago," Alice said. "But it hasn't moved. It's certainly not attacking us. Perhaps the crew is unconscious, as we were when we first emerged from subspace?"

"If it has a crew at all," Sally said, looking wide-eyed up at the spike-covered, roughly spherical black craft floating nearby in space. "Maybe the transit knocked out their central control processers. Whatever, that ship's got what we need! This is great! It's wonderful!"

"Sally?" Alice nervously asked, obviously not understanding.

"If it's not burnt out also—they must have a large DE-generator to allow the whole ship to slip into subspace! That spaceship is even larger than ours."

"What are you suggesting, Sally?" George said, blanching in anticipation of her answer.

"We've got to board it—as fast as possible before it recovers and attacks us."

"But our shuttlecrafts are damaged, and..." Alice began.

"Then you have spacesuits, right? We'll just do a spacewalk over to the spike-ship, grab what we need and come on back. Simple!"

"Oh, that's *not* simple. That sounds very...dangerous," George said, nervous sweat springing up on his bald head. "We're not mentally constituted for war-like expeditions, it's too..."

"I'll go," Sally flatly stated. "Where do you keep your spacesuits?"

"—and I'll go with you!" Dennis firmly added.

"You?" Sally grinned at the big Dinosapien.

"You never know, they might have interesting rock specimens," he humorously stated, his big orange eyes bright and excited. His long tail was flicking back-and-forth, seemingly eagerly.

"On a spaceship?" she laughed.

"Geologists are very adventurous," he solemnly replied.

"Ok, then," she nodded. "Let's go!"

As they headed for an airlock containing "extravehicular excursion suits," Sally was glad to have friends—even if they were big, scaredy-cat Dinosapiens.

Fortunately, at least one of them had some gumption. She was beginning to like Dennis. He wasn't that bad, for a geologist.

But they'd better hurry.

Sally had a feeling that the pursuing alien craft hanging out there in the void wouldn't be dormant for much longer.

Tommy was eager to try and go after Dave. It was taking much too long for the Martian giant intelligent Snakes to set up the subspace transit equipment!

But Tommy understood the extreme difficulty and was not impolite.

Mommy had always taught him to be a good boy, and he was! At least he thought he was...

"Is it ready now?" he meekly asked Snake.

Snake sighed deeply.

"For the twenty-eighth time today, little dude, it's *not* ready yet."

"Why not?"

Before them a large circular apparatus was being constructed. It was in the cavern to which they'd tracked Dave and Breep—and from where the unlikely "dynamic duo" had vanished.

It was a large stacked series of magnetic rings, inside a larger ring through which super-heated plasma would flow. The entire thing was contained by twelve other magnetic rings—with two more superconducting rings encircling the entire thing.

Dozens of Dinosapiens were working there, directed by the Martian Snakes.

Thick cables ran through the tunnel and then out onto the mountainside's slope, down to a large hovercraft sitting on the floor of the valley. Within it, an array of DE-generators would provide the immense energy necessary to power the apparatus and open a Time-Portal!

"It's real complicated, little dude," Snake explained, furrowing his thin brow. "And if they don't get it exactly right, there's no way to follow the subspace trail correctly. You might not wind up where Dave went. Maybe not even on this planet."

"That would be *fun!*" Tommy grinned happily up at the goateed young man.

Snake sighed deeply.

"Not if you end up inside the sun or a black hole, little dude," Snake said in exasperation. "You'd get either fried or crushed. And then you couldn't give Dave his present, right?"

"Oh, right," Tommy nodded. "I sure do need to give Dave his present."

Tommy looked down at the *black gun* he held in his small hand. They'd told him it was the one which originally opened the Portal through which he'd finally reached Dave and Sally—and then again to jump forward a billion years into the future.

It was Sally's gun, his Mother's!

He held it tenderly as a precious family heirloom. It comforted him to have it in his hands.

But now it was depleted of energy and couldn't open another Portal. He asked them why it didn't accumulate energy as it fell forward in time but they just brushed him off. Whatever, it seemed as dead as a lump of metal. But Dave for some reason needed to have it. This was his "present" they were sending him back in time to deliver to him.

"Now be careful with that, little dude," Snake cautioned him. "It's only for Dave and he knows what to do with it. We want you familiar with it also, so you'll not let loose of it in your upcoming time jump— but don't be waving it around. You might hurt somebody if it slipped out of your hand. It ain't 'fully loaded', so to speak—but it's still dangerous."

"Dangerous?"

"Now that it's back in real-time, it's charging itself again."

"Really? I don't detect..."

"It's charging itself!" Snake yelled at him. Then, seemingly catching himself the skinny man replied more softly: "It's slow, that's why you don't sense anything. But you don't know when it might suddenly go off if you were playing with its trigger."

"Oh, right," Tommy said very seriously, tucking it back into the brand new holster at his waist that they'd given him. "But I have a feeling there's something I've forgotten?"

Tommy had vague memories of the Martian snakes taking him into a large operating room where he'd gone to sleep...then woke up with a splitting headache.

They said they'd just optimized the fluid-flow going through his brain, which supposedly was damaged in his transit here from the past. But he was suspicious. Why hadn't they told him advance what they were doing? They knocked him out with some hidden, powerful drugs in his food and then operated on him.

It was almost like they weren't being honest with him.

But that was ridiculous!

They were his friends...

—at least, that's what they kept telling him.

"Oh, it's probably jist you flyin' through all that subspace stuff to get here," Snake reassured him after the operation. "It probably shook loose a few of your robot-neurons or somethin'. Didn't the doctors tell you that you there might be minor side-effects after they cleaned out your brain's artificial blood vessels?"

"Yes," he said, frowning. "But..."

"But what?" Snake solicitously asked.

"Well...I sort of get these...*dreams?*" Tommy cautiously admitted, hesitant to even tell his friend Snake about them.

Snake was immediately attentive, slipping a thin arm around Tommy's shoulder. He led Tommy away from the brightly lit construction site, out through the tunnel to the peaceful mountainside.

"Now you jist tell your good buddy Snake about these bad dreams of yours," Snake said as he sat Tommy on a workbench that looked out over the still snow-covered valley.

Tommy hesitated, thinking better of it.

"Maybe I shouldn't bother you with..."

"Oh come on, buddy," Snake said, leaning close. "I won't tell anyone. It'll be jist between you and me, dude."

"Really?"

"Absolutely!" Snake grinned disarmingly, displaying his nicotine-yellowed, crooked teeth.

Tommy didn't like the bad teeth. They made him nervous every time he glimpsed them. But still Snake was his best friend here.

"Well, ok," Tommy gulped. He lowered his voice so only his friend could hear. "I keep seeing *big round spaceships* covered with *sharp points!*"

Snake narrowed his eyes.

"Out in space?" he hopefully asked.

"No..." Tommy whispered.

"Then where?"

"Here."

"Here?"

"Here on New Earth..." Tommy gulped. "And they're *killing* us!"

Snake took Tommy by his shoulders with both of his hands.

"You're probably jist thinkin' back to those terrible Harvesters spaceships and Reaper Robots that we escaped from back in the 21st Century," Snake firmly stated. "So don't worry none about those nightmares, little dude. Those monsters are a billion years in the past. You jist concentrate on helping us fine-tune the Portal shot, once the containment field's up and running, ok?"

"Ok..." Tommy doubtfully answered. "But my dreams seem really, really, *real!*"

"Well little dude, we can schedule another checkup with the doctors, if you want?"

That sent a chill of dread through Tommy's android body.

"Uhm, no—if you say it's ok then I'm not worried," Tommy forced himself to seem to smile cheerfully.

"Good," Snake said, taking his hands away.

Out in the valley something suddenly "*screeched*"! Nearby, a whole flock of the big black "birds" shot up, their many wings making a thunderous sound...

—as, simultaneously, a dark cloud passed before the sun, throwing the entire landscape into shadows.

Tommy blinked in fear.

He didn't know if he liked this future so well after all. It was starting to seem a lot less fun.

The quicker he could go after Dave the better.

Chapter 9

STRANGE LIFE FORMS

Even just on planet Earth
Life existed in many shapes
From microscopic cells
To gigantic whales
From "dead" viruses
To fluid jellies
From scums on ponds
To towering trees
From creeping tentacles
To wide-flapping wings
From aversion mechanisms
To complex thoughts
From instinctual reactions
To self-and-God awareness
So you should have thought
What variations existed beyond
When you traveled to the stars
Life you might only imagine
If your brains were capable
Beyond your conception
Bringing deadly danger
Not just to your body
Or your fragile mind
But your simple spirit...

Homo sapiens Eulogy, 9:11-15

Dave groggily awoke as they reached the shore.

A net beside him was filled with still-flopping fish.

The sun was just coming up. He'd apparently been on the small boat with the old man all night. The waves thudding into the shore-line were gently rocking the boat under him. He felt a scratchy loin-cloth that the man had apparently wrapped around his naked groin. Plus, a rough blanket was laid over him as he fitfully slept on the floorboards of the small boat.

Still held warmly to his naked chest by both of his hands was the leathery egg.

"Thank y-you," Dave stammered to the man who was outside the boat laboriously dragging one end up onto the sandy shore.

Dave absently noted that the man was old, thin, tall, and had only one arm.

"*Mi milate! Stratiotes erchntai!*" the man suddenly said to him, covering his mouth frantically with his calloused hand.

"Oh...don't talk...ok," Dave said, peeking over the edge of the boat to see a *group of soldiers* approaching the boat.

They all had on helmets, wore cape-like tunics around their shoulders, had short knee-length kilts, with sandals on their feet—and carried small shields and short swords.

They looked very dangerous.

The old man shoved Dave back under the blanket, out of sight.

Dave heard one of them address the old man: "*Ach, Periscus tou Faliru—kali psaria simera to proi?*"

Peeking up from a corner of the blanket, Dave saw the old man grinning nervously, while ducking his head repeatedly in submission, pointing to the net filled with still-wriggling fish.

"*Nai, nai. Mia Kalimera alievmata ichthyon. Parakalo, parte o, ti thelete,*" the old man grinned, reaching into the boat to grab the biggest fish and offer it to the soldier.

The soldier disdainfully knocked the fish to the side while grab-bing the old man by his scrawny neck—as the other soldiers reached in to lift up the entire net filled with fish and start hauling it out of the small boat.

"*Psarema sti nychta pou prospathousan na apofygoun na mas dosei to Meridio mas! Tha parei ola!*"

The soldier was angry about something. He was threatening the old man. Maybe the fisherman wasn't supposed to fish at night?

"*Parakalo min mou kathari. Sas iketevo. Den tha eimai se thesi na sas piasei perissotera psaria!*" the old man begged, grabbing feebly at the net. He clearly was in a panic that his fishing gear was being taken away.

"*Echoume bousel, Periscus,*" the soldier laughed as the other men dumped the fish into bushels they'd brought with them.

Then the leader contemptuously tossed the empty net onto the old man—who floundered around, caught up in it!

The soldiers laughed at his antics.

"*Alla tin epomeni fora pout tha piasei exapatisi sas den tha plironoun mono me dichty sas—alla I zoi sas,*" the soldier icily threated the old man, whipping out his sword to hold it against the cowering old man's sinewy neck.

"*Nai, nai! Lypamai! Pote xana!*" the old man whimpered, tears rolling down his bewhiskered cheeks.

The soldier kicked the one-armed man down onto the sand—where he lay, still tangled up in the net.

"*Ach...kai ti einai afto?*" the leader said. He was looking suspiciously into the boat.

The blanket was swept back off Dave.

Dave looked up in terror at the looming, helmeted soldier! Instinctively he hid his wrist with the glaring Anaconda Tattoo behind his back.

Also, he bent forward over the egg, protecting it from being seen.

"*Einai engonos mou, kyrie!*" the old man said, squirming out of the entangling net to lurch over and protectively stand between the soldier and Dave. "*Mou voitha ta psaria! Ekeinos koimotan!*"

"*Aftos tha borouse na mas kanei ena kalo sklavo,*" another soldier said from the group hefting up the bushels of fresh fish.

Dave understood the threat and the last word—they wanted to take him away as a *slave!*

"*Kali Kyrioi, kali Kyrioi,*" the old man begged them. "*To agori einai adynamos kai ilithios! Aftos einai kofos kai alalos!*"

The old man gestured with his hand by way of illustration, blocking his ears and then his mouth.

Ah—Dave understood. He was too worthless to be a slave for the soldiers. He was, supposedly, both deaf and dumb.

So Dave stared blankly upward, slowly opening his mouth to say: "*Ahhhhhh....*" while letting a little drool leak from the corner of his mouth.

"*Ba! I forologiki sas afxanetai gia ton epomeno mina apo to ena trito eos to imisy tou kathe eidous alievmaton,*" the leader said, turning contemptuously away while conspicuously rubbing his thumb and fingers together.

The old man now was grimacing, clearly just ordered to pay a hefty new tax. But at least the soldiers hadn't summarily executed him and his young "helper" for illegal fishing.

But as the patrol of soldiers retreated into the distance, laughing and hoisting their bushels of fresh fish, Dave knew that even though he and the old man were safe for the moment—Breep was in deep trouble!

Should the egg hatch in this vicinity, the baby dinosaur would surely attract attention and be killed.

He spotted low hills not too far inland.

"Thanks for y-your h-help, Sir," Dave said as he leapt from the boat onto the warm sand and ran!

He had the scratchy blanket still wrapped around him, trying to use it to shield himself from attracting too much attention.

"*Asteri paidi, ela piso!*" the old man called after him.

But Dave was already into the bushes and low trees, tightly clutching his precious egg. It was nice of the old man to protect his "star child," particularly from those soldiers. But Dave had to get away and figure things out.

And before the day got going, with more people coming out and about, he had to find a safe place for Breep to incubate and hopefully be reborn.

"Don't worry, Breep," he said to the still-warm four-inch egg as he ran along on his bare feet, enduring the damage done by the rocks and thorns to the tender skin on the bottom of his newly young feet. "Wherever this is that we made it to, you're going to be ok."

But Dave didn't feel as confident as his brave words implied.

He had clearly traveled to the past, beyond the God-barrier.

But now he was stranded in a place where the police apparently routinely brutalized and stole from the citizenry.

What sort of *savage, uncivilized* place was this, anyway?

Sally was in her spacesuit, about to exit the airlock.

She'd have preferred using one of the small shuttlecraft to approach the dormant spike-ship, but none of them were working. There'd been considerable damage to the hold containing the shuttles during the short battle with the spike-ships. Extensive repairs were needed before any of the shuttles could again fly.

Fortunately, the Dinosapiens—previous to their launch from Earth—had hastily manufactured a spacesuit to fit her diminutive size.

It was snug, but had a big totally clear helmet with its own interior lighting, which allowed her an uninhibited 360-degree view of everything. And on her back was her life-function pack, complete with maneuvering thrusters.

Her normally long, fluffy hair was tied into a tight bun on the back of her head. She didn't like her hair that way. But it was necessary to fit her head into her helmet to allow maximum visibility.

Standing beside her in the airlock—waiting for the air to be sucked out before the hatch opened into space—was the Dinosapien Dennis. He towered above her, firmly gripping in his three-fingered gloves a large bag filled with tools. He was prepared to do his "geology."

Dennis' large dinosaur body was neatly packaged into a form-fitting white spacesuit with short extensions for his three-clawed hands and arms, plus wide trunks for his muscular, thick legs. Another extension of the suit even covered his long, flexible tail. The life-pack on his back, though, lacked thrusters. The danger-adverse Dinosapiens preferred cautious, tethered space-walks. So he was tethered behind Sally.

His illuminated, reptilian head was neatly enclosed in a large, oblong helmet—providing plenty of room for his elongated snout and massive jaws.

He gave her a one-claw-up signal of "ready-to-go"!

"Open the door!" Sally ordered over her communication net.

The air in the chamber had already been pumped out. They were ready to go.

Slowly the hatch leading out into space rotated and then slipped silently to the side.

Outside was blackness, with a faint sprinkling of a few distant stars.

It was *intergalactic space!*

As Sally stepped out into the immense void, floating out into the zero gravity—she was momentary confused half-expecting to see Earth hanging below her...but seeing *nothing.*

And there hanging off at a distance was the dead-black, sharp-angled *Spike-Ship.* It was roughly spherical, but with no actual curved surfaces. Plus, the many flat pieces making up the sphere were studded with long spikes.

To Sally it looked like one of those WWII mines, floating ominously not in an ocean but in empty space. It wasn't a desirable destination for a spacewalk. It was a *threat* to zoom away from as quickly as possible!

But, regardless, she was determined to board it.

The alien ship was difficult to see, however, as there were no close light sources to reflect off its flat black pieces. Thus it was visible only by obscuring the very faint specks of the distant background stars.

She focused her gaze on the "stealthy" ship, mentally calculated a trajectory, and then triggered a long burst of propellant out of her cantered back-thrusters.

"*Can you...me...Sally?*" a voice crackled in her ears. It was George back on the Dinosapien ship.

"I hear you, but your voice is breaking up," Sally said, worriedly. "Can you boost your signal?"

Static and crackles sounded in her ear.

"*...putting out...wide-spectrum...might be waking up. It could be like a radio searching for...*"

Oh, hell! The Spike-Ship was waking up.

"Listen to me!" Sally yelled into her transmitter. "Try to put distance between it and you! Get as far away as possible! I'll call in when we need pickup. Otherwise if you don't hear from us—just try to escape."

Sally listened intently. But there was no reply.

She twisted her head around to see behind her through her clear helmet. But it was difficult. She dared not twist her entire body and thereby risk altering the trajectory of their path—they had limited propulsion gas. If they missed their target they'd float away into intergalactic space...possibly forever.

"Dennis, can you see behind us?" Sally called back to him, switching to suit-to-suit over their connecting tether. "Is our ship retreating as I ordered?"

She heard a babble of *hissing* and *snapping* noises.

"Dennis, please speak in English!" she ordered him.

"Oh yes, sorry, I got excited—it is difficult but I can indeed speak your strange words verbally," came a growling, somewhat-garbled reply in her ear. "I was trying to keep my eyes closed until we got there...but, yes, I can turn backward, looping the tether around me...there...and, yes—our ship is indeed retreating. It is now very tiny behind us...and I fear I am going to vomit my last cube-meal up into my helmet," his voice rose in pitch, clearly panicking.

"*No!*" Sally sternly ordered him. "If you do then you'll breathe in your vomit and die! I *order* you not to throw up! Instead, Dennis," she said, continuing in a calmer voice, "just close your eyes again, relax, and visualize a beautiful place on Earth...are you doing it?"

There was a long pause, then...

"I...I am doing it...a dense jungle area I liked a lot," a shaky voice answered. "I am managing to swallow my gorge back into my stomach where it had risen up into my neck."

Sally had to calm herself on hearing that, feeling her own "gorge" rising up into her own throat in response.

The black, alien spaceship was growing bigger in front of her...

—as Sally saw some of the "spikes" *twitching!*

If it "woke up" and moved before they reached it—yet again they'd be lost in space for eternity! Of course that would be an amazing experience—that is, until their air ran out in a mere eight hours.

Still, that would be a horribly long eight hours to drift through the icy void between galaxies, contemplating their own deaths.

"Dennis!" she said over the tether to keep him alert but even more to detract her own self from the awful fate that might well be awaiting them. "You're from a very old, matured species, right?"

"Yes, Sally, we are indeed," he now calmly answered.

"So what does it take to move from being merely a 'smart animal' like me to being a 'matured' race like you—with whom God, apparently, isn't 'disgusted'?"

"We're not sure," his raspy voice replied in her helmet. "There are definite genetic alterations over time. We've gone back and sequenced younger remains of ourselves. I've participated in some of that research, since fossil reconstructed is considered part of our geology profession. Most of the genetic alterations have to do with expanding our brains—we Dinosapiens have newer brain structures which you *Homo sapiens* mammals lack. But though brain function is certainly related, it does not seem causal to our 'maturity' as you say. Something more has to happen, which we haven't yet quantified. We think it has to do with moving from individual imperatives to a more interconnected group-priority—if that makes any sense to you?"

Sally nodded—though instantly realizing that Dennis couldn't see her gesture.

"So how does that happen?" she asked. "Is it societal, or physiological, or spiritual—or what?"

"We don't know," Dennis repeated, pausing. "And, again, it doesn't seem absolute. In fact, many organisms on earth have intense interactivity, such as ant colonies—and yet still wage mindless war on each other. The maturity that is approved by God might just be an aberration, an evolutionary mistake—like peaceful dogs derived from savage wolves. Dogs in your Dimension were like wolf puppies before they being taught savage survival skills by their parents. Maybe we're just intellectual puppies?"

Sally was happy she'd gotten Dennis to focus on something besides vomiting into his helmet. But the mystery of why God would allow *Homo sapiens* to evolve only to erase it from the Cosmos was as puzzling as ever.

But now Sally's attention was riveted on the ever-enlarging spiked structure. Before, it had merely looked large. Now, it looked massive—the size of a small city! She triggered a couple tiny bursts of propellant to fine-tune their course as they drifted through space ever nearer.

"And what about this monstrosity in front of us?" She asked Dennis. "It's clearly very antagonistic. It wants to eat us without so much as saying 'hello'. Yet it is advanced technologically, enough so to enter subspace. It deliberately rose up from the surface of Kepler-186f to attack us without any provocation. Plus they acted in a highly-coordinated fashion. And now it's managed to track us through subspace to our present location. What do you make of it?"

Dennis was silent, contemplating.

"Perhaps, like you said, it may not even be alive as we know life," he thoughtfully replied. "The level of technology *does* seem to indicate an advanced race, according to our experience in our linked Earth-Dimensions. But as to what can evolve over eons on other planets...who knows?"

"So just what is it?" Sally asked, staring ahead at the ominous spiky structure.

"Maybe it's a planetary 'virus'—looking to latch onto us and drain our energy or technology," Dennis answered. "It might not even be consciously aware of what it does. All that, of course, is pure speculation and..."

"But that *does* make some sense," Sally interrupted him as they floated yet closer. "Earth viruses aren't strictly alive. Outside a host cell, they're just dormant packages of proteins, lipids, sugars, and genetic material. It's only when they attach to, get inside, and take over the genetic machinery of a host cell that they can reproduce. Without a host cell they're inert."

She could now see many more details of the surface of the ship, particularly a variety of different kinds of spikes.

"This thing we're approaching isn't inert, though, Captain," Dennis replied. "It clearly wants to grab onto us!"

"Yes, it's something new to us," Sally agreed, making another small adjustment. She saw puffs of white vapor momentarily appearing behind her back. Her steering propellant was getting very low. She needed to keep enough to slow them sufficiently to not crash into the Spike-Ship. Just a couple more squirts and she'd be without maneuvering capabilities.

But the black craft was looming very large and near. They were almost to "touch-down"!

"Oh, and you don't have to call me 'Captain' all the time, Dennis," she said as they drifted past a huge spike that loomed up ten stories above them. Sally noted with interest the many types of protruding spikes—including the toilet-plunger ones that before had previously tried to drain the power from their ship's shield.

It reminded her of electron micrograph pictures she'd seen of the proteins on the surface of many types of viruses.

"We Dinosapiens are very much regimented, with a set societal structure," Dennis' voice sounded in her ear. "To call you other than Captain would be very difficult for me."

"But George and Alice can do it," she protested as they drifted towards the black surface—too fast! They'd splatter against it at this speed! "So it's possible."

"They've had much practice," he mildly replied. "Besides, they're special."

"Ok...and what, then, is *your* rank, Dennis?" she said as she rapidly calculated their trajectory, speed, and distance to the nearest flat landing site on the Spike-Ships' outer surface.

"In your terminology I suppose I am a 'Commander'," he said in her ear...

—as she touched the keypad on her chest ordering the extended thruster-array to reverse its direction and fire all her remaining propellant!

A condensed stream of solidified gasses suddenly sprang up in front of her so she couldn't see...as she felt the hard push of the reversed thrusters on her body...

—as the tether behind her automatically hardened-up, forcing Dennis to slow down as well...

—and she *slammed* down upon the glistening black surface...followed closely by Dennis now on an automatically softened tether *smashing* onto her back!

"Unnnngggghhhh," Sally groaned, reaching out desperately for a small nearby spike to anchor her spacesuit onto the surface as she *bounced* and *drifted back* into space!

"No! No!" she gasped as the surface retreated. She grabbed for anoter long, slender spike...too far away!

She was bouncing back up into space to be lost forever!

—when she felt a tug and started inching back downward...

It was Dennis, with his long, strong tail firmly wrapped around a thick spike, pulling Sally back by their connecting, strong tether.

"Jesus! I thought I was a goner," she gasped in relief, stretching out her gloved hand to grab onto Dennis' big three-clawed glove. "Thanks, Dennis."

"Just doing my job...Sally!" the Dinosapien grinned toothily at her through his oblong helmet.

She paused a moment to regain her equilibrium. That was the scariest thing she'd ever felt—the terror of knowing she was bouncing back into the void of space to drift forever...

Repulsed, she jerked out of her harness and pushed the now-depleted jetpack off into space. It floated serenely away. It was useless now, unnecessary bulk. But Sally felt an instant regret. They were now fully committed to their daring attack upon the Spike-Ship.

"Whew! We made it. *Now* what?" she gulped, focusing-back on their immediate situation.

"I am awaiting your orders, Captain," he mildly replied, reverting to his more formal conversation. His big orange eyes blinked rapidly at her through his helmet.

Clearly, he was as flustered as she. Sally realized that the float across empty space which they'd just accomplished was a huge achievement for the risk-averse Dinosapien.

"Then we've got to find an entrance into this beast," she said, getting her wits back together. "Look for a hatch or a port."

"Will this do?" he said, reaching into his floating bag of tools to pull out a long, thick wrench.

"Huh?" she said.

As he held her firmly with one arm, still solidly anchored by his strong tail, he used his other arm to SMASH the tool onto the black surface beneath them...repeatedly!

The material beneath them buckled, then cracked, then broke inward.

Dennis kept beating on it until there was a large hole leading into the dark interior of the Spike-Ship.

"How about this entrance, Captain?" he toothily grinned at her. "I've had lots of practice at knocking rock samples out of mountains."

"It will do nicely...Commander!" she formally stated, teasing him. "Shall we?"

"Yes, we shall," he primly replied.

And together—carefully holding onto the sharp edges to pull themselves in without ripping their spacesuits—they both drifted into the interior of the alien spaceship.

Tommy was getting angry.

He knew something was up, but not what!

No one would talk to him.

Even Snake was avoiding him.

The Apparatus was nearing completion. He'd felt a mountain-rattling *VIBRATION* several times now. They were testing it. But they hadn't involved him in the tests, though he knew as much as they did about time-travel dynamics!

At least, he thought he did...

Maybe he didn't?

Perhaps that was what they were trying to hide from him? They wanted to send him backward through an immense stretch of time—a trip that they themselves could not possibly survive—to do their will. But maybe they didn't want him to know enough to come back?

Hmmmm...interesting...

They'd tried to assuage his concerns. They told him that Snake was busy helping design and install a new safety feature into the Apparatus. Tommy hadn't known that his friend Snake was anything more than a talented artist that originally inked his Mom's Turtle Tattoo. But apparently he was a scientist as well. Who knew?

But still it was lonely without a fellow human-looking person to be his friend. He liked the Dinosapiens ok, but most of them couldn't talk English, just their "click/snap" language he had trouble following. And they loomed far above him, physically separated from him, distant! The Martian snakes were even more aloof, hardly even acknowledging his presence.

So he was pleasantly surprised when the Martians shape-shifted him a new companion: *Casandra.*

Casandra's shape-shifted form was as a chunky-looking, short human. She had short-cropped blond hair. She wasn't fat but "beefy." She looked like a female weight-lifter to Tommy, not that he'd known any—but he'd seen pictures in the video histories that he loved to devour. So he was hesitant around her, as she obviously had the strength to grab him and twirl him around her head!

But she wasn't scary. In fact, she was very kind and friendly. It was nice to be around another female like his mother Sally. They were softer and more pleasant than the males, even weight-lifter female ones. And Casandra wasn't as mercurial or flighty as his Mom. This new companion was solid, dependable, and down-to-earth.

But right now she was also away from Tommy in the cavern, helping to get the Apparatus fully operational.

Apparently it was an "all-hands-on-deck" effort to get the new Time Portal working, in order to rescue Dave.

That was nice, although it did leave Tommy all by himself.

The winter outside in the valley was now turning to spring. Only isolated patches of white snow were visible. The rest of the valley was turning from brown to a bright green. The cloudy skies were clearing up. Cheerful sunlight streamed down, warming everything. Flocks of birds were returning, filling the valley with their happy tweets and chirps.

This was just the sort of thing that Tommy enjoyed.

He'd spent so much of his life beneath the dead, frozen surface of Mars that rampant Nature was still a source of endless wonderment to him.

So he skipped along the now well-worn trail toward the central river that ran through the valley. There, he sat on a big boulder and watched the wonderful display of white-water rapids tumbling ever onward.

"Tommy!" a voice sounded from behind.

Whirling about, startled—he didn't think anyone was near him— he saw a *large black bird with four wings* sitting on a fallen log.

It looked at him with four many-facetted eyes which were evenly spaced around its black head.

It had a long, curved-down *red beak* that stood out brightly against its black feathers.

"Did you say something to me?" Tommy smiled at the nice black bird.

"I called your name," the bird said, its red beak "clanking" as it opened and closed out of sync with the words. Yep. It was talking straight into Tommy's mind, telepathically. "We are related, you and I. So I just wanted to say 'hello' to you."

Tommy put his stubby hands firmly on his knees that were covered by his red jumpsuit. He tilted his head expectantly at the talking bird. Tommy's eyes lit up with glee at this new stimulant.

"We're related?" he repeated. "I'm a *bird?*"

"Not so loud!" the bird cautioned him.

Tommy suddenly realized that behind him the river's rushing roar obscured the sound of his voice to any listeners. To unseen observers, Tommy was just marveling at one of the newly evolved valley's species.

The bird had chosen a good place to speak in private to him. In fact, this was the first time that Tommy had wandered completely away from his overseers.

"We stem from the same trunk—the *Goddess Sally Smith!*" the bird said. "She is your Mother. She is our Creator. We waited until now to talk to you because the Intruders would be unhappy to realize that we exist. They are not so happy with you, are they?"

"That's true," Tommy nodded thoughtfully. "They're keeping something from me. I don't know what or why! I've been a good boy. Why are they punishing me?"

The bird cocked its head to the side.

"Just as David King is a past threat to their continued existence—so are you, Tommy Smith."

Tommy grinned at being called his full name. Hardly anyone ever called him that, or even knew it. He wasn't just a human-looking boy robot. He was a unique, special intelligence—just the same as with any other sapient creature.

"I don't want to hurt anyone," Tommy protested, shaking his head from side-to-side in firm denial.

"And yet you are the Prophet that we've long awaited," the bird continued, bobbing its head up-and-down. "And we know that our Prophet will herald the end of this world. Because of your Arrival, the End Times are now upon us. So it has been sung long ago. So we sing now. And so shall it ever be sung: 'PRAISE TO THE PROPHET! CELEBRATE THE ENDING!'"

Tommy was puzzled, not only to encounter a telepathically talking bird, but by what the bird was saying.

"What? But that *already* happened," Tommy protested, frowning. "God wiped out all those *bad* humans. He burned off both planets—Earth and Mars! That's how I came here. God let a few of us escape: me, Mommy, and Mr. King...plus, of course, a whole bunch of the good lizard-people. Uhm, didn't He?" he asked, suddenly confused.

"So...you understand now, do you?" the bird chirped, hopping up-and-down excitedly on its three evenly spaced legs.

"No, I *don't!*" Tommy angrily exclaimed.

Oh, that certainly wasn't his usual cheerfulness speaking. What was happening to him? He was getting very grouchy!

Tommy frowned, putting his small hands up to the sides of his head.

Suddenly he had another splitting headache!

He squinted his eyes shut, trying to block out the intense pain.

And when he opened his eyes, the talking bird was gone.

Chapter 10

ANCIENT GREECE

The "cradle of civilization"

The Roots of Democracy

An Artistic Explosion

An Empire of the Mind

A Birth of the Theatre

Bathed in putrid filth

Addicted to ugly war

Built upon slavery

Subjugating women

And demonizing dissent

Killing its greatest Heroes...

Homo sapiens Eulogy, 10:23-2

Dave avoided people and buildings. He climbed higher and higher up the desolate mountain, cradling the egg. The low mountain was mostly exposed rock, but hardy trees survived singly or in small groves. Low shrubbery covered most of the rest of the surface, clinging stubbornly.

He needed to find somewhere for the egg which would be shaded and secluded. He climbed the steepest slopes he could find, even short cliffs—trying to find the most inaccessible, isolated place possible.

The sun was now high in the sky, starting to burn his exposed skin. The blanket wrapped around his shoulders protected his back—but his face, arms, and legs were turning red.

Was there nowhere he could stash his precious egg?

Ah. There it was. He'd found it—up a very steep slope that few would think to climb. At its top was a rocky peak. But right below the peak was a small, inset cave.

Dave crawled into the cave, finding it damp and cool. A trickle of water ran out of it onto the rocks below, apparently from a crack reaching down to a deep spring. It was perfect.

He went in as far as he could. Then he scooped out a hole and buried the egg two-thirds down into the moist dirt. He left the top third exposed to the air. It was a technique Dave used with his pet lizards and snakes whenever they happened to lay eggs. The blistering heat outside would keep the egg warm. The shade inside the cave ensured the egg would not dehydrate. Then, to protect it from any predators looking for a tasty omelet, he found rocks and built a cap over the egg, with plenty of gaps through which air could still flow. If it should hatch, the baby could easily push itself up through the protecting layer of rocks.

Satisfied, Dave emerged from the small cave and weakly climbed the remaining short distance up to the peak.

There he sat on a boulder and looked out over this strange new world.

He was dizzy from not having eaten for what...a billion years? Also, he felt like he was on the verge of sunstroke—the sweat that'd been streaming now slowed as he got increasingly dizzy—but what he saw *down below him* was undeniably stunning!

He'd been climbing upward so frantically, searching every nook and cranny for a suitable hiding place for Breep's egg, he'd not yet realized his circumstance.

Looking back the way he'd come he saw—stretching from his left to his right—a *dazzling blue, deep ocean!* It contrasted sharply with the green shrubs and trees that marched down the slope of the low mountain to the sea. Rocky islands thrust up off the coastline. In the distance, white mists hugged the ocean. Overhead the sky was light blue.

But it was what lay off to his far right that told him exactly where the Obelisk had brought him...

"Oh, my Lord!" he gasped, stunned.

He saw many small white stone houses—a city! And in the middle of that city was a raised-up square hill. And on the top of that hill sat *white marble temples* glistening in the bright sunlight! The highest

temple was a large rectangle, whose four walls were composed of elegantly curved columns.

"It's Athens," Dave gasped, "*ancient* Athens!"

There was no doubt. Dave was looking at the gloriously adorned,
raised-up hill called the *Acropolis*, located in the ancient Greek city of
Athens—upon which sat the intact *Parthenon*, a temple to the goddess Athena. Dave realized he was in ancient Greece somewhere in
the 5th Century B.C.!

A high wall surrounded the city-proper, leading down to the
coastline. There, a vibrant harbor was safely enclosed by the extend-
ed-out city walls. And in the harbor, amongst many smaller craft,
rode more than a hundred *warships!*

"Those are *triremes*," Dave whispered to himself, in awe. Back in
school he'd always been fascinated by ancient Greece. Though he'd
concentrated on science, history was a close second of his academic
interests, particularly the so-called "golden age" of Greece.

"Oar-driven battering rams, three levels of rowers...the battle-
ships of the ancient world," he nodded to himself, squinting to try and
see more details.

He slumped on his boulder, trying feverishly to remember the
details of this living history into which he'd inadvertently inserted
himself.

"This must be...yes...part of the Peloponnesian War," he muttered
to himself, "when Athens is about to send a fleet to Sicily, assembled
out there in the harbor...which was...414 B.C., yes!—but it's an expedition that will result in absolute disaster, marking the end of the Gold-
en Age of Athens."

So much potential... Many achievements in the arts, science, and
politics—but ground-down and destroyed by endless conflicts, both
with other Greek Empires and with Greek's external enemies.

Why?

Why were they so stupid?—Dave groaned to himself.

Maybe...maybe he was here to learn that answer—if not to benefit
humanity, then perhaps for his own satisfaction?

He winced.

"What the hell?" he gasped, looking down at the Anaconda Tattoo.

It was glowing, *burning* his wrist!

"Alright, alright," he groaned, rubbing the wrist against his naked chest. "I'm paying attention! I see I'm back here for a reason. Who-ever or whatever you are, you who guided me here—I understand! You can turn off the damn Anaconda Tattoo."

So...there was still hope. An unknown Influence was behind his jump to this particular time and place. But why? Why was this hap-pening? Was it, perhaps, giving him yet another chance to *change history?*

It was a breath-taking thought. Dave was suddenly transformed from a desperate refugee forever cut-off from his one true love...back to be a fighter on an incredible Quest: seeking to save the entire hu-man race!

"Can I do it? Is it possible?" he whispered to himself, staring with awe at the distant Greek city at the height of its powers.

Instead of the human race being destroyed in the 21st Century in his timeline—could he still save them from that awful fate? If so, it wasn't just about premature Dark Energy generation anymore—it was about changing the *entire behavior* of mankind!

"Sally tried to do this with Jesus," he nodded to himself. His vi-sion was starting to blur. He was definitely on the edge of heat stroke. But his mind was zipping along a million miles a minute. "But...she tried it from the opposite direction," he muttered around cracking, dried lips. "She tried to 'dumb down' mankind by denying them The Christ...but now I'm 500 years *before* Jesus' teachings. This is at the beginning of scientific reasoning...so what's critical about this time? And what could I possibly affect?"

The vile failures of mankind were obvious.

He'd seen it all. He'd seen with his own two eyes ultra-religious people routinely defile the name of God. He'd seen fathers and moth-ers destroy their own families by turning control of their lives over to addicting chemicals. He'd seen sexual predators deriving their pleas-ure at the pain of others. He'd seen supposedly good-hearted people nonchalantly turning their backs on the sufferings of others. He'd seen otherwise upstanding people happy to destroy the planet so that their monthly utility bills wouldn't be a few dollars higher. He'd seen despots ruling nations with an iron fist at the consent of their own brutalized people. He'd seen self-proclaimed "peaceful" people eager to approve "righteous" wars. He'd seen supposedly devoted mothers killing their own babies with drug-fueled negligence. He'd seen the fruits of science turned into the means to destroy and slaughter on a mass scale. And he'd seen, far too often, worthy improvement efforts mutated into the actual negative thing that they were meant to overcome.

Why was humanity so God-damned stupid?—he agonized.

Perhaps he was here to find the answer.

And he suddenly realized where he might find the Answer.

Looking down at that amazing city—Athens at the peak of its power—Dave knew that one of its residents should be a philosopher who'd become famous throughout the coming ages. Indeed, this man was revered far into the sophisticated future of mankind: *Socrates!*

Surely Socrates—a man of intense intelligence who began the *scientific method* that allowed mankind to question and dissect reality—would know the answer.

Socrates did not record his own teachings and life, which was left to his students and historians to write. So the "real" historical Socrates was largely unknown. Though he was famous for asking incisive questions he gave few answers, at least as described in the recordings of his students. But Dave could now ask the great man *in person*—assuming he actually walked the streets below.

"Jesus H. Christ," he mumbled, stunned by the realization.

Dave was excited and amazed—feeling again a transcendent purpose to his life. But how could Dave ever approach the learned man to find out transcendental Answers? The massive dose of Optimmune he'd taken had transformed him into a young, seven-year-old boy! Also, Dave was a stranger who did not even speak Greek. He was helpless and afraid. He'd already almost been taken away into slavery!

It seemed hopeless. He didn't even know if his guess at the present time-period was correct, or if Socrates really walked the Athenian streets below. Dave's excitement was quickly evaporating like the sweat of his poor body drying-out in the hot sun.

He swayed on his boulder there on the peak of the mountain, feeling his last bits of strength draining away...

"*Asteri paidi—tha einai dyskilo na akolouthisoun!*" Dave heard a cheerful voice below him and dazedly looking down. He saw the old, tall fisherman laboriously clambering up the steep slope.

The single-arm old man grinned lopsidedly, revealing a single, protruding, yellowed tooth. He was sweating profusely, staining his weathered tunic. His grizzly white beard was slick with sweat. His kindly grey eyes were crinkled at the edges. His skin was leathery and well-wrinkled.

He barely managed to top the ridge.

He was trembling from the long, dangerous climb he'd just accomplished.

He wearily sank down next to the boy and reached with his one arm to unhook a flask from his leather belt and offer it to Dave.

—which Dave grabbed and greedily drank from...cool, clear water! It was delicious!

Dave shakily handed it back.

"Thank y-you," he nodded wearily. "Y-you followed m-me? Why?"

"*Periscus...*" the old man grinned again, tapping his own chest with his one hand.

"Y-your name...is Periscus," Dave nodded, understanding. "I am called...I don't know. I'm a *new boy* now. I don't have a name," he said, dejected.

"*New...boy,*" the old man nodded, repeating Dave's words back to him, "*to paidi asteri?*" he said, pointing up at the sky.

Dave sighed, reluctant to claim himself as a god—but why not? If that gave him an edge to survive in this ancient world, why not let the old man believe he'd rescued a fallen god?

Dave nodded.

"*Eisai Astraios?*" the man said in wonderment, reverence in his tone.

Dave thought furiously. Astraios? What was that? He'd heard that name in his historical studies. Who was it? And then it came to him—it was one of the major gods of Greek mythology...the *Titan god* of the stars and planets!

Dave forced his dehydrated, trembling young body to stand up, straight and proud.

He took his hand with the still-glowing Anaconda Tattoo on its wrist and laid it upon the head of the sitting fisherman.

"*Yes!* I am *Astraios!* I have come to Earth in disguise," he grandly proclaimed as "officially" as he could muster with his seven-year-old high-pitched voice. "My snake tattoo affirms this! And you, Periscus, are my loyal subject. I will reward you greatly for serving me faithfully!"

The man raised his own hand to place reverently atop Dave's hand on his head, lightly touching the still-hot Tattoo.

His gaze was awestruck. It seemed he understood Dave's English, at least the tone if not the content.

"*Eimai evlogimenos apo tin emfanisi sas,*" the man stated with absolute sincerity.

"Y-yes, w-whatever," Dave replied, dizzily sitting back down on the boulder, both hands now flat on the rock to steady himself—everything spinning around in a circle.

"*Kai i theia avgo pou diexagetai?*" the man said, curving his one hand into an egg-holding shape.

"Yes, my 'god'-egg," Dave nodded, waving a hand vaguely at the hillside below. "It is safe."

"*Eiste adynamoi. Tha prepei na trote,*" the man said, making hand motions to his mouth and eating noises.

Dave nodded. Yes, he was very hungry. And it was getting too hard to speak.

But he forced himself to ask the essential question to his new protector.

Dave pointed to the city below as he weakly asked..."S-Socrates?"

"*Sokratis!*" the man snarled, his grey eyebrows suddenly shooting up in both alarm and anger!

"Y-you k-know him?"

"*Aftos einai enas apistos pou prokalei tous neous anthropous na amfisvitou tous theous! Eiste edo gia na ton skotosei?*" he asked in an excited, aggressive tone, drawing his finger across his throat in the universal gesture of killing!

"Sure, why not," Dave shrugged, having no idea what the old man was suggesting.

At least in contemporaneous Athens there apparently existed someone with a name similar to "Socrates." That was encouraging, even though Periscus seemed to hate him for some reason.

Dave woozily stood up again, leaning on the arm of the strong old man and allowing him to guide him back down the treacherous, dangerous cliffs and slopes.

Clearly, the old man had a grudge against Socrates. But that didn't matter. All that mattered to Dave now was trying to fit into this new world. He had to learn to speak and read ancient Greek real fast! Only then would he have a chance to integrate into the life of Athens and approach the astute Master.

It looked likely he'd never return to the future. The Obelisk was sunk into the ocean, probably far beyond his reach. This was his world now. But to come all this way through time just to catch fish seemed pointless.

Before he died he wanted *answers!*

And, as they descended past the opening to the small cave, Dave wished Breep all the best.

Should the egg hatch, there were plenty of shrubs and low trees up here to hide a baby dinosaur—and probably plenty of small game for him to catch and eat.

"Goodbye, old friend," Dave whispered. "Be well."

Tommy was anxious...

"*Don't move, little dude!*" he heard Snake nervously admonish him through nonmetallic headphones firmly attached to Tommy's curly blond-haired head.

Tommy was hanging horizontally looking straight down into a totally black, diamond-glittering *maelstrom...*

The Dinosapiens were carefully calibrating his mental EEG readings, mapping finite changes to different Portal-parameters. Electrodes pressed through his hair recorded electrical waveforms from the skin of his skull.

He was in a tight harness suspended above the inner stack of super-conducting magnets of the Apparatus. Around him the larger circular magnets and constrained plasma-flow were contorting space-time—as if he were at the *event horizon* of a cosmic black hole!

Things seemed oddly stretched-out.

He was looking straight down into an opened-up sphere of *subspace!*

The *sizzling, crackling,* and deep *throbbing* noises around him were deafening.

And the heat was causing him to sweat profusely. Clear water cables were wrapped around many surrounding components, carrying rapidly flowing cold water piped from the river—but it wasn't enough to drain the heat generated from the massive amounts of energy. It was getting hotter and hotter...

Plastic fans set around his suspended body were pouring cool air across his face, but it wasn't sufficient to keep him from getting uncomfortably warm.

But it was only a minor inconvenience. He was determined to do his job.

"Ok," he weakly replied into the microphone at his mouth, trying to smile but failing.

It was all fascinating to Tommy.

But he was also very scared...

He knew that if he fell into that whirling black vortex he might as easily be ripped to shreds as thrown into the past or future.

But he'd ridden that wave before, even acquired an intuitive understanding of its movements.

"*Do you see anything yet, little dude?*" Snake's voice sounded faintly but intensely from the headphones.

"No...nothing yet—wait!" he said, frowning. "Yes...there's a trail!"

Yes, he could see *patterns* forming in the flickering diamond patterns—images just on the periphery of his enhanced perception.

It was just like when he'd hunted dinosaurs.

He was floating high above the Earth while it whirled like a top—which he could, at will, freeze in place and dive down into!

It was like being God.

"*Where's it leading?*" Snake eagerly asked.

Tommy was following a faint distortion left from Dave's recent passage from this exact spot along the timeline through the vortex into the past.

"Left!" Tommy yelled out, "Now right...up a bit...hold it there...to the left again—now down three degrees!"

He was following the path that Dave took...now pointing millions of years into the past.

"Yikes! My hair's *on fire!*" Tommy screamed, jerking and twisting in the constraining harness.

Around him *whining* and *screeching* sounds hurt his ears as various components slowed and ground to a stop.

Two Dinosapiens lumbered up beneath him, squirting a stream of *white foam* up onto Tommy.

The intense heat on his head subsided as Tommy's harness was swung over to the side away from the column of circular super-magnets—and then gently lowered.

Snake was right there, looking worried.

Turned over onto his back, Tommy now looked straight up into Snake's thin human face.

"D-did we g-get there?" Tommy gasped as the other Dinosapiens hurriedly unbuckled him, wiping the fire-retarding foam off his body.

"You did good, little buddy," Snake comforted him. "But when the rings get powered up again, we gotta go back. We're still a long ways from knowing where Dave and Breep went. But we're making real good progress! You got the path laid out to about 200 million years into the past. We jist gotta keep you from lightin' on fire, man, to go even deeper. Maybe we kin wrap you up with those cold-water tubes, what do ya think?"

"Maybe," Tommy gasped, feeling up at his head. His trembling hands came away with blackened strands. "I don't like my head catching on fire!"

"Yep, we'll stop that from happening. So you ok, good buddy?" Snake asked.

"Yes, I am ok, I think," Tommy hesitantly nodded, letting Snake help him stand. "So what happens when we get the Portal focused to where Dave went?"

Now they were walking out of the cavern, back to the Valley.

"Well, then you go through the Portal, grab Dave and Breep, and bring them back to us. Easy as pie, right?"

Tommy had never eaten pie, didn't know how it was made, and didn't care. So he kept silent as they walked on down the tunnel. But he was *thinking* furiously.

"Why did you take my gun away?" he abruptly asked.

He no longer had a cute holster at his waist. They no longer wanted him to carry Sally's black gun around with him.

"Oh...it's finishing charging up," Snake replied as they stepped out of the tunnel onto the mountainside. "It's hot enough now it'd be dangerous to have it on your hip, little buddy. We don't want nothin' bad to happen to you, right?"

Tommy deeply breathed in the fresh mountain air. It was nice to be outside again. Back in the cavern it was like his first decades of life on Mars—buried deep beneath its surface. It wasn't bad, but it was boring. There wasn't much there other than the Priestesses. He had work to do which occupied most of his time, but it wasn't the same as being directly exposed to Mother Nature.

Here, Tommy was endlessly stimulated by a fantastic variety of living creatures. Alone or with Snake he often went on extended walks into the wilds of this valley. It was safe enough, even though the Black Birds still followed him—menacingly!

None had spoken to him again.

But they followed him, hopping along beside him on the paths or sitting glowering down at him from overhanging branches.

Tommy even wondered if his prior conversation with the telepathic Black Bird was just a hallucination.

But, no, he knew in his android gut that the conversation was real.

The birds were waiting.

They were waiting for their Prophet to make the next move...

"I want my gun back!" Tommy insisted to Snake.

"What, little dude?"

"Now!" Tommy angrily yelled, plopping himself onto his little rump and folding his arms defiantly over his chest.

"Hey, man, I don't know if it's even ready yet or..."

"*Right now*—or I won't do anything more with that portal!" Tommy shouted out into the air.

Beside them on the mountain slope a flock of Black Birds sudden-ly jumped up into the air, the sound of their many wings making a startling "swooshing" sound!

"Ok, ok," Snake said, sounding flustered. "I'll see what I can do. But if it's fully charged, it'll be dangerous! We'd need to make a new, tougher holster. And they might want for you to..."

"I'm *scared!*" Tommy insisted vehemently. "I need protection. I almost burned to death! I'm just a little boy. I'm not big like you and your friends. Even birds might grab me and eat me up. I need my gun!" he started sobbing, putting his singed head down into his arms.

He kept the sobbing going as he peeked furtively out from under his arms.

Snake stood still—like he was listening to voices which only he could hear.

"Alright, then," Snake said, reaching down to pat Tommy's shoul-der. "They say you can have the gun back. But you have to be very careful with it, keep the safety lock closed. You promise to be care-ful?"

"S-sure," Tommy gasped, catching his breath and looking up with a wan smile. "I'll be *real* careful!"

"Do you want Casandra to come be with you?" Snake said. "I need to go back to the cavern and work on safety measures so you don't light on fire again."

"Y-yes," Tommy whimpered. "Casandra w-would be nice."

"Ok, then, little dude," Snake replied. "I'll call her over."

But Tommy wasn't comforted.

His normally cheerful, trusting self was deteriorating—quickly!

He suspected that once the Portal was focused and calibrated, the Dinosapiens and Snakes wouldn't need him anymore.

He knew they didn't consider him to be a living entity. To them he was just a complex machine. He could see it in their condescend-ing manner to him. And the Snakes—other than his two form-shifted companions—regarded him with naked contempt.

But now he had tangible leverage. And if worse came to worse, his Mommy's super-gun could force a lot of compliance.

He didn't just accept the world as the existing society dictated—he *questioned everything!*

Mother Sally had taught him well.

The "unexamined life was not worth living"...

—a "saying" that the High Priestess taught him, which came from *Socrates* in ancient Greece.

He'd never been there—to Greece—but it sounded like a fun place.

They *questioned* the world around them.

And though he was "merely" a robot, he was a *smart* robot!

And he wished to *survive* to the fullest.

Chapter 11

<u>SELF-PRESERVATION</u>

Brain cells die

As the young head grows

Voluntarily for the good of all

When useful connections are not made

Making room for required, working circuits

In limited space kindly erasing themselves

Neatly and carefully committing suicide

For the good of the completed organism

Creating a precedence not uncommon

Where true cooperation is manifested

And the total good equates to the self

But where self-awareness emerges

The individual organism fights

Its primary instinct to survive

Against all odds, forgetting

The lesson of its own brain

As its Fears take control

And Hate dominates

Killing the Joy...

Homo sapiens Eulogy, 11:5-9

Sally floated into the dark interior of the alien spaceship, the only light a faint illumination from her helmet.

Immediately in front of her she saw a mass of wet-looking cables, with barely room left for her to wriggle deeper.

"Where are you going, Captain?" Dennis politely asked, his small voice coming out of her helmet speaker. "I'm afraid I'm too bulky to follow you in amongst those cables."

She paused, now floating within the jungle of dangling cables, realizing she'd momentarily forgotten about the sapient dinosaur trailing along behind her.

"Oh, I'm just trying to figure out what to do next, Dennis," she said back to him. "You're right—I don't see any clear path forward. I'm backing out."

But when she tried, the cables behind her closed together, blocking her retreat!

"Uh...having some trouble here," Sally gasped, floundering around as the moist-looking black cables stuck to her white spacesuit like leaches!

They were constricting around her like *snakes!* They were crushing her, making it impossible to expand her chest to breathe. Plus they were blocking her helmet.

Sally was panicking, struggling just to get another gasp of air, her vision dimming...

—when she was suddenly yanked backward to safety.

"It behaves like a living creature, doesn't it?" Dennis mildly observed, his big orange eyes staring at her from within his oblong helmet.

She took several deep, ragged breaths of air before answering.

She was now floating just outside the jagged hole that Dennis had smashed into the side of the Spike-Ship's hull. She saw that Dennis had wisely attached a thin line from his spacesuit to one of the knob-shaped spikes, keeping them secure.

"It was trying to kill me," Sally gasped, floating there in her spacesuit, firmly held onto by Dennis.

"It likely perceived you as an invading organism," Dennis nodded. "But that still doesn't tell us for sure if the ship is alive or not. It could still be an automatic defense reaction."

"Thanks for pulling me out," she grinned ruefully at Dennis.

"It was certainly my pleasure," he replied. "But perhaps next time we should be more cautious."

"Agreed," Sally said, appreciating that he had politely said "we" when he really meant "you." She studied the readouts flashing up on the inside of her helmet. "But how are we going to get into the interior to look for its subspace drive mechanism? Just smashing a hole into it doesn't seem sufficient."

"Well, perhaps we should just let it capture us," Dennis dryly replied, motioning over to the side.

Indeed, where before there was only a forest of various fixed spikes reaching up into the vacuum of space, large *tentacles* were emerging.

They waved about amongst the rigid spikes in an eerie, weightless dance.

And one of them was bending fluidly down toward Sally and Dennis!

Sally grabbed Dennis tight around his long neck as he in turn held firmly onto his tool bag, placing it snug against her back.

"I think we attracted their attention when I smashed a hole in the hull," Dennis matter-of-factly stated over Sally's helmet speaker.

"Those huge tentacles look like giant vacuum-cleaner hoses," Sally gulped.

"And that is...?"

"—the big opened end that's coming right down on top of us!" she answered, involuntarily squinting her eyes shut in fear as she convulsively hugged the big Dinosapien.

The circular end of a 200-foot-long tentacle "snapped" down on top of them, totally engulfing them—as Dennis let loose his mooring line—and *sucked* them away!

They tumbled together along a long, dark tunnel—clinging tightly to each other—until they *splashed* into a tank.

A lid above them slid into place, totally trapping them.

The space inside was completely filled with a bubbling, semi-fluid liquid.

"What the hell is this, a stomach?" Sally gasped, floating in the midst of what looked and felt like red jelly.

"I believe that might be an apt analogy," Dennis calmly remarked. "The solution around us is indeed eating through my tool bag."

Indeed, Sally saw that the jelly that they were in was making ever-widening thinning patches on the bag's outer fabric!

"Oh, Jesus," she gasped, "if it's doing that to the tool bag, then...?"

Yes, she saw small flecks of her spacesuit loosening and floating free into the goo.

"We've got to get out of here!" Sally exclaimed, looking around frantically for an opening or exit. "In a few minutes we'll both be dissolved!"

Dennis released her, reached into his disintegrating tool bag, and brought out a gun-shaped device. He grasped it firmly by its handle, where grooves neatly fit his three-fingered glove.

He pointed it at the lid above them.

A *stream of white bubbles* sprang through the red jelly at the lid which buckled and broke upward.

Sally clambered up and out of the acid bath, reaching down to help Dennis climb out behind her.

Seemingly cooperatively, a stream of clear liquid *blasted* into the both of them, knocking them off their feet. It painfully sprayed onto every single millimeter of their white spacesuits.

"Ow!" Sally yelled, trying to block it with her arms.

But then it rapidly drained away into holes in the floor. Simultaneously the damaged lid was pulled away while a fresh lid slid out of a slot and sealed the pool beside them.

"There's artificial gravity in here," Sally thankfully said, getting wobbly back to her feet. "It's not earth-normal gravity, but it's sufficient for us to walk."

"Perhaps that pool was just a decontamination procedure," the Commander observed. "If we'd been more patient, the jelly might have drained away before any permanent damage was done."

"Or we might also be *dead*," Sally snapped back at him. "You took the right course in getting us out of there."

"Fortunately it didn't destroy our tools or suits," the Commander stated, sorting out his remaining tools (though some had dropped out of the crumbling bag and been left behind in the pool) and snapped them securely onto a workbelt at the waist of his white spacesuit.

Sally looked at the readouts projected on the inside of her helmet. Good! The suit was still functioning ok—and the external atmosphere readings also looked promising.

She unlocked the mechanism holding her helmet in place, twisted it, and lifted it up off her head. It swung back on a strap to bob at the back of her head.

She breathed in deeply.

"Sally, what are you doing?" the Commander asked in alarm, looking up from positioning the tools at his waist.

"There's a breathable mix of oxygen in the atmosphere," she replied. "We can conserve our limited air supply."

Reluctantly, Dennis undid his own helmet then tentatively sniffed at the air, baring pointed teeth.

"It smells strange...like rotted vegetables?"

His growling voice was much fiercer and deeper when not coming through Sally's small helmet receiver.

"Well, get used to it," she brusquely ordered him.

"You're being unpleasant, Sally," the Dinosapien sniffed, wrinkling his muzzle in distaste. "I would appreciate you adopting a more considerate tone when giving me directions."

"Well, I'm not used to almost getting dissolved in an acid bath."

"But we did escape. There's no need to dwell on the past, however unpleasant it might have been."

She "huffed" at him, disregarding his complaint.

"And just where did you get that *gun?*" Sally asked. She was inspecting her suit carefully to make sure there were no breaches. "I thought you told me before you didn't have any weapons—not that I'm complaining, mind you."

Her white spacesuit was spotted with red marks, but otherwise undamaged.

"It is not a gun, Captain," Dennis primly stated, doing the same careful inspection on his own suit. He twirled his tail up to give its extra-flexible coverings particular attention. "My 'gun' is a laser-drill, particularly useful in modifying metallic items. It is used both for building or dismantling structures. As such, it was helpful in making an opening through that pool's lid—much as I used my wrench to make a hole into the ship's hull, and..."

"It's a *gun!*" Sally barked at him, reaching over to grab it away from him and snap it firmly onto her own spacesuit's workbelt.

"Captain, that's simply not true," he insisted, now seeming to get angry. "It was specifically manufactured and designed to..."

"Whatever it *was*...it's now *my* gun," She told him, looking around cautiously.

"Your illogical acquisition is most unsettling," he sighed, shaking his big head in denial. "But I suppose that is why the Elders permitted you to accompany us. You see things in a foreign, primitive manner. You even insist on turning common tools into destructive weapons."

"Oh just shut up, Commander," she growled, feeling at the walls of the small chamber they were within.

Something yielded.

She pressed harder.

A previously unapparent *iris* opened, its leaves smoothly folding back into the inner walls of yet another circular tunnel.

It was very similar to the tentacle they'd been sucked into—large enough for them to stand upright within, but made of a pliable, soft material.

It was unnerving that the inside wall of the tube appeared *moist*.

It was like a *throat*, eager to swallow its next meal.

She squared her shoulders and stepped forward.

"Shall we?" she gestured for the Commander to follow, determined to see this through to the bitter end.

He unhooked the tether from his suit, allowing it to coil back onto her suit. She felt it "snap" into place at her waist.

"And what's this, Dennis?" She grinned at him. "You don't want to be stuck with me anymore? Is this a divorce?"

"We don't have your marriage conventions," he seriously replied. "Now that we're inside the alien ship, the tether might hinder our movements. And as to your 'divorce' reference, our mating is conducted as necessary to produce a desired number of fertilized ova for maintaining our optimal population level. The sperm and eggs are from whichever members are selected to produce a desired genetic balance. So, you see Sally, there is no need for divorce amongst our species. We require neither your irrational 'love' nor 'hate' to drive population renewal."

"My how 'romantic'," Sally sneered at him.

Then she laughed, shaking her head ruefully in way of apology. She wasn't being a very good Captain, yelling at and insulting her own people.

She cautiously walked forward into the "springy" tunnel, feeling like she was on a trampoline. She held her new weapon firmly with both her hands. She felt much more confident with the laser "gun" pointed ahead.

"If that's true, then—how do you explain George and Alice?" Sally curtly replied, invoking them yet again. "They certainly seem to have a genuine affection for each other, within the bounds of a permanent relationship."

"They are...exceptions," he hesitantly replied from behind. "Their eggs, from which they were hatched, were genetically modified to be...throwbacks...to a much earlier period in our evolution."

"How come?" Sally said, suspecting she knew the answer, but wanting to hear it from Dennis.

"They were bred to be spies in your Dimension," the Commander replied. "They had to fit into your society, to adapt into your ugly forms—even enjoy such! That's the real reason they kept their shape-shifted human forms on this journey—not just to make you more comfortable interacting with the crew. They actually like being in your hideous bodies—even though they could change back into our beautiful dinosaur forms. We anticipated the need for such trans-dimensional spying long before the end-times came. So some of our people had to sacrifice aspects of their greatly evolved maturity to become...well...retarded and revolting."

"Oh, I 'revolt' you now, do I?" Sally said as she kept moving cautiously forward. "And you think I'm a *retarded* species?"

The tension was getting to her. She was trying to relieve the stress with her jabbering. But things were just getting worse. She felt her throat closing up in growing panic!

"Well, aren't you?"

With each step she sprang up into the air before settling back down.

It was very unnerving.

But it was nice to have some gravity, not just float around helplessly in zero-G.

"No, I'm *not!*" she impulsively yelled back at him.

"Sally, you mammals in our Dimension never progressed beyond rat-like creatures that attacked and ate our precious eggs," he said, making a disgusted, "snorting" noise. "We equate you humans with those nasty little predators."

"So you think I'm just an ugly egg-eater?" she asked him.

He hesitated.

"Well...now that I've come to know you better..." the talking dinosaur behind her carefully stated, "I find you less revolting than previously."

"Wow! What a compliment!" Sally snorted derisively.

Then, more quietly, she added, "Careful Dennis, I think I see a light ahead."

And, yes, there was indeed "light at the end of the tunnel."

They stepped out of the passageway into an open central space. It was a very large, circular room.

Above them, Sally saw many *clear floating bubbles...*

Indeed, there were *thousands* of the bubbles.

"May I help you?" a cheerful, high-pitched voice sounded from behind her.

She whirled around, the laser-drill held steady in her hands.

There, sitting jauntily on one of Dennis' broad spacesuited shoulders was what appeared to be an *elf!*

At least it looked like an elf.

It had one single big "Cyclops" eye on the front of a completely-bald head. Two large, pointed ears sprouted from each side of the bulbous head. It had no nose. But it did have a very large mouth—wrapping fully halfway around its head—adorned with numerous, needle-like teeth.

It also had a chubby little naked body with no obvious genitalia. It had two stubby arms with four-fingered hands. Its two legs were short and fat. Its unshod feet (each with only four toes) were wide and splayed. Its skin color was luminous green.

Dennis—his orange eye on that side of his head opened wide and staring right at the creature on his shoulder—hesitantly raised his clawed glove to grasp it...

—and his hand went right through it!

It was a three-dimensional projection, a hologram.

"I understand your language from a preliminary scan of your neuronal network," it said to Sally. "I perceive you to be the leader of the two, so I'm communicating in your English. Am I speaking it correctly? Though, if you'd like, I can talk in the subservient entity's normal speech?"

A series of "clicks" and "whistles" sprang fluently from the mouth of the elf, though the creature was clearly struggling to produce the harsh sounds.

Dennis reacted like he'd been insulted, making a peculiar "barking" noise through his tightly clenched jaw.

"Subservient?" he growled in English.

"English is just fine," Sally quickly replied. "Both of us understand it. I'm very glad to meet you. We were thinking this entire ship was a machine running on automatic. We hope to convince you we are no threat and you can call off your attack on our ship. Also, we'd like to ask your help for..."

The elf laughed, with a wave of its small hand dismissing Sally's speech.

It hopped from Dennis' shoulder to the floor and came waddling up to Sally to stand right in front of her. It bent way backward to place its hands on its green hips to stare straight up into her face.

It was only two feet tall.

In spite of herself, Sally smiled.

It was very cute—except of course, for that carnivorous fish-mouth.

She felt her guard dropping—it was so funny and harmless looking. But that caused her to be even more suspicious, to clutch her "gun" even more firmly.

"Oh, you won't need that," the elf laughed again. "In fact, why don't we just get it out of the way?"

A bubble suddenly swooped down and *snatched* it away!

"But...?" Sally gasped. Her hand clutched for the weapon as it drifted up beyond her reach, neatly captured in the center of the drifting bubble.

"You might accidently shoot it and cause minor damage," the elf said, motioning for the both of them to follow him.

Stopping her angry reply mid-breath, Sally did as directed, walking silently behind the elf.

She didn't want to unnecessarily antagonize this creature until she knew exactly what she was dealing with.

"Are you the Captain of this ship?" Dennis sullenly asked the elf as he trailed along behind Sally...

—when a large bubble suddenly *swooped down* and *entirely encased* the Dinosapien, snatching him up off the spongy floor to float into the swarm of bubbles above!

Sally stopped dead in her tracks, refusing to budge.

"Give me back my friend!" she ordered the alien "elf."

"All in good time—you will be reunited with him, do not fear," he cheerfully answered in his squeaky voice, continuing onward without a pause. "He was just a distraction. He spoke out of turn. Our business is between you and me, right?"

"I just want to know what's going on here," Sally carefully replied, noting the exact position of the bubble containing the now frozen-in-place Dinosapien as it floated up into the swarm of other bubbles.

She also kept an eye on the bubble containing her gun.

And she subtly edged closer to a wall, putting her side firmly onto it, and began shoving herself along the slick surface...moving quickly, wanting to circle the entire chamber and get a full view of the amazing bubbles floating above.

"I am the *Preservationist* of this vessel's Archive," the elf smiled proudly, now trotting beside her as she circled around the room— apparently not bothered by her exploratory behavior.

His smile again displayed his unsettling array of many sharp teeth.

"Are you alive?" she asked as she kept sliding along the slick wall.

"Not as you judge such matters," he answered, now skipping and hopping along beside her. "I'm an animated projection, as are the other three-dimensional structures you see. Aren't they marvelous?

Please, continue to study them! They are beautiful, aren't they? Do you not find them fascinating?"

The elf waved his small hands around at the floating bubbles as Sally steadily circled the room. The creature was obviously proud of his "bubble room."

And as Sally moved around she did examine them more closely.

She gasped.

Inside each floating bubble she saw entire worlds, living cultures, and distinct works of art. Plus there were individual creatures.

And the details were perfect.

She suspected that the simulations went down to the atomic level. It must require incredible computing power to display such a vast array of projections!

"So these are all three-dimensional holograms?" Sally repeated, in awe at the details of the contents of each bubble.

"Look up," the elf laughed, clapping its hands with glee.

High overhead, a large circular device was set into the ceiling. And it glowed with every color of the rainbow. Indeed, Sally could see it was a super-advanced laser projector—via flickering light streaming out of it made visible by particles in the air from her still-shedding spacesuit.

"So they're not real," she concluded, narrowing her eyes as she returned to the spot on the wall of the chamber where she'd started from, having fully circled the "library" room.

She'd seen everything.

Now she needed to keep moving along the wall, but slower than in her first circuit.

"Oh, no, Captain—they *are* very real indeed. They are the means by which this ship catalogues and preserves its memories."

"But my gun...the Commander...they *are* tangible articles, right?"

"Of course, but they are now in the process of being digitized down to their subatomic particles," the elf happily laughed. "Once those objects are fully analyzed and recorded, the metal and meat will be repurposed or jettisoned. Only their essential information will be preserved as visual replicates—as in the other bubbles. So there will be no spoiling or degradation. They will be immortalized! Isn't that wonderful?"

She frowned at the little creature, realizing that despite its words to the contrary it had no real concept of death or decay.

"So you collect information?"

"As needed, yes—for our continued survival and proliferation," he toothily grinned. "It's much the same process by which your tiny brain catalogues your own environment, but on a much grander scale."

"So you...develop...and evolve?"

"Of course, Captain."

"But you're not alive?"

"Not as a biological being," he laughed up at her. "Metal and meat are very perishable and weak. We long since transcended such restrictions. And what we consume we fully share amongst our particular swarm. Not only are our clients immortalized, they are much amplified! And once digitized they can even merge with each other, *synergizing* into new forms never before seen in the Universe. Is that not glorious?"

Sally was coming to the spot she needed to be at.

"But you still need them...the physical forms I mean—for your spaceships, right?"

"Oh, you are smarter than you look," the elf congratulated her, clapping his small hands together. "Yes, we do need the energy, materials, and resources for construction purposes. But their highest usage is as *templates* for transforming cultures, species, and even worlds. Without such a marvelous Quest—to turn everything into pure, interactive information—we would lack Purpose. We would be nothing more than cosmic, mindless predators. Instead we are the *Repository of the Universe*—collecting and preserving everything, forever!"

"Dennis and I did speculate on your nature," Sally said, trying to keep the elf's attention distracted.

"Oh, but we are far more than the simple viruses of your world to which you compared us," he said, clapping his hands together happily. "And yet we do share many of their more excellent properties."

"So you were listening to us as we approached," she carefully summarized. "You are very advanced, indeed," she congratulated him.

Sally saw that this creature—however virtual and unsubstantial it might be—was enjoying interacting with her.

Everything likes to be appreciated.

She just needed to keep stroking its ego, for just a bit longer, until she reached the exact spot along the wall...

"This is all amazing," she said. "But how did you know we were coming to Kepler-186f? That was an incredible coincidence, unless you were *directed* to do so?" Sally asked, now putting a little distance between her and the elf.

"Yes, you are correct. That was not luck. We are ever vigilant," he grinned. "Having consumed the inhabitants of that entire planet, we eagerly awaited your arrival."

"My goodness, you must be extremely smart and patient."

The elf grinned with pride.

"Yes, we are," he agreed. "We are *very* smart, indeed—especially with where and how we choose to align our interests. A friend of ours told us you were coming there. And then it was so wonderful to see you," he continued excitedly. "You provided us a new Path. That is always a grand achievement for us. You weren't just a one-time collectable, but a *direction*."

"A 'path'—you mean through subspace to here?"

The elf hopped up-and-down excitedly.

"Not just through space, but also through *time*," the elf chortled. "We love to find new leads to fresh acquisitions!"

"What do you mean?"

"We enjoy the chase," he grinned at her with his toothy mouth. "And once we set our sights on a new species or objective, we never fail to obtain it. As such, *you* could not escape us. We've tracked many others through subspace who were trying to escape us. We've never been outmaneuvered. We are quite competent at following subspace trails."

"So you've never once lost a ship trying to get away from you?"

"Hah! Of course not," the little creature chortled. "In fact, we are right now about to capture and consume the spacecraft within which you arrived at this place. We're overtaking it right now. Shortly we will trap and deconstruct it. In fact, if the unexpected length of the jump hadn't momentarily depleted our energy stores—we'd have grabbed you much sooner."

Sally was almost in position as she inched along the wall...

"So where are the rest of you?" she asked, trying to keep him engaged and distracted. "There were *thousands* of ships like this converging on us back at Kepler-186f."

The elf grinned evilly.

"Only one of us was needed to capture you," he said. His voice was low and ominous. "The rest of us, who we'll rejoin shortly, went after a whole new prey—following your time-stream *backward*—that's rich in its maturity and diversity! Our particular flock was getting bored. As I said, we'd long since deconstructed and devoured everything of interest on the planet you call Kepler-186f as we awaited your arrival. But now we have a whole new feast to pursue."

"You mean...?" Sally said in a low, careful voice, trying to keep it from trembling.

"Your home planet, of course," he merrily replied. "Our flock is making a few stops along the way to consume additional targets. But do not fear, Sally—they will soon arrive at your 'Earth', the exact one from which you departed along the time-stream."

Her heart froze inside of her at hearing this devastating news.

"You're attacking Earth?" she numbly repeated.

"Your sub-light path back through time and space was apparent to us once you came into orbit around our latest conquered planet," the little creature chortled gleefully. "And my flock will have no problem tracing your trajectory back to its origin in space-time. But do not be concerned. Your species will finally be freed from its burden of flesh. We will *liberate* you and every other creature on your entire planet. Think of that! You and all other living species of your world will no longer be chained to the indignities of physical existence. And it's all because of you."

"Like *hell!*" Sally growled...

—as in one swift move, she *snapped* the tether from its spool at her waist out like a *whip*...

—"popping" the bubble containing her laser-drill while simultaneously *snagging* it and *yanking* it back to her where she *fired* the focused cutting-laser beam straight into the apparatus on the ceiling!

—which *exploded!*

—raining down a shower of quickly evaporating particles.

"*Nnnnnnooooooooooooo!*" the elf yelled in agony as it faded then "winked" out...

—the thousands of bubbles above also loudly "popping"...

—and Dennis fell with a "thud" from his vanished bubble upon the squishy flooring of the suddenly empty room.

"Unnnggghhhh," He moaned, starting to stir. "What happened to me?"

Sally snapped her helmet back into place, quickly doing the same for him...

—as a *spray of acidic gel* began to rain down from above!

She saw that the shattered super-projector above was starting to recreate its components and reassemble itself! Yep, the Elf certainly wasn't stupid enough to lack back-ups of its vast "files."

"Come *on*, Commander!" she yelled at him through her helmet RF-communicator as she grabbed him by his long neck and tried to lift him up. Even in reduced gravity he was still heavy. "We've got to find the ship's drive! We don't have much time. I doubt this Spike-Ship is going to play any more games with us. We're definitely on its 'kill' list!"

He staggered up to his feet, leaning heavily back on his thick tail for balance.

"W-what happened, Sally?"

"No time, buddy," she said, shoving him over against one wall.

She stepped protectively in front of him as she aimed the laser-cutter at the opposite wall and again pulled the trigger...

—the *powerful red beam* slicing through the opposite wall as if it were butter, spraying fragments in all directions.

Revealed on the other side was a man-sized, metallic globe—covered with short black spikes: all of which attached to a writhing mass of thick black cables!

It was the heart of the "living" ship, its presence *screaming* with pain at their attack!

"Is that...?" Dennis said, twitching his muzzle in excitement.

"It has to be the ship's Dark Energy generator," Sally said, running over to the melted, still-sputtering gap in the wall. Dennis staggered along right behind her. "I felt the vibrations from it as I circumnavigated the room with my side up against the wall. I suspected it had to be close in order to power those incredibly complex bubble-projections."

"So how do we get it out of here?"

"I'll clear a path while you get it loose."

"Right!" he said, unhooking his heavy wrench and lifting it up in his powerful arms.

As he smashed and crushed the cables off of the protruding spikes, Sally took careful aim at the far wall. She sliced a path through it, continuing step-by-step forward through the intervening guts of the ship, burning-away the intervening components.

And as she moved outward, the artificial gravity steadily diminished...

"Ah, we're going in the right direction."

While behind her—rolling the now-freed, large spiked sphere—was Dennis...

—when the inner hull of the ship *suddenly split open* under the withering beam of her laser-gun to reveal...*empty space*...where, floating before them, was their Starship!

"*Jump*, Sally!" Dennis called out from behind her. "I'll be right after you with the generator. Our crew will maneuver the ship to pick us up!"

"Wait!" she said, standing at the steaming gap in the hull and looking outward. "We've got to disable the Spike-Ship before we leave."

"But we have their DE-generator," Dennis protested. "They won't be able to follow us into subspace."

Again, Sally found his lack of war-tactics understanding palpable.

"Oh?" she snorted. "What about their materialization skills? How long do you think it'll take for them to just make a new one, atom-by-atom? And as that's happening, how long do you think it'll take for *us* to figure out how the alien generator works, how to connect it into our power grid, and then to get it all working together?"

"I...well..."

"It might take a *long* time on our side, Dennis," she grimaced. "And in the meantime, with both our ships still stuck on ion drives—

once it's fully recovered from our initial attack, this Spike-Ship will just fire those big spears into us like before. On emergency power, we'd soon be defenseless, destroyed! And if we do succeed in jumping into subspace, what's to stop them from following us again, just as it did before?"

"But..." he said, clearly confused by her annoying battle strategies!

"We've *got* to disable it," she said with finality. "You take the sphere back to our Starship and get out of here. Over time with your existing instruction manuals you and the rest of the crew can proba-bly figure a way to get it working and integrated into the ship. I'll stay behind with the laser-gun and keep slicing this damn place to rib-bons—as long as I can!"

"No, Sally," Dennis protested, coming up beside her and baring his big teeth at her through his oblong helmet. "*I'll* take that gun! *You* take the sphere. You're the best engineer left amongst us. You're needed to get it working on our ship. I'll keep the Spike-Ship occu-pied as long as *I* can!"

"Damn it, Dennis!" she said, pulling away from him back into the wrecked interior, clutching the laser-gun tightly, not allowing him to grab it. "You lack the instincts to put up a good fight. They'll stop you in your tracks before you can do any lasting damage. *I'm* the Captain, remember? You have to take my orders. Now grab that sphere and *jump!* That's an *order!*"

"And *you're* the stupid little mammal who is millions of years be-hind us evolutionary-wise," he angrily retorted. "Captain or not, I'm your superior in all of the most important ways! Now that you've shown me how to use a laser-drill for additional purposes, I'm fully capable of..."

"*People! People!*" a loud transmission crackled over both of their helmets. "*This is Alice! We hear you! We were about to be destroyed by the alien ship. It caught up with us! But it stopped—and now we hear why from your transmissions. You both saved us! But before you attempt to do anything else, please listen to George.*"

A loud, grating burst of "clicks" and sharp "whistles" caused Sally to cringe in her helmet.

"Yes, I see!" Dennis excitedly replied.

He reached to his waist and began unhooking a rectangular tool.

"What's that?" Sally asked, feeling a strong *WHIRRING* vibration building up around her as the Spike-Ship continued powering up its systems that'd been crippled by her destructive march through its guts.

Outside in the blackness of space Sally saw long spikes *shifting their aim*...turning in the direction of the Dinosapien's Starship!

"This is an excavator unit," Dennis hurriedly replied, holding it up in front of his head so he could see by his helmet's light to punch instructions onto its small control panel.

"So?" Sally frantically asked, feeling the *whirring vibrations* around her getting stronger and stronger.

Dennis slapped the unit onto a flat metallic surface where it magnetically adhered. Simultaneously he wrapped up Sally in his strong tail, grabbed the sphere in his arms, and with his powerful legs *flung* the both of them out into the void!

"What...are you crazy?" Sally raged at him, struggling to get free. "As soon as they've reconstituted the damage I inflicted they'll be right on our tails!"

Dennis, intent upon their trajectory through the blackness of intergalactic space, was silent.

"Jesus, you lizards should learn to obey orders," Sally sighed, now relaxing. "But thanks for not leaving me behind, I guess."

They were spinning in space. Sally saw the faint stars, forward Starship and behind Spike-Ship rotating around her.

"I think I'm going to puke," Sally admitted in a low voice.

"Not in your helmet, Captain."

Ah, turn-about is fair play. She detected a certain smug satisfaction in Dennis' voice. She closed her eyes tightly, trying to imagine being back on Earth in Dave's beautiful little valley.

Opening her eyes she saw that behind them the Spike-Ship was shrinking.

The Dinosapien Starship in front of them grew larger, an opened airlock awaiting them—positioned by small jets on the hull to precisely intersect their path...

—as clawed gloves reached out to firmly grasp Sally, Dennis, and the sphere, pulling them inside...

—the airlock hatch "clanging" solidly shut behind them and the Starship activated its ion drive. The spaceship *surged* away from their pursuer, throwing them painfully against one of the walls!

"Gotta get those inertial dampeners fixed," Sally groaned, feeling fresh bruises along the right side of her body.

Air flooded into the small chamber, water vapor forming a mist around them.

Other happy Dinosapiens, clad in spacesuits, clustered around Sally.

Dennis grinned at her from inside his oblong helmet.

"To answer your question...an 'excavator unit' is for us geologists to use in terra-forming large volumes of ground, such as in removing mountains," Dennis calmly replied.

"*What?*" Sally yelled at him, twisting off her helmet to glare directly at him! "Removing *mountains?*"

"Well, it *is* thermonuclear based," he said as he twisted off his own large helmet.

"You had an *atomic bomb* with you all this time?" she yelled again in outrage. "I asked you people if you had any weapons on this ship!" she said, now physically beating him over his scaly head with her small fists!

He cringed back, clearly shocked by her outburst and physical attack.

"But it's *not* a weapon," he protested. "It's an *excavator unit* which..."

A *BRILLIANT BURST OF BLINDING LIGHT* suddenly lit the airlock through its transparent porthole.

Sally was momentarily blinded, rubbing her eyes, trying to get her sight back.

"The enemy ship is destroyed!" the very satisfied voice of Alice rang out through the ship's intercom.

As her eyesight returned, Sally saw Dennis embarrassedly shrugging his reptilian shoulders.

"I'm learning," he confessed.

Sally grabbed his big head in a strong hug, kissing him square on his muzzle.

"So am I," she grinned at him, hugging him again. "So am I!"

Chapter 12

THE SOCRATIC METHOD

Damned old human Curiosity
Can't leave well enough alone
Insisting on tweaking and fiddling
Prompting, poking, and prodding
What if this, that, or the other thing
Might it be better, nicer, or brighter?
But often worse, uglier, and darker
While Master Teachers don't lecture
But prompt students to question
Growing by careful experimentation
The Human Race inching forward
Two steps onward and one step back
And yet another off to the side
Keeping on track is difficult
When the track itself changes
Having a mind of its own...
Beware the Mystery!
Homo sapiens Eulogy, 12:1-4

Dave was getting used to being a young boy in the ancient Greek capital city of Athens.

It wasn't easy.

First, he had to maintain the pretense of being deaf and dumb, just a stupid apprentice to the old fisherman Periscus. His Anaconda Tattoo was provocative, so he covered it up with a wrap—as if his arm was hurt. But much of the time he didn't have to worry about interacting with other people. He lived with Periscus secluded in a one-roomed hut at the base of a low mountain. It was the same mountain where Dave had hidden Breep's egg. The hut was primitive, but had the advantage of being well-away from the rest of the populace, far removed from any other dwellings. Periscus was an outcast, shunned by others of his society. So he preferred disdainful isolation, interacting with others only when he must. But Periscus valued the companionship of his rescued "star-child." And Dave had a place to not have his strange mannerisms attract attention.

Dave kept an eye out for Breep, but the *Pelecanimimus* never showed up. If the egg had hatched, the baby dinosaur likely had no memories of his long pre-egg life. So Dave figured the animal probably just migrated deeper into the interior of Greece, where he'd be even more distant from scary humans and their crowded habitats.

Periscus didn't allow Dave to climb the mountain again to check on the small cave. It was perilous for the one-armed man to accompany or track him should Dave get into any trouble. But Dave had done the best he could for his pet dinosaur. He wished Breep a long, happy life in the ancient Greece wilderness.

Dave picked up the language surprisingly fast. When that's all you hear, it's much easier to learn than sitting in some boring classroom. Plus, Periscus was interminably jabbering on about everything. And when they were alone in their hut or out on the sea fishing, Periscus expected Dave to respond in kind. As such, Dave had a crash-course in ancient Greek.

Learning to read was more difficult. Dave managed to steal a few sheets of loose papyrus while selling fish in Athens. It was from a house that suffered a huge fire. Some of the scroll sheets were burned, but the lettering was still intact. It looked like chicken-scratching to Dave, but was legible.

Fortunately, Periscus had some schooling as a child and could decipher the "scratches." Dave would never be able to write the strange characters, but slowly he learned to read them.

His strange obsession with "advanced" education was explainable by being a god cast down to Earth who was acquiring "primitive" information.

Yes, Dave allowed Periscus to keep the false impression that Dave was the astronomical god "Astraios"—the Titan god of the stars and planets. Living at sea, Periscus was fascinated by the stars. Dave imparted much of his future (godly!) knowledge of the heavens to the old man. Dave was happy to indulge Periscus' interests while cementing his position as a minor god of the heavens. Interestingly, Dave's Anaconda Tattoo fit right into that narrative—since the star-constellation of the snake "Serpens" was said to be resurrected from death by a magical herb. Dave was amazed how well this fit his actual circumstance, having "died" in his trip across an ocean of time only to be "resurrected" by Sally's future "herbal" retroviral-treatment!

But to the world around him—other than when he was with the old man discussing the wonders of the stars—Dave had to remain in the background. He dared not attract attention, at least until he learned "the ropes" and could fluently speak and read the local language and dialect.

It wasn't long, however, until Dave felt comfortable speaking ancient Greek. After all, even though he'd been transformed into a young boy, he still had all his memories intact plus his considerable intellect.

Dropping the pretense of being deaf and dumb, Dave fully expected to be accepted by his peers. But he was wrong. It turned out that fishermen were on one of the lowest rungs of Greek society. Sure, he could accompany Periscus to the Agora, the crowded marketplace of Athens. But as a young boy, clad in rags, dirty, and smelling of fish—he was ignored or shunned. The only people lower than him were slaves, of which there were many.

It turned out that the so-called "heart of civilization" of Ancient Greece, the "magnificent" city of Athens was largely *heartless*. Women were mostly property of males to be kept in their place, or bought and sold at will. Slavery was an unremarkable, common societal institution pervasive not just in Athens but throughout the entire Greek empire. True, a form of democracy had sprung up in the city of Athens—but it was hardly "one person one vote." Yes, the aristocracy was no longer the unquestioned ruler of the realm, but political participation was not a right but a privilege. If you were a "nobody" kid in an ill-regarded profession, you had no status at all.

Dave saw Socrates on occasion...from a distance. In contrast to his lofty expectations, Dave was greatly *un*impressed with the real

man behind the "icon" of modern scientific and philosophical en-
deavors.

The man Socrates, it turned out, was an aging, slovenly character
who'd managed to ride the "democracy" wave to local fame. He made
colorful speeches at the Pnyx, a hillside auditorium located west of
the Acropolis. He always dressed in the same dirty tunic. He insisted
on walking barefoot. Plus he was fat and ugly. He had a stubby nose,
large head, wide forehead, and protruding eyes. He looked like a pre-
human ape. To all appearances he was an odd, garish, brooding town
clown.

But the brutish-appearing Socrates was also a natural performer,
orator, debater, and critic. His speeches were always entertaining,
particularly when he was skewering the establishment. As the
"Ekklesia" political body, which met at the Pnyx, was drawn mainly
from the adult male working-class, many of them delighted in hearing
Socrates castigate the aristocracy. Laughter and applause accompanied the fervent diatribes of the colorful character Socrates. So whenever Socrates was to give a speech, Dave slunk unnoticed into the
crowd of thousands and listened, fascinated.

Though Socrates was a scoundrel, Dave recognized the man's
deep intellect. Dave still wanted to find a way to talk to him.

But even though Socrates attracted a "cloud" of well-to-do young
people around him, he was still not accessible to the young Dave.
Socrates was well-protected and isolated. When Dave tentatively
tried to approach the group, he was casually kicked to the side. Once,
though, Dave did succeed in meeting Socrates in private. After a
drunken night of debauchery, Dave found the "great man" staggering
out of a house of ill-repute into a back alley to urinate. Dave was
there by chance, carrying a heavy load of fish to stalls in the Agora for
the morning crowd of shoppers.

"Master Socrates!" Dave called out to the hung-over, drunken
man, abandoning his fish to run over to the man wobbling forward
against a stone wall. Yellow urine splattered onto Socrates' bare feet
as he leaned against the stone wall. "May I speak with you a moment?" Dave respectfully asked.

The blockish, dirty man turned his head blearily away from his
continuing stream of urine.

"Eh? What do you want, boy?"

The man's face was decidedly ugly. His stubby, wide nose was dripping unwiped snot. His protruding eyes were bloodshot. His bald forehead dripped sweat though it was still the early, cool morning. His scraggly, grey hair was greasy. His short beard was dirty and unkempt. His tunic stank. He looked like an old drunken bum, hardly the father of modern-day philosophy and the scientific method.

"I...I w-was wondering...about how to best p-please God and...?"

"*Piss off*, boy!" the old man spat at him, staggering back toward the rear entrance to the whorehouse. His ragged tunic hung down, soiled and torn.

"But Master...?"

Socrates suddenly stopped in his tracks, turned about abruptly, and stood facing Dave—his dirty hands placed disdainfully on his wide hips.

"Are you *rich?*" the man grated at Dave.

"Well...n-no, sir...but I'm a seeker of Truth, l-like you...and..."

"I don't need any more damn hanger-ons with no money!" Socrates screamed at the cowering boy. "Go get rich—and then maybe I'll consider making you one of my crew. Or, better yet, go get me more wine. I'm thirsty! *Bah!*" he spat again.

With a dismissive wave of a fat hand he turned and wobbled back into the establishment. Dave was left in the alleyway standing beside his net filled with fish, speechless.

This was the "great" Socrates—*really?*

It seemed that all he'd heard from Periscus concerning Socrates was true. The old, one-armed fisherman hated Socrates. In a battle twenty years before—at a place called Delium—Periscus was a low-level squad commander. Socrates was one of his men. Periscus claimed he received orders to retreat to a more secure location. Socrates disobeyed Periscus' subsequent order to his men, choosing instead to single-handedly charge the enemy lines.

This resulted in stories of the great "bravery" of Socrates against the "cowardly" retreat of Periscus. But because of the ensuing chaos as some fighters followed Socrates while others milled about in confusion—Periscus dropped his shield and an enemy's arrow skewered his right arm below the shoulder. A subsequent infection required amputation. Periscus never forgave Socrates. And as Socrates rose in reputation, Periscus' life plummeted. He lost his family, whatever little money he possessed, his rank in the army—and sank to the lowest levels of Athenian society. His only recourse was to eke out a harsh existence fighting against the sea every day to catch and sell a few measly fish.

Dave had considered Periscus' hatred just the complaints of a sour old man who'd gotten the short end of the stick. But Dave now saw with his own eyes that Socrates was not the burnished icon he would become in the distant future. Any hope of getting "Answers to the Great Questions" from the "Master Teacher" faded.

Dave's only source of enjoyment was an old musical instrument that Periscus kept from the days he was a respected soldier with a loving family. It was his family's one remaining old heirloom, a lyre. It had seven strings, similar to a guitar. Also it was strummed like a guitar rather than plucked like a harp. The chords were somewhat difficult to learn since it involved silencing some of the strings with a hand on one side of the instrument while the other hand strummed on the other side. But Dave quickly learned how to make passable chords, sitting outside the hut singing popular Greek songs. Periscus was much amused, grunting along with Dave's sweet boyish melody. But most of each day was filled by getting up at dawn to fish, going to the city with their catch, and returning late in the evenings. It was a hard life broken only by brief interludes of song.

And so the years passed.

As Dave grew from a boy to a young man he grew acutely aware of the stench and filth of Athens, gradually coming to hate it.

Yes, looming grandly above everything were the incredibly-beautiful marble columns of the Parthenon and other Temples, which sat in splendor atop the central high Acropolis. But beneath that glistening magnificence was a crowd of humanity jammed together in a cloistered city. True, the artisans of Athens also produced beautifully-painted vases, but the water carried in them was often contaminated and foul. And, yes, the aristocrats lived lives clad in fine tunics eating fresh vegetables and delicacies shipped by sea from the provinces.

But the rest of the populace was lucky to have a single homespun garment to their name, eating stale bread and dried fish.

Also, some twenty-five years before Dave's arrival a terrible plague had swept through Athens. Hordes of rats came into the city's port when the sea route became the city's sole source of supplies during a self-imposed blockade. The rats carried the plague. Several waves of the horrible disease decimated the city, killing half the population. One out of every two people died in agony. This all happened during one of the frequent wars.

The general and leader of Athens at that time, Pericles, had the idea to make war with Sparta. Pericles thought that Athens could hide behind their strong city walls while the powerful Athenian navy carried the brunt of the battle to Sparta. Like many of Athens' ill-fated "warrior-fantasy" adventures, it was a disaster. Pericles himself ended up dying from the very plague that he'd unwittingly unleashed upon the city!

The old fisherman Periscus complained bitterly and at length to Dave on the privations and horror of war—both on the general population and the affected soldiers. He told Dave how young men ran eagerly to it out of a societal obsession with being a "hero warrior." This was rooted in their mythology. Dave found this fascinating since he'd seen exactly the same thing in the modern world, where young boys were endlessly fascinated with violent video games, bloody war movies, and hyper-masculinity. But from the incessant battles, Periscus angrily chronicled, staggered back the "lucky" survivors—maimed, broken, and sick. And even though the awful results of "heroic" battle were evident, there were always more politicians eager for the spoils of victory, a population seeking bloody revenge to whatever past defeats, and an ever-fresh supply of eager young naïve, testosterone-saturated boys.

And it seemed that the stupid lust for war never changed! That same sad pattern would repeat over and over, on down through the millennia. Dave was amazed at how well Periscus described the terrible effects of war, still seen up and into the distant "advanced" future.

And the great naval expedition to Syracuse in 414 B.C., the year of Dave's arrival in the Obelisk, was a similar horrific disaster. Two hundred ships plus tens of thousands of soldiers "heroically" sailed off to be slaughtered. News of this terrible defeat came back to Athens in 413 B.C., throwing a pale over the entire city. Although Athens struggled on with the war, it was clear to everyone the campaign was doomed. Their enemies got stronger while the Athenian Empire inexorably declined.

Dave, meanwhile, totally gave up on learning anything useful from Socrates. He was now content just to live the life of a simple fisherman.

For good or worse, this was now his home.

Sinking into a grim depression, Dave's songs outside the hut became increasingly gloomy and sad.

He often dreamed of climbing back into the red Obelisk and escaping the filthy, war-torn city of ancient Athens. But though he and Periscus often fished above the exact spot where the Obelisk sank into the waves, it was far beyond Dave's reach. He took soundings with a ball of string attached to a rock. It was over two hundred feet to the bottom. Any attempt to dive that deep without modern scuba gear and decompression chambers was suicide. He'd drown if he tried.

And so the years passed, Dave's depression turning into dull acceptance...

Athens was often under siege. Dave got used to invading armies setting up their camps in the fields around the city, held off by the high walls and still-active Navy at Athens' protected port. The invading armies decimated the fields, burned all habitations, and plundered the surrounding villages. But Periscus was adroit at trading with invaders as well as with Athenians.

Fish were fish. Everyone needed fish. And as long as he was similarly circumspect, Dave found that he could make a decent living helping the old man trade or sell fish to friend or foe. He'd learned the lesson well of his first nearly fatal night on the seashore, now only approaching acceptable soldiers and reasonable situations with his fresh-caught fish.

Plus, Dave realized he could make modest modifications in the primitive tools, fabrics, and processes of the Athenians—using his future knowledge, engineering expertise, and doctorate in physics. He managed to sell these improvements quietly to select merchant men, warriors, and artisans.

In fact, he built and sold the rights to the very first "wheelbar-row"—one wheel in the center front with two studs and two handles on the other end—to a local manufacturer. He'd gotten really tired of hauling heavy nets or trying to use bulky 4-wheeled carts—and fig-ured a good wheelbarrow would make things much easier. So he built a prototype. Dave knew that most future historians attributed the invention to the Chinese of around 100 A.D., some five hundred years in the future. But a few historians suggested that the wheelbarrow was present as early as 408 B.C. in ancient Greece—and Dave was delighted to find that *he* was the one who introduced it!

So he learned to survive "under the radar" in ancient Greece—adapting where he must, improvising in tight spots, and finding nich-es to apply his future knowledge.

But the *Golden Age of Athens* was fast drawing to a terrible end.

Dave heard news of rebellions springing up all across the Atheni-an Empire as subjects chaffed against the now-weakened Athenian state. Sparta, Athens' main Greek rival, continued to press their ad-vantage. A coup overthrew the democratic system in Athens. But a subsequent rebellion then restored democracy to the city. Naval bat-tles continued. And finally the remaining Athenian navy was soundly defeated by the Spartan navy.

In 404 B.C. Dave, now having lived for ten years in ancient Greece—seventeen years old physiologically—witnessed Athens final surrender to Sparta. The great city walls that had protected Athens for so long were torn down. The remaining warships of the Athenian fleet were burned. Oligarchical Tyrants took rule in Athens. This put the nail in the coffin of the Golden Age of Athens.

The whole social order of the city was upended. And this terrible catastrophe was particularly bad for Socrates!

Socrates, once the darling of the unwashed masses, became a scapegoat for the ignominious defeat of Athens. He had never been a fan of the very democracy that allowed him to flourish. Instead he chose to extol the supposed virtues of authoritative philosophers to be Rulers—like him! Dave knew that Socrates' student Plato would ex-pand upon that concept following the death of his master, advocating that political leaders be "Philosopher Kings." Supposedly, these learned men with "enlightened" reasoning would be wiser than mere ordinary people. But despite Socrates' arguments against rule by the "common man" Socrates refused to take any personal responsibility to participate in politics. He was the embodiment of the hands-off "critic."

Even worse, the ever-contemptuous Socrates often made fun of the local gods, choosing instead to invoke a vague "Higher Power"— whom he had the audacity to claim had commissioned him as its very own Heavenly Emissary!

So Socrates loved to "stick his thumb" into the eyes of both the politicians and religious leaders. He was the eternal critic who could always tear everyone else down, but refused to raise a finger to do anything constructive himself.

But the often-amusing "gadfly" of Greece—an ancient "standup comedian" critical of anything and everyone—finally had the tables turned on him.

As the fortunes of Athens grew worse and worse, the populace turned their frustrations directly upon *him*. Socrates was formally accused of treason. He was charged with two very serious offenses: first, *heresy* against the government-sanctioned gods, whom he'd often belittled—and second, *corrupting* the minds of the youth into following his supposed heresies. The *Trial of Socrates* promised to be a great spectacle, with fiery public debates!

It was just what the people wanted: a public spectacle distracting them from their own failings and self-generated disasters.

Dave well knew from his studies in history, back during his undergraduate college years, what would result from the Trial of Socrates. Socrates would be condemned to die by his own hand, forced to drink a cup of deadly hemlock poison.

But instead of this ignoble defeat erasing Socrates from history— as had happened to many other otherwise-forgotten martyrs—it instead catapulted him to greatness! Lionized in subsequent plays, dialogues, and writings, Socrates—the *Great Man Dying for His Values*—became an Icon of Western Philosophy and Civilization.

"*No*, by God!" Dave growled after hearing that Socrates would stand trial for treason, "He'll *not* escape so easily!"

"What's that?" Periscus replied, cupping his ear with his one shaking hand. He was now hard of hearing. The old man could barely get around anymore by himself. Dave did most of the physical work now. But Dave didn't mind. He was grateful to his old friend, helping him into the boat every morning—even though the white-haired, shriveled-up old man just sat there uselessly.

It seemed that Periscus had no reason to live...and had just given up.

They were in the boat now, rocking on the gentle waves of the beautiful Mediterranean. Dave had just thrown out the net and was dragging it in. The sun was warm. It was a poverty-stricken though pleasant life, spent fishing on the deep-blue sea.

The year was now 399 B.C. and Dave had now lived for fifteen years in ancient Greece and was outwardly twenty-two years old. His thick brown hair was back to its adult length, falling to his shoulders. He sported a full beard. His was bronze-skinned, tanned by his many days spent out on the sea. He was well-muscled and slim. He had the hard body of a manual laborer who ate, by default, healthily of vegetables, bread, and fish—with little sugar or fat.

He felt full of youthful energy, ready to *do* something! Yep, if he'd been stupider or less knowledgeable he might well have gone and joined the army to go fight in some idiotic war. Instead, he felt inspired to take up his earlier, abandoned goal.

"*Socrates!*" Dave yelled at Periscus as the boat bobbed along on the waves and the old man dejectedly held onto the side of the boat with his one trembling hand.

"What about that stinking piece of crap?" Periscus answered, scowling.

"He's *not* going to be executed to become famous in history," Dave growled with determination, slowly hauling in the net as he spoke. "And he's *finally* going to give me *answers* whether he wants to or not!"

"Eh?" Periscus frowned, again cupping his ear with his scrawny hand. "What did you say?"

"We're going to *kidnap* that son-of-a-bitch Socrates and *torture* him!" Dave yelled at Periscus.

The old man's normally-dull expression suddenly changed into one of glee! Periscus' one remaining tooth, hanging from the top of his gaping mouth, stuck forward expectantly.

The unexpected prospect of wrecking revenge upon the infamous philosopher seemed to charge Periscus' withered body with a fresh, new energy.

"*Yes!*" the man chortled, sticking his knobby fist up into the air. "Let's go get that fat old bastard!"

Dave kept pulling on the net, bringing it up into the boat. There were only three fish in it. They flopped about helplessly. In a spasm of mercy, he dumped them back into the ocean.

He had a plan.

He'd actually been thinking about it for a long time. Although he never figured he'd really do it, it was a compelling and recurring fantasy. But he'd horded his resources, just in case. And now everything was falling into place.

His hot-headed, youthful body was eager to spring into action, regardless of how foolish or ill-conceived.

Let there be rivers of "heroic" blood!

It was finally time to "do something."

Tommy knew that it was now or never.

They were going to have to answer his questions or face the consequences!

"What is that?" he said, pointing over to the side at a gleaming metallic-looking sphere. It looked like a finished satellite waiting to be launched up into orbit.

"That's just a surveillance drone, little dude," Snake's voice promptly replied over Tommy's headphones. "If we need to, we can drop it into the time-stream. I helped to build it. It ain't metal, but it's near as tough and durable. It can get beat up, unlike you, and still return. We don't want you to get hurt, little buddy! If it looks dangerous, we can send it first then put you through if we're sure it's safe. Understand?"

Tommy just grunted in reply.

He got the feeling that Snake wasn't being fully honest with him— telling him part but not all of the truth.

Once again Tommy was in the harness hanging facedown above the stack of superconducting magnets.

This time, however, a protective suit of clear plastic tubes completely wrapped his head and entire body. Only his face was not wrapped. Flowing through the tubing was a continuous stream of cold water. A clear plastic shield covered Tommy's exposed face. The Dinosapiens assured him he that this time he'd not get burned.

Well, he'd better not!

He didn't like getting burned alive. It hurt too much!

The loud "whine" of the coils powering up around him was deafening.

His vision was getting "sparkly." That meant the immense magnetic fields were affecting his neuronal architecture.

The *subspace sphere* should start forming soon.

"So when are we going to be ready for me to make the time-jump back to Dave?" he asked into the nonmetallic microphone poised right next to his mouth.

Everything on or near him was nonmetallic. Anything metal would be fried or torn away by the immense magnetic fields. Lucky he was a synthetic android and not a metallic robot! Too bad, though, they couldn't just use a monitor screen to access the patterns in the subspace field. But it required his direct visualization for some silly reason. It had something to do with his enhanced perceptions beyond that of a pure biological creature—plus his actual experiences "surfing" the time-stream. So he had to hang right above it, looking straight down into it, in order to guide their exact path back through time along the almost-imperceptible string of perturbations left by Dave's recent passage.

"You can jump just as soon as we get the coordinates straight, Tommy," Snake replied. "We've gone over this plan before, dude. You're doing great! You got us back 200 million years last time. If you can get us back this session to the God Barrier, then we're almost there! So how 'bout that, good buddy?"

Tommy detected a strain in Snake's voice. He now knew Snake very well. He could tell when he was lying. Snake was lying right now. They didn't want to go just to the Barrier. They wanted him to go all the way—which meant that since they wouldn't tell him, they *weren't* going to let him enter the time-stream.

They either didn't trust him, or wanted that metallic-looking sphere to do something he wouldn't!

Tommy realized he might be paranoid. Snake had been nothing but friendly to Tommy all the time he'd been there in the distant future valley. But Snake was still a member of the Martian race that'd invested so much effort in maneuvering Sally into breaking the God Barrier in the first place.

Tommy was certain that Snake's race of intelligent reptiles would do anything necessary to protect their pretty, safe, new world...

—even if it meant *killing* both him and Dave!

Sure, they claimed such violence was impossible for their "mature" species. But Tommy knew better. They might not do it directly, with their own hands. But they could sure do it by proxy.

Tommy had a suspicion that they meant for his gun to do something unexpected if he "gave" it to Dave in the past, probably blow up in his face and kill him!

But after getting to know him, the Snakes surely realized he wasn't just a naïve little robot-boy. He was sure they didn't trust their first plan to work anymore. He'd figured out what they did to his brain: putting in an "over-ride" control such that when triggered he'd obey their every command. Well, he easily dissolved that with some clever specifically modified brain enzymes, in a way that looked natural so they wouldn't suspect he knew. Doubtless they recognized that it was no longer functioning. So now they had a new plan: an automatic, truly-robotic (though still nonmetallic) "probe." They would use Tommy to find Dave then send the probe to finish the job. Hah! He'd show them...

They wanted to "play dirty" trying to tamper with his brain? Well Tommy had his own "ace up the sleeve"!

Hidden in his baggy red jumpsuit was his Mom's *black super-gun!* Supposedly he'd left it at the outer security station in the lock-box for his personal stuff. But using his super-speed hand movement—which he'd deliberately *not* told them he could do—he retrieved the gun after he put it into the box beneath obscuring items.

Yes, it was nonmetallic—so it didn't trigger any alarms as they buckled him into his harness.

And it was positioned right where he could grab it using his super-fast hand speed.

Right now, though, the SUBSPACE SPHERE was forming below...starting out as a tiny flickering dot, then growing steadily larger—then quickly becoming a *five-feet-wide, black globe* that spun hypnotically, positioned in the exact center of the stack of superconducting magnets below Tommy!

He felt hot licks of super-heated air flowing around him, but was kept comfortable in his cold-water suit.

Those hypnotic, *crystalline diamond-patterns* were reforming, plus the faint traces that only he could see.

"Left 2.34 degrees...up one degree...back a half degree...to the right 0.078 degrees," he precisely muttered as he followed Dave's tracks back through time, deeper and deeper and deeper.

And then there it was, the *God-Barrier*: a *billion years* in the past!

On the other side, any human attempts to move forward into the future were stopped. But coming from this side, it seemed ok to move further into the past, if one's "puncture hole" was powerful enough!

And that was just why they'd built this entire, giant superconducting, plasma-powered Apparatus.

Vast amounts of energy were surging through the tangle of thick cables leading out down the mountainside to multiple hovercrafts in the valley below.

Dark Energy was flowing unabated. They were poised to powerfully "punch through"!

"I'm at the Barrier," Tommy spoke into his microphone. "Do you want me to stop?"

"Uhm, Tommy," Snake's voice spoke to him in his earphones, barely audible now that the WHINE of the Apparatus was at a peak volume. "Mission Control says if you're up to it, keep on going. Once we penetrate the Barrier it should take you only a few more minutes to reach back to the exact point where Dave exited the time-stream. Then we'll have the entire path mapped out, so we can..."

"Sure, that's ok," Tommy answered, cutting off Snake's voice. He abruptly *punched-through* the God-Barrier to zip beyond.

He kept muttering tiny changes for the controllers of the Portal...going yet deeper and deeper—*a thousand years...two thousand...two thousand four hundred years*! Then...

"I'm there!" Tommy said again, seeing at the bottom of the immensely long tunnel a *bright blue sea*. "It's very pretty. I see fish jumping. Wow!"

"We're pulling you out now, Tommy," Snake's voice came from a far distance.

He felt his harness starting to pull him off to the side...

—as he simultaneously looked over to see the metallic-looking Probe slowly approaching, being maneuvered to take his place...

"Thank you for being my friend, Snake. Oh, you too, Casandra," he sincerely stated as he jerked his hand under the restraints to grab onto the Gun, firmly *firing* a wide burst through the harness and overlying cold-water-suit...

—and, freed from the shredded constraints, *falling face-first* toward the subspace sphere!

It seemed to take an eternity to reach it, but it was only a split second.

"Yippee!" he shouted as he dived into the black maelstrom.

This was going to be the ride of his life...or the exhilarating means of his own death!

Either way, it would be interesting.

Chapter 13

ENHANCED INTERROGATION METHODS

So when does being tough turn to Torture
And why do you care about the difference
Surely the Ends justify the Means, right?
But then again, squeamish mortals shudder
Their "empathy" mechanism rejecting Horror
Feeling in their own bodies parallel results
Skin being flayed, limbs removed, flesh burnt
Senses, one-by-one, damaged and destroyed
No civilized person wishing that on others
Unless, of course, it were "necessary"
From keen awareness of cosmic Justice
Delivering sweet, appropriate Revenge
Not, you insist, a sin of a depraved madman
But merely consequence of the other's actions
Where their "evil" requires your similar Evil
And you become the thing you claim to abhor
Truly "Justified" only if all humans are human
And you take the same punishment on yourself
Ready to sacrifice everything not just for God
But in support of your own sanity!
Homo sapiens Eulogy, 13:19-24

Dave now knew Athens like the back of his hand.

He knew how to transport anything to anywhere in the city, furtively. He could get whatever he wanted in and out of the town without attracting attention, official or otherwise.

Plus, Dave knew exactly where to wait for Socrates—where the "great man" would be unprotected by his usual gaggle of avid followers. It was exactly where Socrates had so cavalierly brushed off the young Dave fifteen years earlier.

Dave and Periscus quietly awaited Socrates, hidden with their wheelbarrow behind a heap of trash. It was all too familiar to Dave, like a well-worn but still ill-fitting glove. Other than having Periscus with him, the alley looked to Dave depressingly similar to fifteen years ago. It was a nondescript tight space between two stone walls that smelled of urine and garbage.

Dave had carefully tracked Socrates' movements that day. He knew from Socrates' past patterns that he would slip away from his entourage that evening to engage in his addictive debauchery. Socrates was a married man with several grown sons, but he loved to engage in all forms of illicit, casual sex. It didn't seem to matter that he was now seventy years old. Also it didn't deter him that it was just one week until his great public trial.

At the trial he would spout his outrage against the charge of corruption and heresy. He loved to play the part of the wounded martyr of "truth", standing alone against the "hypocrisy" of everyone else! Yet he was the biggest hypocrite of them all. He reveled in his excesses. And this night might well be his last chance to wallow in his perversions.

As the moon rose above in the dark night sky, Dave's patience was rewarded.

Humming a popular tune, Socrates drunkenly staggered out the back door of the whorehouse, a goblet of wine in his chubby hand. His face was more deeply lined than it was fifteen years before when he'd insulted the eager seven-year-old Dave. His hair was whiter. His eyes bulged even further out of his round face. But it was the same old, sour, fat man...

—placing a pudgy hand up against the stone wall he began peeing, as simultaneously he swigged wine with the other hand out of a mug to cheerfully replenish his drained bladder.

Dave began humming in harmony with the drunken man, plucking the appropriate tunes on his lyre.

Startled, Socrates looked back over his shoulder.

"Hey! Remember me?" Dave spoke from within dark shadows cast by the bright moonlight. "Don't stop singing. We've a band going here!"

"What?" the old man started. He dropped his mug to "shatter" on the pavement while jerking around randomly spraying urine. "Who's that...?"

—as Periscus walked briskly up behind him with a large stone and *whacked* the squat, shorter man hard on the back of his head!

Socrates fell into a disheveled heap.

"Yep," Dave grinned down at the unconscious fat man, "I pluck the strings, but Periscus plays the drums!"

Sticking his lyre back in the wheelbarrow, Dave helped Periscus to swiftly gag the groaning man lest he waken prematurely and call-out for help. They tied his arms together behind his back, then his legs, and finally bundled him into their large fish net. Covered with several layers of obscuring netting, they merrily trundled him away in their wheelbarrow.

To any onlookers they were simply transporting a large catch of smelly fish—which no one had the slightest desire to question or inspect.

By the time they exited the city, traveled back down the coastline, and hiked a mile inland to arrive at their secluded hut, it was early morning.

"So, what do we do next?" Periscus grinned evilly. His eyes glittered at the prospect of finally wrecking his revenge upon the squirming fat man still tied up in the wheelbarrow.

"We get some rest before we continue," Dave answered, satisfied with how his plan was proceeding. "They won't miss him for a couple days. He often goes off on drunken binges, usually with other people. But when he satisfies his most-perverted lusts, he does that by himself. He's ours to do with as we please."

"Why not just kill him now?" Periscus growled.

"Would that be as satisfying as *torturing* him?" Dave mildly replied.

"You're right," the tall old man grinned, again revealing his one protruding tooth. "He must *suffer!*" he spat, saliva dripping from the corners of his gummy mouth.

"Oh, he *will* suffer," Dave yawned, going over to his mat and wearily lying down to get some sleep. The seventy year-old Socrates was fat and heavy. It was quite a job sneaking him out of the city and up the mountain slope to their hidden hut. Dave was exhausted. "He'll suffer plenty!"

Snake was horrified when Tommy fired his hidden gun, blew away his constraints, and dropped into the spinning maelstrom! He'd grown fond of the little robot. True, Tommy wasn't a true lifeform, just a computer-derived simulation—but the little guy grew on you.

Snake knew that Tommy's chances of surviving an unprotected freefall a billion years or more into the past, traveling against the normal time-flow, was slim-to-none. Unprotected, he'd be torn to shreds by the incredible forces within the vortex. At least, that's what their best scientists predicted.

The immense jump was substantially different from the "small" jaunts through time that the Tommy-robot experienced previously. This was a fall *against the grain* through the *God-Barrier*—which the Almighty Creator had erected a billion years in the past!

They'd needed the robot's complete cooperation in following the subtle trail Dave left in the time-stream. That's why they promised Tommy he could pursue and "rescue" Dave. But they had carefully prepared the nearly indestructible Probe to do the "dirty work" instead of Tommy.

Rather than "find and rescue" Dave, the Probe's orders were to *locate and permanently terminate!* After having the robot initially map-out the trail, the plan was to send Tommy off to the valley-prison. They wouldn't deactivate or kill him—that would be unthinkable. But he'd be kept safely isolated, unable to disturb the growing societal harmony of New Earth. He wouldn't be lonely. Scientists or tourists would occasionally visit him. Tommy was, indeed, a unique curiosity to be prized, when suitably contained and controlled.

Yes, there had been discussion of putting Tommy into a vehicle similar to the Obelisk, for safe transport into the distant past. But the little robot had proved he was too unpredictable and unreliable. So for a variety of reasons, he couldn't be sent into the past. Even if he survived the journey, there was no guarantee he'd follow orders—even those imprinted without his knowledge in the brain "inspection" they'd originally given him.

Indeed, that neural implant was no longer responding to discrete pings. The Martian Snakes suspected but could not prove he'd consciously detected and inactivated that neural virus-construct. Plus, building another Obelisk was impossible. The Martian Snakes simply didn't have the advanced resources necessary in their hastily-acquired new world. Also, they'd long since lost the advanced knowledge from which to proceed. No, the autonomous, hard-wired Probe was a far better option...

—which they were now preparing to launch, swinging it carefully into position above the throbbing superconductor coils!

"He's gone," Casandra gasped, standing next to Snake in the shielded control room. Around them Dinosapien technicians, supervised by the Martian giant snakes, were busily attending their stations. They were having difficulty keeping the subspace fracture intact and focused.

Snake was startled to see that the shorter, stubby woman was actually crying.

"He wuz one clever robot, that's fer shore," Snake sighed to her compassionately, "Hiding that gun we gave him, now that wuz a slick move! We needed Tommy to feel safe, but I thought it wuz taken from him at security?"

"I saw him put it into the lockbox," she frowned, blinking tears away. "I don't know how he got it back without us observing it."

"Whut's done is done," Snake said, focusing on the immediate situation. "No one's gonna blame you, Casandra. You did your best to control the little dude. He was jist a sneaky little bastard."

The Apparatus was now operating at full power. The sound of its THROBBING vibration was deafening, jarring Snake to the bone.

Plus the *sizzling heatwaves* were growing larger, more difficult to dampen and control.

They had to get that Probe launched before the subspace-fissure blinked-out! The link to the exact point that Dave exited the time-stream in the distant past was very tenuous. To shut the Apparatus down and then try to bring it back online again was a longshot.

Without Tommy there to discern and fine-tune the faint trail, they might never again be able to reach Dave.

And who knew what terrible damage to the timeline Dave might cause? Across a billion years, the gathering ripples of his actions would not be felt immediately. But they'd happen without fail. Dave had already proven his ability to radically alter the future!

He had to be stopped while he could still be reached.

"*Probe away!*" came a telepathic shout in Snake's head—as he saw the metallic-looking sphere drop from its holder toward the central circular magnets...

It vanished into the central stack just as the entire Apparatus *lost power!*

"What happened?" Casandra gasped, the entire cavern thrown into darkness.

Snake heard ominous "*sputters*" and "POPS" as plasma-flows were disrupted, the immense magnetic fields containing and controlling the roiling plasma dying away...

"We've got to get out of here!" Snake said, grabbing Cassandra by her arm and dragging her toward the exit tunnel.

There were frantic *HISSES* and *SCREECHES* as the Dinosapiens and Martian snakes were thrown into panic and confusion.

Snake got Casandra out of the tunnel just as a loud EXPLOSION split the air around him.

Rocks and debris shot from the mouth of the tunnel as Snake dived to the side, Casandra in his tight grasp. He groaned as he landed hard on his side, Casandra on top of him!

"Why did we lose power?" Casandra, ever the practical one, asked. She picked herself up, reaching down to help Snake back to his feet. "The power loss caused the plasma flow to lose containment then explode. How could this happen?"

Snake was greatly shaken, similarly bewildered.

"We *shouldn't* have lost power," he said, standing shakily on the slope. "There were several DE-generators supplying the necessary electrical feeds. If one failed, the backups should have instantly picked up the slack!"

"Oh, my," Casandra gasped, shading her eyes against the still-thick dust and debris blown from the tunnel, looking up at the clearing sky.

"What is it?" Snake said, holding his injured side where he'd been badly bruised.

"Something really...bad..."

He looked up. There, descending rapidly towards them, were *giant black spheres*—with *spikes* protruding from their many-faceted surfaces!

And on the valley floor, looking like harpooned fish, the hover-crafts that supplied electrical power to the Apparatus were crumpled and crushed. Large spikes the size of ten-story buildings had skewered them! Looking up again, Snake saw that there were now *thousands* of the giant, black "spike-ships" descending!

It brought back bad memories of the Harvesters. These space-ships, however, seemed even more ominous. They appeared more purposeful than the mindless Reaper scavenger-robots. These space-ships darted here and there in the sky, actively searching!

"It's...another alien invasion," Snake gasped in disbelief.

"Our people can't deal with something like this," Casandra stated quietly. "We're going to be destroyed."

"Where are Dave and Sally when you need them?" Snake wryly observed, holding his pain-wracked side. "We'd better find a place to hide, my lady! Don't 'cha think?"

She nodded, supporting him as they slid down the rocky slope together, avoiding the well-worn, exposed path.

"Looks like 'poetic justice', huh?" Snake weakly laughed. "We get rid of those bothersome primitive characters only to be left helpless against an even worse evil. We've got no way to fight back."

"Our cities have Dark Energy shields," Casandra calmly observed, as they slunk away into the crags and cliffs of the mountainside. "Our defenses can hold out against those invaders, whoever or whatever they might be."

"Yes, but for how long?" Snake replied. "It doesn't look so much like an invading organized fleet—like the Harvesters—but a whole *swarm*, more like a disturbed nest of hornets! How can we defeat them? We lack both offensive weapons and the knowledge of war."

As if in agreement, a loud "buzzing" came from the sky as a whole squad of the invaders zipped past overhead.

Snake and Cassandra ducked beneath a shielding ledge.

"We *exterminate* them," Casandra forcefully replied. "We're good at producing a well-ordered, clean world—aren't we? They're just super-powerful vermin, right? *Right?*"

"Right..." Snake weakly answered, wondering if she'd just smoked some hallucinogenic substance to reach such a bizarre conclusion. "Well, why not?" he sighed.

Snake was wryly amused at how things could change so radically and swiftly. Just this morning they'd succeeded in penetrating more than a billion years into the past, following an almost-imperceptible trail left by Dave in the ancient Obelisk. It was an incredible triumph. Now, a mere ten minutes later after trying to launch their Probe, their entire hard-won new civilization was teetering on the brink of total destruction!

It was a harsh reprimand.

"We've got to keep moving, get further into the mountainside," Cassandra said, grabbing his hand and dragging him away from the small ledge.

As Snake tottered after her, he had a terrible feeling that the *Creator* was not happy with them for having circumvented His righteous Judgment Day—their punching a hole back through the God Barrier.

Snake had a sickening revelation.

It wasn't just humans who fell short. It was *also* the smug, self-righteous intelligent Martian Snakes, Dinosapiens, and assorted other smart reptiles that made it across to New Earth. They were *all* to blame. Their sins were catching up to them.

Snake looked up and saw one of the Spike-Ships descending right at them! He and Casandra were exposed out in the open. This was the end!

—as simultaneously, around the two of them, a *large flock of the four-winged black birds* fluttered down, completely covering them and obscuring them from any aerial surveillance!

The ominous craft above floated on past, apparently not seeing the two survivors who'd just escaped the exploded cavern.

"That was close," Casandra sighed, hidden beside Snake under the feathery covering.

Snake wasn't sure what was worse, being captured and killed by the new aliens above...or being *eaten alive* by a flock of sharp-beaked birds!

They were *pecking* at him unmercifully with their big red beaks.

"Go away, you crazy birds!" Snake yelled out, jumping up to his feet as the concealing feathery cover erupted upward in a thunderous beat of their synchronized wings.

"What *was* that?" Casandra asked him, standing up and incredulously watching the flock fly away.

"I don't know," Snake groaned, still nursing his injured side. "But whatever happened, they just saved us."

"They tried to eat us."

"I dunno... I got the feeling they were trying to tell us something?"

"I think this New Earth still has some surprises for us," Casandra calmly observed. "While we leap-frogged from the past, the other creatures took a billion years to evolve in new and different ways. Maybe this planet isn't so defenseless after all."

"Oh, you think that those birds will *peck* the invaders to death?" Snake laughed, stumbling on the steep slope.

"That was just a love-tap they gave you," Casandra seriously stated, grabbing one of his arms to steady him. "If they really wanted to hurt us, we'd be scraps of meat."

"Oh?" Snake protested. "I *feel* like a scrap of meat!"

"You're fine," she curtly stated, while helping him limp along across the slope. "So where do we go now?"

He paused, looking out across the central river at the crushed, now-burning husks of their transport crafts. He saw a number of motionless bodies lying near the destroyed ships, skewered by spear-like small spikes. Far off in the distance, he thought he could hear immensely loud "thuds" where devastating *giant* spikes were *hammering* continuously down upon what he feared were steadily weakening city-shields.

Then he looked back the way they'd come at the white-hot fire still belching from the tunnel.

"Maybe there's a *third* way," he hesitantly spoke, gratefully realizing that Sally had taught him more than he'd thought.

"And just what is this 'third' way?" Casandra politely asked, snorting derisively.

"Follow the birds!"

"What did you say?" she asked, tottering on the slope, trying to support him and not stumble herself.

"*That* way!" he said, pointing across the valley in the direction that the flock of black birds had flown.

She shrugged.

"Ok, then," she said, "One way's as good as any other, I guess."

Dave awoke refreshed but troubled. Something *stank*...

Dave was used to the strong odor of fish, of sweat, of freshly-gutted entrails, of infected wounds from dying soldiers, and of rotting bodies washed up out of the sea from Naval battles. But this smell was different. It wasn't just nauseating, it was *disgusting!*

"What the hell is that awful...?" Dave began to complain before stopping himself in midsentence.

Oh yes. Now he remembered.

The sunlight outside was fading. The sun was going down. Their small hut was now in shadows. It was getting dark. But there was enough light for Dave to see the one-armed Periscus standing motionless above the wheelbarrow. He loomed over it like a crane in a swamp eyeing a tasty fish about to be speared with his beak.

In the wheelbarrow, still tied up and gagged, was Socrates. The old man wasn't moving, apparently unconscious. He had massively soiled his undergarments. The awful stench was coming from him.

"Periscus!" Dave barked at him, getting up to his feet. "Clean him up!"

"I *told* you he was just a piece of crap," the thin old man gloated, grinning lopsidedly. "I say we let him stew in his own filth."

"Not just yet!" Dave snapped at him. Then, more kindly, he continued: "I have a more exquisite torture for him than just letting him rot, Periscus. Trust me. We're going to get a lot of satisfaction from that monster!"

Periscus grinned even wider, going outside to grab a bucket and start the mile-long trudge down to the seashore from their isolated hut to bring back seawater.

His happy expression paid testimony to his expectation. After dousing away the filth, Dave knew he'd gladly make Socrates *pay* in full!

Waiting for Periscus to return, Dave grabbed dried fish to munch on, drank fresh water, and sat on a bench looking at the wheelbarrow holding the unconscious but still raggedly breathing philosopher.

Dave then got up from the bench he'd been sitting on and lighted several candles around the hut. Then he sat back down.

And in the luridly flickering light he began to order his thoughts.

After intensely considering his options, Dave started laying out his conclusions verbally—as if he were in a court of law making his case.

"I've pondered on you now for fifteen years," he muttered into the quiet of the hut. "Something brought me here to this pivotal point in the history of the world. I've struggled with the 'why' and I think I've got it. Though you'd deny it, you're important to the development of future democratic governments."

Nothing answered back. The wheelbarrow was silent. Dave feared Socrates was dead. But then Dave again heard an uneven "rasping" noise coming from beneath the fish net.

Good, the old man didn't just now die. That would be a huge waste, since Dave finally had him in his grasp.

"And even though you didn't agree with such governance, you laid the philosophical foundations for independent thought," Dave softly continued, musing to himself. "That's has to be the key thing that got us into trouble. In Sally's Dimension they had authoritative governments and Empires which tightly controlled the people, societies, and science. So Dark Energy wasn't misused. Instead, it was jealously guarded by the governmental powers. Excessive usage *didn't* happen in Sally's Dimension, sending up a 'cosmic flare'! So God didn't turn His full gaze upon us. Mankind might have had the time to mature into a more acceptable species if there'd only been Sally's Dimension containing humans. But because of the overall permissive governments in my...our...Dimension, God noticed us, judged us, and wiped us out!"

A rat scurried across the bare ground of the hut, likely attracted by the awful stench. Dave pondered the grim situation, honing his thoughts, gathering his resolve to see it through.

"But it wasn't just you, Socrates, that set the stage for liberal governments," Dave continue to clarify his thoughts and justification for what would soon occur. "It was also the additional writings and philosophical explorations that you inspired. Because of your example and fundamental conclusions there was *Plato, Aristotle, Alexander the Great, Pythagoras, Antisthenes, Locke, Hobbes*, and many others. You inspired them all. So if you were *not* to die voluntarily in a few days by your own hand for your High Principles—then many others into the future would likewise *not* be inspired by your life! In fact, Plato and your other followers might well be quickly gathered up and likewise executed. And then history would not even remember you and your radical ideas. The *entire future history of Western civilization* might be altered!"

There was no response from the festering wheelbarrow. Dave didn't expect one. It wasn't yet time.

"Sally tried to do this with Jesus," Dave continued his indictment. "She didn't succeed. But I think she didn't go far enough back through time. I'm roughly *500 years earlier* than Jesus. *This* is the key moment to radically alter the history of my Dimension—I'm sure of it!"

"Talking to that bastard?" Periscus said as he slowly edged back into the hut with a full bucket of seawater splashing around. "Gods! It really does stink in here, doesn't it?"

He set the bucket on the floor.

"Now what?" he asked.

"String him up by his hands," Dave ordered.

Periscus brusquely overturned the wheelbarrow, rolling Socrates out onto the floor like a hogtied pig. A few moans came from the fat old man on the floor as Periscus roughly jerked the net away, threw a rope over the top rafter in the hut, untied Socrates' bound hands from behind his back, rebound them together in front with the dangling rope, then started wrenching him upward facing away from Dave.

Dave was amazed at the strength Periscus was exhibiting. Just a day ago Periscus was a feeble old man withering away. Now he seemed possessed, throwing his weight into yanking down on the rope with his one good arm. Surely the prospect of sweet revenge after a lifetime of rejection and degradation was a powerful motivator!

Dave could have helped. But he gladly gave the "honor" of stringing up Socrates to his old friend.

Socrates steadily rose higher...

As the fat man's shoulders began to bear his considerable weight, he finally stirred, groaning pitifully.

"That's high enough," Dave said, still sitting on a rough bench. Socrates now hung stretched upward with just the soles of his feet touching the floor, his back to both Dave and Periscus. "Tie him off!"

Periscus walked his end of the taunt rope around one of the hut's supporting timbers, neatly inserting a fisherman's knot to leave Socrates dangling from the rafters.

"Drench him," Dave ordered.

Periscus effortlessly hoisted the bucket of seawater with his one arm, upending it over the top of Socrates' lolling head. Normally weak and weary, this unexpected redemption of his whole life was certainly giving the aged Periscus a ferocious strength!

Socrates let out a *howl of fear*—twisting and writhing on the rope, not knowing where he was or what was happening to him.

"Get those filthy clothes off him," Dave ordered, lifting his sandaled feet above the rush of dirty water that flooded from the dangling old man.

"Gladly!" Periscus happily replied, ripping and tearing Socrates' tunic off until the man hung there clad only in stained underwear.

"Get your whip," Dave now calmly directed Periscus, pointing at the thick leather strap with several nails set-into its end. It dangled menacingly on a hook in the wall. Normally Periscus used it for driving off rats and other vermin. Now he'd do the same for a similar human rat!

"With pleasure," the thin old man grinned, grabbing it up and *thudding* it repeatedly on the packed dirt floor in expectation.

"Can you hear me?" Dave shouted at the naked back of the dangling fat man.

"What...what is this?" Socrates replied in a deep, guttural growl. "I...demand you release me—at once! Untie me right now and..."

"You will *answer* my questions!" Dave screamed again at him, cutting off the indignant tirade. Then, in a somewhat more controlled voice, he continued: "If you answer well, you will be one step closer to being released. Answer poorly and you will be punished!"

"*Piss* off!" Socrates yelled back.

"Oh, you're in no position to dismiss me so crudely," Dave coldly replied. "Would you please do the honors?" Dave politely articulated to Periscus. "I think *ten lashes* will do for now."

The thick whip with its protruding nails suddenly SLAMMED into the philosopher's naked back!

Socrates *screeched* like a wounded bird—*convulsing* as he dangled on the rope!

Periscus paused, grinning like a little kid getting his first ice cream cone, admiring his work.

Blood streamed from a jagged tear stretching from Socrates' neck down to his butt-crack.

"That's one. Nicely done, my friend. Nine more, please."

Periscus lustily slung the nails again into Socrates' exposed back as further shrieks came from the philosopher...again and again and again and again and again and again and again and again!

Periscus paused, breathing heavily, the bloody whip hanging loosely at his side.

Socrates' back looked terrible. It was crisscrossed with sliced-open sections where blood freely spurted out. He looked like a beached whale being flayed for its fat stores.

Socrates' wails now became agonized groans.

"Now that I have your attention," Dave said more quietly, "I'd like you to meet your happy torturer, who will walk around and face you. This is to convince you that if you refuse to cooperate you will get no mercy."

With an evil gleam in his eyes, the taller Periscus marched around the dangling old philosopher to peer downward into Socrates' contorted face.

Periscus sneered happily at the tormented man.

"You!" Socrates snarled, peering fearfully up at him. "I might have guessed it! You still blame me for your cowardice at..."

Looking from the side, Dave saw Periscus *smash* him in the face with his one clenched fist, *breaking* Socrates already-misshaped nose and splitting his lip.

"*Auuuggghhh,*" Socrates sputtered, spewing droplets of blood out his busted nose and damaged mouth.

At this, the dangling man went limp. But he was still conscious, muttering barely audible curses.

"Good," Dave said, indicating for Periscus to come back around to the backside of Socrates. "Now you know our resolve, Socrates. I know you can hear me. There's no sense in pretending to be unconscious. Be convinced...I am not lying to you! I repeat: answer well and you are one step closer to being *released!* Answer poorly and you will be further *punished!* Are you ready to proceed?"

"Who a-are y-you?" Socrates whimpered. "Are you one of my political enemies? Are you Anytus or Lycon? You're a-about to get me legally executed at court! Why would you t-torture me now, in advance?"

"I am neither of those," Dave smugly replied, pausing for dramatic effect. "I am one of those who you love to defame the most: *a god* in the flesh of a mere lowly fisherman!"

"What...?"

Dave deepened his voice, used his diaphragm for projection, and *bellowed* in his best overwhelmingly "godly" manner:

"YOU DENY THE GODS WHILE PRETENDING YOU'RE SMARTER THAN THE SUPPOSEDLY STUPID COMMON-FOLK!" Dave screamed at him. "SO I HAVE CHOSEN TO TEACH YOU A LESSON! I AM *ASTRAIOS*, THE GOD OF THE STARS AND PLANETS! I BRING TO YOU POISONOUS VENOM FROM ALL THE WORLD'S SNAKES! I AM PUTTING YOU ON TRIAL *MYSELF*— WITH QUESTIONS YOU MUST ANSWER CORRECTLY! FAIL MY INTERROGATION AND YOU WILL SUFFER THE PUNISHMENT OF THE GODS! YOU WILL TASTE MY POISON, WHICH IS FAR WORSE AND MORE PAINFUL THAN THE HEMLOCK WHICH AWAITS YOUR MORTAL JUDGMENT!"

Socrates wobbled at the end of the rope as if he were choking.

But then he began *laughing* uproariously.

"*You* a-are the 'god' of the Stars and Planets?" he cackled hysteri-cally. "You're just s-some stupid fisherman allied with a disgraced soldier who somehow captured m-me. I can smell fish all around me! You're both just pathetic c-commoners who are looking to take a moment of *my* glory. But just release me and I p-promise I won't re-port your outrage. In fact, I'm rather...amused...by all of this...despite the pain and blood that..." his outraged voice trailed off weakly.

"Punish him," Dave coldly directed Periscus. "*Fifteen more lashes* this time, please."

"No...I didn't m-mean for you..." the fat man started to protest— as the whip *tore* again into his naked back, eliciting more agonized screams!

Socrates' hairy, fleshy back was now being torn to pieces. Blood spurted from ruptured blood vessels. Patches of skin hung off of freshly revealed white ribs and backbones.

The one-armed Periscus smirked with pleasure at the groans of the convulsing Socrates. Then Periscus reached fifteen and paused, breathing heavily from his ferocious exertions.

"Shall you receive more punishment, or will you answer my ques-tions?" Dave patiently asked.

"Piss...off..."

"*Punish* him!" Dave yelled at Periscus. "Give him *twenty-five* lashes this time!"

It was a total of fifty lashes. That was a brutal punishment. Dave knew from his Christian upbringing that men often died from such a whipping in Roman days, just as Jesus almost did when he was scourged before his crucifixion.

In fact, Dave was proceeding on the basis of what Sally told him regarding *her* interaction with the *historical Jesus!*

This wasn't just a sadistic exercise in torture.

It was a well-defined, "medical" procedure.

But the splashing "thuds" of Periscus' strong, one-armed blows onto Socrates' already-savaged back still caused Dave to shudder.

When the blows ended, there was nothing but raw flesh on the fat old man's back and upper buttocks. It looked like raw hamburger.

Blood was pouring down the man's fat legs, running onto the floor and pooling at his feet.

"ARE YOU READY TO ANSWER MY QUESTIONS?" Dave shouted with his "god voice" at the man's massively bleeding posterior.

"I...have no problem at all...answering questions," Socrates grated through clenched teeth as he hung suspended from his increasingly-bloating hands. "You...could have asked me...in the marketplace."

"I tried to, old man," Dave sternly reproved him. "But you chose to cut me off!"

Socrates' suspended, tied hands were now turning black from cut-off blood flow.

Dave felt an appalling sense of pleasure at the inflicted injury on the man's hands.

"I'm...sorry I didn't...respect you," the hanging old man now softly replied, apparently sincerely.

"Good," Dave said as Periscus wobbled over to sit beside him on the bench, exhausted from wielding his whip in his orgy of revenge. "Here, then, is my first question: 'Why are people so stupid?'"

Socrates was silent for a minute, apparently thinking how to respond. Dave patiently allowed him time to come up with a considered reply.

"God...made them as they are," Socrates whispered back.

"So you claim it is God's fault that we behave like mere smart animals?" Dave asked.

"Yes."

"Then why did God make us so stupid?"

"It...amuses him..."

"That seems rather trite, doesn't it? You're telling me that God is an egomaniac who delights in torturing people? If that were true, would he not heartily approve the treatment Periscus gave you just now? I've heard you argue at the Agora that the gods are not petty or frivolous!"

"I...speak not of the false gods...but of the...true God."

Dave narrowed his eyes, considering. Perhaps this comic buffoon did have a well of deep wisdom, after all. Dave hadn't actually expected any real revelations from the comic philosopher—but perhaps...?

"And you define 'amuse' how?"

"As in...giving Him pleasure of some sort...perhaps which we can't understand its..."

"—as in our struggle to do better, trying to improve ourselves against near impossible odds? Is that what you are claiming? So it's not just the 'hero' battling in a senseless war, but the Thinker struggling to tame and understand his own Mind?"

"Yes," the blood-drenched hanging slab of meat whispered.

"And *how* do you know that this is true?"

"I...don't."

"But you also claim in your speeches that you were appointed by the true God to pursue philosophy, have you not?"

"Yes."

"Then since you are a self-professed *Master of Philosophy*, why do you now claim ignorance?"

"I am truly 'wise'...only because I know...the abysmal depths of my own ignorance," the man gasped, his voice rapidly weakening from pain and loss of blood.

Dave nodded at this admission, realizing its profound nature.

"And society overall—how can it best improve itself to become acceptable to this Higher Power?" Dave pressed him. "Is it through a personal study of this 'philosophy', or via direction from those who are Masters in the subject, or just by being needled by irritating gadflies such as you?"

Socrates seemed not to have noticed the insult.

"Some...will surely improve through their own study...but most need direction...motivation even, a *trial by fire!*"

The fat, bloodied man seemed to momentarily draw strength from his last statement.

"But you say that most people cannot or will not improve via their own personal initiative?"

"The...unexamined personal life...is not worth living," the limp man gasped-out.

"If that is true—then why do so many people readily accept the traditions, institutions, beliefs, and behaviors sanctified by their present-day society? They certainly appear to *think* that they have worthwhile, fulfilled lives."

"Because they are...they *choose* to be...*stupid!*"

Dave bitterly laughed.

"Ah, so the 'great philosopher' defaults to the weakest argument of all: the 'circular definition' where the snake eats its own tail. We're back to my first question."

The blood-covered back of Socrates did not respond.

"So yet again, Socrates, I ask you: *why are people so stupid?*" Dave pressed him. "And this time don't tell me it's because they were made that way!"

The blood pooling at Socrates' feet was starting to congeal into a thick, red carpet.

"Because...it's...easier..."

"That's not good enough. Try again!"

"And...their stupidity receives...positive reinforcement."

"TRY AGAIN!" Dave shouted in his "god voice" at the man's savaged back.

"And those...that t-try to g-go beyond their own l-limitations...to do otherwise than prevailing s-society approves...to b-be uncommonly smart...get killed," Socrates gasped as his voice grew ever-fainter. "It's not j-just ingrained s-survival instinct...but a c-collective conspiracy to..."

His voice trailed off.

The tortured man was fading fast. Dave knew he had to hurry to acquire the last bit of critical information from the reputably greatest thinker of history!

"So is there any hope for present-day, 'collective' mankind *overall* to become pleasing to God?" Dave said, eagerly leaning forward to hear the answer.

But there was none.

The fat old man was now genuinely unconscious. His head lolled down. His body hung limp, bloated—sliced open like a gutted pig.

"Cut him down," Dave abruptly ordered Periscus.

"What? We can revive him and..."

Dave jumped up, grabbed a fish-flaying knife, and sliced through the rope above Socrates' hands.

Socrates fell with a "thud" into a limp heap at Dave's feet, barely breathing, his savaged back still sputtering up squirts of red blood.

"Go get another bucket of seawater," Dave ordered Periscus.

"But that will take me an hour to..."

"*Do* it!" he snarled at the thin old man.

"Well...if you need it, Astraios," the man mumbled, shrugging.

He picked up the empty bucket and wobbled out the doorway.

As soon as he was gone, Dave spread Socrates face-down upon the floor, his back flattened and pointed upward.

Carefully, Dave used the fish-knife to precisely *slice into his own wrist*, opening up his veins.

He winced at the pain but continued...

—as a steady flow of blood sprang out, carefully directed by Dave down upon the raw flesh of Socrates' back!

Yes, he was indeed following the example of Sally with the scourged Jesus, as she'd related to him in their trek to the downed helicopter. But he wasn't offering major arteries or veins at his neck. Instead, his blood-letting was merely from deep cuts on one of his wrists. The slashes could be readily bandaged, should he not lose too much of his own blood. His youthful, regenerated body was still filled to the brim with a massive dose of the Optimmune retrovirals. The overlapping genetic-enhancing systems he'd taken in the Obelisk would hopefully help him heal quickly...

—and *readily infiltrate* Socrates' body through the massive wounds on his deeply-flayed back!

Hopefully, it would be sufficient...

—to *radically change* future history!

Chapter 14

<u>CONSEQUENCES</u>

Some may claim that Fate rules

While others say they make their own

But in a predestined Universe isn't it sad

That so many creatures don't just give up

But instead torture themselves with strivings

Still fighting for one more last breath of life

If indeed their deaths were already determined

That they had no possibility to delay a moment

Why the futile struggle, heartbreak, and fear

If one's consequences are unavoidable

But if the Creator does rejoice to see

Creatures accepting their greatest Gift

Not just bowing in abject surrender

But fighting, not to win but to improve

Giving the greatest Gift back to their Father

A Godly Creativity ever-appropriate and amazing

Then they could, indeed, find not out of hubris

But in their aspiration to emulate God

A result beyond the probable!

Homo sapiens Eulogy, 14:63-67

Sally was finally ready to run a preliminary test on the subspace drive that they'd taken from the destroyed Spike-Ship. She didn't know if it would even function. It was very different from their own melted-down, destroyed ship-drive DE-generator. But the alien device had indeed opened up a subspace rift large enough for the Spike-

Ship to enter. After all, the aliens succeeded in following the Dinosa-piens to the end of the Universe through subspace.

Sally carefully mapped its interior with high-energy x-rays. She now had a rough idea of the various components within the six-foot sphere and how they related to each other. But she still had no idea about which component did what. And she couldn't take the Sphere apart to study, out of fear of damaging it. However, she did know where its external spikes connected into either input or output inter-nal areas.

One component was particularly interesting to her. While the parts around it were dormant or inactive, it gave off a steady stream of infrared radiation. It was hot! Perhaps it was the palladium core?

Sally attached a multi-spectral meter onto one of the "input" spikes that communicated into the putative core. She was ready to send in a weak oscillatory signal, attempting to give it an initial com-mand.

"Should we have the rest of the crew go to their chambers?" Den-nis asked. He was standing beside her, clearly concerned about what might happen next.

"If it rips the ship apart, it'll likely happen so fast we won't even realize we're dead," Sally sighed. "I've got all our monitoring equip-ment in place. I'm only going to give it a tiny millivolt jolt. If we get any sort of response at all, then we'll know we're on the right track."

"Sally, at the rate you are going it could take us *years* to figure out how to turn on and control this thing," Dennis said in exasperation, stomping his big three-clawed feet in frustration. "We're running out of supplies. We've been floating out here now for over three months. The crew is getting anxious!"

"Well then tell them to go out and find us a nice earth-like nearby planet we can visit with our ion-drive," she joked, carefully adjusting the frequency of her initial test signal to that which Dave had shown her to use with their original "Device."

Dennis whined unhappily.

"You know that our star-charts put the closest extra-galactic plan-et at ten-thousand light years away!" he complained, obsessively "bumping" his big reptilian head onto the closest wall.

"You're going stir-crazy, Dennis," Sally calmly observed. "I thought you Dinosapiens were logical, patient, super-intellects. You know we can't just 'turn-on' an alien ship's engine and expect it to take us wherever we wish. Why don't you go to the hydroponic gardens and help them grow food for us. They always need help to prepare and spread the manure and..."

"Bah!" he sputtered irritably. "You call that 'food'? Those *plants* they're trying to grow from the seed-packs we brought to terraform new planets aren't food. Our *nutrient cubes* are food! The other things are what our distant ancestors ate out in filthy nature. Besides, we're culturing those plants in our *droppings and urine!* That's *disgusting*, Sally! When you proposed doing that to augment our food stocks, I thought then it was a disgusting idea. And I *still* find it disgusting!"

"Then you should be glad I got the nuclear power plant to minimally work, at least supplying the ship with some operating power," she muttered, focused on the read-outs on her computer display. "Without that, we'd have been dead a long time ago. That's what's allowed the grow-lights to give the seeds enough energy to germinate and make crops, potatoes to grow in our dung. So don't whine to me. I'm doing the best I can."

"That's true," he grudgingly admitted. "But the nuclear generator isn't near powerful enough to put the ship back into subspace. I...I suppose I wasn't meant to be a long-voyage astronaut, Sally...I was told we'd only be in space for a few weeks, our time...I'm a *geologist*, damn it! I need a *planet* to put my feet on and my pickaxe into!"

His big head sagged on his thick neck.

"Yes, yes," Sally reassured him. "We'll get there—but not by blowing ourselves up. Be patient, Dennis."

She continued carefully adjusting the frequency and minor oscillations before sending in the first weak input signal. If that was actually the palladium core in there, she wanted to tweak the deuterium ions as Dave had originally done in his garage—many, many years ago in the distant past. Doing so might possibly clue its central computer into wanting to talk to her! The alien generator wasn't just a reactor. It had to have a certain degree of innate intelligence.

If she could directly communicate with it then maybe she could get it to take them home.

"I'm hungry for *real* food!" Dennis moaned, his raspy reptilian voice echoing in the cramped engine room. "I need nutrient cubes, not those soggy, drooping *plants!*"

"Ah...now we're getting to your *true* problem," Sally nodded knowingly. "Your 'ancient' genetics are kicking in, aren't they? Your big sharp teeth want tasty protein, don't they? In fact, I'll bet that little old me is looking very yummy to you right now, huh? And it's driving you crazy! Don't I look just like a nice bloody steak to you?"

He glowered at her.

"I just need *protein*—not meat! Don't be disgusting," he protested. "I wouldn't eat you."

"Well, how kind of you to..."

"—and certainly not those 'plant' things that are growing up in your stinking droppings. Once the nutrient cubes run out I'll *starve!*"

"First of all," she retorted, "it's 'reprocessed organic waste'—*not* 'droppings.' And second, they're not just from me. It's your dung and everyone else's on this ship. And thirdly, it's not urine. It's perfectly-good evaporated and re-condensed water," Sally patiently explained. "You were ejecting your bodily wastes out into space on the voyage to Kepler-186f. That was incredibly stupid. We're a self-contained little world in here. We have to recycle everything if we're going to survive. Even then you couldn't hope to survive only on the limited store of 'nutrient cubes' that you brought along with you for the trip."

Dennis growled in frustration.

"But I *don't want* to recycle everything," he peevishly replied, again stomping his feet. "I'm a *civilized* being—not an animal fertilizing the ground with its own dung. And no matter where you go in the ship now, you can *smell* it. It's awful!"

Sally swung her head side-to-side, exasperated with her picky assistant.

"Jesus Christ, Dennis," she said, looking up at him pacing back and forth with his big tail sweeping along behind him. "Settle down or get out of here! I'm ready to inject the current."

He dropped to his paws, eagerly looking at the readings. His big, oblong dinosaur head bobbed up and down beside her.

"Do you think it will work?" he said, his voice now trembling with excitement.

Yes, he was riveted on the prospect of something happening. Sally was glad to see he was diverted from his protein cravings. She believed his claim to not want to eat her. But those big teeth of his would make short work of her tender mammalian flesh!

"If we see the other components lighting up inside the sphere, then we'll know we triggered it out of its dormancy," she said. "I'm sending notice right now up to Alice that we're going to attempt communication."

She hit the knob to inject a mere fourteen millivolts...

—and the entire spaceship trembled as Sally was *blown back* against the wall behind her!

Dazed but not hurt, Sally's mind was racing.

What happened?

The Sphere was still there. It *hadn't* exploded!

She looked to the side, confused—seeing Dennis *thrashing* about in midair, vainly trying to escape from a deadly grasp!

She couldn't believe her eyes.

That's what knocked her backward?

Holding the heavy Dinosapien easily up in the air by his thick neck was *the Demon* that Sally had fought against long ago beside Dave and Eashoa!

"No...it can't be!" she gasped in dismay.

And yet there it was! It was stooped over in the cramped engine room, fully ten feet tall—twelve feet counting the long pointed horns growing from his big bald head. Its scaly skin was a fiery red. It had long yellow hair covering his groin like a goatish kilt. His feet were large hoofs. From the upper region of his butt a long, red tail hung, twitching excitedly back and forth. The tail was forked at its end.

And he held in his hand a *seven-foot tall, lethal pitchfork!*

"We *killed* you!" Sally now yelled at him, struggling back to her feet from where she'd been thrown. "We left your corpse far away on Earth forever buried behind the God-Barrier!"

"Obviously not," he grinned, throwing Dennis contemptuously away.

The big Dinosapien tumbled through the air like a rag doll to crash into the opposite wall. He slumped to the floor, unconscious and bleeding from the back of his skull where he'd smashed into the bulkhead.

"*Sally! Can you hear me?*" a voice sounded over the ship's intercom. "*What's happening down there? We've got electrical failures all over the ship!*"

Sally touched the communicator disc hanging at her neck, transmitting.

"We...got a reaction."

"Well, please get it under control!" Alice answered again via the intercom. "We're now traveling uncontrollably, spinning around at near lightspeed, about to break up! *Stop* whatever you're doing!"

"I'll try," Sally whispered back, turning the communicator off.

"You...survived?" Sally said, looking up into that which she knew Dave—if he'd been there—would have called *Satan!*

Yes, there was no doubt. Standing before her was the *Demon* that they faced *one billion years ago* in the desert of Judea!

He was the embodiment of the Biblical notion of Satan.

Sally felt chilled to her bones, helpless, and defenseless.

She trembled.

"Oh don't be scared, you silly little girl," the towering Demon hissed at her, motioning for her to stand up.

She was furiously thinking as she slowly got back up to her feet. Behind her, the alien generator was visibly vibrating. She certainly had succeeded in activating it!

"So..." she hesitantly replied, "this isn't just a weird cosmic accident then, my running into you *thirty billion light-years* from Earth—while lost in intergalactic space?"

He laughed, revealing pointed yellow teeth.

"I've been hard at work for a billion years, hoping you'd someday reappear from your little time-jump, Sally," he matter-of-factly replied in a scalding-hot voice. "After all, you and your friends caused me a great deal of pain when your Day of Judgment slammed down upon me! Fortunately, my fleet of Harvesters had already escaped Earth's orbit, so they weren't destroyed. But it took months for them to retrieve me from the wastelands. It was quite *boring* there on that burnt-off, little planet. That's reason enough for me to want sweet revenge, isn't it? And then I couldn't follow you into the future because of the God Barrier. I had to reach you through the normal course of time moving along at a snail's pace. But now my sweet revenge will be worth the wait."

"You knew this spaceship was traveling to Kepler-186f—with me on it?"

"Of course," the Demon leered. "I placed beacons on Earth to alert me if you ever reappeared. But before I could return to grab you, your lizard friends launched you up into space. And so I arranged a 'welcoming' party to greet you at your destination. But you cleverly escaped them. And then I had to step in, take charge, and come after you myself."

"You were inside the Spike-Ship's generator?"

"Yes I was...recharging myself, actually—even though I'm not a biological being, it still takes considerable power for me to do my clever tricks. But when you so rudely ripped it out by its roots, I was momentarily trapped inside."

"—until I reconnected and reactivated it?"

"Yes," the looming satanic head nodded. "And now I'm free. And now we're going on a little trip, just as soon as I can get the Drive properly connected and controlled...I'm surprised you couldn't get it working properly...it's actually quite simple," he said.

—as in a blur of movement, he reconfigured the entire engine room to incorporate the now-THROBBING spike-generator!

"So!" he grinned evilly at her. "Are you ready to leave, my lovely?"

"Where are we going?" she asked, feeling totally helpless.

"—to where there's *infinite prospects* for New Beginnings!" he laughed. "Isn't that wonderful? It sounds practically *inspirational*, doesn't it?"

"You're...going to kill us?" she gasped.

"Don't be silly," he snorted, walking back over to the black sphere, running his red hands lovingly along its knobby surface. Then, he began grabbing and adjusting various other engine room components, building piece by piece an elaborate control station.

"This isn't just about revenge, then, is it?" Sally suspiciously stated, afraid to move from the spot where she was standing.

Twin puffs of black smoke came from his flared nostrils as he again loudly "snorted."

"Of course not," he stated, fixing her in the unblinking gaze of his bright-yellow eyes. "You're a key part of the Project I've been working on for several billions of your earth-years. I *need* you."

"Me?"

"Yes! You—the *'Girl with the Turtle Tattoo'*—you're central to my Plan."

"But I'm just a human, one of the last two humans in existence."

"Hah!" he cackled. "That's funny! Sally, I like having you back with me. You make me laugh!"

"I don't understand."

"Yes, you don't," he agreed snidely. "Suffice it to say that you—in all your different incarnations—are somehow favored by the Creator," he said as he finished the control station above the sphere.

"I'm that important?"

"Fortunately and unfortunately, yes," he cryptically sighed, "which is why I've been forced to delay my plans for so long. I've been patiently awaiting your much-anticipated re-emergence."

She shook her head in firm denial.

"I don't understand any of this—and don't believe anything you say!" she defiantly concluded. "This is just too fantastic and melo-dramatic. I think that maybe I'm really just sleeping in my bunk, hav-ing a nightmare that's..."

He stepped forward and grabbed her roughly by her chin, forcing her to look straight up into his glaringly bright yellow eyes.

Then he *slapped* her hard across her cheek!

She fell backward to the hard deck.

"No, little girl, it's *not* a nightmare," he hissed at her. "It is quite real. I explained all of this once before to you, but of course you don't remember."

"To another version of me?" she hesitantly replied, holding a hand to her smarting cheek as she sat on the floor looking up at the towering Demon.

"One just as annoying as you," he grated as he lifted her up and casually tossed her over to the side, where she landed with a "thump" upon the still-unconscious Dennis.

Poor Dennis—he was getting battered from all directions, back and top!

"But that's behind us now," the Demon cheerfully said as he returned to the control console and punched in coordinates. "Let's just be thankful for what we've got, shall we? Instead of you and your pitiful crew of talking lizards being lost in the vastness of space, I'm 'rescuing' you! Now isn't that nice of me?"

He spun his pitchfork around his head like a giant cheerleader's baton.

Sally tightly hugged the twitching Dinosapien beneath her as *RE-ALITY WAS TURNED INSIDE-OUT AND SHE FELT HERSELF SIMULTANEOUSLY STRETCHED TO INFINITY AND CRUSHED INTO A TINY DOT!*

They must be back in subspace.

And this time, it was incredibly *painful...*

She didn't know where the Demon was taking her and her friends. But she was certain that she would *not* like it.

It was wonderful!

At first it was like flying in orbit around Earth! It was exhilarating! It was God-like!

Everything was neatly laid out to each side, above, and below.

Unencumbered by any protective vehicle or shield, Tommy knew he could literally reach out and grab anything he wanted. He saw everything simultaneously within his physical reach! But trying to collect souvenirs would only slow his journey.

He knew he had to get to Dave straightaway, without any detours.

After all, there was nothing to stop that ominous Probe from following him. In fact, it could right now be hot on his heels!

"*Wheeeeeee!*" he cried-out in glee...

—as he continued to *freefall through subspace*, going faster and faster along the path that Dave and the Obelisk had traveled before him, along the groove he'd already laid out as he was suspended above the subspace portal...

"Uh oh," he gulped to himself, realizing that this wasn't just an expanded amusement-park ride.

—as he felt *crackling waves of searing energy* jarring against his android body, *ripping* off his clothes, *peeling* off his outer skin, and *torching* his hair while *battering* him mercilessly...

He SCREAMED as he felt his face *burnt off!*

—his body being *vibrated apart* on a molecular basis, almost to the point of disintegration...

—and felt one of his eyes *yanked* out of his head...and an exposed hand *seared to a crisp*...and one leg twisted so sharply that the bones in it all *simultaneously snapped!*

"*Nnnnnnnnnnooooooooo!*" he yelled into the ether.

Afraid he could stand no more of the immensely prolonged de-structive fall *against the flow of time*, Tommy despaired of complet-ing his mission...

—when he suddenly SLAMMED INTO WARM WATER THAT FELT LIKE SOLID CONCRETE...

—and floated up to the surface, barely alive, feeling warm sun playing across his flayed and crushed body.

The salty water *burned* into his many terrible wounds.

He couldn't move.

He just barely managed to suck in enough air to keep his mangled body buoyant....

—as he let the waves wash him gently toward a distant shore.

He was content to know that in his one intact hand he still firmly held Sally's super-gun.

Tommy knew that Dave would be glad to get it...

—that is if Tommy didn't drown in the depths of the warm sea...

—or have his bloody remains eaten by a passing shark.

"Clean him up, but not his back," Dave ordered Periscus. "Get all the blood and wastes off the rest of his body. Put fresh underwear on him. Tie a loose bandage over his back. Then rinse out what's left of his tunic and put it back on him."

Periscus had just returned to the hut, lugging the bucket of sea-water with his one good arm.

"What happened to you?" Periscus fearfully asked, seeing Dave slumped into a corner, his wrist bandaged and bloody.

Dave was so drained he could barely move. He feared he'd given too much of his blood. But he wanted to make sure that the retroviral overlapping immune-optimizers would infiltrate into Socrates' "tenderized" back.

But now Dave was pale, shaking, and incredibly weak.

"Please just do as I say, my friend," Dave said. "Clean him up. We'll be taking him back into town tonight. Don't bother tying him up. He'll be out for quite a while—I've drugged him enough so that..."

"We're taking him back?" the thin old man gasped. "But that's too dangerous! We barely got him out of the city undetected. Why not just dig a deep hole and push him in?"

"DO AS I SAY, PERISCUS!" Dave shouted at him in his "god-voice," feeling too woozy to argue. But then he forced himself to explain. More softly, Dave continued: "This...is all...part of my 'godly' plan—so don't question the dictates of *ASTRAIOS!*"

"Of course not, my young Lord," the old man hastily replied, setting the bucket down as he searched for rags.

Dave's weary eyes closed. He fell into a fevered sleep. In his delirium he felt he was falling down a deep well while being ripped apart by sharp spikes stuck along its walls.

But that was just his imagination...wasn't it?

He couldn't allow himself to succumb to the pain of continued existence. He'd not yet accomplished his ultimate purpose with Socrates. When that was finished—if it succeeded—he could die in peace.

After the incredible distance he'd come—everything he'd been forced to give up—the *Trial of Socrates* was all he had left.

Chapter 15

<u>FRIENDS</u>

Important to humans are friends

Though of many varieties and shapes

Often irritating, disappointing, and annoying

Still the nebulous definition of close relationship

Holds a certain comfort against the dying of the light

That when all else is lost and hopeless, one shares

A sense of companionship, related experience,

That where you go, so do these other ones

If not an ultimate loving selflessness

Then still sympathetic, helpful

Holding hands in the dark...

It's a quaint custom.

Homo sapiens Eulogy, 15:58-61

Dave and Periscus had a difficult time getting the brutalized body of Socrates back into the city. It wasn't because of risk of discovery—the old man's bloated body was well-hidden under layers of fish net on which fresh fish were added for good measure—but because Socrates was so fat and heavy.

Dave had done more damage to his own body than he'd intended during his splurge of blood-letting upon the scourged back of Socrates. He really needed several days to recuperate, but couldn't take the time. To accomplish his plan, they must return Socrates to where they'd captured him, that very night. To delay longer risked a hue and cry, a search, and the course of history perhaps being prematurely altered in Socrates' favor. So Dave took one arm of the wheelbarrow while Periscus handled the other.

Periscus was also drained of energy, exhausted by his extreme exertions torturing Socrates.

Thus instead of being wheeled along by a well-muscled young man, as in their journey out of the city—two weak, exhausted men now staggered along. They just barely managed to keep the wheelbarrow upright.

It was getting towards dawn when they finally made it to the narrow alleyway behind the whorehouse.

"Good," Dave gasped, leaning weakly against a wall, trying to catch his breath. "Dump him and let's get out of here!"

"I still don't understand why we can't just kill him?" the thin old man peevishly said as he removed the top layer of fish. "We beat him within an inch of his life! He'll be dead in a few hours anyway."

Dave could hear a few people out on the street. The darkness was lessening. The city was awakening.

"Get him out from beneath the netting," Dave quietly said, slumping against the stone wall behind him, trying to regain his depleted strength. "And...put him over where we found him. They'll discover him soon enough...and think he just wandered off drunk and got mugged."

Periscus tossed aside the netting, yanked Socrates out of the wheelbarrow, and let him fall to the ground. The fat man's tunic bunched to the side. The bloodied bandage on Socrates' savaged back—pieces of an old tunic tied with rope—also came loose.

"What's this?" Periscus gasped, loosening and moving aside the bloodied bandage.

Socrates' torn-apart back was almost completely healed! Just a patchwork of red welts remained.

"You did this?" the thin man gasped in shock, tossing the bandage away. "But *why*, Astraios? Why did you restore him to his health?"

"He...must stand trial...by his peers," Dave determinedly stated, struggling to get his breath. "His fall from grace must be complete. Plus, since the severe injuries are gone, without further evidence even he will think what happened to him was just a drunken nightmare."

"Oh, I see," Periscus reluctantly agreed, clearly not convinced. But as ordered he dragged the heavy body of Socrates over to the urine-stained wall to position it up against the yellowed stones. The old philosopher was breathing shallowly. He was still alive.

"This blowhard idiot *should* be shamed before the *entire* community!" Periscus now agreed. Then he continued more enthusiastically. "Yes, he must lose what he values the most—the praise and adoration of other people. Good. I will very much enjoy seeing it with my own eyes!"

"No, my friend, you won't," Dave said, painfully getting back to his feet. He grabbed onto one of the wheelbarrow handles.

Out in the city, he heard roosters starting to crow.

"What do you mean, Astraios?" Periscus plaintively said as loaded back into the wheelbarrow the net and concealing fish.

"You can't go to the public trial," Dave flatly stated. "If Socrates recognizes you in the crowd and chooses to make a fuss, call the authorities, it could change the whole dynamics. Instead of him being on trial he could shift the focus to you and his political enemies. He might curry favor, even sympathy for his abduction and beating. The verdict is likely to be close as it is. That might swing the vote in his favor! If you're not there to remind him, he will have no evidence that his torture wasn't just a nightmare he had while collapsed drunk in the street."

"Oh...yes," Periscus muttered as they pushed the bouncing wheelbarrow along. "He did see my face, that's true. I wouldn't want that to..."

"And from here you must go alone, my friend," Dave said, abruptly stopping in the middle of the street in front of a city inn.

Periscus just looked at him in bewilderment.

"Now that the fat idiot is gone, you should be able to get the gear and fish back to the hut by yourself."

"By myself? But...?"

"I'm staying in the city."

"But...Astraios!" the old man cried, tears welling up in his eyes.

Dave didn't want to hurt the old man, his dear friend who was like a father to him, who'd saved his life. But there was much more to accomplished, which Periscus would not understand nor agree with.

"I have something for you."

Dave reached into a pocket of his loose, rough-woven tunic and pulled out two small pouches.

He handed one to Periscus.

"What is this?" the thin man said, taking the deceptively heavy pouch in his one hand.

"Open it."

Periscus set it on the netting and loosened the drawstring.

Inside was a mound of *silver coins*.

"It's...a fortune!" the old man gasped.

"Oh, not a fortune," Dave demurred. "But it will help you perhaps have a modest retirement. You no longer need to labor from sunrise to sunset. You can live out your life in peace, my friend."

"Where did you get all of this?" Periscus said in disbelief, his well-wrinkled face now highlighted by a shaft of the arising morning sun.

"These last fifteen years I've been setting aside what you gave me of our profits—plus doing trading and selling on the side, whenever I had the opportunity. I also sold some of my, uhm, 'heavenly' knowledge—improvements in this or that of your primitive tools and such. I'm the one who came up with the idea of this handy wheelbarrow that we now use all the time. I never got a lot for those ideas from the builders and merchants I sold them to, but when saved up it's a tidy sum. I have an equal amount in my own pouch. What I've given you is your half of my earnings—in gratitude for your many kindnesses to me."

"I...don't know what to say," Periscus gasped, his eyes wide in amazement.

"And I don't know what's going to happen to me in the next few days," Dave quickly explained. "But I want you to be rewarded for your faithful service to me. So, if you wish, make yourself a better life. You might want even choose to travel to another city, see more of the world. Whatever, be well my friend!"

Periscus slowly pulled the drawstring taut, slipping the pouch full of silver coins under the netting to hide it away.

"Where are you going now—back to the stars?" he said, his voice trembling. Dave saw tears dripping from the old man's eyes.

"I have a part to play at the trial of Socrates," Dave said. "I was careful that he never saw my face. He won't recognize me. So I'm staying here in the city. Don't worry about me, Periscus. I'll be fine."

Periscus lurched forward and grabbed Dave in a tight one-armed hug.

"It was the finest day of my life when you fell from the stars," he sobbed. "You've been like a son to me."

Dave patted the old man's thin shoulders with his hands.

"And you like a father to me," Dave said, his voice trembling as well. "I have learned much from you—about hard work, dignity, and true bravery. Please go and live out your life in peace. Goodbye."

Dave abruptly turned and strode to the door of the inn. He entered, not looking back. He wanted a clean break with the old fisherman. It was better that way.

If anyone ended up taking the rap for the abduction and torture of Socrates, it would be Dave. His plan was a longshot. Likely he'd be brought down along with Socrates. But so be it. Somehow—whether by luck or design—he'd been given another chance to set the future world straight.

And he was going to take it.

Snake was not used to physical suffering. He found it quite unpleasant.

"We could change back to our true forms," he said to Casandra, who was cuddled up next to him in the chill of the night. Her back was plastered against his thin chest. He had his arms wrapped around her waist.

They'd traveled all day down the long valley, moving from the protection of high boulders to clumps of trees to ravines—anything to hide them from the still-searching Spike-Ships!

They'd succeeded in evading the circling aliens, but not the privations of being on foot in the wild. All day long they'd had nothing to eat, little to drink. They'd dashed and climbed up and down steep slopes. They were sweaty and dirty. And now they were getting so cold that their human teeth clattered loudly.

"N-no..." she replied, ever the practical one. "That w-would take t-too much energy to accomplish. B-besides, in our snake f-forms we're exothermic...once our b-body heat fell, w-we'd be helpless."

He hugged her compact, strong body close as they lay in a grassy nook hidden under an overhanging small ledge. He felt the stirring of physical passion in his body. This surprised him. He didn't think that his human form could impose upon his advanced mind such primitive impulses, especially since it was getting so cold. He'd only felt a similar reaction before toward Sally. But even then it was more emotional than physical. But then again, Casandra was the only shapeshifted human female around for eons! And she was there, warm and cuddly, in his arms.

"You k-know, since we're probably b-both going to be k-killed to-morrow by those marauders anyway," Snake softly said, his face bur-ied in the short blond hair of Casandra's small head, "we might as w-well have some physical f-fun—and who knows, it might even help us keep warm?"

"You m-mean *sex?*" she said in disbelief. "How can you s-say such a thing?"

"Oh, y-you're right," Snake hastily replied, now starting to shiver uncontrollably. "The whole n-notion of mammalian coupling is un-thinkable...I apologize. Actually, I was just j-joking—trying to keep our spirits up."

"Well..." she said, holding tighter to his encircling arms as they lay alone in the wilderness, the stars twinkling down from the cloudless night sky, "I was 'actually' thinking more of the somewhat unappeal-ing female form that I deliberately a-adopted. I wanted to be a n-neutral figure to Tommy, rather than the sexy teenager that Sally h-had become. You know, to draw a sharp contrast—more like a m-motherly figure. So to think that y-you found me physically attractive caught me by s-surprise."

Something "howled" further down the valley in the darkness, making Snake think that perhaps his larger snake form might actually be preferable to the small human body he now inhabited.

"And y-you are!" he congratulated her. "You are a v-very proper, reassuring, no-nonsense, p-powerful female-human p-presence."

"Shut up and kiss me," she said, sliding around on the thick grass to hug him face-to-face.

"What?" he gulped. He felt her warm breath on his neck.

"Let's g-generate our own h-heat," she said, slowly undoing his shirt.

Sally felt like she'd been boiled in a pressure-cooker.

Woozily, nursing a fierce headache, she pulled herself off the now-stirring Dennis.

Every nerve in her body was *screaming* in pain! Her eyes throbbed in their sockets. Her teeth ached. Her guts felt like she'd just endured a month of the most terrible flu. Even her fingertips recoiled from touching anything, like they'd been cooked on a frying pan!

"W-where's that S-Satan guy?" she stammered to herself. Blinking rapidly to try and clear her vision, she got up and wobbled toward the alien subspace drive.

It hung there, suspended by attached cables, in the center of the engine room.

A *red haze* surrounded it. Waves of blistering heat rolled off of it. Sally couldn't even get near its control console.

The Demon had, indeed, gotten the alien generator to work. But it looked unapproachable and uncontrollable! And just where was the Demon, anyway? It wasn't anywhere to be seen. Had it gone back inside the stolen subspace drive?

"*Sally!*" she heard a shout behind her and spun around fearfully.

But it was just Dennis, staggering drunkenly to his feet, his powerful tail flopping back-and-forth haphazardly.

"What...happened?" he gasped, cringing back from the blistering heat waves.

"We went into subspace," she said, running over to support his heavy body with her own. "Let's get out of here! We don't know what lethal radiation might be coming out of that generator along with infrared heat. And we've got to get up to the control room to find out where we've gone!"

"Right..." he agreed, allowing her to help him to the exit tunnel. "But...shouldn't we... Hey! Where's that *big red monster* that tossed me around like a toy?" he yelled-out in a panic.

"I don't know," she soothed him. "It claimed to come from the Spike-Ship, hidden inside their Subspace Drive. It connected and activated the sphere to our system. Maybe it went back inside of the DE-generator. I don't know."

"Ok, then..." Dennis gasped, saliva dripping from his big, slack jaws. "It caught me by surprise. If it was still here, I'd go over and *kick its ass!*"

"Uhm, sure..." Sally diplomatically agreed. Her violent human ways were certainly wearing off on him. In fact, she was "contaminating" the entire crew. The big Dinosapiens were all swaggering around like lizard cowboys! Fortunately, George and Alice retained their human forms and seemed immune to Sally's "macho"-inducing influence.

And then they were back in the Starship's control room, looking out the transparent dome at an incredible sight!

"Oh...my...God," Sally gasped.

The blackness of space above them—which in the intergalactic void was mostly empty except for faint, distant galaxies—was now filled-in with a dense presentation of *stars of all sizes and colors imaginable!*

The largest, nearest ones were mostly reddish—old, dying stars, as Sally recalled from astronomy specials she'd seen on TV. And as their Starship slowly and uncontrollably spun on its axis, Sally saw coming into view behind them a HUGE, SHIMMERING, FLATTENED SPHERE—with an "accretion disc" of matter and stars streaming towards its gigantic, glowing surface!

"Sally, that's a..." Dennis incredulously began.

"—'*Black Hole*' she finished his sentence. "It's incredible...but I thought they were invisible?"

"I think what we see is called the...'event horizon'. That's what's making light we can see it by," Dennis softly replied, squinting his big orange eyes in concentration.

"Right..." Sally nodded. "Past that point nothing can emerge...but atoms are being torn apart up to that point—producing light...ok then."

It was a Monster known by scientists to exist at the center of most galaxies. It was both fascinating and horrifying at the same time!

And very close off to their right was an *old, red, bloated star.*

And beneath them was a *planet*—shrouded with orange clouds beneath which were vaguely visible red-looking continents and strange-looking green oceans.

They were in orbit around the planet.

"George, where are we?" Sally said as she left Dennis behind and ran up to the bald-headed, chubby professor.

He was busily working at the astro-chart station. Alice was beside him, looking very worried.

"Oh, Sally! Thank God you're alright! We thought you and Dennis might have been killed in the engine room. Nothing is responding to our commands! We're drifting aimlessly and..."

"—we're back in the Milky Way!" George interrupted her, trembling with excitement. "Whatever you did, Sally, you got us back home. We're at the center of our Galaxy!"

"It wasn't me," she softly replied, looking up again at the crush of blazing stars above her.

"No?" George asked. His previous delight was now replaced by a frown of deep worry.

"It's apparently an 'old friend' of ours."

"What?"

"It's the Creature that sent the Harvester invasion that decimated Earth...and I fear it's waiting for us on the planet down below."

Alice grabbed onto her husband's chubby shoulders, dismayed.

"If that's so...what does it want from us?" she asked, her voice trembling.

"Well, it's certainly not to kill us," Sally said, fluffing-out her long red-brown hair while closely scrutinizing the foreboding planet below as it swung past in their view (as the Starship kept slowly spinning). "It could have destroyed us long before if that's what it wanted. It was waiting in ambush for us on Kepler-186f, then came after us in the Spike-Ship. Whatever its plan, it wants us alive."

"So what do we do?" Dennis asked as he staggered up to drop to all fours beside them, his big head still bleeding from the gash he'd suffered in the engine room.

"I think we have to go down to the planet," Sally said, squaring her small shoulders in determination. "Do you happen to have any more of those 'demolition units,' Dennis?"

He grinned toothily, pushing himself determinedly back to his feet.

"I sure do," he said, his reptilian voice raspy with excitement. "And I'd love to do some prospecting!"

"But you're injured."

"It's nothing!"

She frowned at him.

"Really! My skull is much thicker than your little human heads. It's just a superficial cut. I'll get a bandage."

"Well...then let's do it."

"Captain?" Alice asked, awaiting orders.

"Ready a shuttlecraft!" Sally grandly directed with a flourish of her arm.

"But they're not operational," George said.

"Give it a try. I suspect that they're now working just fine."

"Oh...you're right!" George exclaimed in surprise. "One of them is indeed responding to my commands—while nothing else on our ship is doing so. What's happening?" George asked in amazement.

"Clearly, the Demon wants us to go to him," Sally nodded.

"And who else is going on your 'away-mission'?" George asked from behind her.

"Clearly, you watched too many 'Star-Trek' programs while you lived among the humans," Sally called back. "It's just me and Dennis. That way only a minimum number of us will be in harm's way. Plus, the two of us make a good team."

"Bandage my head, we're on our way!" Dennis grinned toothily.

In a few minutes they were approaching the shuttlecraft hanger.

"Do we?" Dennis asked, trotting along beside her toward the hanger bay, a big square bandage taped to his head.

"Do we what?"

"Make a 'good team'?"

Sally tried to keep a straight face.

"Well, you laugh at my jokes," she shrugged, not wanting his swollen head to get any bigger.

"Yes, I do...sometimes," he grinned.

"And besides, you might find some real food down there."

"Ahhhhh...now *that* would be delightful!" he said, his orange eyes lighting up with excitement.

"I have a feeling our 'host' will want to keep us happy," Sally now grimly stated. "It's tested us enough. Now it wants to *use* us."

"For what?" Dennis replied.

"I knew once, but I forgot."

"What?" Dennis asked, puzzled.

"Never mind," she sighed as they reached the hanger bay. "Just go load up whatever you think we'll need. I'll check out the shuttle."

She wasn't that eager to follow the lead of Satan, particularly when his intentions were unknown. But perhaps she'd have a few surprises for him as well.

Apparently her "other self" had thrown him a few loops. Maybe she could do so as well?

She knew he was still testing her. She was on trial. She was probably going to be found wanting.

But she was determined that it wouldn't be for lack of her effort.

Chapter 16

THE TRIAL OF SOCRATES

Often humans did things for unobvious reasons
The immediate stimulus just a convenient excuse
Driven by something other than the supposed Problem
Motivated often beyond their ability to even perceive
Still just a collection of 20,000 or so interacting genes
A complex, self-aware, yet largely unconscious Machine
Dancing spryly to the tune of an unseen puppet-master
Did they dare look beneath the superficial Purpose?
Only if they were brave enough not to kick and cry
When all they could finally claim was: "I tried."

Homo sapiens Eulogy, 16:8-10

The proprietor of the inn almost threw Dave out on his ear. Dave didn't blame the man. To him, Dave was just a smelly, impoverished fisherman dressed in sweaty rags standing in the doorway of his fine establishment. But when Dave held up a couple of *glittering silver coins* on his fingertips, the angry innkeeper's disdainful countenance abruptly changed.

"And what can I do for you?" the man hesitantly smiled.

"I want your finest room," Dave replied, affecting a haughty manner. "I am *Davos of Corinth*, here in disguise! I am a wealthy poet and actor. I am here for the trial of Socrates, having first gotten the common man's viewpoint on the street in my present fisherman guise. Now, I wish to regain my proper status. Please have one of your people go out and purchase good clothes for me. I will take a bath in my room to clean off the dirt, grime, and fish-stink."

Despite the absurd story, Dave knew that in any time-period money talks.

"Yes, *Sir!*" the man now enthusiastically answered as Dave tossed a couple more silver coins up on the counter. "Your room is on the top floor. Shall I show you to it?"

"Yes, please," Dave replied, allowing the now-solicitous proprietor to lead him into an opulence he had not seen for many years. Dave's last fifteen years were spent living in a poor fisherman's hut. And before that he'd lived for several years in his own shabby hut in the future Dinosapien world. And previous to that, he'd been in desperate "apocalypse"-style group dwellings. A fine hotel for ancient Greek Aristocrats was a new and expensive experience!

But Dave knew he had to act the part.

He immediately got scissors and carefully trimmed his lengthy beard. Likewise, he cut his long hair to be merely stylishly full on the top of his head.

Now he looked very different from the young shaggy fisherman that had entered the city that morning.

Later, having leisurely bathed for the first time in many years, perfumed and well-clothed in fine wool and linen, Dave felt clean and suitably prosperous. He made sure the sleeves of his tunic hung long enough to cover his Anaconda Tattoo—in case others who'd glimpsed it on the young fisherman might connect him with his prior persona.

Then he went out to eat in a fine restaurant, beginning to establish his identity as a visiting young aristocrat. He was worried he'd be recognized by those to whom he'd sold fish in the marketplace now for the past fifteen years. But that fear was unfounded. As long as the tattoo on his wrist was well-covered, they saw only his supposed wealth, fine clothes, and elegant manners.

Yep, money talks.

So he quickly and easily established a presence in the upper society of Athens.

And only a couple days later the Trial of Socrates began...

It was an all-day affair, a combination circus, rock-concert, and picnic. Thousands attended, crowded into an open area in the Agora of Athens called the People's Court. Dave had attended many other similar events there over his fifteen years in ancient Greece. These were grand, public spectacles. They consisted of rousing speeches and tense drama. In this case, a jury of local male citizens was chosen by lot—five hundred strong! It would be accusers' job to convince each of the jurors that Socrates was guilty of the charges, Socrates' task to defend against the charges.

Dave sat with a group of well-to-do Aristocrats. He'd met them the last couple days at fine restaurants. They'd accepted his story of visiting from Corinth without question. Now, they embraced him as one of their own. They, like the rest of the citizenry, had differing opinions concerning Socrates. Some saw him as an amusing clown. Others hated him because of his arrogant dismissal of their own intellectual power. Still others saw him as a dangerous instigator of insurrection against the stability of the city. Yet others saw him as a religious heretic who railed against the established state-sanctioned gods and traditions. And a few were intrigued by his deep, though biting philosophical insights.

Regardless, the crowd was in the mood for *blood!*

Dave knew that there, in 399 B.C., the crowd was only five years removed from the horrible humiliation and defeat by Athens at the hand of Sparta and her allies. The once-great Athenian Empire was destroyed. Socrates, though not overtly siding with Sparta had, nonetheless, often held up the authoritarian government of Sparta as superior to so-called "common" people directing Athens' affairs.

But even worse, the Athenian democracy was briefly overthrown twice in recent history—from 411-410 B.C. and from 404-403 B.C. And in both cases, the leaders of the insurrections were former students of Socrates! They'd been inspired by his insistence that educated Elites should be society's Rulers. The leader of the first revolt, Alcibiades, even allied himself with Sparta. The leader of the second revolt, Critias, was particularly vicious and bloody. He confiscated the property of many of the Athenian aristocrats, banished thousands of the citizenry to exile, and summarily executed hundreds.

And now they have someone to squarely place blame upon for all those terrible events—Dave observed to himself—not themselves or their leaders, but Socrates!

The charges were read against Socrates. The first charge was "corrupting" the youth of the city. The second charge was "false-teachings" against the city-approved religion. So Socrates was squarely labelled as both an insurrectionist and a heretic. Then, in a three-hour presentation, a detailed case was made against Socrates in support of the charges, consisting largely of quotes from his own speeches. The evidence against Socrates was damning.

Socrates was then allowed three hours to make his own defense against the two related charges. But Dave was shocked that Socrates did not attempt to shoot down the evidence brought up against him. Rather, Socrates appeared to be deliberately needling the jurors: making obscure arguments regarding the proper definition of "piety", brashly invoking his times as a soldier for Athens and the battles he'd fought supposedly heroically, proudly acknowledging his questioning the "virtue" of the people of Athens, and invoking a higher God rather than the so-called "false gods" that the people revered. And as to leading his students astray, he hid behind the "defense" of being a mere "asker-of-questions" rather than a didactic Teacher espousing a particular philosophy.

He knows he's guilty of the charges—Dave mused to himself. *He's getting high on all the attention. And rather than trying to "get off" on some technicality, he prefers that the people condemn him!*

Although it was customary for the accused to bring his family forward as evidence of his good character and solid citizenry, Socrates' wife and three boys were notably absent. Dave took this as further evidence of the fat old man's perverted death-wish.

Dave felt a degree of measured pity for Socrates. The old fat philosopher finally had his "chickens coming home to roost." He'd been tweaking the people with his pious denunciations for a long time. Now, *they* could tweak him back in the worst possible way.

And following Socrates' allowed three-hour defense, it was time for the 500 jurors to vote.

The vote was "guilty"—280 to 220. Yes, it wasn't unanimous. There were still many people to whom Socrates was a revered local celebrity. But the rest were tired of his pompous ways and saw him as a deserving scapegoat for their present troubles.

The only thing left was to determine his punishment.

Both the accusers and accused were then required to suggest an appropriate penalty, upon which the jurors would again vote. The accusers flatly demanded *death*. Socrates, however, had the audacity to demand that his "punishment" should be free meals by the state for the rest of his life. He blatantly claimed himself to be a "hero" of the state whose "penalty" should actually be a reward!

Throughout the crowd around Dave, the people were simultaneously amused and outraged. They either laughed or shouted out their derision!

And, indeed, the jury was not amused. In fact, they were clearly infuriated with Socrates' defiant stance. So they demanded that he and his defenders propose a real punishment.

Socrates shrugged and then proposed that he be fined one piece of silver, a relatively modest fine considering the alternate punishment on the table. This was yet another insult to the jurors, who were even further enraged against him!

At this, Dave abruptly stood up and loudly shouted over the roar of the crowd: "I will add to the fine that Socrates should pay—*ten more pieces of silver!*"

The crowd was momentarily quieted, their attention now focused on the fine-looking young aristocrat holding up high in the air ten silver coins in his hand.

This would deplete Dave's remaining money. But just the offer alone caused him to appear solidly in the camp of the Socrates-supporters.

"And I also will donate to the fine!" another supporter elsewhere volunteered, holding up his hand with some coins.

"And I... And I... And I...!" the cries rang-out across the crowd.

Altogether, a total of *thirty silver coins* were pledged to pay as the penalty for Socrates' guilt. It was a fairly hefty sum of money, equivalent to an average man's wage for ten years.

But it was not to be.

On a vote of 360 to 140, the jurors voted for death over the fine.

A mockingly smirking Socrates was led off to jail.

He'd been condemned to drink a cup of hemlock, which would painfully paralyze and kill him. Thus his outrages against the dictates of the State would be terminated permanently—whether the State was defined as an entity derived from the people or from despots. But by this very act of defiance Dave knew Socrates would be cemented in history as the *principled first martyr for free speech*, thus setting a solid stage for Western individualism in both thought and action!

And so the foundation would also be laid for—in two-and-a-half millennia—the discovery and misuse of generated Dark Energy. That would, subsequently, attract the full attention of the Creator. And thus would arise Judgment Day, the denunciation of *Homo sapiens* as a failed experiment, and its incineration by a solar super-storm. So by getting rid of the irritating clown Socrates, Dave knew the Athenian society was indirectly assuring the doom of all humanity!

Dave was certain that this was indeed a pivotal point in history, one that still could be changed.

"That was quite noble of you, my friend," a young man fervently said to Dave as the crowd started to mill away, "offering a means to save the Master, even though it failed. Are you one of his disciples from afar?"

It was a person about Dave's age, in his early twenties. His thin lips were trembling in rage, tears dripping from his eyes. He had a short beard plus a band around his head, from which curly locks protruded down over his eyes.

"I am Davos of Corinth," Dave politely bowed to the young man. "I am a poet and actor, come to witness this sad but notable event. Socrates is a great man. It pains me terribly to see him treated so poorly—and by his very own people!"

"My name is Plato," the man said, holding out his hand.

Dave gripped the man's hand firmly. "It is a pleasure to meet you, Plato. I have heard of you. You are one of Socrates' most learned and talented disciples—are you not?"

The young man blushed with pride.

"Would you join our group in comforting the Master?" Plato said, his voice trembling with grief. "We have a plan to save his life, but he is very stubborn. An outsider like you might be able to affirm our urgings, perhaps even guide him to a new life elsewhere?"

"It would be my honor," Dave humbly replied. "I am happy to help in any way that I can."

Then, walking beside Plato through the dispersing crowd in the direction of the jail to which Socrates had been taken, Dave smiled to himself.

As a poor, common fisherman Socrates' group hadn't given Dave the time of day—indeed, casually kicking him to the side of the road. Now, as a supposedly rich visiting artist, he was welcomed with opened arms.

It was working out just as Dave had hoped.

Periscus shuffled along the seashore, bitter and dejected.

It was several weeks now since Astraios departed. Periscus hadn't ventured back into the city. He was too miserable. Without his "son" with him he had stopped making daily expeditions out upon the sea to gather fish. So his meager income was depleted. But with the money the god-child gave him, he purchased from travelers passing along the beach enough goods to satisfy his meager needs.

That seashore was now deserted. It was peaceful and beautiful.

The sun was almost set—the colors all around Periscus getting warm and mellow. Even the pounding of the waves on the shore seemed muted. Small crabs scurried out of his path. The sand under his sandals felt softer than usual, his feet sinking into the grains. He heard a flock of seagulls cawing loudly, circling above. They were hunting for dead carcasses washed up from the sea, to drop upon and greedily consume.

"And what of *my* life?" he muttered to himself.

He'd heard that Socrates was convicted and sentenced to death. But it gave him no pleasure. He'd finally gotten to wreck his own personal revenge upon that monster—and yet it left him with no satisfaction! He felt empty, cheated.

That old fool would die with dignity in the near future, still the center of attention of the entire city!

Periscus, in contrast, could go jump off a cliff and nobody would even notice him falling.

But he and the renowned-but-disgraced philosopher now shared something in common. They were both old men, their days of glorious battle long gone. The world had moved on past them. And now they were both just looking for graceful exits from this harsh, cruel world.

Periscus knew he could take the small fortune Dave gave him and travel. But what was the point? Everything he knew and enjoyed was right there in Athens. That was where he was born, raised, dis-graced—and now would die.

Sure, he could keep on fishing. In fact, he'd finally gone out that morning and come back with his net filled. But it gave him no pleas-ure. Nothing did. Now that his "son" was gone, it was just too quiet. He hadn't realized how lonely he'd been before the Star Child fell from the sky. His self-imposed solitude hit him even harder than be-fore.

He might as well face it. His life was finished.

The only question was whether his death would be slow or quick.

And suddenly Periscus knew what he had to do. He felt a lift in his step. It was fitting and heroic. And even though none of his fel-low humans would ever know of it, the *gods* would know!

He would go out in his boat, get out of the small ship into the wa-ter, take the deepest breath he could—and dive straight down toward the giant red spear that'd brought Astraios from the stars. There he would leave what remained of the pouch of silver coins as an offering to the gods. In his youth, he'd been quite good at pearl-diving. As an old man, though, it would be very difficult for him to make a descent, especially that deep. But it would be a fitting final accomplishment since there was no way he'd make it back to the surface.

He'd try to reach the bottom of the sea and drown there. It'd be quick. He wouldn't suffer all that much. And it would be heroic!

Periscus grinned, his one remaining tooth protruding. Yes, this was a good plan. He could beat Socrates to the afterlife—and be there waiting for him! Hah! And it would not be a kind welcome that the famous philosopher received. No, it would be *a cold slap* in his dead, fat face from his most-belittled enemy. Hah!

He would finally beat Socrates at something!

Filled with new-found excitement, Periscus started to turn back to where his boat was moored when he noticed something strange ahead of him.

The flock of seagulls had descended and landed on the beach. Now they were clustered around something on the sand ahead—*pecking* and running, *pecking* and running.

"What is this?" Periscus said to himself, frowning. He wanted to turn back, get to his boat, climb in, and get about his final task—but, despite his eagerness to die, he was intrigued.

He'd never seen seagulls act this way before.

"Eh?" he said, puzzled. Taking a few more minutes before going back to the boat wouldn't matter in the long run. He knew that Socrates' execution had been delayed by a month for the city to observe an annual religious rite. Socrates' death wasn't to occur for a few more days. Thus, Periscus knew he had plenty of time left to beat the old man to the afterlife.

So he shuffled on down the seashore. The waves lapped at his sandaled feet as he got closer to the prancing flock of white seagulls.

He saw in the center of them what looked like a torn-apart squid. But, then again, the "squid" had *an arm and hand*...holding something black and shiny.

"Get away! Get away!" he yelled at the birds, sending them flapping up into the sky.

He squatted next to the still-living thing sprawled there on the beach.

It was a bloody mess, raw and putrid-looking. But it was clearly alive. And it had *one white eyeball* peering up at him! And there at the middle of the bloody mass was a strange *iron tool*—the likes of which Periscus had never seen before. Was this...could it be...another fallen god? Twice in his lifetime was he favored to encounter a true god from the heavens?

"Just what are you, strange sea-creature?" he asked rhetorically, not expecting any answer. "*Are* you another god, like my friend Astraios?"

"G-Greek...you...speak...Greek?" came a weak, moist reply from somewhere in the middle of the bloody heap. "A god...you say...Greek god...of the sea...?"

Periscus jumped back, almost falling over!

"Yes, of course I speak Greek!" Periscus weakly squeaked, still not sure if he should stay or run. "We are near Athens, the heart of Greece—or, at least, it used to be before our Empire was destroyed. And you...are you...a *Triton?*"

Periscus knew that Tritons were mermaid-like sea creatures descended from the god of the sea, Poseidon. Tritons could be male or female.

The answer was so faint Periscus the splashing of the waves on the shore almost drowned it out:

"Yes...I am...damaged...in a great battle."

"How can I help you?" Periscus gasped in amazement.

"Help me...find food," the small voice came from inside the bloody tangle of raw flesh. It indeed was speaking Greek, though the accent was very strange. Periscus could not place it. But that was not surprising. After all, this creature was a minor god of the sea!

"Food?" Periscus dumbly repeated.

"Anything..." the sputtering voice replied, becoming even weaker. "Preferably...protein...I must...rebuild myself."

"Would fish do for you?" the old man asked.

"Yes..." the thing replied, now so faintly that Periscus could barely hear it.

The fisherman took off his tunic and carefully wrapped it around the bloody mess. He managed to keep the ripped-up parts together, lifting it up as one piece. Cradled in Periscus' one arm, the creature and its iron hammer were surprisingly heavy. Also, the iron thing was HOT—with a *pulsating glow* emanating from it! But he managed to carry the fallen god and its iron tool without dropping them—all the way back to his hut.

There, he placed the quivering, bloody heap tenderly into his wheelbarrow before covering it over with a thick layer of fish that he'd caught that very morning. Then he covered everything with a woven blanket. He could still see the red glow from inside shining up through the fabric.

He had no idea what would happen.

But he was intrigued. The thought of suicide was no longer so compelling.

He had something to live for. He had in his possession yet another god!

Take *that*, Socrates! For all your jabbering, did you ever have in your hut not one, but *two* gods?

Periscus lay contentedly on his mat as the night descended upon him. He was exhausted, his well-exercised one arm strained badly—but he felt mentally exhilarated!

Perhaps he didn't have to die after all? Was he no longer merely a walking corpse?

For the first time since Astraios had left him, he was happy.

Chapter 17

<u>THE WALKING DEAD</u>

Did they not struggle?
To live just another day
To breathe another breath
To stave off death and decay
To barely manage to survive
When it'd been so much easier
Just to give up and decay-away
Admirable quality of persistence
Those pesky humans so hard to kill
Swarming with life-energy replete
Not just as individuals but species
That even when they fell and died
They often got back up again
Insisting on resurrection
In one form or another
Rising to walk yet again!
Homo sapiens Eulogy, 17:26-30

Sally and Dennis were ready to go.

They were in a small shuttlecraft just large enough to hold them plus some cargo. It was an elegant craft with a tail section, short wings on each side, large clear canopy cockpit with stations for a pilot and copilot, and a small sitting or storage area right behind them. In that seat was piled a number of tools and other supplies.

It was not much bigger than a small sports car. Everything was of one piece, molded out of a plastic-like substance. According to Dennis it was powered and protected by a very small DE-generator that projected a thin external force-field. Thus the shuttle didn't need a durable frame.

It had stopped functioning when they encountered the Spike-Ships at Keplar-186f. But now it worked fine!

Sally found it all very suspicious.

"Exactly how did your people ever manage to build all these things in the few years that you've been here in the future after escaping through the Portal from the distant past?" Sally asked Dennis as they sat waiting for the shuttle bay to de-gas before lifting the exit door to space. "You have starships and shuttlecrafts and sophisticated tools and even cities. There's no way you could bring all that through the Portal."

Dennis grinned at her toothily, his big dinosaur head nodding in agreement. They were both in their spacesuits, not having any idea what environment they'd discover on the planet's surface down below. Dennis was in the pilot seat, since he claimed to know how to fly the shuttle. The seats were spacious to accommodate the big Dinosapiens. A slot was even cut through the back of the chair to allow their thick tails to stick through and curl up behind the seats. Even with the seatbelt at its tightest, Sally still felt unsecured in her own roomy seat next to Dennis.

"We managed to bring through a few key *duplicator units*," he replied. "That plus our extensive specification manuals-files were enough to allow us to quickly manufacture the parts to larger duplicators and so on."

"What's a 'duplicator unit'?" Sally asked, intrigued.

"With unlimited energy—as from our DE-generators that are far-advanced beyond what your people ever constructed—anything is possible," Dennis stated. "A duplicator unit uses massive amounts of energy to construct, atom-by-atom, an exact replica of whatever is in its database. You could think of it as one of your people's '3D-printers' but at an exponentially greater level. Does that answer your question, Sally?"

"Wow!" she gushed. "That's incredible! It sounds very much like the Spike-Ship bubble-displays. So you just give it matter to work with—say a pile of rocks or dirt—and the atoms are rearranged to become a house, a shuttlecraft, or whatever?"

"Well...it's far more complex than that," Dennis shrugged, "but that's the general idea. And, yes, the bubbles we encountered were of a similar nature, though they were mostly holographic. Also, when they were reconstituting their ship it seemed to me that pieces appeared out of nowhere. I think they were converting energy directly to matter, not just reconfiguring existing matter like we do. So whatever technology they're using is far advanced from ours. But we still manage to produce actual physical replicas, within limits, of course."

"Such as?" Sally asked.

"Well, we can't replicate living creatures, something to do with their unique quantum signatures," the Dinosapien patiently explained. "If we try to do so—even for simple viruses or single cells—they emerge looking like the original, but dead. Beside that limitation, however, most everything else is replicable."

"Even food cubes?" she asked.

"Of course."

"Then why are we in danger of starving?" Sally eagerly asked.

"Sally, it takes immense amounts of energy to power the duplicators. Changing dung directly into food cubes is very energy intensive. So for the moment, sadly, primitive cultivation is our only option."

"Oh, right," she nodded, understanding. Since the Starship's central generator was destroyed, they didn't have the mammoth power necessary to directly produce food cubes.

"But then why not use the shuttlecraft's power units since this and maybe others are now working?" she persisted. "Couldn't we...?"

"—because they're 'all-of-one-piece', Sally," Dennis impatiently interrupted. "When the shuttles were themselves duplicated from our files, everything in them is dedicated to specific purposes. Parts can't just be taken out, diverted, or repurposed. I wish they could, but they can't. Everything's dedicated to specific integrated functions."

"Oh," she nodded again. "I guess mass manufacturing does have drawbacks."

She shrugged, eager to launch.

"The air in the hanger is down to near-vacuum," Dennis observed, looking at the few, simple readouts on the control panel. "Are we ready to depart?"

"You remember our plan?" Sally asked.

"Of course, Sally," he answered. "I have a photographic memory. Our contingencies are clear. But...I suspect and fear that we have not anticipated everything. We may need to improvise, an activity that you are by far my superior."

"Nice of you to admit I'm better than you," Sally glibly replied.

"In *some* ways," he tartly observed.

"Then I'm ready to go," Sally huffed in reply, firmly nodding in her helmet.

She had room to move her head in the helmet since her fluffy red-brown hair was again tied up in a bun at the back of her head.

"Alice, please open the shuttle bay door," Dennis spoke into his own helmet.

"*Opening...*" came the static-ridden reply. The ship's intercom in the shuttle bay was still sporadic. A few of the ship's systems were now operating, in particular (thankfully) life-support. It seemed the Demon down below didn't want them to die just yet.

As the large hanger door in front of them started pulling upward, the star-studded crowded space around them was revealed in all its glory.

"Wow!" Alice gasped again as their craft floated out of the hanger and into space.

Hanging beside them was their still aimlessly rotating spaceship, passively orbiting the planet below.

Down below them was the planet, from which *a focused, polarized* BLUE LASER BEAM extended from somewhere on the surface up through scattered orange clouds to intersect with the ship!

"It appears we are being summoned," Dennis said, aligning the craft with the beam.

"Then let's go knock on his door," Sally eagerly agreed.

Taking the steering lever firmly into his three-clawed glove, Dennis fired the rockets in the rear of their craft that plunged them into the orange clouds!

Blazing fire sprang up around them as they hit the atmosphere, superheating the air with the speed of their passage.

"W-will the s-shield protect u-us?" Sally stammered as the craft rocked back and forth violently as they plunged ever deeper into the atmosphere, shedding their orbital speed as kinetic energy.

"Do not fear, Sally," Dennis replied, his hand steady on the control stick. "I am a good pilot."

"H-how m-many t-times have you d-done this?" Sally gasped as she was whipped back and forth in her seat.

"In simulations, more than a dozen times," the intelligent dinosaur replied.

"And in r-real life?" she asked.

"This is my first actual trip," he mildly replied. "We are not in danger of exceeding the shield's capacity to deflect the heat. We are only at 95% of its absorbance."

Yikes!—only 5% tolerance left! Horrors! Sally was suddenly not so confident that they'd ever find out what the Demon was up to. She and Dennis might end up as a bright flare in the orange sky!

But then they emerged beneath the acrid orange clouds—now arching instead of plunging, traveling at a high rate of speed across a broken, crater-scared, rocky plain.

The ride became much smoother.

Great gashes and canyons stood out below. Nowhere was there any sign of greenery or any other evidence of life.

To Sally it looked very much like the surface of Mars. In such a vast desolation, where was their destination?

But the blue laser beam was still guiding them.

"Look there!" Dennis said, pointing with his free hand.

Indeed, by following the blue path in the sky they were fast-approaching what looked like an enormous ancient Temple. It had mile-high transparent columns of strange spiral shapes that went at odd angles. It was truly gigantic, the size of a large city on Earth. And at the top of the columns was a supported, flat plateau made of the same transparent material.

As they fast approached it, Sally saw at the center of the flat plateau the source of the huge, pulsating blue laser beam: a house-sized, shimmering *blue globe*.

"Hang on, Sally!" Dennis warned her.

He was bringing them in fast for a *hard landing!*

—as with a loud BANG they dropped the last few feet in free fall, *bouncing* once upon the transparent surface before settling down!

Banged-up but otherwise unhurt, Sally finally relaxed—looking out at the house-sized blue Globe looming in front of her.

The blue laser blazing up into the sky abruptly blinked-off.

"They know we're here," Sally gulped.

It seemed oddly familiar, as if she'd been there before?

"Well, we made it," Dennis sighed, turning off the shuttlecraft engine.

"Then let's go," Sally said. "I'll take that laser-drill 'tool' of yours."

"Of course, Sally," he answered as he popped up the canopy.

He reached behind his seat for the drill, handing it to Sally. Then he took several other items from the back seat to attach to the workbelt at the waist of his spacesuit. Finally he lithely hopped out of the pilot seat to the ground below.

"We could probably breathe this air," Sally said from above him, still in her seat. "The analyzer says it is thick with sulfur, but still has enough oxygen for us."

"But we'll be *very* cautious, *won't* we Sally?" Dennis firmly insisted, walking around to her side to help her step down. "We'll keep our helmets on, right?"

"Quite right," she agreeably answered. "That monster might have hallucinogens or sedatives in the air to greet us. Our suits offer protection."

The surface was perfectly smooth, difficult to walk upon without falling. But, supporting each other, they managed to shuffle to the house-sized blue Globe.

As soon as Sally placed the white glove of her spacesuit upon its surface, a circular door opened in its side.

"Shall we?" Sally invited Dennis.

"It's why we came here, isn't it?" the Dinosapien stated.

Sally entered into the Globe, closely followed by Dennis.

Immediately the opening sealed itself shut behind them.

Inside, Sally was astonished. It seemed like they'd entered another world.

Although the Globe externally looked no bigger than a small house, inside it expanded out into a large valley filled with huge, flourishing flowers of every color imaginable!

The giant blossoms loomed up above their heads.

A gentle breeze was blowing, stirring the tall flowers. Overhead, a sun much like Earth's seemed to hang in a blue sky. Mountains lined the valley, upon which greenery glistened. A few white clouds drifted past in the sky.

Strange, gossamer-winged "butterflies" flitted around them.

"Dennis, where are you?" Sally barked out into her helmet, suddenly realizing that he was no longer with her.

"Do not worry about him," a kind, quavering, elderly voice pleasantly replied from her helmet speaker. "He is quite fine, I assure you."

Walking out of the vast Garden was an old bald oriental man wearing dark-rimmed glasses, clad in a simple red robe! A touch of orange at his shoulder accented his appearance. On his feet were simple sandals. He was smiling in a beguilingly friendly way.

Sally recognized him. It was the spitting-image of the 14th *Dalai Lama* of Tibet!

"I'm sure you are more comfortable with this visage than the evil satanic one I used previously," he gently smiled at her. "I must apologize for my bad behavior, Sally," he continued, slowly approaching her. "I was out of sorts, you having trapped me in that generator far away from my normal power sources. I reverted to my worst nature. But I want to make amends, so..."

"Where is *Dennis?*" Sally fiercely yelled at him, grabbing her laser drill to point straight at his "kindly" face.

"I just sent him back to his little transport vehicle," the Creature replied, now sounding a trifle irritated. "He is of no consequence, Sally. Is he not just your glorified chauffeur? This is entirely between the two of us. I assure you—*again*—that he is perfectly fine. I am not looking to harm either you or your friends. Is that not obvious? I could have easily disintegrated the lot of you while you were up in orbit, but I did not."

Sally continued to hold her gun on him, not convinced by his slick words. Indeed, she remembered all too well battling him to the death in the Wilderness of Judea. This was not a kindly religious leader, but an ancient, evil monster masquerading as such. If he didn't kill them immediately it was only because he needed them for something, *not* out of any kindness.

"How is it that you are so much more powerful here?" she asked, keeping her gun pointed at his bald head.

"You saw my power-source from orbit, did you not?"

"What?"

"It's the Black Hole—you saw the accretion disc? It fills half the sky. You could hardly miss it!"

"You draw power from it?"

"In ways you cannot even imagine," he grinned. "I am the remaining Essence of a very powerful race, left to fulfill a marvelous Mission—one in which you play a pivotal role. You, from a disgraced and destroyed race, should feel honored to be in my Presence, *not* angry at me."

"Just what is it you want from me?" Sally crisply asked.

"Oh, before we get down to business I have wonderful things to show you—which I'm sure you will find very extremely interesting," he obliquely answered.

"I doubt that."

"And do lower that silly weapon," he laughed gently, turning to quickly stride back in the direction he'd come from. "It can't harm me and it looks heavy to hold out for so long in front of you. Please follow me, Sally."

Reluctantly, she lowered the laser drill and attached it back to the workbelt at her waist. She walked forward with determination, her eyes darting about, and then having to sprint to catch up to him.

For an older man, he was quite spry!

It only took a few minutes walking beneath the looming, giant flowers to arrive at a plain, wooden house.

"Please come inside, Sally," he invited her from the doorway. "This is where I keep my most-prized possessions. You will find my Collection fascinating, I assure you!"

Suspiciously, she clomped forward in her spacesuit, walking up short concrete steps to enter the house.

Inside, on a table, were laid out what appeared to be fresh bread, jams to put on the bread, sliced meats, roasted potatoes, pies, and tankards filled with a frothy, golden beverage.

"It's just a snack for you," he graciously indicated for her to sit on one of the human-sized chairs. "Please, remove your helmet and eat.

The drink is similar to your honey-flavored wines, I think, though containing no ethanol—suitable to your religious beliefs. The Animists of your extinct race only used stimulants in high-ceremonies, right? I made this meal after reading your mind. Is it acceptable?"

Sally was tempted. For far too long she'd been surviving on spongy nutrition cubes plus a few cultivated vegetables. The feast set out before her looked delicious!

But she regarded it with suspicion. She wasn't going to let this ancient Beast beguile her.

"I'm not hungry," she firmly stated. "If you must do so before we 'get down to business' then show me this 'collection' of yours. And stay *out* of my head! You may be my 'superior' intellectually, but you neither impress me nor win my cooperation by invading my privacy."

The kindly Buddhist figure nodded agreeably. "Perhaps you'd like to eat later, then. I can bring your friend in for that. Indeed, I can bring down your entire crew! Wouldn't that be fun? But..." he quickly continued, seeing her angry expression through the clear helmet that she still had firmly sealed upon her head, "it can be after you have the 'big picture' that you so desire. And I was only trying to be hospitable to you, reading only your superficial emotions and random thoughts. Since I want—and need—your unreserved cooperation, I will gladly do as you ask."

He stood up from his chair and motioned for her to follow.

As she stomped forward in her spacesuit she snatched a couple well-done steaks from the feast on the table, stuffing them into an outside pocket of her pants.

And so they walked down some stairs into a basement area. It was huge! It was lit by a pale green light.

"This is my private collection, containing my most-prized specimens," he proudly said. "Please, take a look around for yourself."

There were transparent *tubes* standing upright everywhere that Sally looked. Each tube was ten feet high and four feet in diameter. The inner surfaces were fogged up. But here and there were clear patches that allowed one to see into the interiors.

Sally gasped, shocked at what she saw in the nearest tube.

"It can't be," she gasped, looking closely.

But, yes, it was *herself!*

Frozen in place, staring sightlessly back at Sally, she saw a slender girl: five foot four inches tall, slim, in her early twenties, with long fluffy brown hair, and bright green eyes!

And on the woman's wrist, just visible through the fog on the inside of the tube, was a green-glowing *Turtle Tattoo*.

"What the hell *is* this?" she sharply asked the Creature, turning to glare at him out of her transparent helmet.

"Why, it's you, of course," he smiled benignly back at her, his oriental eyes mere slits now.

"Is this a hologram information-storage image—like on the Spike-Ship?" she barked at him.

"No nothing like that. It's actually..."

"—or is it a dead replica, like Dennis' Dinosapien race can make?" she pressed him.

"Oh, it's very much alive, I assure you—though at the moment *frozen in time*," he nodded politely at her.

"So you made...a *duplicate* of me?" she said. "Why? And why did you make it older than me? I'm only a teenager!" she said, peering closer at the woman through the fog inside the tube.

"Oh, no, Sally," the Creature said, walking up close behind her to stick his kindly Buddhist-looking face alongside of hers to peer at the motionless figure in the tube. "It is *not* a duplicate of you."

"Stop playing games with me! Stop telling me lies!" she yelled at him, jerking back away from his ominous presence at her shoulder.

"Well, perhaps looking further will convince you of the truth of the matter," he mildly stated, walking to the next tube and gesturing her to come over.

Reluctantly, she stomped over in her spacesuit, peering closely...

—to see an *older* version of her own self, possibly in her late twenties...with a particularly sour expression on her frozen face!

"And, last but not least..." the red-robed figured gestured again for Sally to follow to yet another tube.

Looking in, Sally gasped out loud.

Inside was *yet another version of herself*, this time clearly middle-aged—with wrinkles around her eyes and at the corners of her mouth!

"Do you like my Collection so far?" the image of the Dalai Lama now imperiously stared at her.

Sally looked around in the dim green light at the many other tubes. What or who was in the rest of them? Were they really alive? Were the different versions of her truly real or just three-dimensional representations?

"Explain!" she snapped at him.

He spread his hands as if to calm her.

"From my powerbase here, perched on the edge of the Black Hole, I can reach through time and pluck out whatever I wish. There are constraints on me, of course—but within reason I can take what I wish if I substitute an exact, dead facsimile in its place."

"So these women...?"

"Yes, Sally, they are the actual 'you' from three separate timelines. The first early-twenties version of you is the heroic version I fought against in a Harvester—who caused the crash that destroyed your Cheyenne Mountain military base...incidentally triggering your Nuclear Winter," he grinned. "She was just like you, spunky!"

"—and the second, somewhat older one?" Sally prodded him.

"Oh, the late-twenties you is the Sally that collaborated with Dave to start the Dark Energy revolution before being killed in an explosion trying to steal the head of a Reaper robot...hah! That was quite entertaining," he coyly giggled. "She was a real pistol!"

"And the third, middle-aged woman?" Sally asked, not ready to believe his incredible claim but still fascinated.

"Oh, I grabbed her out of the Cheyenne Mountain Nuclear Bunker just as the Harvester smashed into it. She was you before you started your Mars retreat nonsense, before you traveled back in time to interact with your historical Jesus, turning into your present teenaged self," he grinned again. "She had 'charisma' as you say—leading a war of fanatical nuns against the 'evil' Dark Energy scientists, as you did. But she was sidetracked from your timeline by the invasion of the Harvesters. She faced death trying to stop the launch of ten Dark Energy ballistic missiles. She thought that doing so would stop God from noticing you filthy little humans! Hah! Fat chance..."

Sally backed off a few steps, glancing at her oxygen gauge projected on the inside corner of her helmet. She still had several hours before she'd have to lift up her helmet and breathe the surrounding air. She didn't want to do that. She liked being isolated from the Creature, with a barrier between her and him, even if it was only the plastic of her helmet or the tough fabric of her spacesuit.

"Why?" she softly asked. "Is this just pandering to your own ego, collecting souvenirs? Or is there some method to your madness?"

Faster than she could follow with her eyes, he was at her elbow, grabbing her and then dragging her upstairs.

He casually threw her into one of the chairs.

"I HAVE BEEN WAITING PATIENTLY FOR A BILLION YEARS TO START MY OWN NEW UNIVERSE!" he *screeched* gleefully at her as his form changed from the kindly Buddhist priest back to the demonic form of *Satan!*

His booming voice shook the walls around them.

He happily flourished his giant pitchfork up in the air!

"What do you mean...your *own* Universe?" Sally whispered, her eyes narrowing.

"My plan is to *poison* the *White Hole* that's forming on the other side of our galaxy's Black Hole! But my plan was put on hold by the Creator," he seethed, prancing back and forth, his horns raking the high wood ceiling. "So my Harvester that's filled with millions of you ugly humans has been orbiting incredibly rapidly right outside the Event Horizon—the *time dilation* effect from the immense gravity of the Black Hole keeping the ship in effective stasis."

"You...y-you have...*millions* of us?" Sally gasped. "And I thought that Dave and I were..."

"—the last of your wretched species?" the snorting Demon laughed, "Hardly! I salvaged plenty of your vile kindred off your Earth's surface, right before the God Barrier dropped! I meant to populate a whole new, developing Universe with your kind. But God saw fit to stop me in my tracks. If I attempt to insert them into the Black Hole they'll be snuffed out...but...*not* with *you* aboard, my dear Sally!"

She cowered back in her chair, shuddering. This was unthinkable. This was impossible. But...then again...the fact that she was here a billion years in the future, on a planet in the Galactic Core—was itself rather "impossible."

"Me? How could I possibly be so important? But...is that why you snagged the other versions of me?"

"Ah, now you understand," the Demon grinned, slamming a big red fist upon the table, *crushing* it to the floor and scattering the dishes of food. "I was hoping the other versions of you would be enough. I was prepared to launch the orbiting Harvester into the Black Hole with them as insurance against its destruction. But I wasn't certain. Somehow, the *original you* is valued by the Creator above all the rest. You hold a special place in the 'heart' of the Creator. So I held off—hoping that someday you would reappear...and here you are! I'm admirably patient, am I not?"

"I'll never help you," Sally said, rising slowly up from her chair and turning toward the door. "Kill me if you want. Duplicate me if you must. But whatever your evil scheme I'll not..."

"NO!" the Demon *roared* as he yet again changed his form once more...becoming a duplicate of the cheerfully smiling Tommy-robot!

"Mommy!" he said in a sweet little-boy voice. "Please help the nice Monster! He just wants his own Universe to rule all by himself, where God won't come because it's so filthy and ugly! But you can stop the humans from being erased! They can live in the nice Monster's other Universe! You can be there to guide them, Mommy. You know how to make them be good. You're a good Mommy. Please help him!"

Sally jerked up her laser-drill and fired directly at the Tommy-figure, who staggered back, clutching his burnt-off face in dismay!

She ran towards the door, trying to escape.

"That was a good try," the Creature said, blocking her exit now as a *giant, octopus-like creature* with waving green tentacles!

She recoiled in disgust.

His red, spider-like eyes stared unblinkingly at her. They were scattered around several especially-lumpy appendages. Blue filters that looked like layered gills fluttered periodically, sucking in air. Crinkled ceramic-looking plates protected a brain-like area.

A mucous-covered slit in the middle served as a mouth.

It flopped open and closed, open and closed...

"This is my true form—many millennia ago when my people swam the warm green seas of this planet," a raspy voice emanated from several membranous orbs. "I show it to nobody. You are the first. It is a token of my respect, you *Twister of Time!*"

"Thank you so much for the honor," Sally sarcastically replied. "But I'm allergic to shellfish!"

She stepped backward, avoiding the thrashing tentacles.

"But I have *more* inducements for you other than multiple versions of yourself plus millions of your fellow humans to save," the oily voice sputtered. "I have *much* more that *will* persuade you to voluntarily help me."

"What do you mean?" she glared at him.

"I've also snatched other long-lost humans from the timelines, those with a special connection to you and your other incarnations," the revolting Creature wetly-spoke. "Down in my special collection I have time-frozen, living versions of...oh, let me remember here— Ivanna and her dear, sweet husband, Professor Volodymyr...and Dave's mother...and, oh yes, even your *own* mother!"

Sally sank into a still-standing chair, her thoughts swirling. "They...they're still alive...the *real* ones?" she whispered.

"Yes! And they can all be with you again, in a new world, where your dinosaur and reptile 'friends' won't be trying to keep you from breeding! Indeed, I *WANT* ALL YOU DISGUSTING, VILE ANIMALS TO REPRODUCE WITHOUT LIMIT," he roared up at the ceiling, "TO FILL UP A MILLION, BILLION, TRILLION WORLDS!—THE MORE THE MERRIER—TO REPEL A SUITABLY DISGUSTED CREATOR WHILE PROVIDING ME WITH ENDLESS AMUSEMENT!"

The tentacles all thrashed wildly at this loud declaration.

"You're *sick!*" she glared at him.

"No!" he laughed. "Hey, I *love* you putrid little rat-mammals! You're my kind of people! And you're going to be my new army to conquer and keep subjugated a whole new Universe. So surely you can see where your allegiance *must* be placed? I could just take you without your consent—which might be sufficient for my purposes. But having you *want* to join the Harvester will *definitely* stop the Creator from interfering. I want your *willing* participation, Sally. Think of all you've got to gain! Surely that's better than your stilted existence under the thumb of intelligent snakes and lizards? They're just *tolerating* you until you die-out."

"But...to leave my own world behind..." she gulped, the persistence of the Creature starting to wear her down.

She was confused. It was hard to think straight. It was getting hot in her helmet. Her head was spinning. She was getting very weak, slumping in the chair. And the one thing she wanted most he couldn't offer her.

"Oh, are you thinking of your little boyfriend 'Dave'?" the sputtering sea-creature seemingly kindly asked.

"No...he's long dead now...over five hundred years in the past," she reluctantly admitted, tears forming in her eyes.

"Phaw!" the creature spat, writhing its tentacles. "That fool—soon after you left on your spaceship—found a way to slip back into the time-stream," the octopus-like creature sputtered angrily. "I haven't yet located him...but not to worry, my dear Sally!"

"Gone?" she said, shaking her head in total confusion. Dave had vanished back into the time-stream? But he was supposed to be dead, five hundred years in the past! Did that mean...somewhere, some *when*, he was *still alive?*

"Oh don't bother your little head about that would-be lover, your 'number two timeline' Dave," he sputtered again at her. "In my collection...I've also got one of *him!*" he exclaimed in triumph.

"What...how?" she gasped.

"It's the *original* Dave that you refused to shoot in the head, right before you altered the timeline the first time," he evilly laughed. "Yes! It's your very first little boyfriend, snatched from gaping stupidly at you at the podium of the United Nations General Assembly chamber! Just like you, he's an 'original.' *Think* of it, Sally! You can be with your own dear Dave again in a whole new *Homo sapiens* planet of your very own making. Under my benign oversight you can be the *Queen and King* of your very own world."

Sally swiftly contemplated her options, sitting silently in the chair. On the floor of the wooden house, the tentacles of the revolting sea-creature writhed expectantly. She knew that she could not trust this vile Demon. She knew he wasn't telling her all the truth. He was leaving something out, something critical. But then again, what choice did she have?

She made up her mind.

It would be an incredibly painful sacrifice, but she could not let this vile Creature succeed!

"Alright then," Sally sighed, setting her teeth together tightly. "*Do it!*" she shouted into her helmet transmitter.

"What...?" the sea-creature said...

—as a HUGE EXPLOSION ripped-through the garden-Globe, *tearing the wooden house to pieces and fracturing the sky!*

—as Sally sailed off into the air, blown-away by the blast, turning and flopping-about, spinning uncontrollably, being battered by debris...

—while around her the only thing she could see was an *inferno of fire and smoke*...with only her tough spacesuit momentarily protecting her!

—as the *shuttlecraft* appeared out of the flames beneath her, strong claws snagging her hand and dragging her into the cockpit, the canopy slamming shut above her...

—the small spaceship continuing to rise into the sky past the orange clouds, turning on its side to insert itself back up into orbit...

—as Sally looked to the side, observing the unmistakable *mushroom cloud* of a huge NUCLEAR EXPLOSION punching up through the roiling clouds beneath them.

It was lit with every color of the rainbow, a sizzling caldron of the most primeval force of them all.

Sally looked now at her blackened, superficially shredded suit. Fortunately, its multiple tough layers plus her helmet had saved her from being killed in the initial blast. Its integrity had not been violated. Those Dinosapiens sure did make good spacesuits!

"You...positioned your 'excavation units' quite nicely," she managed to gasp-out into her helmet transmitter.

"Thank you, Sally," Dennis graciously acknowledged to her from the pilot seat as they exited the atmosphere of the dead planet back into space. Ahead of them she saw the welcome sight of the Dinosapien Starship floating against the blazing panoply of the many close-packed stars. "I did try to focus the different nuclear explosions to hopefully leave the center of the plateau relatively intact, at least for a few seconds. Did I succeed?"

"You succeeded brilliantly," she sighed, finally reaching up to take off her helmet and breathe freely. "For a nonviolent species, you created a marvelous maelstrom!"

"Thank you, Sally," he nodded his big head, still inside his large oblong helmet. "I'm learning. And you apparently did a great job of distracting Satan from monitoring my efforts. We make a great primitively savage team!"

Sally sighed deeply, happy for the back-handed compliment from the pacifist dinosaur.

"Oh, I brought you a snack..."

She pulled out the two smashed-up steaks from her side pocket and plopped them on the dashboard in front of Dennis.

"*Protein!*" he shouted, snatching them both up as he snapped his helmet back, cramming them into his toothy mouth.

Apparently "meat" was not as distasteful as he'd made it out to be.

"You're welcome," she smiled, hearing him loudly gulping them down.

She gazed forward as the Starship grew ever larger. They still would have to tame the alien subspace-generator. Then they'd have to find the time-dilated Harvester that was in close-orbit around the Black Hole. And then they had to get those millions of humans back to Earth—and then back in time to *her* Earth. It all seemed impossible, but she'd already accomplished the seemingly impossible multiple times over!

She hoped that the Creature momentarily vulnerable inside its mushy, soft ancestral form had finally been killed, once and for all.

But it had a disconcerting habit of resurrecting itself.

All she knew was that with the help of the kind-hearted Dinosapien sitting next to her, they'd escaped the Monster's clutches. She'd sacrificed the possibility of reanimating her dead friends and relatives. But...in truth they had already died, respectfully and heroically. They didn't need to be resurrected. They'd completed their lives with honor. Now, they could rest in peace.

But *she* was still alive. And she had a defined task to complete—the first step being to cement their escape!

There was no time to lose.

Chapter 18

<u>RESURRECTION</u>

Don't discount the future

Even when the present is killed

Sure, you might not get there intact

But even broken there's a way forward

Maybe not what you hoped or expected

But even in an entirely different form

You might again see the light of day

From a whole different perspective

With a completely new attitude

Rejoicing rather than crying

Celebrating not moaning

A fresh, new Creation!

Homo sapiens Eulogy, 18:59-62

As the sun arose—casting long shadows while illuminating the valley in its warm glow—Snake was dreamily contemplating the superiority of mammalian to reptilian sex.

In his previous Dimension sexual coupling was a highly regulated, ritualistic endeavor. It occurred only during the appointed breeding season, between select individuals. Typically it involved a single mating event properly supervised and authorized by a governing Board of Reproduction. Love did not enter into the equation. It was a clinical procedure driven by necessity rather than passion. Also, it was rare for a male and female to have a lasting relationship. It was similar to their remote snake ancestors. Reproduction for most wild snakes is a yearly occurrence between otherwise-isolated, solitary individuals.

Snake found his sexual encounter with the human-form Casandra entirely different from that of his reptilian society. There was genuine affection. It wasn't just for procreation, but recreation. It wasn't a mandated necessity, but a mutual joining. And once it was over it wasn't finished—Snake was surprised and pleased to feel additional stirrings in both his loins and mind!

Casandra was cuddled in his arms, still sleeping, as they both lay naked beneath the sheltering blanket of their piled-up clothes. Fortunately a thick layer of grass beneath their backs provided a comfortable, insulating bed. True to their stated intention, they'd survived the cold night warm and well.

"Ahhh..." Casandra sighed, her blue eyes flickering open to look at him tenderly. "That was...very pleasant."

He laughed, kissing her on her forehead.

"Want to do it again?" he whispered enticingly, moving a hand to caress her thigh.

"I wish..." she sighed again, slipping out of his arms to get to her knees. She hunted amongst the pile of clothes for her underwear and started putting them on. "But we have more urgent matters to address," she concluded firmly.

Realizing that the moment had passed, Snake reluctantly pushed up out of the warm nest they'd made. He shivered in the morning chill—starting to pull on his own clothes.

The sun was beginning to warm the air. Also, the sunlight cast a cheery glow on the greenery below.

Now standing outside the overhanging ledge, looking back on the valley, they saw that the fires of the burning shuttlecraft had gone out. Only wisps of black smoke were still rising. Off in the distance, the "thudding" had stopped—either because the bombardment had been unsuccessful or the cities had fallen.

"I wonder if either our people or the Dinosapiens have launched a counterattack?" Casandra said nervously. "We have the means to probe and analyze those alien ships. Surely there's some weakness we can exploit?"

Snake shrugged, taking the shorter, stouter Casandra in his thin arms and hugging her tightly.

"I don't know," he said, putting his goateed chin affectionately upon the top of her head. "The attack was such a surprise I doubt our scientists even had a chance to consider what was possible. We may be the last two of our kind alive. How about that? Our ancestors migrated here from Mars as the last survivors of a dying world. And now we end up here on Earth, yet again the last sapient indigenous creatures?"

"But we're certainly *not* dead. We are still alive," Casandra stated with firm determination. She brusquely moved out of his arms to survey the land around them. "And even if we are the last of our species—masquerading in human form—we've a duty to persist."

At the moment, none of the Spike-Ships were overhead. Yesterday, Snake and Casandra were dashing from hiding place to hiding place as hunted fugitives. Now was their first chance to pause and take stock of their situation.

Overhead, a flock of the black "birds" that'd saved them from discovery were circling lazily.

They began "cawing" loudly.

Casandra and Dave looked up. As they did, one of the birds dropped out of the flock and *zoomed* down at them.

They ducked as it barely missed their heads and lazily flapped away...toward the end of the valley.

"Snake, just what is beyond this valley?" Casandra asked. Her blue eyes narrowed in concentration.

"Well...I don't know, my dear Casandra," he shrugged again. "In our Dimension this valley was located in an arid desert with no nearby inhabitations. In the human Dimension it was called the Wilderness of Judea. It was part of what was called the Holy Land, fought over by their various religions. I think—in the direction which that bird flew—was the Earth city of *Jerusalem*. Of course, that was a billion years ago. What with tectonic shifts, continental drift, the upthrusting of new mountain ranges, and natural weathering mechanisms..."

"—probably nothing of that ancient city remains," Casandra finished his thought. "But at least it's a destination. We can't go back to Dave's hut or to our cities. Those aliens would catch and kill us for sure."

Snake nodded.

"You know, there might be tunnels or caverns still existing in the Jerusalem area," he mused. "Jerusalem was known for its extensive underground networks, carved out of soft limestone."

"Then that's where we'll go," Casandra firmly stated. "We can follow the river out of the valley. It'll give us plenty of fresh water to drink. But what will we eat? I'm getting very hungry."

"The river should have fish in it," Snake observed, taking Casandra's hand and leading her on down the slope toward the gushing mountain river below.

"Meat?" she grimaced, clearly appalled at the idea of eating the flesh of another living creature.

"It's still too early in the spring for any wild fruits, nuts, or vegetables," he observed. "The other land animals are too fast for us to grab or trap. I think fish are our only option. We can use some of the thread in our clothes to make a fishing line or even a small net."

"Do we have to?" she said, shuddering.

"We no longer have beamers to inject nutrients directly into our bloodstreams," he reminded her. "We're going to have to revert to our ancestral habits. Actually, in the years I spent in the human Dimension I acquired a taste for 'smoked catfish.' "

"You smoked fish?" she gasped in amazement. "Wouldn't that be an impractical way to assimilate their nutrients—sucking their burnt remnants into your lungs?"

He laughed.

"Nope," he said, stepping carefully around loose rocks as they walked along. "You suck into your lungs 'weed' not fish. I did that also...but for fish you build a fire from wood and let filets simmer in the heat and the smoke. That's of course after you split the intact animals open, remove their inner organs, and flay off their scales and skin. I worked in a restaurant, my dear. I've done it many times."

"But it's so *disgusting*," she grimaced. "I don't know if I can eat like that."

"Oh, there's a 'secret ingredient' that will make you love my smoked fish," he knowingly nodded.

"What's that?"

"*Starvation*, my dear lady," he replied grimly. "Just a few days of not eating and you'll be happy to gobble-down even worms straight out of the ground."

She gagged, almost throwing up.

This time he didn't laugh at her. It had taken years for him to adjust to the savage, uncivilized ways of humans. He could certainly be considerate of her automatic revulsion.

"I'm cold, dirty, and *already* starving," she replied. "But somehow I'm happier than I've ever been before. Why is that?" she said in wonderment, gazing with her big blue eyes up at the sky.

Snake breathed deeply of the cool, mountain air.

"We have a new life...together," he said, squeezing her hand as he helped her climb down a particularly dangerous decline. "It's a peculiar mammalian phenomenon."

Below was a dense patch of forest. They'd be safe there, hidden from aerial detection. There was plenty of wood to build a warm, carefully hidden fire. And the river ran right beside the trees. Dave knew they'd find lots of fish.

His mouth was already watering in anticipation.

Periscus awoke with much anticipation.

The sun outside was soft, fading. It was late in the afternoon. He'd slept all day long, exhausted from his unaccustomed labors of the night before.

Then he remembered the incredible events of the last evening.

"And what of my little merman?" he grinned, elbowing himself up off his mat and walking over the few steps to his wheelbarrow...

—which was empty!

Where was the mangled god-creature he'd put into the wheelbarrow the night before? Where was the pile of fresh fish he carefully laid over it? Was it...could it have been...just a dream?

Periscus felt his inner excitement collapsing back into the familiar pit of internal depression and despair.

It was just like him to imagine some miracle! Who was he to be visited by the gods? He was just a poor, stupid, used-up old soldier who...

"Good morning," he heard a young, boyish voice from behind him.

He whirled around to see a grinning boy no more than five years old. He wore a neatly-tailored short tunic apparently cut from Periscus' old garments, held securely at his small waist with a short

length of rope. On his feet were child-sized sandals obviously fash-
ioned from the fisherman's castoff footwear. The boy's cherub-like
face was topped with a mop of blond curls.

The boy was carrying a plate of freshly roasted fish filets.

Periscus' mouth hung open in amazement, dumbfounded.

"My name is Timotheus, what's yours?" the young boy grinned up
at him, speaking in perfect Greek.

"I...I...I'm P-Periscus," the old fisherman stammered. "But...are
you the Triton that I found on the beach?"

"Yes, I am," the boy happily replied, handing the tall old man the
plate of steaming fish meat. "I really do appreciate your giving me all
that fish. I used its energy and building-blocks to reconstruct my
body. Wow! I was really in bad shape, huh? But I had some left, so I
went out to your outdoor fireplace and cooked you breakfast. Did I
do well?" he finished hopefully.

Periscus accepted the plate in his one hand and sat cross-legged
on the dirt floor, placing it alongside him. Then he raised the white
meat to his mouth in his trembling hand.

It was delicious, cooked perfectly.

"Thank you," the man mumbled, stuffing the rest of the steaming
meat into his mouth, "You're a very good cook!"

"No, thank *you*," Tommy graciously replied, making a little bow
to the old man. "And, yes, I *do* cook really well. I have the details of
many occupations inside my head. Well, I mean inside my brain—
which fortunately was the last thing to be damaged in my journey
here. So the true 'me' survived relatively intact. At least, I think so?"

"And...*why* did you come here?" Periscus asked, still not sure he
wasn't dreaming.

"I'm looking for a friend of mine," Tommy happily answered.
"Perhaps you've seen him? His name is Mr. Dave King and he came
here in a big red pillar of rock that..."

"—the *Red Spear* from the *Stars*," Periscus gasped, sputtering
fish-bits out of his gaping mouth. "Yes, Timotheus, he is *Astraios!* I
raised him from a child, like you!"

"Like me? He was a young boy?"

"Yes!" he nodded fiercely. "I rescued him from the sea where the Red Spear fell and sank. He almost drowned before I could pull him into my boat. Then he lived with me for the last fifteen years. But..."

Tears now welled up in his eyes as all the memories of past and recent events came flooding back.

"Please tell me!" Tommy urgently asked. He put his small hands on the seated old man's hunched shoulders and looked him square in his face. "Is this 'Astraios' man still alive? Is he here?"

"He...left me...to go follow after that piece of crap, Socrates!" he angrily spat, turning his face away from the young boy. "I think he just used me until he could make himself rich and well-connected. Well...that's alright. He was a good boy...like you...and I wish him the best."

"And where is he now?" Tommy smiled gently at him, reaching with his small hands to turn Periscus' face back to him.

"He's in the city...Athens. He's bumping elbows with all the rich, stuck-up people...I guess."

Periscus was startled by Tommy doing a little "jig" dancing around the insides of the cramped hut.

"Hurray! Yippee! Hurray!" the boy shouted, sticking his small arms straight up into the air above him. "Mr. Dave is still alive! Yay!"

Periscus was glad for the boy but also dejected.

"So I guess you're going to leave me too?" he frowned, looking forlornly at the floor. "But that's alright...you go find him. I'm just glad I could help you. I'm not important...just an old, stupid fisherman."

"No!" Tommy suddenly said, hopping back over to sit next to him.

"No?" Periscus said, surprised by the boy's intense answer.

"I can't help Dave by myself. I need something that's much bigger and stronger. You say that the Red Spear which fell out of the sky is out in the ocean? Do you know its location?"

Periscus nodded.

"Yes, Timotheus, I know exactly. It sank into the ocean nearby, in an area I regularly fish. But it's deep, beyond reach from..."

"Not from me!" Tommy laughed.

"Oh, of course that's right...you're a merman," Periscus nodded knowingly. "You can breathe water."

"Well, something like that," Tommy snickered. "And I can swim real good! At least, I've got instructions in my mind on how to do it."

"So...you're going to dive down to it?"

"Yep."

"But...why?"

"Well, silly—to bring it back up!"

Periscus looked at the magical boy with an even deeper appreciation of his god-powers. Truly, this was a wondrous day for an old fisherman. It was just like in the stories that Periscus enjoyed hearing as a child. It was a *heroic journey*. This was marvelous!

"I am happy to help you however I can," Periscus solemnly promised. "But I'm just an old man with one arm. I don't know how much I can do for you, Timotheus, to..."

"Oh, right—you have only one arm," Tommy interrupted him, apparently only then noticing.

"Yes, Timotheus," the man nodded. "I lost it fighting as a soldier in a war, long ago. Plus I'm a weak old man that..."

"So it's an amputation?" Tommy interrupted him again, reaching his hands toward the stump below Periscus' shoulder. "My Mommy taught me a lot about medicine. She made sure that my body is capable of manufacturing lots of good drugs, 'on-demand'. And I know all about being a doctor. I've got lots of medical treatments in my mind."

"Then I hope your medicine is better than they do it in Athens," Periscus growled, involuntarily cringing back from the boy. "Those bastard doctors butchered me!"

"They cut your arm off?"

"And a poor job at that," the old man sighed. He now allowed the god-creature to feel gingerly at his stump. "I almost died from the loss of blood, let alone the horrible infection from the arrow that..."

"Oh, I can fix it," Tommy matter-of-factly stated.

"What?" Periscus frowned, not understanding.

"You just lie down on your bed, close your eyes, and let me put you back to sleep," Tommy cheerfully ordered the man, leading him over to his dirty mat.

"But I just woke up...?" Periscus protested.

Things were moving very rapidly. What was the boy trying to do? Periscus was perplexed and surprised. But he wasn't afraid. There was something infectious about the boy's good cheer.

"Do you have more fish?" Tommy asked, ignoring the man's objections.

"There's some drying in the sun out behind the hut on rocks, leastwise drying today—it's getting to be evening again...?" Periscus said, totally bewildered why the god-child wanted more fish.

"That'll be fine," Tommy said, putting a now-hot hand upon the old man's temple. The small hand at Periscus' forehead suddenly felt *slippery*. "Now, I'm secreting something that will make you very, very sleepy."

Feeling a peculiar, woozy sensation, Periscus felt his eyes closing...

If this was a dream, he didn't want to wake up.

Chapter 19

ZOMBIES

Sometimes resurrection is a bitch
Especially when the undead are mere shells
What once before animated, now departed
Those cold, lifeless eyes darting here and there
When the clammy skin should lie motionless
It's a horror unlike any other imaginable
A jerking, twitching, stumbling and bumbling
A tortured shuffle where once the person ran
A peaceful, dignified ending often desirable
Versus that awful indignity of continuing onward
Past the point where it should all have ended
The cycle of life aborted, tossed to the side
Can have consequences unanticipated
Be grateful for what you once received
Rather than always wanting more.
Homo sapiens Eulogy, 19:37-41

The execution of Socrates was looming, yet his inner circle still did not fully accept "Davos of Corinth." Dave didn't blame them. They'd been with the Master for years. Now, approaching the end of their interaction with Socrates, they were a tight, close-knit group wary of outsiders.

But Plato lobbied hard for Dave's inclusion in their group.

Although the young man had not yet made good on getting Dave allowed to visit Socrates in prison, he "clicked" with Dave. After all, they were of the same physiological age, with similar interests. So they had long discussions on music, writing, and philosophy. Together they sang harmony on popular songs, accompanied by Dave on one of Plato's fine collection of vintage lyres. Plato was from one of the wealthiest and most politically connected families in Athens. He was well educated. Dave, holding a future Ph.D. in physics with considerable engineering experience—plus a lifelong love of singing and playing the guitar—got along with him famously.

And unlike the acerbic Socrates, Plato had a very sweet and agreeable disposition. He was polite and considerate. He was a prolific writer who'd already written several, though as-yet not performed, plays. Dave, pretending to be an actor himself, made a point of reading and lavishly complimenting Plato's nascent scripts.

Plato was also an athletic young man. He wrestled in formal leagues. He regularly won awards at the Isthmian games staged every two years at the Isthmos of Corinth. Since he claimed to be from Corinth, Dave had another strong connection to Plato. Dave, very strong and fit from his fifteen years doing physical labor as a common fisherman, was happy to arm-wrestle the young man whenever he wanted—though careful to lose more matches than he won.

Thus he quickly gained Plato's total confidence.

Dave knew that "unmasking" Socrates as a blatant, self-promoting fraud would have a dire "spill-over." It would badly tarnish Socrates' students, including Plato. But this was all part of Dave's plan. He knew that Plato, along with *his* future student Aristotle, if undeterred would subsequently lay the foundations for Western science. Delaying that development would likely push back the discovery of Dark Energy-generation by centuries, perhaps allowing mankind time to develop beyond its animal underpinnings.

So—though Dave hated what he was doing to his new friend—he proceeded with his plan to *poison* Plato.

It had to be done.

"Tomorrow the Master dies," Plato sobbed. They were dining at an exclusive restaurant. Dave was still playing the part of a rich kid from Corinth, although he was now down to his last few silver coins. It was a good thing the whole charade would end soon or Dave would have to slink off back to his lowly fishing "career."

"It is an unspeakable tragedy," Dave sighed in commiseration. "I'd hoped to be there, to document and memorialize the travesty in

my own poetry and acting. But I completely understand that the
great man would allow only his beloved inner circle to be present. I
am respectful to the wishes of the group in not being allowed to attend. You, though—his most beloved and talented student—will document it in your future plays. You will force the world to confront
their ignominy! I know you will stay strong. Socrates depends on you
to carry forward his memory, teachings, and vision."

"You are so kind and supportive," Plato sobbed, reaching for his
nearly empty wine glass.

"Here, let me give you a different vintage," Dave said, pouring
from a small jug of his own rather than that supplied by the restaurant. He filled Plato's cup to the brim. "It is a particularly bitter wine
come from the Nemea vineyard not far from my home in Corinth. It
memorializes Hercules killing the vicious lion. Similar to Hercules,
our dear Socrates will triumph in the end—placing Virtue above mere
survival. I think this vintage suits our sad occasion. It is powerful yet
poignant."

"Thank you, my dear friend," Plato said, accepting the cup and
quickly upending it, drinking it in one long gulp.

"How was it?" Dave asked, solicitously, pretending to drink from
his own cup.

"It does...have a strange tang to it...?"

"Have another," Dave said, pouring more. "We must toast our
great and venerated Master!"

"If you insist," Plato said, his head starting to wobble. The curls
at his forehead were trembling in a strange way.

In his eagerness to properly dose Plato, Dave forgot about keeping the sleeve of his fine tunic pulled down over his wrist.

"What...is that?" Plato said, staring at Dave's revealed *Anaconda
Tattoo*. "It...looks familiar—have I seen it before?"

"I don't think so, my friend. It's unique—done by a traveling artist."

Plato wobbled in his seat, frowning as he swigged down the refilled glass of wine.

"But I'm sure that I...in the Agora? But you can't be...?"

Dave quickly refilled Plato's cup a third time, his own as well
(having poured out his previous cup beneath the table into a plant-

containing vase). Dave could not have Plato connect him with the fisherman boy that he'd undoubtedly seen many times in the Agora. Plato could not be suspicious of him! But, not much chance of that—it was already too late for poor Plato.

As they brought both of the cups again to their lips, Dave again only pretended to drink his own.

Dave had "doctored" the new jug with a carefully calibrated concentration of *arsenic*, purchased in disguise at a local, illegal apothecary. There was sufficient poison to make whoever drank from the jug deathly ill for a few days—with intestinal cramps, vomiting, and bloody diarrhea—but not enough to kill.

Dave suspected that killing Plato would cause totally unpredictable ripples forward into history. But for him just to be sickened, unable to attend his Master's execution—well, Dave's future history had *already* recorded that Plato was not present due to illness.

And instead of Plato attending Socrates' execution, *Dave would go there in his place*—claiming to be sent by Plato. The inner circle wouldn't be shocked that one of their own had "food poisoning." Such was common in an era where refrigeration was unknown. And, in their shared grief, they'd finally welcome Dave into their presence as one of their own.

"I...don't feel so good...?" Plato frowned, setting his wine glass down on the table.

"Should I help you back to your room?" Dave solicitously replied.

He'd make a suitable replacement for Plato, even sobbing convincingly.

Yes, Dave's tears at the execution would be real. He actually admired the old rascal for his many accomplishments. After all, Socrates was born not into easy aristocracy, but a hard-working stonemasonry family. He did have some status as a member of a local business, but his rising to a prominent place in the newly democratic society was solely due to his own genius and persistence. Even Socrates' death was a testament to his "Living-by-Principle": refusing to turn his back on the rules of his society while simultaneously defying underlying hypocrisy.

But Dave knew Socrates had to be totally "exposed" as a "pompous fraud." It was essential that he be discredited, regardless of the truth of the man's convictions! Only in this way would Socrates' existing long track record of potent influence—and subsequently that of his students—be totally discounted and lost to history.

"Yes...please," Plato weakly replied, his normally tanned face turning pale.

Dave helped his "drunk" friend back to Plato's room at the local inn located near the jail where Socrates awaited execution. Plato was already delirious and very sick. So before departing, Dave "kindly" volunteered to inform Plato's friends of his sudden illness. Plato agreed, even thanking Dave for doing so, having forgotten all about that distinctive, troubling Anaconda Tattoo.

Everything was falling into place.

Dave was guardedly optimistic. But there was still a lot that could go wrong.

As Sally wearily climbed with Dennis out of their shuttlecraft into the hanger of the Dinosapien Starship, she had a sense of foreboding.

Something wasn't right.

There'd been no answer to their hails. This was not unexpected as they'd not been gone for that long. The crew was probably still trying to get the fragile systems operating again throughout the ship, particularly communications.

But Dennis and Sally had to trigger the hanger doors themselves in order to get them to open, rather than having it gaping ready to accept them. One the hanger repressurized, no technicians came out to help them disembark. Everything was quiet...*too* quiet!

"We've got to get up to the control room," Sally gulped, wobbling in the weak artificial gravity. She was still beat-up from her passage through the nuclear maelstrom. But she had to put her aches to the side. "There's trouble here, Dennis—*bad* trouble."

"They may be completely engaged in trying to correct the spin of the ship and get the other systems on line," Dennis cautioned her. "I wouldn't be too worried...yet," he added.

But it was obvious to her that he was likewise concerned.

The adrenalin-rush from their successful destruction of the lair of the Demon and their dramatic escape was fast wearing off. Sally felt drained of energy—wanting nothing more than to go to her cabin, lie down, and sleep for a week.

But she knew they didn't have the luxury of time. They had to get out of orbit around that evil planet as soon as possible. Who knew what automatic defense mechanisms might be triggered by the destruction of the Demon's lair?

So she summoned up the energy to sprint through strangely empty corridors—carrying her helmet, not taking the time to remove her battered, burnt spacesuit.

Dennis had to trot to keep up with her as she ran quickly into the control room.

"Oh, there you are!" the towering Demon cheerfully greeted them. "You both certainly took your time returning. It only took *me* a split second to get here."

Yes, it was the Creature from the planet, now regally attired in his full Satan-suit. He sat on an improvised throne made of ripped-apart control consoles, staring upward through the transparent globe at the awesome display of packed stars—with the ominous accretion-disk of the Black Hole hanging off to the side.

His bright red skin glowed. His pointed horns reflected flashes of light. His black hoofs, planted firmly on the floor, were impatiently tapping out a rapid beat. The sharp white talons on each of his fingers glittered. His red, forked tail stretched to the side, twitching impatiently.

And leaning against one of the walls was his seven-foot-long, ominous pitchfork.

Looking terrified, George and Alice stood silently trembling at his side.

Most of the other Dinosapiens were either dead or dying, splattered against the walls in bloody sprawls—as if they'd been hurtled there with incredible force! A few intact survivors were cowering in the corners.

"Well, let's get going," the Demon growled at the stunned Sally and Dennis. His bright yellow eyes seemed to pierce into their very souls as he sat regally upon his improvised throne.

"But...we killed you...?" Sally said, struggling to get her scattered wits together.

The Demon threw his head back and laughed deeply.

"Oh, you just destroyed all your dearest friends and relatives tucked in their little tubes!" he cackled gleefully. But then, more seriously, as if commiserating with Sally's devastated expression, he continued: "No, no, Sally. I'm only joking with you. At the same time I teleported myself up to your ship I also brought my personal Collection along with me. All the stasis-tubes are quite safe in one of your holds, rest assured. I definitely didn't appreciate your destroying my Palace, but I've got many more scattered throughout the galaxy. Now with the past behind us, we can move forward on our grand Adventure, right? There's nothing to hold us here. It's full speed ahead!"

Sally was hit with simultaneously conflicting powerful emotions. The Creature was—yet again—resurrected! But he'd brought along Sally's dear friends with him in their time-freeze tubes. She hadn't sacrificed them! It was a great relief but also a terrible prospect: that they all were now under the total domination of an insane, ancient Alien. And together with him they were about to poke a finger into *God's eye...*

She felt sick to her stomach.

"They're all here?" she managed to gasp out.

"Yes Sally, your Mom, friends, and all the rest of your nasty little incarnations are safely packed away in a cargo hold down below," the Demon grinned evilly. "Did you really think I'd let you destroy my prized Collection with your little fireworks? Hah! Now that you've gotten your rebellion out of your system, your tube-friends will insure your continued cooperation—and, incidentally, add additional weight to my defiance of the Creator."

"I...will never cooperate...with you," Sally grated at him through clenched teeth, narrowing her eyes.

The Demon sighed deeply, reaching out a claw to lightly scratch Alice's throat—as George tried to intervene but with a gesture the Demon froze him in his place.

A trickle of red blood dripped from the cut.

"Really, now?" he said. "Must I nip off the heads of your remaining friends, one by one?"

Sally shuddered.

"No," she admitted in a small voice, looking down at the floor in defeat.

"Good! Then we'll have no more false bravado, shall we?"

He turned to George.

"I've restored all your ship's functions, so pilot us to our destination. I've already placed the coordinates in your files. And fetch me my pitchfork to prod you with if you deviate in even the slightest way from my commands!" he imperiously ordered the bald-headed professor.

George hesitantly walked over to the wall where the heavy pitchfork leaned, wincing from its internal heat as he grabbed it and lugged it back to the Demon.

Then George walked over to the remaining intact control console and dejectedly sat down. Alice followed him to put her hands tenderly on his slumped shoulders. Sally chose to walk up to the Demon and look him square in his hypnotically shining yellow eyes.

"Where are we going?"

Behind her, Dennis suddenly ran at the Demon with his *claws outstretched*...only to fall, unconscious, to the floor.

The Demon didn't even give the Dinosapien the courtesy of acknowledging the thwarted attack.

"Isn't it obvious from what I told you down on the planet?" he grinned, his voice sizzling with excitement. "We're joining a time-dilated Harvester in orbit close to the Event Horizon."

"And then?"

"And then, using your spiffy new Subspace Generator that I've revved up to full power—we're going into the Black Hole! Then we'll *spurt* out through the *White Hole* on its other side to mold a whole *new Universe* into my own image!" he screamed into the chamber, revealing yellow-pointed teeth. "It will be the *Big Bang* of a new Universe, occurring exactly as *I* design it. In my new Creation there will be new Laws of Physics, set according to *my* dictates."

"You won't succeed," Sally defiantly stated. "I'll find a way to stop you."

The Demon swatted her away like an annoying insect. Only her stiff spacesuit saved her from broken bones as she smashed into the nearest wall. As it was, her head bounced off the wall distressingly hard—the helmet held in her hands rolling across the floor with a loud clatter.

"Don't irritate me," the Demon warned her, half-rising from his throne. "I need you *alive*, little girl—*not* undamaged."

Sally felt hot blood running into her eyes from a cut on her head as she slumped to the floor, afraid that the Creature was correct. Despite her brave words, she knew that there was nothing she could do against the ancient monster. It was just too powerful.

Like it or not, she was headed straight into the *Black Hole* at the center of the Milky Way!

It was the day of Socrates' imminent execution.

Periscus opened his eyes to see morning light streaming through the hut's open doorway.

His first thought was that he should be ecstatic that his lifelong obsession with the fat philosopher was finally coming to a satisfactory end. But an even greater joy consumed him, eclipsing his elation at Socrates' looming execution.

On a stand to the side of the hut's doorway was the Triton's strange-looking, iron hammer.

It was *shimmering...*

It seemed insubstantial—as if it were from this world but not *of* this world.

It reminded Periscus that he was in the midst of something far greater than sweet revenge.

Also, Periscus felt very woozy. Strangely, he could remember no dreams. Usually he had nightmares, mainly of being back in the Hoplite army, submerged in an endless sea of bloody turmoil, shouting and fighting—struggling to find his sword but failing—as numerous arrows thudded painfully through his arm!

It was an awful, recurring nightmare.

But this "sleep" had been different. He'd closed his eyes and then reopened them. There was no intervening time at all. What had happened?

"T-Timotheus?" he woozily asked, raising a hand to his head as he reached out with his other hand for a jug of wine sitting beside his mat...

—his *other* hand?

"By all the gods!" he yelped, leaping up off the mat to stagger back against the thatch wall of the hut.

He now had *two* arms! One was old, thin, and liver-spotted—but the other was the arm of a young man. It was clean-looking, with smooth unwrinkled skin.

His eyes stretched wide, Periscus held up his new hand in front of his face. He opened and closed it. He twisted it around so he could see its back. The veins on it were big and thick, pulsing with blood.

"Ah, you're up, Mr. Periscus," Tommy cheerfully said as the little boy stepped into the hut, a wide smile on his round face. "How do you like your new arm? Oh and while I was at it, I fixed your teeth also— and then revved up your metabolism a bit, stuff like that. I sort of gave you a 'tune-up'," he shyly snickered.

The old fisherman felt at his gaping mouth...teeth! He had a full mouth of teeth in his head. It was yet another miracle.

"Thank you!" he gasped, completely astonished.

"Oh I'm happy to help," the little boy grinned. "But now I'd really like to go see that 'red spear' you said dropped out of the sky. Can we go now, please?"

"Anything that you want!" Periscus grinned widely, still looking in awe at his new, perfectly functioning arm. "We'll cook and eat something and then go to my boat and..."

"I've already made breakfast for you," Tommy happily interrupted him. Tommy held out a plate of perfectly fried fish and crispy bread. "So as soon as you're ready...?"

Grabbing the plate of food and stuffing it into his mouth, Periscus gleefully motioned for Tommy to follow him back to the beach.

The fisherman noticed that Tommy was now carrying the strange metal hammer-looking thing. It must be a magic talisman. And, yes, it still had that pulsating glow.

They strode out onto the rocks of the lower mountain, headed toward the distant beach. Periscus was certain that this would be a day to remember...the most magnificent day of his entire life!

With a new vigor in his steps, it seemed but moments for Periscus to reach the beach.

And as they pushed off in the small fishing boat onto the beautiful, clear waters of the Mediterranean—Periscus was deliriously happy. He now had two arms and a mouth full of teeth. He felt like a new man. It was like he'd been *reborn!*

He paddled the boat vigorously, not even bothering to raise the one sail.

Then, above the very spot where he'd found his Star Child, Periscus pointed down. Through the clear waters, there was a hint of *red* deep below.

"Ah, I see it," Tommy grinned.

He handed the iron hammer to Periscus, who winced at the heat it was giving off.

"This is very important for us, so please take good care of it," the boy grinned.

Periscus nodded.

"But don't play with it," the little boy cautioned him. "It can hurt you real bad if you're not careful!"

"Alright, I won't play with it," Periscus solemnly replied, gingerly holding it by its cooler though still-glowing handle.

Then the boy took off the short tunic that he'd made for himself, unloosened his small sandals and stepped out of them. Then clad only in a small loincloth he dived off the side of the boat.

The "splash" was loud, startling.

Periscus watched over the side of the boat with amazement as the little boy dove like a dolphin deeper and deeper before being lost from sight in the depths.

A flurry of bubbles erupted out of the waves by the side of the fishing boat...then nothing.

Periscus did his best to keep the small boat over that exact spot, paddling now and then to offset the gentle waves. He expected the boy to reemerge any minute. As the minutes, however, stretched into *hours*—Periscus got more and more concerned.

Had the boy drowned? Had other sea creatures grabbed and eaten him? Did the merman go back to his heavenly realm?

The sun was sinking in the sky but Periscus was determined to wait as long as necessary.

He would not abandon his young friend.

He fingered the iron hammer in his hand. It had a handle where a hand would fit. On the handle was a movable part that a finger could manipulate. And on its top was a cap that moved back and forth. Below the cap was a dial with one-to-five stars beside it.

Should he try to use the magic hammer? Perhaps it could save Timotheus if he were in trouble in the depths?

But...he knew better. The Triton ordered him to not fool with it. It was dangerous!

But if the boy didn't return soon...what then?

Periscus would try to use the hammer. Perhaps it would attract the god Poseidon to save his merman descendant.

Yes, that was a good plan.

But Periscus was growing increasingly impatient.

The mourners headed for the jailhouse as a close-knit unit. They did not welcome the intruder, Davos of Corinth, who confronted them on the busy street.

Dave was suitably sad but insistent.

He told them Plato had sent him in his place. Plato was very ill and in bed from food poisoning—yet wanted everything documented and reported by a certified writer such as himself.

Reluctantly, the group allowed "Davos" to accompany them.

In the jail, Dave found Socrates to be almost jovial, cavalierly accepting the new young man in their midst and his reason for being there. Clearly the old philosopher's mind was elsewhere, resolutely preparing to take his permanent leave from this life.

The attitude of those attending, though, was not at all jovial. There was much crying and wailing by the assembled witnesses. But Socrates rebuked them all, saying it was unseemly to carry on so! Particularly devastated was his wife, Xanthippe, who he'd married late in his life, and who carried in her arms his youngest son. Dave had thought that Socrates' family didn't come to the trial out of embarrassment—since Socrates was such an infamously unfaithful rogue—but he learned Socrates ordered them not to attend, again thinking it unseemly to use them to beg for mercy.

Also, it turned out that Xanthippe was somewhat of an argumentative shrew, who Socrates claimed he'd married not out of love but out of his love of verbal competition! Socrates truly loved to argue and debate. Apparently Xanthippe not only humored him but readily engaged with him. It was a match fit for a confirmed philosopher. But then again, her family had money—and the jobless Socrates not only could not support a wife and family on his own, but typically sponged off relatives for his livelihood.

But Dave's disdain for the foul old man was again tempered by Socrates' abject refusal to escape the city—even though his friends told them they'd bribed the guards to let him escape. One of them, Crito, begged Socrates to leave—insisting that Plato also wanted it this way. But Dave saw that Socrates was not afraid of dying, indeed seemed to look forward to it...if nothing more than to cut short the indignities and pain of further ageing. After all, Socrates was now seventy years old—at a time when the average life expectancy was around forty years.

Dave had grim satisfaction seeing the pompous Socrates preparing to drink his cup of hemlock. It was a terrible thing to witness the execution of another human, even though that person seemed to welcome it. Xanthippe was especially distressed, weeping unconsolingly in a corner of the jail cell. Socrates, seeing his wife huddled miserably there, either took pity or was tired of her wailing—and ordered her to leave.

One of the others volunteered to take her home. Only then did Socrates consent to having his shackles removed. He washed his own body carefully in order to save the other women present the trouble of later readying it for burial.

A couple of the guards were preparing the hemlock poison. Finished, they handed it to him. Without hesitation, Socrates took the cup and gulped it down, asking how soon it would take effect. They told him to get up and walk until he felt numb. He staggered a few steps, lay back on the bed, and then coolly began describing the effects of the poison: a spreading, painful paralysis.

"Davos"—true to his cover story—was carefully taking notes, as he'd done from the moment they'd entered the jail. He was making marks on a clay tablet, small enough that the others didn't see he wasn't actually writing with Greek characters. Though he could speak and read the language now quite fluently, he'd not had the occasion to learn to actually write it.

Socrates squirmed and moaned pitifully. Beads of sweat sprang up on his wide forehead. His normally popped-out eyes now seemed to be bursting from his face. He breathed in ragged, uneven gasps.

It was horrific for everybody present, including Dave.

Soon Socrates could only move his head. His last, gasped-out words to Crito were: "We owe a rooster to Asclepius...please, don't forget to pay the debt."

And then the old philosopher died.

In the hush of the jail cell, his friends quietly discussed what Socrates meant by his final statement. True to their philosophic obsession, they took this opportunity to debate Socrates' last words. Some thought that since Asclepius was the Greek god for curing sicknesses, Socrates meant that a sacrifice was to be made in gratitude for his death, the ultimate cure of any illness. Others thought that Socrates was emphasizing his martyrdom for Athens, curing his beloved city of its ills. Others thought that Socrates was kindly referring to an actual debt to a real person—though he routinely was in debt to everyone, so that didn't make much sense. Regardless, Socrates was now but a motionless fat corpse sprawled on the jail cell's one stark bed.

Gradually the talking and debating quieted.

The group simply wasn't used to being without their Master's garrulous needling, his dynamic and robust presence. Dave viewed their abysmal loss with sympathy. But now that the "deed was done" he had to keep his focus. There was more he needed to accomplish.

After confirming his death, the guards allowed Socrates' disciples to take away his body. Socrates, it turned out, had already instructed his followers not to go through the normal ceremony of having a public viewing on the second day, followed by burial or cremation on the third. Dave's admiration for Socrates grew again, realizing that the old man didn't want to endanger his followers any more than necessary with a protracted funeral. Instead, the old philosopher had ordered his body to be buried immediately in a private ceremony at an undisclosed location.

So the attendees wrapped the body in a bed covering and carried it away. Dave was one of them—holding onto one of the heavy corpse's shrouded fat legs. And so they took the dead body out of the city, into the countryside, and set it down beneath a secluded grove of trees. The glade was located to the side of the very mountain where Dave had initially hidden Breep's egg.

It was now evening. The light was soft and yellow. The gathered young men all pitched in to dig a grave, using several shovels they'd brought with them. It was difficult as the ground was full of rocks and boulders. They only managed to dig down four feet before they had to quit. But it was deep enough to put a couple feet of dirt on top of the corpse. That, plus rocks piled on top, would be sufficient to conclude Socrates' time upon the earth.

Socrates' youthful followers tenderly lowered Socrates' lightly shrouded body into the grave. A prayer to the Higher Power was solemnly intoned. Then they started to put the dirt back into the grave on top of the body...

"*No!*" Dave loudly yelled out, springing forward and ripping his fine linen tunic off his back. "I'll not have the Master's body soiled! Take *this*, dear Socrates. Let my own cloak comfort and protect you."

He dropped the wadded-up cloth upon the already concealed face and chest of Socrates' upper body. Then Dave collapsed in a heap at the head of the grave, loudly and uncontrollably sobbing!

Unobtrusively, he was careful to shield his now-revealed wrist from view by the other participants. He needed them to focus on his own "unselfish" and "heartfelt" example, not the suspicious Anaconda Tattoo.

Also, he covertly pushed with one of his feet a shovel beneath a bush, in case he needed it later.

Then, one by one, the other followers were moved by his unexpected example to do the same—until a pile of fluffed-up tunics completely covered Socrates' body.

Then, clad only in their loincloths, as the sun set, they finished burying Socrates. Finally, they rolled several boulders over his grave to prevent any predators from digging up the body, while also obscuring its location.

Dave sat with his bare back positioned against a tree, crying quietly.

"We initially doubted your dedication and conviction," Crito said, laying a hand on Dave's bare shoulder, "but clearly we were wrong. Come with us to the tavern. We will discuss our next moves. The Master has not truly died. We will spread his Teachings far and wide!"

"Thank you," Dave continued to sob, burying his head deeper into his arms, "but I cannot bear to leave the Master just yet. If it is permissible, could I stay here for just a bit longer?"

"Of course," Critos nodded. "Stay as long as you like, Davos. Just do not let others know of this location when you return to the city. We will be glad to have you join us later or whenever you wish. You can help us spread the news of his heroic death all across Greece—and from there to the *rest of the world!*" he triumphantly concluded.

"Yes, that is my wish also," Dave convincingly lied. His head was still buried in his arms, his fluffed-out hair concealing his tattoo. "Thank you—I will see you, my dear new friends, later."

And so they left.

As soon as he was sure they were gone he jumped up and rolled the heavy boulders off the grave. Then, satisfied that the contents of the grave weren't being squashed, he went back and sat against the tree. It was getting chilly. He missed his tunic. But he knew that it and the other garments buried in the grave were doing what he'd intended.

The process took several days with his mother. But her body was being refrigerated. He didn't know if it would work—or how long it might take—with Socrates.

He couldn't dig up the body because other mourners might appear unexpected at any time. But the hidden shovel was there should he need it.

So he settled down to wait until he knew for sure, one way or the other.

After all, what else did he have to do?

Only the whole future survival of mankind hung in the balance!

Chapter 20

THE GRAVE

Both final resting place and disposal pit
Tombs forever engulf their victims
If auspicious a lasting Monument
If not, the charnel house of bones
Flesh melted off, personality lost
All the little humans meet in defeat
Dissolving back to where they came
Calmed the hate, stilled the wars
Complex molecules decayed
Until only dry dust remains
Telling a sad story of huge struggles
Where titanic, grand Visions surrendered
Death's final grasp holding sway
Taking everything away...

Homo sapiens Eulogy, 20:14-17

Sally wiped blood from the cut on her head with the back of her hand. She was concussed from being thrown into the hard wall of the control room by the Demon. But she was too confused and depressed to care.

Through the transparent canopy above she saw the black rectangular surfaces of a gigantic *Harvester spaceship* set in stark relief against a glaringly white background.

Both they and the Harvester were orbiting at near-lightspeed right outside the Event Horizon of the Black Hole located at the center of the Milky Way galaxy. And a huge panel was opening in the side of the Harvester leading into one of its cavernous holds.

The Dinosapien Starship floated up to and drifted into the hold...the huge panel sliding shut right behind them.

"As soon as air floods the hanger, we can get out and go up to the control room of the Harvester," the Demon calmly observed.

"How are we alive?" Sally dully asked, seated on the floor, leaning back against the blood-splattered wall.

"And just what do you mean, my pretty little pet?" the Satanic figure said, looking over at her with real curiosity.

"The radiation here next to the Event Horizon has to be astronomical," Sally replied. "I don't see how that even our ships' force fields could possibly withstand it."

"Normally you'd be right," he shrugged, now standing up—bending so his horns didn't scrape the ceiling. "But the Dark Energy generator you so cleverly took from the Spike-Ship is far superior to what you and your little reptile friends ever built. Oh, it won't do much past the Event Horizon, mind you, but here it provides sufficient protection for us—as does the force field of the Harvester. Don't you worry your pretty little head, Sally. We're quite safe, for the moment."

Dennis stirred, groggily wobbling up to his own feet. "And then...*past* the Event Horizon, what happens?" he said, defiantly standing straight, blocking the Demon's path out of the control room.

"When the Harvester passes the Event Horizon," the Demon calmly replied, grinning at Dennis evilly, "it will be cloaked in a *sub-space* cocoon. That's how you're going to travel to the heart of the Black Hole and beyond, you silly little reptile. Don't you trust me?" he "sweetly" concluded.

Dennis slowly backed away to stand beside Sally, putting a three-clawed glove protectively on her shoulder as she still sat with her back to the bloody wall.

Sally now realized that the Demon could not be defeated. But the comfort of having the beefy dinosaur at her side was appreciated.

"What do you want from us?" Sally wearily asked, too tired and hurt to resist.

"Just go down to the cargo hold and make sure the tubes are well-secured," he ordered them. "I transported them rather hastily—oh, due to some irritating gnats biting on my neck, *you!* Anyway, all's forgiven, right? We're 'good buddies' now, right? So since we all realize that there's bound to be turbulence as we transverse the Black Hole, just make sure the tubes don't bounce around and get smashed. I'd hate to lose any of my prized specimens."

"You value us that much?" Sally weakly asked as Dennis helped her back to her feet.

She reached over and snatched up her helmet, latching it onto the back of her spacesuit at her neck so she didn't lose it again.

"I care not if I lose tens of thousands of the millions of humans already tubed in this Harvester," he disdainfully laughed at them. "But you and your fellow Sally-creatures will prevent the Creator from meddling with our little trip. I hold you and them as hostages. So yes, you still have value. Just don't overstep my patience with you again!"

Having said that, the Demon stalked out, leaving them alone with George and Alice in the control room.

"Should we try to do something?" Alice asked.

"What can we do?" Sally shrugged.

"For now, you two go and do as that Demon ordered you," George prudently directed them. "I'll keep an eye on Satan. He didn't know it, but I put a micro-chip on the handle of his pitchfork when he ordered me to get it for him. So unless he notices it, I can track his location out in the Harvester. I'll let you know if anything significant happens."

"Good thinking, George," Dennis said. "We'll go check the cargo hold."

Sally let Dennis lead her into an adjoining corridor.

"I still don't believe that we're near as valuable as the Demon claims," Sally sighed, leaning on Dennis' strong upper arm. "And I don't believe that even in a subspace bubble we'll be able to traverse a Black Hole. The gravity is so immense that everything at its center is squashed into subatomic plasma! God, we don't even understand the physics of what happens there. Subspace bubble or not I think we're headed straight to our doom."

Dennis sighed deeply.

"Our astronomers and physicists have puzzled over the physics of Black Holes far longer than the scientists of your human society,"

Dennis replied. "And yet we are not much more advanced than you in our understanding. Classical theory predicts a singularity at the core where gravity becomes infinitely strong. That supports what the Demon claims—that from the pinpoint of the Singularity will explode a fresh Big Bang into a new Universe that's outside our own! But such a singularity—or 'white hole'—would by definition destroy even quantum information passing through it. That means everything that makes us who we are would be erased."

"But I thought that Quantum Mechanics claims that information can't be lost?" Sally frowned. "It can be converted from one form to another, but *not* erased, correct?"

"Yes, Sally," Dennis answered as they continued shuffling along down the corridor. "That theory supports our presence somehow 'coloring' the plasma to determine the new Laws of Physics on the other side after exiting the White Hole in the new Universe. But our ship could never survive intact, just as you said. I agree that the Demon is lying to us, Sally. It can't claim we'd survive into the new Universe. By everything we know about physics—it's simply impossible. If we enter the Black Hole *we die*, even if some 'essence' of ours does manage to pass on through."

"But the Demon is going with us," Sally mused, starting to regain her strength. "Why would it go on a suicide mission through a singularity? It claims to be the remnant an ancient galactic race. Its one dominant compulsion seems to survive and rule!"

"Maybe it *isn't*," Dennis softly said as they entered the cargo hold.

"Isn't what?" Sally asked.

"—isn't going with us!" he barked angrily. "Maybe he was just lying about going with us, to fool us into cooperating peacefully. He *does* seem to need you and the other Sally-figures to keep the Creator from intervening. Also he needs the rest of you 'awful' humans to 'flavor' his new Universe. But if he abandons us to the Black Hole then he must have another way to enter the new Universe once it's formed."

Yes, right before them in the cargo-hold Sally saw the many people-sized tubes. They were still intact. None were smashed or broken. But they were jumbled up, lying on top of each other. And there were *hundreds* of them.

"How can we ever get these sorted and secured in time?" Sally asked, confused.

"We can't!" Dennis suddenly exclaimed. "This was just a ruse to distract us. Sally, put your helmet back on. We'll try to communicate with George and Alice privately."

Sally did as ordered, though it hurt her cut and bruised head to get the helmet back into place over her fluffy hair.

"George, can you hear me?" Dennis said, his voice coming over Sally's helmet speaker.

"Yes," George's small voice came back.

"Where is the Demon right now?" Dennis urgently asked.

"Well, it's up in the central control room of the Harvester...wait, that's wrong," George sucked in his breath in alarm. "He's now transported himself into one of the Harvester's shuttlecrafts. He's *exiting* the Harvester!"

"Jesus!" Sally gasped. "You were right, Dennis! He's leaving us here on our own. We've got to get back to our own control room and somehow get our Starship to smash out of this hanger before it's too late!"

She and Dennis began running back as fast as they could.

"George!" Dennis yelled into his helmet transmitter. "Power us up! If you have to, *ram* us through the hanger door! We've got to get out of this giant Harvester spacecraft before..."

And just as they skidded back into the control room of the Dinosapien Starship, Sally felt herself *turned inside-out* as the entire Harvester dropped into subspace and crossed the threshold of the Event Horizon—headed *straight into the depths* of the Black Hole's interior!

A horrendous "SCREECH" filled the air, vibrating even into Sally's helmet.

"Our subspace generator plus the Harvester's are working in concert!" George yelled over her helmet receiver. "We've got no control! All I can do is link a viewscreen to the Harvester's so we can see what's happening outside!"

Hearing his words, Alice quickly unfolded a large viewscreen and set it up at the front of the control room. All that the clear canopy above them showed was the dark interior of the large hanger in which their ship resided.

"You were right, Dennis," Sally sobbed, holding onto the big Dinosapien for dear life as her head seemed to spin in all directions at once. "He's abandoned us so we can die 'flavoring' his new, perverse Universe. He had no intention of our surviving the plunge into the Black Hole! Once the new Universe forms he must have some other means of entering it."

Everything kept elongating, further and further and further.

And from what seemed a million miles away she heard the Dinosapien's reply:

"Past... the... Event... Horizon... nothing... can... escape... a... Black... Hole's... gravity..." he said, his words stretching-out in a terrifying way.

"It's..... been..... nice..... knowing..... you....." Sally replied, her voice in her own head growing fainter and fainter.

"And.......... you........... also........." Dennis answered from a billion, billion, billion miles away...

Sally looked in fascination and fear at the viewscreen.

It showed what looked like an external view of a surrounding SOLID BLACK BARRIER COBWEBBED WITH RED-GLOWING FRACTURES that were getting larger and larger!

It was a stunning picture, *screaming* "kiss your rear end goodbye" into Sally's spinning mind.

It seemed that the Demon wanted them to travel as deep as possible into the Black Hole before they were crushed into subatomic particles.

But the *subspace shell* protecting them wasn't going to last for much longer!

Sally knew that this was the end—not just of her, but also her timeline replicas.

What a strange and remarkable ending for *the Girl with the Turtle Tattoo*—falling to her death within the Black Hole at the center of our Galaxy!

And, as if to add injury to insult, *her wrist hurt.* Say what?

Dave was shivering in the secluded grove of trees beside Socrates' grave when *Xanthippe* appeared out of the darkness.

Overhead, a half-moon shone down. The black night sky sparkled with a million brilliant stars. A cool breeze was sweeping across the mountain.

Instinctively, he hid his Tattoo by moving that arm behind his back.

His Anaconda Tattoo was *glowing* again. In fact, it was hurting his arm! But it felt different than before. Now, it was sending out pulsating waves of heat. Was it trying to "signal" something?

Dave had a sick feeling in the pit of his stomach. Things seemed to be going so well, but now the Anaconda Tattoo was acting up...and Socrates widow was here!

He had to get rid of her.

"You must be very cold," she said as she handed him a fresh neatly folded tunic and outer garment. "Please, Davos, put these on. The other young men told me of your valiant final gesture for my husband. I wanted to visit his grave once he was safely buried—and thought to return your kindness if you were still here."

Despite his gathering panic, Dave wave was struck by the beauty of the woman. She was still relatively young, in her early thirties. She had an elegantly tall, lean body. Her face was long and fawn-like. She had large brown eyes. And her hair in the cool breeze flowed about her head like medusa-snakes.

She was a classic Greek beauty.

"Thank you," Dave said, stiffly standing up from where he'd sat leaning against a tree. He gratefully accepted the clothes, slipping them on over his loincloth. "I'm so sorry about the terrible injustice done to you and your family by..."

"Oh, don't be sorry for me," she interrupted him, sighing. She shrugged her delicate shoulders. "I had no love for the man. Respect, yes—but never love. And it's amazing he lived as long as he did without severe repercussions. He insulted everyone he ever met. I've long anticipated finding him lying face-down in a dark alley with a knife sticking out of his flabby back."

Dave kept silent. Her brusque words sounded shockingly discourteous. But everyone grieves in their own way...?

She walked over to one of the big boulders he'd rolled off of the grave earlier, sitting down on it. Though desperate to send her on her way, he was still curious of her motivations. He went to another bolder right beside her, sitting on it as well.

"You are a very attractive young man," she softly addressed him. "You say you are from a wealthy family in Corinth? Your girlfriend or wife is very blessed."

Ah, so that's it then...this is why she came here—Dave thought to himself. *But it can't be true! Surely I must be misinterpreting her actions and words. I'm just too wound up with tension to think straight.*

He sighed, rubbing at the now painfully pulsating Anaconda Tattoo safely hidden under the sleeves of his fresh tunic and overcoat. "I am not married, my good lady—and my girlfriend is far distant," he sadly replied, trying to appear the grieving mourner. "I doubt I will ever see her again. She is as lost to me as is our dear, departed Philosopher Master."

"And yet you are true to her memory," she nodded knowingly, ignoring his comment about Socrates.

"She was...*is*...a very unique person," he falteringly said, feeling tears welling up in his eyes remembering his forever-lost Sally. The events of his remarkable journey to ancient Athens all erupted into the front of his brain, making him careless with his words. "In fact, I am doing all this for her—it's very kind of you to discern this."

He choked up, unable to continue.

She placed a warm hand tenderly on his shoulder.

"We do so much for those whom we truly love," she sympathetically stated as moonlight fell through the swaying branches above, bathing her in a silvery glow. In any other circumstance this would have been incredibly romantic.

"I feel the same toward my three boys," she continued. "I'd do anything for them. I fact, I put up with my horrible husband for years for their sake. Any other woman would have left him long ago. But now that he's gone, well...I'm both legally and morally free to seek new alliances."

Dave was stunned to realize she was, indeed, trying to seduce him. This was not unusual for the sexually liberal aristocratic Greek society, who all seemed ready to jump into anyone else's bed at a moment's notice—but it further shocked Dave to be personally involved. Xanthippe was an incredibly attractive woman. But to be propositioned by her, however delicately, there beside the fresh grave of her newly buried husband...Dave knew that her advances were simply wrong!

He had to get her to leave the forest glade, perhaps by unburdening herself concerning the fat old philosopher. Then, freed from Socrates' rhetorical chains, she might leave Dave to "mourn" in peace.

"Why did you marry him?" he cautiously asked her, dodging her advance with a sobering question.

"Oh..." she sighed, withdrawing her warm hand from his shoulder, "I don't know. I was brought up to be a strong woman with an inquiring mind, in a well-to-do family. I was drawn to Socrates' radical teachings. Even at the time, though, he was already old— divorced, lewd, and insufferably rude! But he was also endlessly fascinating. And when I dared to say that I wanted to be one of his followers, instead of rebuffing me—as do so many elite men to smart women—he *encouraged* my intellectual pursuits. Of course I couldn't be 'one of the boys,' but he allowed me into the fringe of his group. I was young and impressionable. So when he then offered to marry me..." her voice trailed off.

Dave knew exactly what she was saying.

He'd seen the same thing happen many times during his years of study at the University. Young female "cuties" were swept up in the supposed prestige and intellect of their "lofty" Professors. The "lucky" young ladies then got to marry their much-older Advisors while the previous, aging wives were cast aside. *Un*lucky young females just got to have sordid brief affairs.

Dave was sympathetic of the still youthful-looking woman. But he had no thought of "hooking up" with her, either temporarily or permanently. But now he realized she wasn't a kink in his plan at all. Indeed, if his plan did actually work, she could play a key part in spreading *righteous outrage* throughout the Athens community!

He relaxed, now happy to have her present. He just needed to keep her talking as long as it took until...

"Your grief at his execution was quite convincing," Dave spoke into the quiet of the mountainside.

"Was it?" she flippantly replied. "I actually wanted to cheer at the old fart finally getting what was due to him. But I was determined to be the 'good wife' to the end. As to my 'crying'—that was my public fake-wailing required for all respectful funerals. But now..."

A "scratching" and "scrabbling" sound came from somewhere nearby, punctuated by muffled "moans".

"What's that?" she said, turning...

—as *Socrates* surged up out of the thin layer of dirt that covered the air-filled layers of fabrics to *lurch* out of his grave!

His arms flailed about aimlessly as he staggered upright, his head lolling back, dirt falling from his head...

Xanthippe let loose *a blood-curdling scream* and toppled over backward, fainted dead-away!

Involuntarily, Dave grinned at the absurd comedy playing out in front of him. That "wail" certainly wasn't faked.

Then he realized that the woman might be hurt, quickly kneeling over her.

She'd hit her head on a rock, but was still breathing. Good. Hopefully she'd regain consciousness shortly. She'd make a totally convincing witness.

Calmly, Dave stood up and grabbed Socrates' fat, floundering arm, helping him to finish clambering up out of the shallow grave.

"Wait...what...*where* is this?" the man grunted, looking about wildly. Catching sight of his wife, he *shouted* in fear: "Is this the Underworld, to be tortured forever by my shrew of a wife? Are you the god 'Hades'? I didn't think you really existed!"

Dave wanted to laugh giddily in triumph—the protective and regenerative Optimmune transfusion had worked even better than he'd hoped. Socrates was back from the dead in only a few hours! But instead of dancing with joy and relief, Dave placed a concerned expression on his face.

"No, it isn't—and I'm not Hades, the god of the dead," Dave quickly informed him. "But you *do* remember my *voice*...don't you?"

Indeed, instead of the high-pitched speaking and crying he him-self had faked at the execution, he was speaking just as he had in the hut when he'd tortured the man.

"You're...*not* Hades?"

Socrates steadied himself, looking uncomprehendingly down at his fainted wife.

Then he staggered, almost falling back into the grave! Only Dave's supporting arm kept the man's overweight body upright.

"*You*...yes, your voice *is* familiar—in the fisherman's hut! So that *wasn't* a wine-induced nightmare? You...you are really...*Astraios?*" Socrates said, panting rapidly. "But...I drank the hemlock...?"

"I brought you back to life," Dave stated matter-of-factly, steering him over to a boulder for him to sit weakly upon. "You answered my questions at the fisherman's hut, Socrates. So after allowing you to be appropriately punished for your crimes against your fellow men by your vengeful government, I chose to reprieve you!"

"I'm...really alive again?" Socrates said with wonderment, feeling shakily at his heaving chest and face.

"Yes," Dave patiently explained. "And now you will go back into the city with your wife, who was here mourning at your graveside. You will let them know that the god Astraios *returned you to life.* Xanthippe will bear witness to this miraculous event. And then, with the undeniable imprimatur of the gods upon you, you can return to your prior life, more respected and revered than ever before!"

Socrates' eyes seemed to be popping from his head as he looked jerkily about him.

His dirt-drenched body looked every bit a reanimated zombie.

"Return—to my old life?" he gasped, clearly still not understand-ing...or agreeing.

It was obvious to Dave that despite his ghoulish appearance, the keen intellect of Socrates' mind was still functioning. He was pro-cessing the situation from every angle. He was coolly analyzing this, the most bizarre of situations!

"But...then...all of my Teachings...?" he gasped, frowning in the moonlight.

"Don't worry about that," Dave quickly comforted him. "It will all work out. Be thankful for the gift of Life that I've given back to you. Once your wife regains consciousness, return with her to..."

"*No!*" he shouted, surging up and away from Dave. He staggered but quickly regained his balance, wobbling threateningly with fists clenched. "I see what you are doing here—whoever you are! No one will believe that I was 'resurrected' by some god."

"Now just calm down," Dave tried to reassure him. "You're jumping to conclusions. Everyone in Athens believes in the gods and their great powers to..."

"—which I've loudly disclaimed and denied! Even if they did believe this fantastic story I'd be made a fool for having denounced the very beings that supposedly saved me. I'd be a laughing stock!"

"No! Not at all, Socrates! Sure, you'll have to be a little bit humble, publically change your position on..."

Socrates' already misshaped face was twisted up in ferocious anger.

"The people will come to a much more logical conclusion—that I somehow *faked my own death!*"

This "resurrection" was turning into a disaster. Dave had to find some way to get things back on track!

"But many witnesses, official and otherwise, saw you drink the hemlock and..." Dave tried to protest, holding up his hands in a pleading manner.

"Instead of being remembered as a *Great Man* who *died for his Principles*," Socrates continued, undeterred, "I'll be *forgotten* as yet another fake sorcerer who only really cared about his immediate, ephemeral reputation."

"No, no!" Dave said, desperately holding up his hands in a calming gesture.

"Instead of a Great Thinker I'll be deemed a *shallow trickster!*"

"But you *are* a great debater," Dave desperately protested. "You can persuade any doubters that they're wrong!"

But the dirt-encrusted old man now *shouted* in outrage at Dave: "This is what you wanted to happen, right? Somehow you *weakened* the poison so I only appeared to die! This is the revenge of that coward, Periscus, isn't it? Well I won't let you make me into a mockery of my true self! I'm heroically *dead* and I'm going to *remain* dead!"

Dave backed off a couple steps, suddenly fearful at the suddenly super-charged, maniacal philosopher. Dave's plan was falling to pieces! In confusion, Dave turned to run away...

—as out of the corner of his eye Dave saw Socrates snatch up the half-hidden shovel and SLAM it into the back of Dave's head!

Dave dropped like a stone, not unconscious but still knocked silly....

He dazedly saw Socrates hurriedly scooping the fabrics and dirt back onto the empty trench in the ground. Then with seemingly super-human strength he easily rolled the boulders back atop his reconstituted grave.

"When my wife regains her wits, she'll see the 'undisturbed' grave and think that she tripped in the darkness, knocked her head, and had a nightmare," Socrates growled, now turning back to Dave. "But you and your smelly friend, Periscus—that's another problem entirely."

"Stop...please reconsider!" Dave managed to gasp out, his head pounding, making it hard to think. "Don't throw away this chance to start up your life again. You've got to go back to Athens! It'll be a great triumph for you to..."

"No, 'Astraios'—*no!*" Socrates growled, advancing on the fallen Dave with the shovel held menacingly in both his meaty hands. "My final, greatest triumph is behind me. But before I can sneak off in disguise to another city to live out what remains of my life as just another nondescript beggar on the streets, neither you nor Periscus can remain to make 'false' claims to tarnish my legacy!"

He lunged at Dave with the shovel, swinging hard at Dave's exposed neck.

Weakened and groggy, Dave just managed to jerk to the side, barely avoiding the slicing shovel's descent. Then he lurched up to his feet, dashing away into the surrounding undergrowth.

But close behind him, Dave could hear *heavy stomping* as the enraged, revitalized Socrates fast gained ground!

Dave's scheme wasn't quite going according to plan.

Things were getting a wee bit complicated.

Chapter 21

<u>ENTANGLEMENT</u>

Many humans did not believe in Fate
Until they found their way blocked
Not by an Evil Hand but by their own unbelief
Locked into a self-destructive spiral
They refused to look up, only ever-downward
Until their Savior so far away
Across the vast span of the Universe
Held out a hand of sympathy
And they chose to reach out and up
And felt that strong grip in their own
Pulling them to safety...

Homo sapiens Eulogy, 21:3-6

Periscus was lightly dozing in the gently rocking boat, the hot hammer cradled in his lap, when Tommy *erupted* out of the water and *flopped* up onto the deck!

It was the middle of the night.

The half-moon shone down from above, made the waves shimmer and glitter.

"I got it!" Tommy sputtered happily to Periscus.

The "iron-hammer" dropped from the startled fisherman's lap onto the deck. But he snatched it up protectively.

"I was getting very worried," Periscus moaned in relief as Tommy shook the seawater off of him. "Did you find the Red Spear?"

"Oh, even better than that," Tommy said, sitting on the seat beside Periscus. "I got *this!*"

Periscus frowned in the dim moonlight, squinting at a flat square metallic thing in Timotheus' lap.

The boy set it aside as he put back on his small tunic and sandals. Then he grabbed-up the flat thing, causing it to *split open* with a *glowing window* appearing on the inside of one of the two halves!

"What is it?" Periscus gasped, cheered by Timotheus' relentless good humor.

Strange colors and shapes flitted across the window. It was a magic mirror! It could show the spirit world!

"The Obelisk was settled into the sand, with the side that I needed to get into buried," Tommy hurriedly explained while poking at a whole series of magic buttons on the other inner side of the split square. "I had to dig a tunnel through the sand in order to get to the doorway. And then I had to dig out a big enough pit to get the doorway open. And then I finally got inside and found Dave's Laptop."

"Whose what-top?" Periscus asked, bemused.

"Oh, this is what controls the Obelisk," Tommy snickered. His short hands flew over the magic buttons. "It was dead, of course—its battery long drained. But I got it plugged into the Obelisk and recharged. The Obelisk on arrival was itself drained of energy. But over the last fifteen years you say that it was in the ocean, it's recovered. The DE-generator was offline, of course. But I think I can trigger it to reinitialize. Of course I couldn't do this down at the bottom of the ocean, so I brought the laptop back up here. Aren't I clever?"

Periscus didn't understand half of what the boy was saying. He figured that Timotheus was speaking in a god-language. But that didn't matter. The Triton found the thing for which he was looking. And now, he was going to get it working!

"Yep! Yep! Yep!" Tommy laughed, peering intently at rapidly changing lines and colors in the magic window. "Good! It's powering up. Great! And now..."

The ocean suddenly *heaved* beneath the boat.

Periscus was immediately apprehensive. It felt like a *whale* was rising up beneath them!

But then he relaxed. He had a *god* in his boat. *Timotheus the Triton* wouldn't let anything damage their boat.

At least, Periscus hoped not...

—as out of the ocean beside the boat a LONG, RED TOWER began rising up...

It was encrusted with coral and seaweed. It was a hundred feet long, twenty feet wide, twenty feet deep. It was massive!

And as the sea water poured off, it didn't stop rising—but floated *up into the air* above the waves!

Periscus stared in awe.

"Wheeeeee!" Tommy shouted in triumph. "Let's go back to the shore!"

Periscus put the black-hammer down and started rowing.

And as they splashed along through the rolling waves, the Obelisk floated in the sky behind them like an obedient giant seagull.

...until, at the seashore, it up-ended itself and SLAMMED down into the sand, positioning itself there at an angle, pointed up at the nighttime sky.

Tommy hopped out of the boat as Periscus pulled it onto the shore. He ran over to the Obelisk where a panel now hung open, sea-water pouring out of it.

"Tommy! Is that really you? Did you just bring up the Obelisk?" a shout rang-out from over at the edge of the woods as the astonished Periscus saw *Dave* come bursting out, running rapidly toward them!

"Dave!" Tommy happily greeted him. "Your friend Periscus just helped me go get the Obelisk out of the ocean. It's powered up! I even got your laptop working. Wow! Aren't I clever?"

"*So* clever! It's amazing to see you, Tommy!" Dave called-out as he reached the robot boy, grabbed him up in a tight hug, and spun him around in a circle—as Tommy held tightly onto the still-opened magic mirror!

"*Astraios!*" Periscus exclaimed, happy beyond measure. He was delighted to have his two gods there together with him on the beach!

"Your arm! Your teeth!" Dave exclaimed in return, grabbing his fisherman friend by his shoulders and hugging him together with the boy.

"Timotheus fixed me!" Periscus happily began to explain...

—as bursting from the woods behind them came an ill-kempt, dirt-smeared, *squat figure*...

"I'll kill you all!" the nightmarish figure screamed at them, brandishing a shovel as he bounded toward them with demonic energy.

Periscus was astonished to see the undead Socrates. But his amazement instantly turned into raging *ecstasy!*

"*Socrates!*" Periscus snarled. He stepped away from Astraios and Timotheus to hurtle himself in the direction of his hated adversary, while still clutching tightly the magical iron-hammer...

Dave looked up and saw a *sparkling, spinning, metallic object* dropping rapidly out of the night sky at them!

"Oh, no!" Tommy grimaced, simultaneously catching sight of it. "That's the 'Probe' that the Martian snake-people sent behind me! I think it wants to kill you and me!"

Indeed—at that moment—a *brilliant red laser beam* flashed out of the Probe, narrowly missing Dave!

"We can activate the Obelisk's force field," Dave said as he snatched Tommy up and ran over to the open panel. He flung both Tommy and the laptop in first before following. "It'll protect us while we figure out how to defeat the Probe!"

Behind him, Periscus heard all the words—yet not understanding their meaning. But it didn't matter. He was intent on stopping that vile, undead Socrates. He was going to *crush* the evil creature's head, once-and-for-all!

He was vaguely aware that a new god-thing was circling overhead, apparently trying to shoot its magic beams at Astraios who was now inside the Red Spear with Timotheus—the "Obelisk" which now was *glowing* a shimmering, bright BLUE!

But Periscus had more urgent things to worry about.

Socrates was welding the shovel that he carried like a combination sword and battleax, with all of his considerable past-warrior's expertise.

"I'll kill you!" the stocky Socrates screamed, *SWINGING* the shovel up at the tall, thin Periscus—who parried it with a CLANG from his iron hammer...

—as something *snapped* on the hammer...

Periscus looking down at it momentarily, seeing that the cap on its top had broken off...

But the shovel was swinging at him again. It knocked the hammer to the side...as Periscus dove under Socrates' flying shovel right into the old man's ample gut, knocking him to the sand!

"This time Astraios can't stop me," the fisherman snarled back at Socrates. "I'm going to rip out your heart!"

And then they fought each other hand-to-hand.

Kicking, *screaming*, *biting*, and *bashing* each other with their fists they rolled over and over in the sand, trying to *choke* and *gouge* each other—*poking* each other in their eyes, *pulling* at each other's tongues and hair—until, finally...totally exhausted...they disengaged and lay bruised and bloodied, gasping for breath beside each other on the sand.

Up in the dark sky, Periscus was dimly aware that the "Probe" thing was still darting-about frantically.

Did it kill his two pet gods?

His eyes darted over to the Red Spear—which was gone! It had vanished! What had happened?

"You've still got some fight...left in you," Socrates gasped, staring with his bulging eyes up at the sky, "for an old man, that is."

"And...you as well," Periscus responded weakly. He was too drained to reengage just yet in their fight-to-the-death battle. "But...I thought that...they *killed* you yesterday?"

"They did. But your friend Astraios...got me out of my comfortable grave—the little *prick!*"

Periscus laughed. "Yes, that is what he loves to do, mess with orderly nature. Hah!—as does that little boy, Timotheus, who..."

His exhausted musings were cut short.

The Probe was descending to float right above their heads!

A series of bright lights flashed in Periscus' eyes as it hovered there.

Then it floated to the side, extended three skinny "legs", and settled down upon the sand.

"WHERE DID TOMMY AND DAVE GO?" a strange, clipped voice boomed from out of the Probe, speaking passible Greek with a thick accent. "REPLY QUICKLY AND I WILL NOT KILL YOU."

Socrates and Periscus glanced at each other, communicating non-verbally.

Then they both *surged to their feet* and *launched* themselves at the metallic creature!

—encountering a blinding, *solid-red wall!*

Groaning, they were both tossed backward, again prone on the sand, staring up at the Probe.

"W-what happened?" Periscus gasped.

"It slapped us down," the stocky man angrily spat, blood from a busted lip smearing the sand.

"How'd it do that?" Periscus asked, wiping blood out of his eyes with both his hands from a cut on his forehead.

"It's got some sort of magic light—hard as a rock, I tell you!"

"Yes, it did a number on my head also," Periscus agreed, reaching up again with both hands to wipe the continuing flow of blood out of his eyes.

"Hey, how'd you get two arms?" Socrates glared at him.

"The Triton did it!" Periscus grinned. "That's a wonderful little god-boy, I tell you."

"Well, I'm glad to hear it," Socrates nodded grudgingly. "I always did feel bad about you getting that arrow in your arm back when..."

"I WILL GIVE YOU ONE MORE CHANCE BEFORE I KILL YOU BOTH!" the harsh-sounding Voice from the immobilized Probe interrupted them, now sounding impatient with their mutual jabbering.

"*Piss off!*" Socrates shouted at the Probe, his attention apparently once again focused upon their common enemy...

—as the *sizzling red beam* shot again out of the Probe to the side of the two men, this time advancing relentlessly across the sand at their prone bodies, fusing the sand into melted glass as it went!

"REPLY QUICKLY BEFORE I SLICE YOU INTO..." the Probe's voice ominously ordered them...

—as a *GIANT LIZARD* hurtled into the Probe, knocking it bouncing down the beach!

"What *is* that?" Socrates gasped at the creature which now pranced before them on two powerful legs, its two small arms grabbing at the air. Its small bird-like head darted back and forth as it swung its powerful tail to again SMASH into the Probe!

"It must be a *lizard-god*," Periscus marveled. "This is wonderful! *Four* gods, Socrates! I've been visited by *four* gods! And this latest one is *saving* us yet again!"

—and to think that just yesterday he was going to commit suicide!

"I think not," Socrates said as he scrambled to his feet. "These are not true gods. They're just natural monsters! We've got to escape. That lizard-thing is just slowing the flying globe down. It's going to kill us all!"

Indeed, red light bursts were *zapping* into the sand just where the giant lizard had last been as it scampered around the Probe, apparently trying to distract the Probe's attention from the two men.

But a glancing "zap" caught the creature in its leg, causing it to flop onto the sand.

The Probe rose back into the air—retracting its "legs"— and floated menacingly toward the downed lizard...

"And I *also* think *not!*" Periscus grimly said, running over to grab up the still-glowing "hammer" from where it'd fallen onto the sand. He saw that the circle on top was now pointed at "five-stars," presumably its highest power. The covering cap had already broken off.

He pointed the "hammer" at the Probe which was relentlessly advancing on the lizard-god, and with a finger pulled the movable part on its handle...

—causing A MASSIVE WALL OF ENERGY to *SLAM* into the Probe...crushing and *incinerating* it!

And in its place was left a twenty foot-wide, circular *black maelstrom* exhibiting *glittering diamond patterns* in its swirling matrix!

—which hung in mid-air above the sand.

It was *THRUMMING* with incredible Power—but steadily shrinking...

"What is that thing?" the squat Socrates gasped, walking fearfully up to it and peering tentatively inside.

"It must be a *magic doorway*—perhaps to the heavenly realms of the gods!" Periscus gasped. He still held the smoking gun in his hands as he came up to stand in awe beside the shorter Socrates. Together they stared into the mesmerizing, spinning black depths.

"If that's true then it's my gateway to the underworld!" Socrates grinned widely. "I'm not so stupid as not to admit when I've been wrong. The gods are real! And I'll go there to pay for my many sins while my legacy is protected for all of future human history. Get out of my way, you old fool!" he said as he roughly shoved Periscus to the side.

Regardless of having been a momentary ally, Periscus was rudely reminded that Socrates was still a *royal ass!*

"*I'll* say who goes through *my* magic doorway that *I* made!" Periscus exclaimed. He lurched forward to grab the shorter Socrates by his neck with one hand as he still clung tightly to the "magic" hammer with the other.

"Let loose of me, you old fool, or I'll kill you!" Socrates shouted again. He reached up to grab the taller Periscus' neck in both his meaty fists.

"*No*, I'll kill *you!*" Periscus sputtered back. He *slammed* the still-glowing black hammer into Socrates' fat belly, while continuing *throttling* his old enemy with his other hand.

—as Periscus glimpsed the big lizard rocketing up behind them both, limping on its damaged leg, and then *knocking* them all into the whirling vortex!

Periscus felt the magic hammer jarred from his hand, seeing it spinning away into the surrounding maelstrom...

—as the also-falling, spinning lizard stretched out its long neck and *clamped* his jaws firmly around it...

—and the Portal "winked"-shut behind them.

In the dawning light of the morning, on a lonely beach outside of Athens, Greece, in the year 399 B.C.—there remained only scorched sand and an abandoned fishing boat bobbing in the waves.

That was all to note the passage of the world's greatest Philosopher, the world's most obscure fisherman, and an extinct dinosaur into the realms of the gods.

Such that, despite Dave's heroic effort, history was *not* changed.

The "noble" martyrdom of Socrates to Individual Freedom, his *Right to Question* everything, and the power of *Self-Defined Virtue* continued unabated.

His position as a historical Icon was assured.

—and the sun, oblivious to it all, still shone brightly down.

Chapter 22

<u>SURVIVAL</u>

"Don't give up!"
What a crock...
Humans did so
By the millions
Every day they existed
They'd lie down to die
Deeming life too hard
The way ahead too difficult
Even doing it to themselves
With a gun to their head
Or a noose to their neck
Or gulping handfuls of pills
Or jumping off a bridge
All to stop the pain
Of tiresome existence
It's so easy to do
So hard to keep on fighting
When options are exhausted
And you're bone weary
Just wanting the pain to stop
In final, peaceful rest...

Homo sapiens Eulogy, 22:42-47

Dave and Tommy were squashed together in the tight storage chamber of the Obelisk, Dave struggling to get the laptop screen up in front of his eyes.

They could see by the glow of the screen.

Tommy was uncomfortably smashed against Dave but simultaneously fascinated. What a ride! He'd fallen back a billion years in time, almost died in the process, got regenerated with the help of that nice fisherman, and now was inside the Obelisk going somewhere else!

But he could feel their motion—as they tumbled end-over-end, without any obvious destination.

"What happened?" Dave asked in Greek.

"Once the panel closed, Mr. Dave," Tommy cheerfully replied, now speaking in his more-familiar English instead of ancient Greek, "—the Obelisk launched!"

"Yes, but to where?" Dave replied, still speaking in Greek.

"Maybe to nowhere," Tommy ventured, shrugging his small shoulders. "Maybe the nice Obelisk was just trying to save us."

"I...think...you're right, Tommy," Dave said, also now speaking in halting English. "It apparently recharged itself down at the bottom of the ocean the last fifteen years. But where are we going? I'm trying to get a vector on our laptop but all I'm pulling up is a six-dimensional map."

"But..." Tommy gulped, "*six* dimensions? Are you sure? That sounds like a whole lot of dimensions?"

"*Up, down, depth, time, subspace...*and something *else*," Dave gasped.

"Oh...that's *very* scary," Tommy said. His head was pressed against the side of Dave's as they both looked at the strangest graph he'd ever seen.

It gave Tommy a headache just to look at it though he had lots of time-travel experience. Somehow, though, he knew he needed to find in the graph a *pattern*.

Tommy concentrated all his considerable android computing power on "connecting the dots."

"I think...there's a *blinking space* in its center—like an empty co-ordinate?" Tommy suggested. He squint his eyes tighter to try and decipher the complex information the Obelisk was sending them through the laptop's limited interface.

"You're right," Dave said, his voice trembling with excitement. And it's tied into everything else on the graph. I think I can increase the resolution and enlarge that section."

And then there it was, right in front of both of their noses.

It was a bright green, smiling baby turtle.

It was Sally's *Turtle Tattoo!*

"Jesus Christ!" Dave gasped. "How can this be? What should we do?"

"Can you get your own tattoo up next to the keypad?" Tommy brightly suggested, grinning widely. "Snake told me all about it. Yep, he *bragged* about it."

"Maybe, but why...?"

"I think they want to grab onto each other," Tommy snickered.

Looking down at their squashed-together arms, Tommy saw that Dave's Anaconda Tattoo was *pulsating* at his wrist.

Tommy saw Dave wince as he struggled to maneuver his wrist up next to his face and place the *Anaconda Tattoo* directly onto the laptop screen...

—when *BLAZING WHITE LIGHT* surrounded them...

Everything was whirling *within and through each other*—like nothing Tommy had ever before experienced in any of his previous subspace or time-jumps!

Whatever was happening, Tommy was now incredibly frightened.

The *whole fabric of space-time* was being freakishly *twisted!*

Sally was sitting dejectedly on the floor of the wrecked control room when the *Red Obelisk* came crashing in.

"Watch out, watch out!" Dennis said, running over to snatch her up in his strong arms and whisk her to the other side of the room.

They were both thrown to the floor as a *phasing-in-and-out* Obelisk fully materialized, with a loud "screech" of torn plastic and metal *skewering* the control room and several decks below!

It was positioned upside-down, the lower access panel now at the end sticking up out of the smashed floor of the control room.

As George and Alice hesitantly walked up to touch the still-glowing, red crystalline surface—the panel popped open and *Tommy and Dave* tumbled out headfirst!

"Dave...?" Sally gasped in disbelief.

"*Mommy!*" Tommy called out, hopping up to his feet and running over to hug her still-spacesuited legs.

She put a shaking hand on his bouncing blond curls, bemused at his little Greek tunic and sandals—he was as cute as ever!

And Dave was...*alive!*

She handed Tommy off to Dennis and stood over the tumbled-down Dave. She just stayed there a moment, wavering in front of him, not daring to believe it was really him.

Then she undid her helmet, letting it pop back off her head to dangle by its strap behind her back. More than anything she wanted to hold Dave in her arms and *kiss* him!

"I got a new tattoo," he wanly grinned, holding up his arm.

The sleeve of his Greek tunic fell back, revealing the fierce-looking *Anaconda Tattoo* wrapped around his wrist.

"Snake gave it to me."

"I like it!" she exclaimed in delight. She held up her own wrist as the two tattoos met—giving off a radiant burst of *rainbow colors.*

Then Dave slumped backward, held up only by the slanted red surface of the protruding bottom-half of the still-smoking Obelisk.

"Dave!" she said, grabbing him in a tight hug to keep him from slipping back down.

The Starship was trembling and jerking, rocking violently back and forth.

Sally looked over at the large viewscreen.

The subspace bubble outside the Harvester ship was fast crumbling. What started as a cobweb of red lines was now a network of *large, fiery fissures!* And the black substance of the protective bubble itself was frothing and buckling inward.

It wouldn't be long until it collapsed, crushing them to subatomic particles—minutes, perhaps only seconds...

"I'm so glad you're here at the very last," Sally sobbed, burying her head in Dave's chest, pushing aside the laptop that he was still fiercely clutching. "It must be a final gift to us, by whatever's been guiding us all this time."

"What's happening?" Dave gasped, looking down fearfully at the floor bouncing under his and Sally's feet.

Dennis walked up, poked his big dinosaur head between the two of them, momentarily separating them.

Sally thought that was rather rude of her dinosapien friend. Was he jealous of Dave's amazing appearance and presence?

She gently moved Dennis' big head to the side and again latched tightly onto Dave.

"Hi, I'm Dennis," he grinned toothily at Dave. "I never had a chance to meet you on Earth before we launched, though I wanted to do so. I really admired your scientific achievements. Sorry we have to meet under these sad circumstances."

"What's *happening?*" Dave urgently repeated, now speaking to the big dinosaur as he continued to hold the tightly clinging Sally.

"Well—long story short—we've been thrown into the Black Hole at the center of our galaxy," the Dinosapien quickly summarized. His steady tone was betrayed by a hissing rasp as the words spat past his big pointed teeth. "Perhaps you've brought a means of escape, given your timely arrival?"

Sally just stared blankly at her big dinosapien friend. She'd already given up. She didn't see any point to his jabbering about escaping the inevitable. She just wanted to hug Dave and wait for the end.

"Can you fall out of the Black Hole into subspace?" Dave asked, clearly trying to understand the desperate situation.

"We're already there," Dennis said. He pointed one of the claws of his spacesuited hand at the big viewscreen at the front of the wrecked control room. "Our spaceship's inside a Harvester. Both its subspace generator and ours are working in concert at full power to put us into a subspace bubble...but it's just not enough protection."

Sally glanced again at the buckling, writhing inner surface of the subspace bubble on the viewscreen. It was very depressing.

"Nothing can escape a Black Hole past the Event Horizon, Dave," Sally dejectedly ventured in a small voice. She patiently continued her explanation: "Our subspace bubble around the Harvester has delayed the inevitable, that's all. Despite it, we're slowly being crushed and..."

"But *how* did this happen?" Dave gasped. "The last I heard from our captors on Earth you were traveling at near lightspeed to the nearest star!"

"The Demon that almost defeated us at the God Barrier came back, Dave," Sally said in a small voice. "It wants us to penetrate deeply into the Black Hole before we're smashed into pure energy—to somehow 'flavor' the new laws of nature that form on the other side of a White Hole in a new Big Bang so God stays away. He's using millions of us 'nasty' humans it has stored in Tubes that've been time-frozen since the Harvester escaped Earth a billion years ago! So we're just screwed, Dave. It's the end."

She quietly sobbed, tears now running freely down her cheeks.

"But...but..." Dave frowned, pressing a hand hard against his forehead.

Sally absently noticed through her tears that Dave looked different. He was no longer the middle-aged, distinguished Professor. Indeed, he was now a lean, strong young man in his early twenties! In fact, he looked very sexy.

She sighed. Probably no time remained for any "couplings" other than friendly hugs.

It was a real shame.

But she had a passing thought that being a Ph.D. physicist he probably was perversely enjoying this chance to be inside the unknown environment of an actual black hole!

Yep, his eyes had that distant look he got when he was deeply engrossed in a fascinating new physics puzzle.

"Dennis...Sally...Tommy," Dave addressed them all, his eyes stretched wide. "What if we activate *another* subspace bubble while we're *already* inside subspace?"

"You mean...?" Dennis gasped.

"Wow, that's an idea!" Tommy grinned widely, hopping up-and-down with excitement.

Sally narrowed her eyes, blinking away her streaming tears—her mathematical-genius brain starting to reengage.

"I suppose..." she tentatively ventured as the entire ship again shuddered, almost throwing them all off their feet. "It *is* theoretically possible that there might be a *sub*-subspace—but that's just wild speculation, isn't it?"

"Activate the *Obelisk!*" Dennis excitedly said. "Its field is powerful enough to contain both us and the Harvester, isn't it? Use it to throw us into *sub*-subspace—whatever that might be!"

Tommy groaned.

"Tommy?" Sally asked, concerned.

"It's drained!" he said, stomping a small foot on the buckling floor in frustration. "It depleted itself of energy getting us here. And now it'll take a long time to get recharged. Oh, I'm so *mad!*"

"Then what about using your ship's DE-generator...oh, right," Dave groaned, "you said it is already fully engaged along with the Harvester's main drive to..."

"But...there *is* something else," Sally suddenly remembered. "Dave, is your laptop still functioning?"

He glanced down at the screen—which Sally could see was still brightly glowing.

"Yes, it's doing fine, but..."

"Then come with me!" she yelled, grabbing his hand and running across the twisting, jerking floor.

Still in her spacesuit, it was cumbersome trying to run. Her helmet on its short strap bounced against her back. But none of that mattered. Every second counted!

"What about us?" Dennis yelled at her, grabbing Tommy's hand as he almost toppled over from the shuddering flooring.

"Just keep us intact! Juice up the generators! Fine-tune their interactions! Whatever! Just give us *a few more minutes*," Sally yelled back at him.

She dashed along shaking corridors that were no longer straight, but *bending* like long, twisting snakes! She practically *danced* down their interiors, barely keeping erect and moving—Dave right behind her.

They exited into the engine room. The alien generator was there *pulsating* in the center of the chamber, casting off searing waves of heat!

"The radiation...?" Dave gasped, seeing the generator was on overload.

"We can survive it for a few minutes, ignore it!" Sally said, dragging him under some large cables over to a haphazard jumble of connected spare parts in the corner.

"What's this, Sally?"

"We were stranded, our regular generator destroyed, and I was trying to cobble together another one from spare parts," she said, running her words together as she dived into the innards of the large clutter of connections and components.

She reached out her hand to Dave.

He tenderly grabbed it in his own.

"*No!*" she yelled at him. "The *laptop*, give it to me!"

"Oh," he said, withdrawing his hand and slapping the cool rectangle into her grasp.

"It was the main missing piece, a CPU central control unit!" she yelled out of the tangle at him. "I don't know if the laptop will replace it, but...if I can just get it in place...damn! I can't reach!"

She tried to squirm deeper, her loose helmet catching behind her.

"And it probably won't even work, Mommy," Tommy's voice unexpectedly rang in her ear as he crawled up beneath her. "It'll take a long time to interface it, get it to communicate with all the other parts, and take precise control, right?"

Jammed up into the entrails of the tight-packed cables and components, Sally realized the truth of what Tommy was saying.

"Yes, I guess it's hopeless," she moaned as she felt the entire Starship convulsing around her.

"But you just need to turn the machine on, right Mommy?"

"Yes!"

"Then maybe *I* can do it," he said, as he squirmed past her into the tighter spaces, pushing the laptop aside.

The shaking around them was getting worse and worse! Large pieces of equipment in the engine room were crashing down. The already intense heat was rapidly rising. The radiation intensity must be increasing exponentially.

"I think I can grab the right wires," Tommy said, reaching even deeper. "And maybe I can generate electricity from my internal mechanisms...and use my artificial neuronal circuits to sense and adjust the different flows..."

"But even if Tommy can turn it on," Dave said from behind Sally as a *large explosion* coming from the outside corridor almost brought the entire engine room down upon their heads, "can it produce a field large enough to contain both your ship and the Harvester?"

Sally was partially deafened, her head spinning.

A terrible, grating *roaring* and *whistling* noise continued all around them!

"I don't know!" Sally yelled back at him, now reaching out to grasp his hand firmly in hers while still holding tight to the little boy's tunic in front of her with the other. "But if Tommy can somehow...?"

The world suddenly collapsed upon itself and *inverted...*

—and Sally discovered the three of them *floating* in a FEATURE-LESS WHITE SPACE, still clinging tightly to each other.

Periscus and Socrates—still with tight strangleholds on each other's necks—found themselves face-down in a luxurious meadow.

Sputtering and growling, they disengaged from each other, rolling over onto their respective backs.

Overhead, Periscus saw a bright blue sky. Flapping along leisurely across his field of vision was a large flock of black birds. A few white, fluffy clouds drifted sedately higher above. The sweet scent of many flowers permeated the air. Soft, green grass cushioned his back.

Periscus was sure that he'd died and gone to the *Elysian Fields*—the afterlife paradise of the gods, the righteous, and the heroic.

But why were there *children?*

Staring down at the two old men were the round, cherubic faces of a surrounding gaggle of young kids.

There were red-headed toddlers, dark-skinned ones, fair-skinned ones, chubby and thin ones—little girls and boys of every type and shape imaginable.

There must be dozens of them!

"What is this, a schoolyard?" Socrates gasped, slowly sitting up to brush the still-clinging grave dirt from off his bloodied tunic.

The surrounding kids giggled at his language and ran away, yelling out unintelligible words to someone in the distance.

Periscus sat up also, amazed to find that he was still alive.

"Well," he observed pragmatically, firmly levering himself up to his feet. "I suppose we can always kill each other later. Perhaps we should first find out where we've landed?"

"I don't like children," Socrates groused as Periscus reached down with a strong hand to help him up to his feet.

"But you have three boys," Periscus laughed, feeling a cool breeze gently caressing his brow.

He was giddy with relief to still be alive in a marvelous new land.

"Like I said..." Socrates growled, "That's women's work. The little monsters don't give you any respect."

Across the field, walking hand-in-hand, a man and woman were approaching.

It was a taller, thin man sporting a goatee at his chin. The woman was stouter but not fat, with short blond hair. A little boy happily skipped up to the pair, jumped upward, and was caught in the woman's strong arms.

"Who are they?" Periscus wandered.

"I will find out," Socrates said, stepping forward.

Periscus blocked him with his newly formed, strongly muscled arm.

"No, *I'll* greet them!" he insisted, glaring at the fat old man, ready to renew their fight to the death.

Socrates' angry expression looked like he was also eager to pick up where they'd left off...then softened.

"We'll *both* greet them together," Socrates relented, reaching over his pudgy hand to grab Periscus firmly by his thin shoulder.

"That's...acceptable," Periscus sniffed, "for now."

And in the flower-adorned meadow, arm-in-arm, they walked forward to discover their destiny.

They certainly weren't friends.

But—somehow—they were no longer deadly enemies.

Chapter 23

<u>GOD</u>

How could you deny God?
When all The Creator wanted was your love
But you insisted on returning indifference
The very worst insult of them all
Such an incredible Gift he gave you
Little smart-animals to be like Him!
Endowed with His Godly Creativity
You scratched in the dirt to eat and nest
As if you'd never even seen the stars above
Your collective societies squandering Power
Fighting with each other over who got what
Allowing your rich heritage to dwindle
Losing the Light, overcome by the Dark
And you were left with nothing
Except for your own regrets
At what might have been...
If only man and woman
Had just appreciated
All that they held
In their hands
That precious
Spark...

Homo sapiens Eulogy, 23:68-72

Dave looked as bewildered as she felt.

They were floating weightless in *a featureless white void!*

His tunic drifted around him. Her spacesuit clung tightly while the helmet on its strap bobbed to the side of her head.

"Is this *sub*-subspace?" Dave gasped, clinging to her hand.

She looked down at her feet.

Tommy was floating there, one hand latched onto her shoe while the other tightly grasped the laptop.

"Don't let loose, either of you!" she urgently ordered both of them, grabbing Dave's hand even tighter. "We don't have any idea what might happen if we get separated."

"I'm scared, Mommy," Tommy called up at her.

"Just hold on tight!" she cautioned him, trying to figure out a course of action.

"But where's your dinosapien Starship—or the Harvester?" Dave asked. "There's just the three of us here!"

"I was afraid of this," she groaned as they floated in the void. "I knew the only field we could make with those spare parts would be small," she said as they drifted onward together, slowing spinning. "Apparently it was only large enough to let the three of us fall through to..."

"And that's a bad thing?" a friendly voice interrupted her from a short distance.

Appearing out of the white fog around them, leisurely walking toward them on nothingness—was *Eashoa*.

He looked just as Sally remembered him from when they'd fought together against Satan a billion years earlier: with a ramrod-straight back, a black eyepatch over his right eye, his skin wrinkled and leathery, and sporting a pure-white beard and mustache.

He wore the tattered uniform of a Resistance fighter, even carrying slung over one shoulder a battered assault rifle.

"Jesus!" Sally smiled broadly at him, almost letting loose of Dave's hand as she continued floating in the white void, not surprised to see the religious icon walking on clouds. "So this is heaven and you've come to greet us? Instead of entering a new, deeper level of reality—we're all dead, is that it? The generator blew up and killed us?"

He laughed as he walked right up to both of them, casually waving a hand to materialize a wooden table plus rough-hewn chairs.

"Please, sit down," he said, taking his place at the table and motioning for them to join him.

Caught by his power, Sally and Dave floated down to sit across from him, still firmly holding hands.

Tommy scrambled around to sit right next to Eashoa, hugging him briefly with a small arm.

Sally noted that the little boy was still loyally clinging to the laptop.

"Hi, Tommy," Eashoa nodded affectionately at the little robot. "You were a real terror there back at the Battle of Armageddon. I liked those dinosaurs you brought. That was a riot!"

Tommy ducked his head shyly.

"Is this the dining room table from Victor and Ivanna's Vermont home?" Dave keenly observed, finally letting loose of Sally's hand to run his palms along the familiarly rough wooden surface.

"Yes, it is," Eashoa replied, putting his gnarled old hands together on the table before them. "I thought it might make this place seem more...friendly."

"But weren't you killed when the God Barrier swept over us?" Dave asked.

"Oh that," Eashoa grinned, dismissing it with a wave of his hand. "That was just a game. Please don't take it personally."

"And are *you* actually the Commander Eashoa M'Sheekha alongside whom we battled Satan—or are you just another 'comforting' illusion, like this table?" Dave incisively asked, continuing to interrogate him.

"I'm no illusion, I assure you," Eashoa smiled gently. "But 'comforting'—I certainly hope so! Are you not more relaxed, now that I'm here?"

Sally just enjoyed seeing him again. She'd spent thirty-one years of her life back in the first century growing up beside him. He was a religious giant, a conduit to the Almighty, yes—but foremost a dear friend.

"Where are we?" she simply asked.

"Just where you intended to go," he cheerfully replied. "You are in the fabric of reality that *underlies* the 'subspace' which supports each Universe. This is indeed the 'big picture' writ large. Do you wish to see more?"

"Yes," Dave eagerly replied. "Please show us!"

Eashoa lifted his hand above his head and waved it casually in a circle.

Immediately the surrounding white became opaque, then transparent. To Sally it was like looking through a thinning white veil. All around them—appearing above, below, and to each side—came into view a *vast array of joined, shimmering black ovals.*

As far as Sally could see in all directions, the complex network of joined ovals stretched. There were short and long chains of the deep-black ovals. And not only were the spheres joined in long, spreading chains—they also budded off of each other. Some of the ovals were bloated and large. Others were just tiny dots. But they all looked to Sally like *shiny black pearls* of many roundish shapes and sizes, glaringly dark against the ever-present background of stark white.

And they *weren't* stuck in place.

The branching, intertwined chains slowly *twisted* and *touched, merging then separating*—as if they were alive!

"What are those things?" Dave gasped.

"They look like fractal equations," Sally observed in awe, instantly recognizing a *visualization* of mathematical formulae which constantly formed, merged, and reformed inside her very own mind. "Does it actually look like this—or are you just putting them in a form that my mind can grasp?" she asked the grizzled old fighter.

"Well..." Eashoa began.

"To me they look like budding chains of bacteria," Dave interrupted him, his eyes stretched wide as he gazed all around.

"It's a big octopus with a million arms!" Tommy enthusiastically added.

Eashoa smiled paternally at them.

"Each of the individual 'black pearls' that you see is a *complete Universe*," he mildly stated. "Yes, Sally, I did read your mind—and the others as well. Sorry. I didn't mean to pry, but you already know that *I* know *all* things. And I especially liked your imagery, viewing the many Universes as chains of precious pearls. Each individual Universe is contained and supported by the black of its own subspace. And all of the many Universes are supported in what you call *sub-subspace*—which to your eyes is a field of endless white."

"That's...almost beyond comprehension," Dave gasped.

"It's one big animal!" Tommy laughed, clapping his small hands together in glee.

Sally was awestruck.

"It *is* beyond our comprehension," she quietly stated.

This was the "*Multi*verse" that physicists of her time theorized might exist beyond her own *Uni*verse. And now she was looking at it with her own two eyes.

It was stunning.

"So the Black Holes at the center of the many individual Galaxies inside each 'pearl' can keep budding-out new Universes?" she gasped. "In that manner you get these linked chains and branches?"

The white haired old man nodded. A kindly smile of approval shone from his wrinkled face.

"Some do...and there are other processes which can also form new 'pearls'—but from a 'big-picture' scenario it's not definitive or assured," Eashoa added.

"What do you mean?" Sally asked, fascinated.

"Oh, you can see for yourself that some of the 'pearls' out there are big and diffuse—those are old Universes, dissipating after many billions or trillions of their internal 'years,' due soon to 'pop'...and the reddish-looking smaller ones?" he pointed with a finger at several close examples. "Those are Universes where the resultant Laws of Physics and Nature are royally screwed-up. They are turning inward on themselves, decaying and dying. Others naturally shrink and disappear by other processes over time."

"That's incredible!" Sally said, astonished by these new super-cosmic insights.

"Yes," the genial old man continued. "And others will just explode and break their particular chains. Others will crash into each other and mutually destruct. Still others will merge with their neighbors, scrambling everything inside both of them. And of course there are multiple Dimensions and Timelines everywhere, so what you see here is a simplistic 'flat' view along just one linear time-span...it's all a marvelously chaotic scramble! And, governing the whole thing, there are certain mega-Laws that guide their interactions in a sort of super-cosmic Evolution, if you will."

"So...this goes on forever?" Dave said, still looking in amazement around him—above, below, sideways—at the immense field of joined floating chains of black dots receding in every direction off into the distance.

"Oh, that's a quaint term that doesn't apply here," the kindly old man gently stated. "I'm afraid you don't have the mental capacity to comprehend what's really happening. I've translated it into terms you can deal with, just as I've allowed you to physically be here in an atmosphere suited to your bodily needs. If I hadn't protected you, your bodies would be gone. In fact, you'd right now be on your way to a yet higher—or rather from your perspective, *deeper*—realm."

"So there *are* other sub-levels?" Sally tentatively asked, frowning. "What we're looking at here *isn't* the sum total of Reality?"

The old warrior laughed again, pleasantly.

"Yes, of course," he cryptically replied, "But that which surrounds and contains—on and on—is far beyond your limited ability to recognize let alone understand. Just feel fortunate that your minds are complex enough to perceive this small fraction of my Totality."

"So..." Dave swallowed hard, looking Eashoa straight into his one visible eye, "you're God?"

This time Eashoa didn't laugh.

He merely nodded.

Sally was thrilled to her bones. She'd heard Jesus say, back in his sermons in the first century, that if people saw him then they saw God! She'd thought at the time that his claim was merely symbolic, in the sense that anything seen in the world revealed an aspect of its Creator. But she hadn't actually thought that God would really come to her world as a little baby, growing up to experience personally the heartaches and problems of tiny little humans!

But here was her confirmation.

"I'm as much of 'God' as you can grasp," Eashoa patiently explained. "It is impossible for you to put me into a tiny little box of your own mental construction. I appear in this container of flesh as a courtesy to you. But regardless, feel free to ask me any question you want. We can stay here forever or for only one of your nanoseconds, it matters not to me. Please put your concerns to rest."

At this incredible invitation, Sally was paradoxically dumfounded. She had fought so hard with Dave to "put things right" that now she had difficultly even formulating her core concerns.

But Dave was not so hindered.

"Why do you hate *Homo sapiens* so much?" he urgently asked.

"But I don't!"

"You *incinerated* the surface of our entire planet and *prevented* mankind's escape into the future!" Dave angrily accused him. But then he softened his tone: "Yet...to be fair...on the other hand you allowed Sally and me to be supposedly 'saved'—only to then be irrevocably separated! Why did you toy with us so cruelly? Sally and my endgame was the same as for the human species: finally and completely, to be *destroyed!* I don't understand."

The old man smiled, reaching absently up to adjust his black eyepatch.

"You *mis*understand, my friend," Eashoa grinned. "That which you decry so vehemently *wasn't* a punishment. It was a reward."

Dave's mouth hung open in shock, seemingly unable to mount a reply.

Sally smiled ruefully, looking down at her wrist to see her Turtle Tattoo gently *glowing*.

Looking over at Dave, she noticed that his Anaconda Tattoo was likewise also glowing.

"So you were behind it all from the start, weren't you?" she smiled. "It was really *you* that caused our tattoos to sway us this way or that—not just the Martian snakes?"

He nodded politely.

"Yes, you were not simply dancing to the tune of alien intelligent snakes."

He laughed, kindly.

"But *why?*" she urgently asked. "Why did you do this for us?"

"That's my question also," Dave grimly added.

"I told you both before," Eashoa quietly stated, his one brown eye twinkling at them.

Beside him, Tommy nodded, grinning widely.

"So it's just a game?" she sincerely asked, puzzled.

"Of course..." Dave grimaced, shaking his head in disgust, "it's just like the ancient Greeks and Romans envisioned the 'gods'—where us humans are just pawns in their cruel games!"

"Oh, it's not 'just' a game," the old warrior precisely replied. "Your whole existence was a tiny but incredibly important part of an endeavor beyond your scope to understand."

Sally saw Dave rise angrily from his seat, *glowering* fiercely at Eashoa.

"Oh, I understand perfectly," Dave grimly spat. "It's a *war* game. That's why you appeared to us before just as you look now—as a soldier. The ancient Greeks were correct...the 'gods' are just *capricious monsters* cruelly torturing us little humans for their own twisted amusement!"

"No, Dave, that's simply not true. We're..." Eashoa began...

"—and so our 'reward' as a species was to be 'heroically' *burned alive* in battle," Dave bitterly interrupted the rifle-toting Deity.

"Dave..." Sally tried to calm him, reaching up to lay a hand on his arm...

—which he shrugged-away as he *shouted* across the table at Eashoa: "And all the awful *pain* and *horror* of the Harvesters, the *nuclear winter*, the *religious war*, the terrible *atrocities* done by evil sadists upon the innocent, the nightmarish *illnesses* and *injuries*, the *starvation* and *sickness*, the *hate* and naked *evil*, the *suffering*—and then the countless *failures* of those who struggled futilely...all of that over and over and over...those were just for your *amusement?*" He finished, panting heavily, out of breath.

Dave sagged back down in his chair, seemingly exhausted.

Eashoa looked at him sadly.

Then the old warrior suddenly began to sweetly *sing*: "Swing low, sweet chariot...coming for to carry me home. Swing low...sweet chariot...coming for to carry me home!"

Dave stared at Eashoa as if he'd gone totally insane.

The old man stopped, now holding out an instantly materialized *sparkling-golden lyre* out to Dave.

"Don't you want to join your voice with mine?" Eashoa smiled. "You can play your beautiful Greek 'guitar.' I'll sing base if you'll sing tenor? And Sally and Tommy can 'join right in there'! What do you say, my friend?"

For a moment, Dave looked puzzled then tempted...but grimly shook his head back and forth as a firm negative, his eyes glaring *hatred!*

He slapped the lyre contemptuously to the side, where it floated away into the endless white expanse.

"Please, Dave," Sally tried to soothe him.

"It's exactly what Socrates said to me," Dave moaned bitterly, dropping his head down into his arms. "That old reprobate was right all along," he sobbed.

"You met Socrates?" Sally gasped, reaching out to hold Dave's hand—which he angrily slapped away!

"But Dave..." she said, hurt.

Eashoa pushed back from the table.

He slowly stood up.

He sighed regretfully.

"I'd hoped the both of you would understand somewhat—and might even want to rise to an even higher level! But it appears you're not ready..."

"No!" Sally said, standing up also and reaching out a loving hand towards Eashoa...

But he was already fading back into the reforming featureless white fog...

The vast network of black pearl chains fading also, obscured by bellowing white mists...

"Goodbye!" Eashoa called out to them from a far distance. "Perhaps we will meet again."

Sally, Dave, and Tommy were suddenly *thrown* into the white expanse: the table *whipping* in a circle, *knocking* them away in three different directions!

"Mommy!" Tommy cried-out pitifully as Sally saw him flung into the obscuring white clouds, still clutching the laptop in both his short arms.

"Dave!" Sally cried-out, *grabbing* for him...

But Dave was beyond reach, spinning rapidly away into the weightless, white void, disappearing...

Sally felt an infinite sadness—as if she'd just lost her best friends. And she had.

Chapter 24

<u>CONCLUSIONS</u>

All things human must end

As with so many other transient species

Developed upon the back of many deaths

Dynamic evolution may pause, but not stop

And that which once dominated evaporates

As do mighty planets, stars, and galaxies

Even the Universe inflating to dissipate

Mammoth Black Holes decay and fade

How could humans think otherwise?

Complaining as they did so sadly

That they were badly mistreated

Too little time in the Universe

Unfairly limited, held back

What monumental Hubris

Yet applaudable Spunk!

You will be missed...

Homo sapiens Eulogy, 24:3-7

Sally dazedly looked up at Dennis' big dinosaur head. He was frantically dragging her out of the superheated engine room. Her helmet was firmly back on her head protecting her, steamed up from within and scorched black on the outside!

"Dave and Tommy...?" she gasped, struggling to get loose and run back into the engine room.

"No, it's too late for them," Dennis growled at her, restraining her.

Indeed, the INTENSE RED GLOW from the room behind her was proof-certain that the radiation level had risen to lethal levels.

"We've got to get back up to the control room!" Dennis urgently barked over her helmet speaker. "Whatever you, Dave, and Tommy did in there worked. We're in some new aspect of space itself. We're still falling into the Black Hole but now we're somehow *outside* of subspace!"

"What...our entire Starship...even the Harvester?"

"Yes!"

"And...is it *white?*" Sally gasped, climbing painfully to her feet.

She felt like she'd been run over by a truck. Every inch of her body ached. If this was what eternity felt like, she didn't want it.

"Yes, it is. How did you know?" the Dinosapien gasped, again affirming her suspicions. He supported her body as they staggered away from the lethally glowing engine room. "Once you triggered the spare-parts drive, we slipped out of the buckling black cocoon into a misty-white, stable cloud. Our failing ship systems normalized. But we're still trapped inside the Black Hole. We're plunging deeper and deeper."

"But...Dave and Tommy?" she asked yet again, refusing to believe they were lost.

"When you didn't respond, I came after you," he breathlessly explained as they limped along. "There was fire breaking out everywhere. I just hope that the spare-parts ship's drive you managed to cobble together and turn on will keep working long enough to see us through. I was barely able to find you in the spreading fire in the engine room. You were unconscious on the floor, but fortunately had your helmet back on."

What? But she hadn't...oh...

"I'm sorry, Sally," Dennis continued. "In the few moments I had in the smoke I couldn't see Dave or Tommy—and the radiation was getting worse and worse! Even my tough reptilian hide was in danger of being permanently damaged. But you're just a soft little mammal.

I'm sorry, Sally, but I had to drag you out of there. There just wasn't any more time to..."

So, her amazingly alive Dave was again lost. Her cute little "child" Tommy was also gone. *Again*, she felt like totally giving up.

But...maybe everything wasn't lost?

Tommy, after all, was just a glorified robot.

And didn't that vile Demon say that the very first Dave was still alive in one of his "private" collection-Tubes?

So...she *could* continue onward...and try to save everyone, including her very own mother. The situation seemed impossible, what with the blistering heat still bathing their backs. But what she'd just experienced would in anyone's experience be deemed impossible. Did she just talk with God Himself? Or was it all just a radiation-induced delirium?

Whatever, if they were to somehow survive their plunge into the Milky Way's central Black Hole, it was time for her to again take control.

She squared her shoulders, pushed Dennis' supporting claws away from her waist, and *sprinted* for the control room. In it she saw George, Alice, and the surviving Dinosapiens hurriedly repairing salvageable control consoles. Through the dome above she saw that the Harvester's large hanger was still intact around them.

And in the viewscreen still linked to the Harvester's outside perspective was *roiling red plasma*—but held-off by a shimmering *white curtain!*

It was an awe-inspiring sight. But she ground her teeth together and resolutely snapped her eyes away.

Jerking off her helmet she let it again dangle on its strap behind her head.

"I think we're almost to the *Singularity* at the center of the Black Hole!" George gasped upon seeing her entering the chamber. Naked awe was apparent in his shaking voice as she staggered up to his station. "As far as I can tell, Sally, the standard Laws of Physics out there are combining—being reconfigured—and *changing!*"

He was hysterical. His voice was cracking with intensity. This was beyond his experience, beyond anyone's experience!

"Can we make it through?" Dennis urgently panted, staggering up behind Sally.

"I have no bloody idea!" George yelled, now looking fearfully over at the viewscreen...

—where, in a blinding-white FLASH—accompanied by a soul-wrenching VIBRATION—their combined vessels EXPLODED-OUT the other side of the Black Hole and revealed...

—space-time expanding from a tiny pinpoint White Hole...into *an ocean of elemental particles*...and from that cosmic soup, large-scale structures started to emerge!

"What's happening?" Sally breathlessly asked George, clinging to his trembling back and to Dennis' solid shoulder...

—as the entire, gigantic Harvester, still clad in its own protective white curtain, began *spinning* and *jerking*-about violently!

George was hanging onto the console desperately, trying not to be tossed aside despite their inertial dampers struggling to keep them intact.

"I think I know what we're seeing!" Dennis breathlessly yelled at Sally's elbow. "The time-dilation effect is running in reverse for us. We're witnessing eons passing by in a flicker. This is the Big Bang process in a *new Universe* happening right before our very eyes!"

Sally was dumbfounded. It was Cosmic Evolution played out at a super-fast speed...

—as suddenly *everything went dark* in the viewscreen. Then, just as suddenly, *stars burst forth* in splendiferous glory! The vast hydrogen clouds were coalescing and growing as gravity smashed the atoms together to ignite into countless new suns. And Sally saw on the viewscreen yet larger structures forming—the stars grouping themselves together as globular galaxies that matured and spun themselves into elegant spirals. And the galaxies clustered themselves together, the clusters then forming mega-clusters...

—many of those stars within their galaxies *burning out and exploding* as SUPERNOVAS, scattering their cooked-up heavier elements to form yet newer stars...

—as many *planets* took form out of the accretion discs spinning around the stars...

—when Sally's entranced attention was diverted by a violent EX-PLOSION from within the Dinosapien Starship, tossing them head-over-heels inside the control room!

Sally staggered to her feet, smelling and seeing thick smoke.

"What happened?" she gasped, choking and coughing.

"The automatic fire fighting suppression systems are still work-ing!" Alice yelled over from a control console she'd crawled back to. "The fire will be out in moments. But our engine room below is a dis-aster! It's been destroyed, Sally. And the Obelisk has gone complete-ly dark! We're totally dependent upon the Harvester's drive. And that's also been heavily damaged by our passage through the Singu-larity. We're spinning out of control!"

The gigantic Harvester began spiraling into the gravity well of a nearby planet...which grew larger and larger in the, thankfully, still-functioning viewscreen.

"Hold on, we're going to crash!" George yelled out to everyone in the control room.

—as the giant Harvester spaceship containing the much smaller Dinosapien's Starship went *zooming through the atmosphere below*, fire blazing in the viewscreen, just-skirting a wide blue ocean to SMASH into an expanding landmass!

Sally was grateful still to be alive.

True, most of the major systems of the Harvester were destroyed in the crash-landing, but the precious Tubes were still intact—both in the Harvester and in the Dinosapien's hold. Mankind could start all over again...this time on a fresh new world—in a whole different Uni-verse! True, they were forever cutoff from their previous Universe, but at least they weren't dead.

She stood with Dennis on a high hill overlooking the crash site. They both were now out of their cramped spacesuits. The air smelled strange. She knew that the unpleasant stink was due to an abundance of sulfur from many active volcanos scattered around the surface of this new world. But there was sufficient oxygen. They could breathe.

The gravity was less than that of earth. She and the other scien-tists hoped the planet's smaller iron core would remain fluid, continu-ing to produce a strong magnetic field, deflecting the worst of their sun's hard radiation. That would ensure survival of the atmosphere, allowing any life on the surface of the planet to endure.

They were orbiting closer to their parent star than had the Earth around its sun. So the new "sun" in the sky appeared larger than Sally was used to. But fortunately, the output from the star they'd chanced to encounter was redder and weaker than Earth's. The planet they'd crashed on was thus still in the "habitable zone" of the new solar system, where water could remain liquid.

Plus there were *three* moons up in the sky—two smaller ones and another ten times the size of Earth's moon.

The tidal dynamics in the oceans here were likely horrific, contributing to violent volcanic activity.

So life might still flourish—if not endemic then from the precious cargo of the crashed Harvester and Starship.

"We've got a lot of work to do," she sighed to Dennis.

"And when did that ever deter you?" he laughed.

Down below, a number of Dennis' fellow Dinosapiens were romping around, skipping and hopping, mock-dueling with their powerful lashing tails.

Yes, they're learning from me—Sally thought to herself, amused, *maybe all the wrong things!*

Their desperate situation definitely needed more work and less play.

The Harvester was a crushed mass of wreckage strewn out across a stark landscape. But key parts were still intact. Some of the equipment was salvageable. And the Dinosapien Starship was relatively intact, protected during the crash by being inside the big hanger of the Harvester.

So they had an interplanetary spaceship with a functional ion drive. True, its DE-generators were toast—but with time to tinker, who knew what might be repaired?

Many humans lay time-frozen in their Tubes, scattered across the rocky plain. So repopulation of the human race wouldn't be a problem. But that would occur on a reasonable schedule. This society wouldn't be a haphazard mess, as was Earth's. Their wiser Dinosapien friends would certainly insist on an orderly, reasonable expansion.

And her past great companions, who'd seen her through so many incredible adventures on Old Earth, were all there waiting to be revived...

—including the original Dave! Sure, he was a middle-aged Professor versus the sexier, younger version who was tragically lost helping Sally save the Starship. But she had fond memories of the older original version. And who knew where that might lead?

Sally couldn't wait to see his expression...snatched in an instant from her about to shoot him in his head at the United Nations General Assembly Chamber...to *this!*

Hah! He'd be so *amazed* when Sally told him everything that happened.

Sally should have been deliriously happy to be alive with prospects of reviving humanity...but she wasn't.

She knew—along with her fellow survivors of the crash—that the Laws of Nature here were *different*.

Not only had the Rules been subtly changed, they were now *unpredictable*.

Already, a Dinosapien drinking water at a pool had been *launched up into orbit* as the gravity at that point suddenly reversed.

And yes, the poor fellow didn't have on a spacesuit.

They'd have to learn how to anticipate and avoid such awful surprises in the future.

But that wasn't the worst.

Sally was grimly aware that lurking behind everything was their new Master—the Demon!

This was *his* Universe. And from what Sally had experienced in the White Void, it seemed the Creator would *not* be interfering.

But perhaps Satan might leave them in peace for another billion years into the future?

Or, then again, he might appear tomorrow.

Regardless, Sally knew without a doubt that the Demon had plans for his "vile" human victims.

But she wasn't going to let that happen!

Whether it was her or her distant descendants, the human race would always fight back.

She now realized that behind everything there was an actual *cosmic war* going on between what she simplistically knew as "good" and "evil." This conflict wasn't just a vague generality, a catch-phrase, a religious doctrine, or a flexible societal construct. No, it was very real and irrevocable.

From both sides terrible forces were arrayed against the crash survivors.

And yet Sally was convinced that the human race—despite its many failings—would prevail.

She thumped Dennis playfully on his scaly shoulder with a closed fist.

"Let's go make some mischief," she grinned at him, turning to run-like-the-wind down the slope.

As the big Dinosapien "thumped" along behind her, she heard him call out to her: "Sally, wait up! You little mammals are too fast for us!"

Yes, that was the problem...and also the solution.

Versus the pragmatic, logic-driven Dinosapiens, other intelligent lizards, and Martian Snake Overlords she and her fellow "little mammals" always found an excuse to *play*.

Truly, it was humanity's one irrefutably redeeming virtue.

Regardless of what the future held—what evil Creatures they must face—Sally was determined that they were going to have *fun!*

She snickered to herself as she swerved and jumped, darting into and through a crowd of the plodding Dinosapiens.

After all, she was the *Girl with the Turtle Tattoo*—and she wasn't afraid to dance with snakes!

THE END

[continued in: *The Girl Who Flew Too High*]

Thank you for reading!

Dear reader,

I hope you enjoyed **The Girl Who Danced with Snakes**. It was fascinating for me researching ancient Greece then transporting the real Socrates into the distant future. And moving into *sub*-subspace to have a talk with God was an amazing high. The sequel to this book, **The Girl Who Flew Too High**, finds Sally dying of cancer, stranded in an imploding, corrupted Universe.

I hope you are intrigued by the sequel's eternal question: "How do you survive death?" One answer is that you birth a new, female, baby Messiah!

Finally, I need to ask you for a favor. If you enjoyed this book and would like to encourage others to read it, **a review written by you** on the Amazon page for this book would be greatly helpful. It's hard to get reviews nowadays and your support will be very important to both me and other readers. If you'd like to do this, I sincerely thank you in advance for your time. It can be as long or short as you wish.

Thanks again for reading my **Girl with the Turtle Tattoo** books and experiencing with me the awe of "driving the equation to its limits."

Sincerely,

About the Author:

Daniel Basil Lyle holds a Ph.D. in Biology, is a lifelong amateur herpe-tologist, taught medical immunology at a University, completed a career in cell biology research, lectures on how to apply theological and psychological principles in practical ways, and has a strong interest in all aspects of cosmology and physics. From a small kid he was fascinated with dinosaurs. As such, he has always lived with exotic creatures, including harmless snakes, all housed in his own homemade habitats. Some of his tame pet pythons and anacondas ranged up to twelve feet in length. He is the author of over thirty books, many of which are religious in nature. His writings go beyond the ordinary, exposing deeper aspects of life. His books are meant to be fun, conversational, and helpful. His various works are available at LylePublishing.com and Amazon.com. The "Girl with the Turtle Tattoo" science fiction series was inspired by paintings done by his mother, movies adapting Stieg Larsson's crime novels, and various men and women sporting spectacular body-art tattoos. The author hopes that you, the reader, find his characters spontaneous, quirky, surprising, and even thought-provoking—just as did he!

www.ingramcontent.com/pod-product-compliance
Lightning Source LLC
Chambersburg PA
CBHW070547260626
47161CB00002B/530